Leland's Journey

Journey

A Tale of Toil Amid Gangsters and Massacre

Darrel Knobloch

outskirts
press

We all tell lies and the person we lie to the most is ourselves.

Introduction

Some of the tale that follows I take from books on Williamson County, Illinois, and from my conversations with a former miner who lived next door when I attended Southern Illinois University in the early 1960s. I came to know this elderly man living in Carterville, Illinois, who was in the later years of his life and spent most of his days sitting on his front porch, when the weather would allow. Living in a rented room in the house next door, I spent many hours sitting on the porch with him. He enjoyed telling the wide-eyed student stories of his time working in mines in the early 1900s—although I don't believe all the stories were the exact truth. But, after reading about the history of Williamson County, I believe he must have known about many of the events that transpired, since he was certainly not a person who was an avid reader. He also related some of his memories of the people living in that time.

Over the years I have come to better understand what this man was telling me about the history of that area. While this story is complete fiction, I have tried to draw on historical events to embellish the telling of this tale. Several books cover the Herrin Massacre and gangster activities. The mining accidents described here are taken from historical records; many of the Italian references come from various publications. I have tried to weave my characters into these events.

An important element of the telling of this story would be the people and events in the history of Williamson County, Illinois. Knowledge of this history is needed to understand how this tale unfolds.

The story of Williamson County begins in the early 1870s. During this time four families living in the area became embroiled in a dispute that led to the killings of many members of all four families and some other people who were associated with them. The killings were accomplished by road ambush, hangings, open shootings on the streets of the cities, and the ambush of people in their homes. Some of the men suspected of killings were never tried, or were tried without being convicted, by the local authorities.

This era became known as the Bloody Vendetta—a name it was given by a newspaper reporter from St. Louis. People across the country read the articles many reporters were writing about the county. They were appalled by the lawlessness allowed there by the authorities. The Vendetta reached its climax in 1875 with the hanging of a Marshall Crain.

During this time, members of the Ku Klux Klan made their first foray into Williamson County. After the Vendetta was settled by the hanging, the Klan seemed to slip off until it reemerged in the 1920s.

In 1899, the city of Carterville was the scene of a riot between a group of nonunion men working a mine north of that city and the striking union miners they were replacing. The men working the mine were all Negros. On Sunday, September 17th, a group of thirteen black miners walked to the train station in Carterville. They were met there by a group of striking union miners carrying rifles. The miners began to shoot the Negros—five were killed—in front of many witnesses in the city. At least twenty miners were arrested and held in jail, but were later released without trial because no witness could be found to testify against the miners.

The Daily Free Press of Carbondale reported on the incident this way:

Had the white miners of Carterville not lived under constant apprehension of violence from the negro non-union miners, this unfortunate tragedy would probably never have occurred. But having been at high tension so long it was but natural for them to think that the first shot would mean a signal for a general scrimmage. However this may be, it is the general opinion of the people of Carterville that quiet will not be restored there until the imported darkies leave, of which there is no immediate probability.

It should be noted that Carterville, like most cities in Southern Illinois, had a sundown curfew for black people; that is, black people were not allowed to be in the town after the sun went down. Also notable is that men were allowed to kill other men in Williamson County without being held accountable: the rest of the country was taking note of this, especially the gangster elements.

The county was quietly producing coal for the next twenty years. The rise of the United Mine Workers Union did improve the lot of the coal miners in this country, both with higher wages and with safer working conditions. The Midwestern states of Illinois, Indiana, Ohio, and western Pennsylvania had plenty of bituminous coal under the surface of the earth. Herrin, Illinois, in Williamson County was the center of much of the coal-producing activity. The city grew from 1,560 in 1900 to 6,900 in 1910 to 11,000 in 1920, mainly due to the opening of many coal mines in that area.

In the early 1920s the mine operators began to push back against the power of the unions representing the working man, especially in the coal and railroad industries. The United Mine Workers Union went on a nationwide strike on April 1, 1922. Shortly after that a Mr. Lester, who had a strip mine located between Herrin and Marion in Williamson County, brought in nonunion workers to begin extracting coal for shipment. The striking union workers took up arms as the ones in Carterville had done earlier, resulting in the massacre of about twenty-five union miners and scab workers. This action was covered by newspaper reporters from outside Southern Illinois, calling it the Herrin Massacre, and Williamson County was again given the moniker Bloody Williamson.

As in Carterville in 1899, union men were arrested, and this time they went to trial, but with the same results. The members of the juries—there were two separate trials—were people who had worked in mines, or were related to people who worked in mines, or they were familiar with the miners' situation in some way. Even the state's attorney said in a press interview before the trial that he didn't expect to get convictions because of the relationship of all the people in the county to the mining people.

The lack of convictions caused many national newspapers to refer to Williamson County as "the Black Spot on the State of Illinois." Williamson County, and Herrin in particular, gained such an ignominious notoriety that any of its citizens traveling outside Southern Illinois needed to shield their connection to that area, lest they be ostracized.

At one point the national vehemence reached the White House. In an address to Congress on August 28, 1922, President Harding said about Herrin:

> My renewal of this oft-made recommendation is impelled by a pitiable sense of Federal impotence to deal with the shocking crime at Herrin, Ill., which so recently shamed and horrified the country. [Applause.] In that butchery of human beings, wrought in madness, it is alleged that two aliens were murdered. This act adds to the outraged sense of American justice the humiliation which lies in the Federal Government's confessed lack of authority to punish that unutterable crime.

Had it happened in any other land than our own, and the wrath of righteous justice were not effectively expressed, we should have pitied the civilization that would tolerate and sorrow for the government unwilling or unable to mete out just punishment.

I have felt the deep current of popular resentment that the Federal Government has not sought to efface this blot from our national shield; that the Federal Government has been tolerant of the mockery of local inquiry and the failure of justice in Illinois. It is the regrettable truth that the Federal Government can not act under the law. But the bestowal of the jurisdiction necessary to enable Federal courts to act appropriately will open the way to punish barbarity and butchery at Herrin or elsewhere, no matter in whose name or for what purpose the insufferable outrage is committed. [Applause.]

It is deplorable that there are or can be American communities where even the arecitizens, not to speak of public officials, who believe mob warfare is admissible to cure any situation. It is terrorizing to know that such madness may be directed against men merely for choosing to accept lawful employment. I wish the Federal Government to be able to put an end to such crimes against civilization and punish those who sanction them.

His administration had been attempting to aid in negotiations in the mining industry and in the railroad industry. The President then continued with an attack on big-business interests for their treatment of labor:

In the weeks of patient conference and attempts at settlement I have come to appraise another element in the engrossing industrial dispute of which it is only fair to take cognizance. It is in some degree responsible for the strikes and has hindered attempts at adjustment. I refer to the warfare on the unions of labor. The Government has no sympathy or approval for this element of discord in the ranks of industry.

During this time, the Ku Klux Klan was again becoming active in the area, as they were across much of the country. The Marion Illinois History Preservation website describes it thus:

> It should be remembered that Williamson County in 1922 was in the throes of lawlessness. The Herrin Mine Massacre occurred in this year, Prohibition and bootlegging were in full swing and gangsters were in full control of prostitution, alcohol distribution and gambling houses. Numerous local, county and state officials were known to be on the take or under Klan control and many of the county's citizens were fed up with local authority's lack of control. Williamson County was ripe for the Klan's picking.
>
> National wire services in 1922 and 1923 carried several stories about KKK activities throughout the country, collectively providing an indication of the Klan's increasing strength. Perhaps because they attached no importance to the articles, perhaps because Williamson County's own story occupied so much space locally, the *Daily Republican* and other area newspapers did not use the stories. In 1923, the Ku Klux Klan was on their doorstep, and its hooded presence could no longer be ignored.
>
> That presence was first manifest in area churches, usually during evening services, when several hooded members would appear, hand the minister a note and a small sum of

money, and then leave quietly. The substance of these notes was that the Ku Klux Klan supported the work of Protestant churches in the community and stood for "the highest ideals of the native-born white Gentile American citizenship," which they held to be:

'the tenets of the Christian religion; protection of pure womanhood; just laws and liberty; absolute upholding of the Constitution of the United States; free public schools; free speech; free press and law and order.'

Whatever the reason for its success, the Ku Klux Klan was already more firmly entrenched in the county than anyone except the Klan itself, realized. On May 25, 1923, five thousand Klansmen gathered in an open field near Marion and initiated two hundred members.

To counter the Klan influence, some men formed a counter-group called the Knights of the Flaming Circle. Most people of the county were aligned with one group or the other. Feelings ran high on both sides as to the lawlessness in the county.

Violence flourished in the area in the 1920s and beyond because the people didn't have a culture of respect of the law. To a point, they felt this was justified because of their treatment by mine owners and by the local civil servants who were taking graft as a matter of course. The laissez-faire attitude of many elected officials opened the area to illegal activities, which encouraged an influx of gangsters from other areas, such as the Shelton gang and Charlie Birger.

Leland Vance had a tough beginning to his life in the mountains of Kentucky. Then he had an opportunity to make a fresh start in Herrin, Williamson County, Illinois. Here is how he remembers his story.

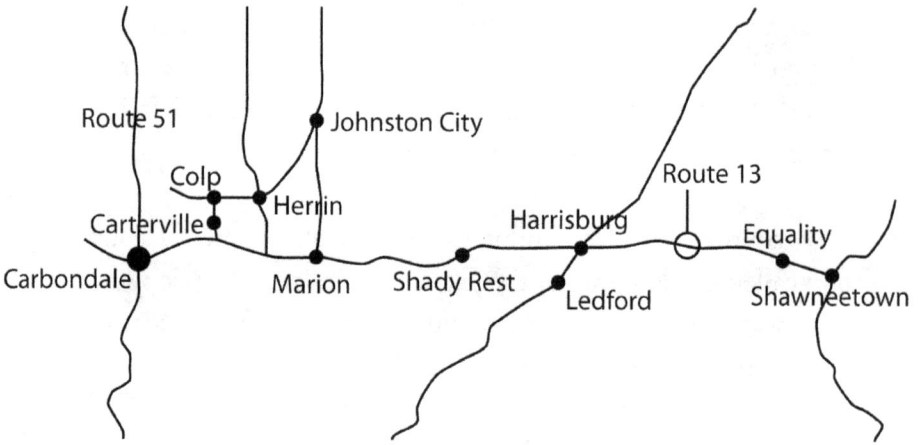

Southern Illinois – Circa 1920

Illinois Counties

Chapter 1

"This guy's just bad news, and he's not going to get better; let's send him out of here, maybe he'll have better luck the next place he lands," Agent Valdic shouted out in frustration. The agents of the Internal Revenue Service had been chasing this "guy" for months, but they couldn't get him incarcerated for any length of time. He just kept committing small crimes of bootlegging that gave them headaches and hurt their arrest records with their boss.

"That would solve our headaches—we can send him off to somewhere else and let them deal with him." Agent Rohn shook his head and slapped the table. "We can write off some cash to give him. That and a train ticket to Louisville. The boss will see an improvement in our incarceration numbers over the next few months and then he won't complain about the amount we're spending."

Rohn looked up with another thought. "Maybe get him a haircut too? He looks like a weird mountain man with that long hair. At least that would give him a chance at his next stop."

Valdic laughed. "Hell, no, he almost broke the jail barber's arm when Ernie went in his cell to give him our free haircut!"

"Fair enough then, let's give him the night to let him sleep off whatever he's been drinking. We can get the money and ticket together tomorrow, then put him on the afternoon train. But we have to be sure he understands that this is a one-way ticket—he's not to return to Mule Shoe ever again." The two agents nodded their agreement, then left for the day.

By noon the next day they had the money and ticket ready. They brought Leland to the front of the police station and gave him the news.

"This is your lucky day, Leland. We're giving you the chance to get out of Mule Shoe—way out of Mule Shoe. Here's a train ticket and some money to get you a fresh start somewhere else. You take this as an opportunity to start a new life, but remember, we don't ever want to see your face in this town again. Do you understand?" Valdic was looking directly into Leland's eyes and telling him his instructions as serious as he could be.

Leland pushed his long black hair back out of his bloodshot eyes. He looked at the money and ticket he was being offered. "Yes, sir, I sure do. Where you sending me anyway?"

"This ticket will get you to Louisville. Since you're a miner, you might want to go on to Herrin, Illinois—the newspapers say there are new mines there and plenty of work for miners like you. How you get from Louisville to Herrin is up to you, but you've got enough money here to make it some of the way. We just want to make sure you understand that you can't come back here—ever."

Leland looked up at the sky as he talked further. "Sure, I understand that. And if I can get a job someplace else, I sure don't want to ever see this place again."

"Now, do you have any kin you want to say 'so long' to, before you get on that train?"

"No, I ain't got no kin at all. But, if I could see Mrs. Goshen for just a few minutes, that's all I need. She lives nearby the station."

The three men walked the short distance to Mrs. Goshen's house. The agents waited outside the door as Leland went inside. Mrs. Goshen was surprised to see him. She listened to Leland tell her what was about to happen, that he would never see her again after today.

She pulled him to her as tears started to run down her cheeks. Holding him tight, she said quietly, "Leland, you're a good man inside there somewhere. I know, because I helped raise you when you was still young. You just got mixed up with some bad people over the last few years and lost your way. But I know you can get your life back on track if you can get away from the people around here, I just know you can. Wherever you go, will you promise me you'll try to change what you've become? Can you do that for me?"

"I guess you're right, Mrs. Goshen. I did lose my way after I moved away from you. But these men are giving me a way out of here, so I know I need to try to make me a better life where I'm going."

Mrs. Goshen released her hug and put her hands on his shoulders, looking in his eyes. "Just remember all the things I taught you and Abel, how to live a good life, and you'll be all right. Promise me you'll stay away from men who want to do bad things, will you?"

"I'll do my best, I'll try to make you proud of me again, I promise." Leland kissed her cheek. "Bye now," he said softly, and turned to go. He wiped his eyes before going out to join the agents. They continued their walk to the train station. Leland got on the waiting train; the agents stayed on the platform until the train pulled out.

—⊃(((◊)))⊂—

I had been on the road for four days, riding trains and barges, then hitchhiking. From Louisville, I caught a ride on a coal barge down the Ohio River to Shawneetown, Illinois, where I started hitchhiking. The last ride was on a truck going across Route 13 headed for St. Louis. I got off a little south of Herrin and began walking north the last few miles. A man in a Model A surprised me by pulling over to offer me a ride. As I got in the seat, the man offered me a cigarette.

"Are you new around here?" He had a metal lighter which he opened and worked to get a flame.

"Just getting here, now."

"Well, then, welcome! Where you from?"

"Kentucky. This sure is a nice car."

"Thanks, I just got it a few weeks ago. Brand new, it is. A 1920 Ford, I'm real happy with it, yes sir! You look like a coal miner, that right?"

"Why'd ja say that?"

"Plenty of the men around here are miners and you have the frame of one—medium height, sinewy muscles, no extra weight. And with your good looks, I'm guessing you do all right with the womenfolk too, since you look like Billy Colman, except for your hair. Suppose you haven't stopped for a haircut for a while."

"Well, you're right on the coal miner, I don't know about the second part though. And I never heard of Billy Colman—who's he?"

"He's in the moving picture shows. He has long black hair combed to one side, a strong nose and steel gray eyes like you."

"Yeah, well, see, I'm trying to get to the Madison Coal Company office. Do you know where it is?"

"Sure do, I'll drop you at the door."

After telling the Madison Coal hiring agent about my background in the Kentucky mines, the man told me I would be working as a pick miner at the Number 12 mine starting tomorrow morning.

"Any idea where I can get a room in the area of that mine?"

"Number 12 is on the north of Carterville, so go see Mr. Huntsman on North 14th. It's about two blocks from the Interurban. You can ride that over to Carterville. Lots of miners do that."

This was going easier than I had expected; people in Kentucky weren't as friendly as the local people here in Southern Illinois. And the land was so flat, I could see it would be easy to walk most anyplace. The boardinghouse was nearby so it took just a few minutes.

The address was a three-story building housing an office at the front. Standing behind the counter was a gray-haired man reading a magazine while smoking.

"Afternoon. Can I help ya?" Mr. Huntsman put down the magazine.

"Can I get a room to rent for a short while?" I asked.

"How long is a short while?"

"Well, I start working at the Number 12 mine tomorrow and I need someplace to sleep until I can get an idea of this city. Maybe a few weeks would be about right."

As he slid a registration sheet across the counter, I could see the man looking me over; his face had a frown. I started filling out the form.

"Where you from, if I can ask?"

"Kentucky."

"Where 'bouts?"

"Mule Shoe, Kentucky."

"Did you work mines there?"

"Some."

"Were you in the army any?"

"Naw."

"Most of you 'Kentucky crackers' live over in Saline County—why'd you want to be here in Herrin?"

"My people told me to stay away from there."

"You don't talk much, do you? Got anything you're trying to hide?"

"Nothin'. In the mountains we don't need to talk to strangers and we don't like strangers asking questions of us. I just like to be left alone. I don't cause no trouble and I won't do no harm to your property."

"I'd like to know how old you are and if you intend to have anyone else in the room with you."

"Well, I'm twenty-two years old and no, there won't be nobody else in there with me."

"There's a room open upstairs on two. You share the washroom with the three other men and I don't provide any of your meals. Two dollars each week, in advance. Do you want it?" Mr. Huntsman put out his cigarette in the ashtray on his counter.

"Sure do. Can I take my bag up now? I'd appreciate the chance to get some rest tonight before work tomorrow."

I went to a nearby restaurant for a bite, then back to the room. As it got dark I heard some guns being fired and I heard the people in the other rooms come and go, but I was so tired I soon fell asleep. It was the best night's sleep I had experienced in a long time. Before going to sleep, I thought about my new surroundings. The people here in Herrin seemed nice and friendly, so I should be able to start my new life easy enough. I just needed to follow Mrs. Goshen's advice: live on the straight and narrow, stay away from bad people, and concentrate on doing a good job at whatever work I do. Then I should be able to convince people I meet that I'm the kind of person they can trust and will want to be associated with.

The work in the Number 12 mine was the same as the work I had done in mines previously. The workers in this mine belonged to the United Mine Workers of America, the same as the union workers in Kentucky; I later found out most of the people in Herrin were laborers of one kind or another so they were favorable to unions; some even belonged to their respective unions—iron workers, railroad workers, printers, or others. One change I noticed was the people in Illinois seemed to want to talk more than Kentuckians. I would have to get used to that.

On Saturday, I worked in the mine till 1:00 in the afternoon. Jumping off the train at the 14th Street station, there was a crowd of people on the streets. At first I wondered if something important had happened, but, as I walked, I realized from the voices around me people were going about their Saturday shopping, meeting with friends, going to the cinema, or just walking around. Some of the people were dressed similar to the folks I had known in Kentucky, and their faces had that same dull look. When I heard them talk, I was sure they had lived near Mule Shoe, or somewhere in the mountains. Perhaps these were some of the people Mr. Huntsman had mentioned, the ones that lived in Saline County. These folks were dressed in worn clothing and the children, some without shoes, that went with them were shy and walked quietly, trying to stay close to their parents. These people had dark skin, dark hair and eyes, and walked forward looking at the ground ahead of them, not seeming to notice others nearby.

As I walked north on 14th, the crowd changed slightly, and by the Madison corner many of the people were dressed nicely; I thought they might be Herrin residents. Some youngsters heading west on Madison were talking about the latest motion picture, *Manslaughter*, playing over on Park. On the north side of Madison was the Ly-Mar Hotel. When I reached the rooming house, there were two men sitting on the porch so I decided to join them. Albert offered me a cigarette and held the match.

Sam had a room on the main floor. "Guess you just got off work, what ya think of all the people on the street?"

I took a seat on the last empty chair on the porch. "You bet, it really surprised me. I ain't seen so many people in one place in all my born days! Seems there's more people on the street by the station than there is in all of Mule Shoe."

"See, Saturday's when the folks what live in the poorer towns near the mines comes to Herrin to spend some of the money they made last week. Herrin's got the bigger stores and cheaper prices then the small towns got, that's why they all come here. They'll most all leave later this afternoon to git home for supper, yeah, this here's the big day in town fir most-a 'em. The men probably work in the mines over in Harco or Harrisburg. The coal's deeper there, so the mines ain't as productive as they are here in Williamson County, or in Franklin County, to the north. Since most mines pay by the weight of the coal produced, they don't make as much money over there. You're lucky you decided to come to Herrin."

Sam looked over the street as he took out another cigarette. Then he looked at me. "If you want to know a good barber to cut that long black hair of yours, you ought to go over to the pool hall on Park to see ole George Johnston. He's a good ole boy, and he knows everything that goes on around Herrin."

"Thanks, yeah, I need to get a haircut, for sure." Albert occupied the room next to me. "Might-a noticed the different folks what come from other countries, like Poland, Hungary—the coal mines call 'em here from ever'where."

Mr. Huntsman came out to join the group, so we enjoyed the pleasant Herrin weather while we tried to solve our city's problems. After a while, we each went separate ways, but sitting on the porch as a group became something we did often. It usually ended by my going to my room to get cleaned up and take a nap.

That evening I had my weekly bath, walked to a nearby restaurant for a bite, then to the moving picture house to see a show. As I stood waiting outside the theater, I watched several families—mom, dad, and their children—who were going to see the picture. Also, several young couples who may or may not have been married were there. The men and women in each case seemed to be genuinely enjoying each other's company; this was new to me and I liked their apparent relationships. I determined that I should find a woman who would be like that with me. I'd be a man with a wife, and maybe some children, who went to the movies on Saturday night: then, everyone would see me as a good Herrin citizen.

The following Saturday I went to the pool hall on Park Avenue Sam had mentioned. There were several men sitting in chairs in the front, so I nodded to the barber and stood against the wall to watch. I guessed the man cutting hair was the George Johnston Sam had mentioned. He was about my height and weight and stood very erect as he worked his scissors on the hair of the man in his chair. He looked like a good barber: his brown hair was neatly combed, and even his eyebrows appeared as if he combed them. He seemed like he took good care to buy nice clothing; even his shoes had a bright shine. I guessed he must be about forty. He was clean shaven. I thought he was a good advertisement for his shop.

After he recognized my entry, he continued to carry on a banter with the man getting a haircut, resuming their talk about baseball. The two men waiting in the chairs were reading the magazines or newspapers strewn on the side tables. At times, other men came through the door, nodded to George, and headed back to the pool table area; a half wall separated the two sections. On the other side of the divider, over in the corner, stood a short counter with a man behind it taking the money from the men who came to play pool. Next to him was a large cooler with drinks, for anyone who wanted one.

Mrs. Goshen had cut my hair in Mule Shoe, so this was a new experience for me. I can't recall that Mule Shoe even had a barbershop, it shore 'nuf didn't have a pool hall, we had to go to Booneville for those things. I guess the people back there weren't as well off as the people in Herrin. Getting a haircut would change my looks from an unkempt "mountain man" to the more civilized version of me I was attempting to achieve in my new surroundings. The reduced alcohol intake was a shock to my body at first, but I was now accustomed to it.

When my time came, George welcomed me as a new customer. We exchanged pleasantries as we got to know each other a little. I told him where I was from and how I had traveled to Herrin.

"Well, I've been living here in Herrin since 1899. I came here with my parents and two brothers from Kentucky, around Paducah. We heard Herrin was coming to be the center of coal mines, so people would be flocking into here and my dad thought we could get in on the action. One of the barbershops was owned by Dave Wilkerson and he was looking for a young barber. He said he'd teach me the business, so I went to work with him."

"I guess you haven't worked in the mines then?" I asked.

"Naw, I worked on the farm in Kentucky, then became a barber here. There was about five barbershops in Herrin in those days. After a few years, I bought the shop from Mr. Wilkerson when he left town."

"Guess you've seen a lot of changes to the city."

"Sure have, there was board sidewalks at first—not like the concrete ones we have today. Being a small town everybody knew everybody else, so we would sit on a street corner, under a shade tree, and drink some beer together. Everyone was welcome, not like now."

"Well, it looks like you're doing a good business these days."

"I like to think so, I stay busy most of the time. I keep the latest newspapers here for you to read and most usually you'll find men sitting here wanting some conversation. Oh, you can find out what's going on in Herrin if you stay long enough.

"So, I'm very glad you picked me to be your barber, I just hope I can keep you satisfied with my services. Now tell me how you want me to cut your hair. I'll remember for the next time you come in, so you won't have to tell me each time. That's one of the services I provide my regular customers."

"I've always parted it down the middle, so my barber used a bowl to gauge where she cut the ends, but I like the way your hair looks— can you get me something like you've got?"

"Sure can! It might make you look a little older—that would

be good, don't you think? Who knows, you might have the women knocking on your door then." He looked at me in the mirror and smiled.

George gladly told me of Herrin's history; he seemed to know a lot about the city and its people. I told him a little of my story—just the good parts, of course. Afterward, I went back to watch some men playing pool. I soon decided I needed to come over here on my days off to learn this game. It would give me a way to meet other men in a friendly setting. I later found that women wouldn't be seen in a place like this; not that they weren't welcome, it just wasn't something that a respectable woman would do, to come into a pool hall, unless they needed to get their man who was there to get away from other obligations. Even then, they would generally just open the front door and call out his name. That would be enough to embarrass him into submission.

Chapter 2

By Friday of the following week, I had become more familiar with some of the other miners, so I approached one of them. "Joe, I hear you men talking about going dancing at the local clubs. Mind if I join you on Saturday evening?"

Joe Petrie was about forty years old with black hair that was mixed with a little gray, the same as his heavy mustache. His body was thin, but strong, like most miners. He always wore work jeans with suspenders that held the top of the jeans around his waist. The denim pants had a short inseam and there were cuffs at the bottom, which he sometimes used for his cigarette's ashes. It seemed he always wore a flannel, long-sleeved undershirt; once it was probably white but the years of wear in the coal dust made it a dark gray. His choice of words and inflections made me think he sounded like someone who had lived in the area most of his life.

"Sure, you can come along. You got a girl you want to bring?" he asked.

"Naw, I don't hardly know a soul here in Herrin. I only been here for 'bout a week. You men are the only people I've met—well, except the men at Huntsman's boardinghouse. I'd like to start getting around to meet people and see the area, though."

"Where you from?"

"Kentucky."

"Are you particular to any kind of folks?"

"Guess I don't know what you mean by that."

"Well, around here, people usually socialize with their own kind. The Italians have their social clubs where those people tend to meet up, there's a few German folks that have a roadhouse over toward Carterville, like that. Most of us here at Number 12 don't mind where we go, we just want to dance a little and drink a lot. Just have some fun, you know?"

"That sounds like what I have in mind. Say, I don't have a car yet, can you give me a ride?"

"I sure can. You said you live at Mr. Huntsman's place, that right?"

"That's right, over on North 14th Street."

"All right, I'll be there around nine tomorrow evening."

Joe pulled up on North 14th Street at 9:10. "Pretty nice auto you've got, Joe." I glanced around the interior of the car. It was a 1919 Ford sedan, a five-seater with a little wear and Joe's personal items strewn about. He had on clean jeans and a somewhat white long-sleeved shirt. He had brushed the coal dirt off his shoes so they looked decent. His suspenders were also different from the ones he wore at the mine.

"Yeah, I won some money in a card game last fall and used it to pay for this. Ain't nothin' great but it gets me around. And the girls like to ride in it too."

"I don't play cards no more, so I guess I'll have to work awhile before I can buy one," I told him.

"What you mean you don't play cards no more? If you need to borrow some money to get going, there's a gentleman I know you can borrow from."

"No, that's not it. I've had a little temper problem and it got me in some trouble in Kentucky. I was playing cards with some other miners one night and I caught one of 'em cheatin'. Well, I guess I got a little too mad about it and beat the man pretty bad. The judge made me promise not to play cards again. I still think that's a good idea."

"The way you handle the pickax in the mine makes me think you must be pretty strong in the shoulders. Do you like to fight?"

"No, I don't like to, I just don't allow nobody to take advantage of me."

"You know as the evening gets late sometimes a miner or two will have too much to drink and then they like to get into some action, start pushing people around, arguing over a whore, you know? I like to get to the back and watch—not enter into the fracas. But some evenings the whole joint gets out of hand, so those times we just try to stay out of the hospital. Most usually the man behind the bar has called the sheriff to settle things down. I never get hurt too bad," Joe said smugly.

We had arrived at the Easy Time roadhouse on West Herrin Street and looked for a place to park. The parking area was already full and the music was loud inside. All the windows were open and people were sitting at tables on the patio outside. Joe parked the car near others on a grassy field in the back. As we walked toward the patio, Joe saw people he knew sitting at a table. A pleasant-looking blonde woman in her twenties was talking to a couple in their thirties and another man.

Joe interrupted, "Evenin', folks, this here's Leland, we work together at the mine. This here's Penny, this is Carl and Mrs. Worth, and that's Catfish, he works at the service garage. Catfish is a good mechanic—he fixes my car when I need it." Both men put out their cigarettes and half stood as they nodded at me. I noticed the two men had heavy mustaches, like Joe. Maybe I should grow one to fit in, I wondered.

Penny smiled at me. "You're not from around here are you, Leland? Where you from?" She had a round face, blonde hair, and light eyebrows, so I assumed the blonde hair was her natural color.

Her hair was pulled off her face to a ponytail at the back of her head. It was a roundish head and from the side, I noticed she had a sunken chin. She had an easy attitude, like she felt comfortable in her surroundings.

"Kentucky."

"That's a pretty big state, can you give me anything more?"

"Mule Shoe, Kentucky, in the mountains. I worked in the coal mines there." I pulled up a chair from another table and sat at an open spot, near Penny.

Penny pulled my arm back so she could see my waist. "I'm guessing you're about five foot ten inches tall and weigh about a hundred-fifty pounds, am I right?"

"You're a pretty good guesser, aren't you?"

"Well, I work at the hospital and one of my jobs is to weigh people coming in, so I have a little experience guessing people's weight. But most of them aren't as easy to look at as you are, Leland. You remind me of an actor I saw in a movie once—wavy hair parted on one side, a strong nose. Anyone ever tell you you looked like someone in the picture shows?"

"Yeah, somebody else told me I looked like an actor, but I don't remember his name."

"Where'd you get your good looks?"

"Can't rightly say. My father died when I was four and we didn't have pictures of him but my aunt says we don't look similar. Mom died when I was six, but I don't resemble her at all.

"You from around here?" I asked her.

"Born and bred right here in Herrin. South Side Elementary School and Herrin High School. Been working at Herrin Hospital since then." Penny emptied her glass and put it down on the table with a sigh.

"So that's a nurse's outfit you're wearing." I got up to go to the bar. "I'm gettin' a beer, would you like another one?"

"Sure, I've got time," Penny said in a lighthearted voice with a smile.

As I went into the building I had to squeeze through the crowd to get to the bar. The room was filled with cigarette smoke and everyone was talking loudly to be heard over the music. When I asked for two beers, a somewhat inebriated woman bumped against me.

"Sorry about that," she mumbled. Looking up, she realized that she hadn't see me before. "Hey, you're new here, aren't you? I'm Mary, what's your name?"

"My name's Leland."

"Where you from, cowboy? Wait, let me guess. You're from Kansas, aren't you? You look like you've spent a lot of time in a saddle."

"No, I ain't from Kansas, Mary. But it's been nice meeting you." The woman was pushing her body into me and making me feel like she was offering too much, so I turned to take the beers outside.

Mary made one last try: "Hey, wait, don't you want to talk to me? Don't ya want to ask about my saddle?"

I set Penny's beer in front of her and took a drink of mine as I sat down.

"So, tell me Leland, what do you like to do for fun?"

"Well, Penny, I don't have much time for fun."

"You ever go to the movies, that's fun."

"A little."

"How 'bout going dancing, that's fun too." She snapped her fingers in the air, like she was dancing.

"I did dance some back home."

"What kind of dancing did you do there? Were you at a roadhouse?"

"No, just on occasion we had something like the Fourth of July dancing at the hall over in Booneville."

"Did you have a special girl you would dance with, maybe a girlfriend?" She nudged my elbow with hers and winked.

"You sure ask a lot of questions, Penny. Now tell me about what you like to do."

"All right. First, though, I like to ask people questions to find out about you. It's a part of my job at the hospital and I'm good at it because I'm naturally nosy. Now, I like to dance and go to see moving pictures and sit around talking with my friends. I enjoy my job at the hospital and all the people I work with there. Well, except my boss, he's a real asshole, if you know what I mean." Penny paused a moment, but then pushed on. "Sometimes in the summer, when it gets hot we go to the lake to go swimming. Can you swim, Leland?"

"Sure. My friend Abel and I went skinny-dippin' in the creek a few times. I guess anybody can swim."

"So you had a friend named Abel. Tell me about him."

"Ain't much to tell. We were the same age and went to the same school, the only one in Mule Shoe. I lived with his family for a few years when I was young. We both went to work in the mines when we turned twelve. His daddy was dead, so we helped his mom pay the bills."

There was another pause. I couldn't understand if she was waiting for me to talk more, or just what she wanted. I sure didn't want to bore them by talking about me; I didn't have much excitement in my life anyway. And, I sure wasn't going to tell the real story of my life in the mountains—no point in telling that part of me.

Mrs. Worth asked, "Joe said you were living at Huntsman's place. How you like it there?"

"It's alright. I can walk to the train from there, so that's good."

"Tell me your last name—Leland what?"

"Vance."

Catfish was next. "You rode over here with Joe. Guess that means you ain't got no car?"

"No, never did own a car myself. We didn't need one in Mule Shoe."

"Well, we get some in at the shop once in a while, used cars that people sell, or we take for the money they owe us. There ain't any right now, but if you get interested in a good deal, I can help you out."

Joe leaned forward and lowered his voice. "The one I got came from a man out of St. Louis. He comes down here once in a while with a good deal for a car. You just can't ask too many questions about the car, though. He don't appreciate people asking questions—just take the good deal and be glad you got it."

A Model A Ford pulled into the parking lot and the horn *ah-ou-ged*.

Penny put her arm on my shoulder and leaned close to my ear as she got up. "Don't listen to them, Leland. You don't need to get involved with no stolen cars. That's what they're talking about, don't you know."

"I ain't never drove a car anyway. I'd need to learn how to drive before I can think about buying one," I responded.

"I'd be glad to teach you how," Joe said.

Penny thanked me for the beer, said her good-byes, and walked over to get in the Ford and left.

Joe finished his beer and suggested he should take me down to Vinny's Bar south of town. "Leland should get to know our Italian friends!"

"Can you drop me and Clara off at home? We're living a couple blocks down 19th Street over there," Carl asked.

"Sure, let's go if you're ready."

On the way Clara asked me, "Why did you decide to come to Williamson County, did you hear about the murdering miners and decided you wanted to join in?"

"No, I heard about the new mines here, so I was pretty sure I could get work, that's all."

As we arrived at the Worth home, Carl explained, "We put the kids in bed and walked up to socialize a little. It's a nice spring night and we need the exercise, you know?" We all said our "Evenins," then the Worths opened their screen door and walked into their house.

"Now we're going to stop at Vinny's for a drink or two. Have you ever been around Italians, Leland?" I shook my head. "They're great people! Very friendly once you get to know them. And they make great wine. Have you ever had Italian wine?"

"Naw, in the mountains we only drank moonshine or rotgut beer. We didn't have no wine around."

"You got to try some wine then. This will be some they made themselves so trust me when I tell you it's going to be good. You might not think so at first, it's different from anything you been drinking. The important thing is you shouldn't show you don't like it. That might hurt their feelings, you know?"

"Sure, I can do that."

"And don't be surprised if some of 'em wants to give you a hug. That's just the way they are, they don't mean anything untoward by it."

"Now that, I don't think I'd like. I don't like people touching me, 'less they're want'n to shake my hand."

"Uh-huh, well, we'll work that out if it happens."

I felt I had to ask, "What was Clara talking about back there, when she asked if I'd heard of the murderin' miners?"

"Oh, you haven't heard about that, eh?" Joe lit a cigarette and smiled, then started his story.

"Well, back in '88 and '89, there was a man named Brush over in Carbondale who bought some land north of Carterville and he hired some of us to dig a coal mine. We just had the United Mine Workers of America come in this area and they unionized all the miners. We got better wages through them. Well, Old Man Brush didn't want to pay us the extra money, so we went on strike. It shut down the mine for a while, until he decided to bring in some strikebreakers. Damn, they weren't just any strikebreakers, no, they was darkies. In those days, black people couldn't stay in most Southern Illinois towns after sundown and everybody knew it, so Brush built some houses and had them all stay out at Dewmaine, right at the mine.

"Now, ole Brush lived in Southern Illinois all his life, so he should-a knowed that people around here don't need much to get their gander up, and taking our work away from us and givin' it to scabs always does that to us. So most all the miners got our guns together and got ready for trouble.

"Well, the next day he brought 'em into town on the train. We had heard they was comin' and we ambushed the train. We poured rifle fire at the coaches and we killed one of the women. I was just a kid then, but I remember it like it was yesterday.

"The police called in the National Guard unit from over in Carbondale to keep the order. Now, the scabs were working at the mine and living there, so we couldn't get to 'em. We got a wagon loaded with guns and ammunition and waited. After a few weeks it seemed peaceful in Carterville again, so the troops left. Within a few days we got our chance." His voice lowered and he leaned toward me, like he was giving me treasured information.

"A group of 'em came walkin' down the road toward town and we had the wagon waitin' for 'em. We opened fire on 'em and killed a bunch of 'em, two or three right there. The others ran into the woods. I know I hit at least one of 'em. They had guns too and shot at us, but none of us got hurt. Some a' us got arrested, but they dropped the charges before we went to trial. There weren't no witnesses, so they couldn't prove anything on a-one a' us.

"Old Man Brush had to shut down the mine and finally sold it to Madison Coal Company, I think that was around aught six. It's the mine we're working in now!" Joe laughed and slapped his thigh—he enjoyed telling the story. And it was quite a story. I began to wonder what I had come into, here in Williamson County!

Vinny's Bar was off South Park Avenue at the south end of town. Again, there wasn't no parking spaces near the bar, so we had to walk a short distance. I was beginning to feel like I was in another country, not in the United States. Even the aromas in the neighborhood were unfamiliar. As we entered Vinny's, I noticed wall posters with writing I didn't understand and the women in them showed more bulging breasts than I had seen in posters before. The room wasn't as smoke filled as the last place. The music here was a little slower in tempo and a man was singing what appeared to be something in Italian. The other patrons were talking in low tones so those that wanted could enjoy the vocalist standing in front of the band. I noticed the band had a violin, not a fiddle, and another person was playing an instrument that was metal and looked like a shiny pipe going to the side, and the woman playing it was pushing flaps along its length. The piano and guitar I was familiar with, but the people playing them used a different technique. While the sound was different, I had to admit the music was very pleasant to listen to.

One of the men at the bar had seen Joe come in. "Hey, Joe, over here." As we approached, I recognized him as Anthony Garagiola, one of the miners we worked with, but, of course, he looked different with his street clothes on and the coal dust washed off his body. I imagined Anthony looked like a typical Roman: smooth dark skin, black wavy hair, dark eyes, and a strong body. Now that he wasn't working in the mine, he smiled a lot and generally looked very happy. I could see that very few of the men here had mustaches, so maybe growing one myself wouldn't be necessary after all.

"What are you guys drinking?" Anthony asked.

"I told Leland he needs to have a glass of Italian wine. He's never had wine before so we need to get him one he'll like. What do you recommend?"

"Vinny has a great Lambrusco that should be good for him." Anthony waved Vinny over, then put his hand on my shoulder.

"Vinny, don't you think a glass of Lambrusco would be good for Leland here? He's never had a glass of wine before so that should be a good starter, don't you think?"

Vinny looked me over with a quizzical look. "You must be what, twenty, twenty-five years old and you never had a glass of wine? Where you from, if I can ask, that you have never had a glass of wine?" For the last sentence he shrugged his shoulders and raised his eyebrows as he lifted both hands with the palms facing upward.

Joe jumped in. "No, see he's from the mountains of Kentucky where they drink moonshine and stuff like that, so no, he won't have tasted wine there."

I smiled weakly at Vinny and nodded my head.

"Well, since this is your first glass, I'm going to pour a Chianti for you. It's more mellow than other wines. I think you'll like it. And, since this is your first glass of wine, I can't charge you for it—that's a tradition from the part of Italy where I lived."

Now I was smiling and anxious to taste my first glass of wine. Vinny made a big production of wiping the bar in front of me with a towel, setting the empty glass on the bar, opening the bottle of Chianti, and pouring the wine out as he raised and lowered the bottle. Then he used two fingers to push the glass across to me.

"Salute!"

Anthony translated, "That means enjoy, or good drinking. It's just something Italians say to each other when we drink."

I could feel some other men watching as I picked up the glass. Even men further down the bar had become interested in this. I really wanted the wine to taste good so I could present a genuine smile. And, as I drank it, I had to admit that it was very smooth and had a good taste! So my smile was genuine as I pulled the glass away from my lips. It sounded like the whole bar was cheering for me! I was feeling warm all over from the embarrassment of everyone's attention.

I nodded my head as I smiled. "Now that's not at all what I expected. But this is very smooth and tastes like grapes. I really like it!"

More encouragement from the entire group!

"Maybe we can make an Italian out of you!"

"Salute!"

"Buona salute, Paesano!"

Many of the people patted my shoulders or shook my hand. It felt like I had passed a test and they were happy for me!

Joe gave me a knowing smile and nodded his head. I was liking this new atmosphere very well indeed. It appeared these people were seeing me as acceptable.

"Look, my friends, there's a table in the back we can sit at. Bring your drink with you, Leland." Anthony put his arm through my arm and one through Joe's and guided us through the crowded bar to the table. Again, Joe caught my eye and smiled. I smiled back and nodded reassuringly.

As soon as we were seated, a waitress in a black dress with a white apron approached the table. The black dress matched her black hair and dark eyes perfectly. The thick, short hair was done in curls, like many women wore their hair these days. This style revealed her ears, which had earrings that stuck through the lobes—something I hadn't seen before. Her ankles showed below the hem of her long dress and I noticed how smooth her skin appeared. I guessed she was about twenty years old, if that. When she smiled at me with full, red lips, I felt like her whole face lit up and it made me feel warm all over.

"Tony, who do you have here—well, of course I know Joe, but who is this gentleman?" she said as she put a hand on my shoulder.

"Maryanne, this is my friend Leland Vance. He works with us at the mine. Leland, this is my sister."

Maryanne moved closer to me so her right hip was pressed against my left bicep, then she put her right hand to my right shoulder in a semi-embrace.

"Welcome to our home, Leland! I'm glad you came," she said with a smile in her voice. She had an Italian accent, though she was easily understandable.

I glanced around the room and noticed that most of the people here had dark hair and dark eyes. Even their skin was darker than the people I was familiar with in Kentucky. Also, as they talked they moved their hands a great deal—another new trait.

"Well, Leland, I see you already have a glass of wine—Joe, do you want your usual beer?" she asked, still looking at me. She moved her body around to be more in front of me and leaned forward to ask, "Leland, I heard a minute ago that you're new to our place. Have you ever tried our food?"

As she leaned forward slightly to be more easily heard, her blouse opened a little and I could smell the perfume she was wearing. She struck me as a very attractive young girl, one I could easily get to know better.

"I don't know, what's your food, anyway?"

"No, I mean have you had rigatoni, or spaghetti, or antipasto? Things like that? My aunt is the cook in the kitchen and she makes great-tasting meals."

"Can't say for sure that I've ever had any of those things. In the mountains of Kentucky, we don't have much to eat but fried pork, beans, and cornbread. Oh, chicken and eggs, too."

"You say you're from Kentucky? I went to Paducah one time, is that near where you're from?"

"No, that's a long ways away. I'm from the eastern part, where the mountains are."

Joe tried to interrupt: "That beer sure would taste good right now."

"Is it pretty there, in the mountains?" she asked.

"No, not really. Well, in the springtime the trees come back to life and the flowers bloom, so I guess that's pretty. And in the fall when the leaves on the trees change color, that's a pretty time too. I guess I didn't take the time to look at the mountains that way."

"Isn't that sad? Beauty all around you but you didn't take the time to enjoy it!"

I realized she was right, I didn't take time to really look at my surroundings back then. I just gave her a weak smile. I hadn't looked at life that way.

Maryanne put her hand on Joe's shoulder without looking at him. "There were mountains in Italy, where I grew up, well most of the people in here are from that part of Italy. I thought the mountains were beautiful." She turned to go get Joe's beer.

"You'll have to excuse my sister, she likes to talk a lot." Anthony put his hand on my back; again he was touching me.

I shrugged my shoulders. "That's alright, she seems to mean well."

Joe offered us a cigarette; everyone took a deep draw and we got comfortable in our chairs.

Anthony started a story. "Yeah, she has an idyllic view of Italy. She was young when my family left to come here, so she doesn't remember the hard times. I left Italy to go to the Ruhr valley in Germany to work in the coal mines because I couldn't find work in Italy. That's where I learned to be a shotfirer. Digging the coal is hard work, so blasting the coal gives me a break from that."

I frowned with confusion. "Why did you leave Italy for Germany? Wasn't there work you could do in your hometown?"

"I was just getting old enough to realize how corrupt the people were there. The thing that really set me off was when a friend of mine in school—he was really smart—wanted to get a job at the silk factory as an accountant, but it was denied to him. The man who got the job wasn't really qualified, but he was from a wealthy family and they used their money and influence to bribe the factory owner. So my friend and I decided to leave Italy and go to Germany, we thought it would be better there. The German government paid our train fares because they needed men to work in the coal mines. But we soon found out the situation there was similar to Italy. So much of the government bureaucracy was corrupt. And we could see that the German people were anxious for a war. If we stayed there we would be caught up in it, so we saved our money and came to America. That took a little time because we had to bribe the German officials to get exit visas, but we did it. When we got to New York, I read in the papers about the new coal fields here in Southern Illinois, so I came to Herrin."

Maryanne returned with Joe's beer and set it in front of him, but she was smiling at me. She turned and went off.

Joe quoted a man he had read in the newspapers: "Go west, young man?"

"Something like that. But, as I get older I realize that people are the same everywhere. As more people came here from Italy, our families wanted to open businesses here in Herrin. But to do that we were required to pay the same bureaucrats as we were required to do in Italy and in Germany. It doesn't seem fair, you read in the children's books as you grow up that you should always be fair, but when you get older, you find out that life's not fair in the real world.

"What about you, Leland, why did you leave Kentucky?"

"Well, I just decided it was time to leave. I had worked in the coal mines since I was twelve, so that was the one thing I knew how to do, and people there told me about the new coal fields in Herrin. I came here by train, riverboat, and hitchhiking, so here I am." I had been practicing this explanation and it came out better each time I told it.

Anthony turned to the last man at the table. "What about you, Joe, what's your story?"

"I ain't got no story. I grew up on a farm over at Fredonia. When the early mines started opening up, that's where I went to work. My older brothers were going to get the farm when the old man died, so I thought I needed to find some honest work. Hard work in the mines don't bother me—hell, I worked just as hard on the farm all summer. They was longer hours and in the hot sun all day! Naw, mine work ain't any harder 'an that."

Maryanne returned again with a plate of food which she put in front of me. She wiped the edge of the plate with a towel to clean off some of the spillage.

"Leland, you said you hadn't had any Italian food before, so I brought you a plate of several types to try. I want to know which one you like best! I'll be right back. Tony, why don't you show him how to eat the spaghetti?"

Anthony gave a short chuckle. "You'll see Americans cut the spaghetti with their knives and then eat it with their fork, but Italians use a spoon with their fork, then spin the fork to grab the spaghetti like this. It's the traditional method, but you can do whatever you like."

I tried to pick up the noodles by spinning the fork, but I gave up and cut the noodles first. When Maryanne returned, she asked me for my selection.

"I liked all of it, but the spaghetti would have to be my favorite."

"You Americans are all alike. It takes a little time to enjoy the other dishes, of course, but it's worth the trouble to enjoy good Italian cooking. Why don't you come back tomorrow night and eat here, I know you'll enjoy yourself," she said with that smile that lit up her whole face. I thought she was a quite pretty girl, one who was very outgoing, friendly with everyone. While she was younger than me, she sounded more experienced talking with other people than I was; she probably wouldn't be someone I could get involved with right now.

As we three men enjoyed another smoke, a young man walked into the restaurant. Anthony called out his name and waved for him to come over.

"That's my younger brother, Caesar," he told us. "Caesar, come on over!"

But Caesar just waved and walked to the bar to talk to a young woman. He looked like a younger version of Anthony; his body moved easily as he walked and he had a look of confidence about him. He was dressed nicely and the woman appeared to know him well, since she offered her cheek for him to kiss as he greeted her.

"He has a mind of his own, that one," Anthony said, shaking his head. "He's only twenty but he thinks he knows everything—well, you men were young once too, so you know what I mean. It's just that he gets into moods sometimes. He'll be happy and easygoing for a while, then he acts like he hates everyone. The whole family worries about him."

Chapter 3

I had been living at the Huntsman rooming house for four weeks, when, on a Saturday, as I returned from work I noticed a strange man talking with Mr. Huntsman.

Mr. Huntsman held up his open hand. "Say Leland, can you give us a moment? This is Mr. Wilson. He'd like to talk with you, if you have time."

"Yeah, sure, I have time now."

Mr. Wilson was about forty to forty-five years old and dressed in slacks, a white shirt, and held his straw boater hat in his hand. He seemed tired to me from the way his shoulders slouched forward, but he introduced himself quickly and got right to the point.

"Hello, Leland, nice to meet you. Mr. Huntsman here has told me a little bit about you already. The reason I'm here is this: my mother lives further up the street here, in a two-story house. She's seventy-five years old and lives alone, which isn't good, as you'll understand. We had a young man living with her for the past few years, but he's now gone on to another city, so I'm looking for someone else to live with her. In these situations, when I'm looking for someone for her, I depend on Mr. Huntsman's recommendation and he's suggested you. Can you tell me if you might be interested?"

Mr. Wilson paused as I thought for a few seconds. I had planned to find another place to live after a few weeks living at Huntsman's, and this would be good timing. And, I would be living with a local person, so it could help me understand the people here.

"I guess that might be something I'd be interested in. What does it cost and what are the rooming arrangements?"

"You'll find the cost reasonable, five dollars a month, which will include a private room and one meal each day. But there's a little more to it than that. Mother is a widower—my dad passed over about ten years ago. She was a schoolteacher here in Herrin for forty-some years while Dad worked for the State. She is adamant about living in her house, so I try to make that possible for her. Now, here's where you come in: you will need to help her to get her groceries, help with the heavy chores, things like that. Your room will be on the second floor—she lives on the first and really can't manage the steps any longer, so you'll be left alone when you're up there.

"Is this something you might still be interested in doing?"

"Sure is, I can do everything you've mentioned so far. Last place I lived in Kentucky, I helped Mrs. Goshen like that."

"Good, so far, so good. I've been listening to you talk, that's going to be another aspect of living with her. She taught English at Herrin High and she likes for you to speak proper; in fact, she enjoys working with you young men on proper speaking, so you would receive another benefit living there. At least humor her on this and you'll get along fine. So, do you have time to meet her now?"

"Yeah, but I need to wash the coal dust off first. Can you wait fifteen minutes?"

"Why don't you walk up 14th here when you're ready. I'll be sitting on the porch with Mother, waiting on you. It's the second block up, second house on the right."

I quickly washed up and put on decent clothes, then walked to the house. It was an older house with a brick exterior and many flowers in the front. The rear appeared to be fenced in and contained a large garden. As I approached the front steps, both people rose to meet me.

"Leland, I'd like you to meet my mother, Rosemary Wilson. Mother, this is Leland Vance."

I took off my hat and bowed slightly. "Nice to meet you, ma'am."

"Well, it's nice to meet you too, young man. Can I offer you a cool drink?" Mrs. Wilson was a slight woman, perhaps five feet four, who stood very erect and seemed to move easily. She had a head of gray hair, which was thinning on the top. She wore a long brown dress with a clean, colorful apron over it. Her black shoes were laced and she had on white stockings that went up past her hemline. She did indeed look like a schoolteacher, although that had ended ten years earlier. She turned to her son. "Charles, let's go inside and get this young man something to drink."

Through the front door we went, stepping into the living room which extended to the right. A large opening in the middle of the wall to the left was the entry to the dining room. Rosemary led the way directly through the living room into the kitchen. I immediately thought this was an old room because there was a pump for water situated on the counter next to the sink. Near a back door was an icebox, still in use. A doorway to the right led to Rosemary's room.

After pouring three iced teas, Rosemary led us out the exterior door and onto the back porch.

"This is my outdoor workroom. You can see the vegetables I'm preparing. Here's the bathroom we'll share, you'll have a washstand in your room to use for cleaning yourself. Over there is the stairway to the second floor where you'll stay. It has a lock on the door up there; Charles, it does work, doesn't it? Well, you don't really need to lock it, we've never had a problem here. Although, the drinking problems that have come with the prohibition thing are starting to change Herrin. Do you drink, young Leland?"

"Yes ma'am, with a meal, for instance, but not unless I'm with other people, you see."

"Well, I don't have a problem with drinking alcohol, I drink a little wine at times myself.

"Now, the only rule I have is that you not bring a woman upstairs with you. I don't have the problem with that, it's the people in the neighborhood that get concerned. You may have noticed that Herrin is a very religious community.

"I need groceries on Fridays, I will give you a list and you can walk, or take the car in the garage there. Do you drive, Leland?"

"Not yet, ma'am, but I'm just about to learn from a friend. He has a car he said we'd use for that."

"That's fine, you can walk while the weather's nice anyway. My doctor's in Marion, I won't need to go there for a few months, I hope, so we'll talk about that later. Charles, will you show Leland his area and tell him about the money he pays. Can you start tomorrow, Leland?"

Charles gave me the tour of the second floor; it contained the two bedrooms Charles and his sister Betty lived in growing up. It looked ideal to me—some privacy in a quiet room and a landlord that seemed compliant—so we made the final arrangements. I thought it was a good sign, too, that Mr. Huntsman had considered enough of me to recommend me to Mr. Wilson. Perhaps I can become the upstanding man Mrs. Goshen thought I could be.

On Sunday I carried my clothing and personal items in two trips up the street. Mrs. Wilson had a Sunday dinner ready at 1:00. I thought it was delicious, perhaps as good as the best I had ever eaten, although it was composed of some vegetables I hadn't tasted before, probably items she grew in her garden.

"I enjoy cooking and Sunday calls for an especially good meal, don't you think?" Rosemary asked. "My husband Johnathon believed Sunday was the best day of the week. We used to go to church and then come home to a good meal. After that we might talk or read for a while, then he would take a long nap. After working six days, he needed the rest, especially as he got older.

"Do you attend church, Leland?"

"No ma'am, I wasn't raised in a Christian family, I guess. I became an orphan at six, so I lived with several different families till I moved in with Mrs. Goshen. Guess the people in Kentucky aren't as religious goin' as you folks here."

"Well, I was raised in the Pentecostal church over in Carterville. Johnathon and I were raised in families of that church. He went off to the Normal College over in Carbondale, then a year later I joined him over there. We both learned a lot about the world, of course, that's what a college does for young people." Rosemary lowered her voice and glanced out the window. "We learned about evolution there but the folks here in Little Egypt don't think that idea is true, so we don't talk about it with anybody else around." Then she returned to her normal voice. "Johnathon was hired by the State of Illinois when he graduated, so we stayed here with his work, but most of the other people we went to school with left here to go to the bigger cities. See, Southern Illinois cities don't have much to offer to people with college degrees. Well, when we started our married life together, we were attending the Presbyterian church. The folks there are a little more open minded than most of the folks here in Herrin.

"I got a job teaching English at Herrin High School, did that all my life until Johnathon died. We raised our two children right here in this house. Betty went to college at the state university up in Champaign, then got a teaching job in Decatur, at Millikin University. Charles went to school in Carbondale for a while, then went to work for the railroad in the office over there. Of course, he looks after me when I need help, which isn't very often—I can take care of myself just fine.

"Enough about me, I just talk a little too much, I know. Tell me about yourself, Leland. How did you wind up at the rooming house down the street?"

I filled Rosemary in on my activities, giving some information about my time in Kentucky, at least the items I felt she needed to know—I left out the parts about the moonshining, bar fights, and my time in jail. Then I talked a little about working in the mines each day, but again, just enough to satisfy her curiosity. I wanted to be on good terms with her because this living arrangement could turn out to be ideal. As the two of us got used to each other over time, it was indeed a good arrangement.

Chapter 4

A few weeks later I had saved enough money for another night of dining and drinking with my friends. On Saturday night, the trio of us—Anthony had joined Joe and I—planned to go to the Black Forest Inn, a restaurant and bar located on the west side of Herrin. During the week I had purchased a new white shirt for the occasion; also some new jeans and a belt.

This evening Anthony was driving the Ford Model A he had purchased in the spring. "It hums along up to forty miles an hour," he said proudly. He still had a fresh look to him, like he did at Vinny's. Joe, again, had on a white shirt, probably the one he wore last time. I suspected he just had the one "dress" shirt.

As we entered, Anthony asked to be seated at a table served by Fraulein Bertha.

Anthony and Joe had eaten here many times and they had me primed to expect a great meal. The music in the place was much closer to the music I had heard in the mountains. The musicians had a fiddle, an accordion, and a guitar. Most of the walls were made of wood and in the posters on them, the women wore blouses buttoned more so than the Italian women I had noticed in the posters at Vinny's.

A small dance floor was located before the band and the people there were moving somewhat similar to the way people danced in the mountains—quick short steps, the men turning the women in different fashions. Also, more lighting made it easier to see than at the Italian restaurant. Again here, there was some cigarette smoke in the room, but not as much as at the Easy Time Bar. I had seen some of the people who were eating here before, either in the town or going to the mines, and this made me feel more comfortable. I could detect a little German being spoken, but mostly the people spoke my familiar English.

We were seated at a table away from the dancing, nearer to the kitchen and toward the back of the restaurant. Bertha came to the table with a pleasant smile on her face, but her eyes looked weary. Her chestnut-colored hair was pulled up in a bun on the back of her head and she wore a long brown dress, covered by a white apron. I thought she was about five feet, five inches tall and couldn't weigh over one hundred pounds; probably about my age, or a little younger. One distinguishing feature was a scar on her right cheek about an inch in front of her ear, but it was barely noticeable.

"Gut evening, gentlemen, vat would you like to drink tonight?" Bertha had a good command of English, but a little of her native language still remained.

Anthony asked for three beers in his best German. Bertha smiled at his attempt. "Besides three beers, would you want pickled eggs, or sauerkraut, perhaps?"

Anthony and Joe shook their heads, but I ordered the pickled eggs. "Yes, we'll have an order of pickled eggs. I haven't had any since last winter in the mountains! Have either of you eaten pickled eggs?"

Both men shook their heads with a sour look on their faces. Bertha picked up on my comment about the mountains.

"What mountains are you talking about? Where did you live in the mountains?"

I had to smile at her interest. "I'm from eastern Kentucky. I lived in the Appalachian Mountains until I moved here. Are you a mountain girl?"

"Yes, but from the mountains of Germany. I really miss them."

"There are mountains to the southwest of here," Joe spoke up.

"I've heard talk about them," I replied. "They ain't far away but they ain't very high, not like Kentucky."

I guess Anthony sensed a comradery between Bertha and me. "Leland, why don't you borrow my car tomorrow and take Bertha for a ride to the mountains south of Carbondale?"

I got a quizzical smile as I looked at Anthony. Then I turned to Bertha, who gave a quick grin, then returned to her business face, nodding. "Sure, but I have to work." She turned around, heading for the bar. Even though her face looked tired, her step was quick and she stood very erect.

As I watched her go, I noted a familiar voice to my left. Turning, I saw Carl and Clara Worth sitting at a table with Penny. I motioned to my two friends to look at the other table, then asked about Penny.

"What do you guys know about Penny, she's been with the Worths both time I've seen her. Is there some story here?"

Joe responded, "Oh, yeah, see, Penny and Clara are sisters and Penny was married before the war. Her husband Danny went off to be a soldier over there. He survived the war, but on the ship coming back he got the Spanish flu. He didn't live to get back to shore. So Penny lives with Carl and Clara now and she works at the hospital."

Anthony nodded. "Sure, everyone around here knows about that. Herrin is a small town so we all know about things like this. I asked her to go for a drink with me last month, but she said she isn't ready to see anyone else yet. She still misses Danny."

Joe added, "We all tried to make her feel comfortable when the news came in, but she took it really hard. I remember her saying that she would rather he died in a trench by a German shell than to die on a ship from the dreaded flu, that dying that way must have been awful for him."

"Joe, you worked in the mines with me; Leland, did you go over there?" Anthony asked.

"No, miners didn't have to go into the service."

Bertha returned with the beer and eggs. She looked at my eyes and smiled as she put the eggs before me. "Prost!" she said and walked away.

Anthony was happy to explain, "That's what the Germans say, it means good health or something like that."

The beer was darker than I was accustomed to drinking, but I liked the robust flavor. I offered eggs to the other two so we all belched and farted from the gas of the eggs and beer. As the evening progressed, we ordered more beer and plates of Rouladen with boiled potatoes and sauerkraut.

When we finished eating, Anthony noticed Harry Fisher, another miner at Madison Coal, at the bar and called him over to join us. Harry was a typical miner, a little taller than me; he had a lean, muscular frame and he had a full mustache like Joe. His eyes seemed calm, but, to me, his mouth appeared to have a permanent sneer. I had seen him around the mine on occasion—he was the miner who was called on when there was a problem with the equipment. One thing I remember about him was that he had sarcastic things to say about the company we worked for. But here, he was a friendly person, he liked to tell jokes, so he and Joe started trying to outdo each other with funny stories.

Bertha came to our table to see if we needed anything, so Harry told her a joke that was a little on the racy side. Her cheeks turned red as he gave the punch line and she gave a polite chuckle. Then Anthony told a joke about a Lutheran minister, a Catholic priest, and a Jewish rabbi. For this one she gave a hearty laugh, saying she was Lutheran in Germany and heard a similar joke there, she just didn't know how to translate it to English. She had a hearty, genuine laugh; I liked hearing it.

"If no one needs anything else, I'll leave you alone to tell your dirty jokes," she said with a smile and left us to our stories.

After enjoying a final cigarette, we called Bertha over for our check. She asked how we liked the food.

Joe and Anthony claimed it was the best they had had.

I was more complimentary. "It was better than my friends said it would be. I'll be back here next week for more!"

Bertha gave me a friendly glance and winked at me. "When you do, be sure to ask for me to be your server."

"I sure will." I was confused as to whether she was just wanting the business, or did the wink mean more? But I did like her interest in me, so I took the wink as something more. I don't know why, but this woman interested me. She was pleasant looking, had a strong voice and very pretty eyes. Her reserved manner appealed to me.

I slept well that night.

Chapter 5

The following Saturday night I went to the Black Forest Inn alone, somewhat later in the evening. I asked for a table in Bertha's area. When she came to the table, she recognized me with a smile and a friendly greeting. She looked a little less tired tonight—maybe she hadn't had to work as hard this week—but her dress was the same and her hair was still in a bun on the back of her head.

"So you've come back for more of our delicious food?"

"No, I'm here for some more of your good beer. I haven't had German beer before, only the rotgut beer we had in the mountains." I thought mentioning the mountains would jog her memory and I might get her talking about them; perhaps we could get a conversation going.

"I believe your friend, Anthony, asked for the dark beer. Is that what you had in mind?"

"Sure, that sounds like the beer we had last week, can you bring me one?"

She turned and went off to get it. The room was less crowded tonight, so the talk was more subdued. Very quickly she returned with the glass of brew.

As she set the glass on the table, I remarked on the number of customers this evening.

"Yes, well, last week, when you were here, we were exceptionally busy, I don't know why some nights are like that. Of course, it's good to have many customers, but the amount of work is very tiring for me. I like it better on nights like this." Her voice was brighter sounding than last week—she seemed to be in a better mood.

"How long have you worked here, it sounds like you've been here for quite a while?"

"Well, let's see, I came to America in 1914 to work for my cousin Carl, so I guess I've been working here for about six years. At first I worked here all the time, but the last two years, I've been working at the Rogers' Tailor Shop during the week and I help out here on weekend evenings."

"How did that work out, you coming from Germany to a place like Herrin?"

Bertha noticed another table that needed service, so she told me to wait a moment. While she was gone I tried to think of other questions that would keep her talking; I was enjoying her talk and, I think, she was enjoying talking with me. She returned shortly and resumed her story.

"My grandfather in Germany owned a very successful restaurant in Kempten, near the Swiss border, in the south of Germany. He had twenty-four grandchildren and, at one time or another, most of us worked in his restaurant. He said he wanted for as many of us as wanted to be able to go to America. He thought we would be better off here than in Germany because the people there seemed to always want to go to war with their neighbors. He said Emperor Wilhelm II was building a war machine and that a war would be bad for us. That's why we were being sent to America."

"Does this restaurant belong to your cousin?"

"Yes, Grandfather helped him come here in 1912 and start this place. Two years later, when I was fourteen, I was able to come over to join them. Just in time too—the war started later that year."

"Did any other family members come over too?"

Bertha got a sad look and her shoulders sank a little. "No, just the three of us, Carl's wife is the cook here. My father and one brother had received notices to report to the army before I left. They were both killed in the war. My other brother went into the army but he survived. After the war, he moved to Selesia with his wife and my mother. I still write to my mother often, I really miss her, but things aren't good in Germany now, so I guess we won't be getting together for a long time."

"I'm sorry to hear that, I'm sure it makes you sad, but at least you made it to America. That's good for you!" I wanted to brighten the mood, not let her feel sad.

"You said you came here from the mountains of Kentucky, didn't you?"

"That's right, I moved here several months ago." So she remembered me—good. "I worked in the mines in Kentucky, but living there was real hard, so I decided to come to Herrin. I was told miners got better pay here, so I got on a train and left Kentucky." I didn't think it would be good for her to know the real reason I left just yet—no need to scare her off while we were enjoying our conversation.

A new group of men came to a table nearby, so Bertha went over to help them. The more I was finding out about her, the more I thought she was a really nice person; she had gone through some hard times, but she seemed to be coming out better for the experience. As I drank my beer, I tried to think of other ways to keep her focus on herself—I didn't want to have to say too much about my past.

After delivering the drinks to the new table, she went to another to wipe it off and reset it. After a few words with the man at the bar, who, I assumed, must be her cousin Carl, she worked her way back to me.

"You're still here? I thought my boring life story would have scared you off by now." She cocked her head to one side and smiled at me; it made me feel good.

"I like to hear you talk, especially about Germany. You're the first person I have known from overseas, anywhere. I like the way you talk, it's different, but nice."

Bertha pulled back a chair and sat at the table with me.

"We aren't busy tonight, so Carl doesn't mind if I take a break here a little while. Why don't you tell me more about you? I like to hear what Americans think about living in Herrin." While she said she was sitting down for a break, I thought she was sitting very erect, not relaxing at all, which was a little confusing to me.

"Sure, I like living here in Herrin. The people are nice, they're helpful and friendly. But, what I find very different from Kentucky, is how much they talk. We didn't have people who liked to talk like this in the mountains. Do you think it's different from the people in the mountains where you lived?"

She thought about this for a few seconds. "No, I think the people there were at least as open as the people here. When I would walk in the mountains with my friends, we always talked about everything. On Sunday afternoons my family would play games or read together, especially in the winter, those were fun times. Didn't your family do things like that?"

Damn, I thought, not going the way I wanted! "To tell the truth, my father died when I was four and my mother was sick with consumption for the last few years of her life, so, no, we didn't have good family time like you did. But even the other children around me, at school or playing around, didn't have families that talked much. That's just the way it was in Mule Shoe."

"Did your mother and father talk with you when they were alive?"

I felt this might be a turning point in our relationship, if there was to be a relationship, so I decided to take a chance on her mercy. "I'll tell you the truth, which I don't usually share with other people. My father wasn't a good person. He would usually be drunk when he came home, if he came home at all. Then, he would treat my mother terrible until he passed out. He would have beat on me too if my mother didn't protect me by hiding me under the bed. We would be very quiet as we got ready for bed so we wouldn't wake him. In the morning he might have coffee and toast before he left for the mine. So, no, we didn't talk much at home."

Bertha leaned toward me with a sorrowful look. "I'm sorry to hear this, but thank you for telling me about it, it must be hard to recall. I wish there was something I could do to help." She put her hand on my arm and squeezed it.

I nodded. "There's not really nothin' anyone can do now. I just accept that my early life wasn't as good as most people's, but I try to not let it get me down. My life now is pretty good, so I think I have come out all right after that beginning."

"That's a good attitude to have. When I was traveling here from Germany, at times I would become afraid of the surroundings on the boat or the train. Then, I would try to concentrate on something good and tell myself that it will be all right in the end, and it always was. When I look at you now, I think you look like a good person, Leland, someone I would like to get to know better, so, yes, you've overcome your unfortunate start in life."

I felt relieved she wasn't shaken by my story. If anything, she was more taken with me because of it. "Well, enough of my history, let's talk about something good!"

We talked briefly about the mountains in Germany, then she had to return to her duties at the restaurant. I left for the evening, with a promise to return soon.

Chapter 6

*R*emoving coal from the earth continued unabated. In fact, the number of mines in the country produced more coal than was required, which kept prices low. Union contracts mandated the companies to hire more men than needed, so there were 200,000 more mine workers employed than were necessary. Consequently, the mine workers divided the work, resulting in an average work week for most men of around three days, but they were each paid a full wage. The mine owners were caught in union contracts that required them to employ extra men and to pay all workers the same living wage.

The country was using lots of coal and Williamson County was an integral part of the production to meet that need. But, there was a hazard to the lives of the miners working underground. Usually, the horizontal mine shafts, many over a thousand feet long, had small railroad tracks for the wheeled bins to ride along, some being pulled by mules. Miners would be killed or injured by the movement of these rolling containers in the close areas. And then, some mines produced a gas that would cause an explosion or ignition, or it would asphyxiate the men down there.

For example, there was a mining accident in Johnston City, a nearby town—an explosion which killed five men. The Herrin Christian Church announced a memorial service for that Saturday. It was one of the bigger churches in the area, so it had the best chance of holding the large crowd that was being expected. A religious service would be held and donations *taken for the families of the deceased. While three of the miners were single, the other two left a total of seven children. Mining companies considered these accidents to be just a part of the job. Working in coal mines had always been a high-risk endeavor, so they didn't provide any benefits to the survivors. The union had a small fund that helped out a little, but only briefly. It was getting to be late September so the families would welcome the help to get through the winter.*

It was a touching service; the widows sat in the front with their children. One family of the single men was a member of the church, but all the victims were well known in the community. Attendance was so large, many people were standing on the street outside waiting to see the victims' families.

After the service, a potluck dinner was held in the basement of the church. The feeling in the room was as if everyone was part of a large, extended family. It wasn't just the miners who were in attendance, but all different union workers as well as business owners and public officials. All parts of the community were represented: Baptists, Methodists, Catholics, wet, dry, even non-Christians came to honor the deceased. A rather large amount of money was collected in donations and the families said they were most appreciative. Of course, the political people were there to shake as many hands as possible, since the next elections would not be far off.

I intentionally arrived a little late so I could stand outside, but still be a part of the memorial service. Afterward, I went with my friend Caleb to the pool hall down the street. I got a haircut first, before joining Caleb at the pool table. As I sat in George's barber chair, I noticed a short and slender, attractive woman walk past the front window.

George noticed her also. "That's Bertha, she works in the tailor shop next door. If you ever need some sewing done, she's a good person to see. She does fine work!"

"Yeah, I know who she is, but I thought she's a waitress at the

Black Forest Inn. Oh, that's right, she did tell me she worked at a tailor shop too." As I realized who she was, I sat straighter in the chair and looked closely at her. I hadn't seen her in the daytime before. I thought she was more attractive in the daylight—or was it just that she wasn't tired looking from working until late at night? Her complexion was clear and she stood very erect as she walked. Her chestnut hair was lying loose with a curl at the ends, near her shoulders. The hat she wore looked like a beret—very foreign looking. She must have seen someone she knew ahead of her, because she smiled and waved. I wished it had been me up there.

"Yeah, she helps her cousin at his restaurant on Saturday nights, but she works at the tailor shop during the week. She's from Germany and very industrious—well, you know how those Germans are."

"I have a tear in my winter coat that I need to get fixed before it gets cold, guess I could take it to her to mend."

"Sure, do that. And tell her I sent you over, we like to help each other out here in Herrin. Now if you need a good grocery store, Old Man Jacobs over on 14th Street is a good man to see. He's a little bit conservative in his beliefs, but if you tell him I sent you over, he'll give you a good deal."

"I believe I've seen his ad in the *Miner's Weekly*, but, I live with Mrs. Wilson, so I go to her grocer."

"So you live with Rosemary; she's a great old gal. Now, have you been to Vinny's Bar on South Park? That's good Italian food, for sure."

"Yeah, Vinny is the uncle of my friend Anthony Garagiola. We've been there a few times."

"Oh, Mr. Anthony Garagiola, he's becoming quite the man with the Italians here in Herrin. He came in here last week soliciting for the annual Columbus Day Parade. It sounds like that will be a great event this year. Has he told you anything about it?"

"Just that he's working on it with some people. I don't know if they're his relatives or not—with all those three-syllable names, I can't keep them all straight."

George chuckled at the humor. "I know what you mean. And there's getting to be so many of them moving here, we better get to know how to pronounce their names. They're moving here from Murphysboro, Carbondale, all over Little Egypt. And from Italy too, of course." George went on about the happenings in his hometown.

"Now, there was an article in the *Herrin News* about some action in Milan, Italy. That's where most of them come from. You know, the man that runs the Hippodrome, Mr. Marlow, married one of the women from over there. He hadn't met her till she got off the train!"

"My friend Anthony is talking about quitting the mines and opening an Italian grocery. He says Mr. Marlow will give him money to get it started."

I watched through the window as a man wearing a suit and black tie approached a car parked at the curb. The man paused before getting in and looked at the pool hall window. Then he came to the door and called inside. "Anyone need a ride back to Johnston City? I'm about to leave for there."

A young man sitting in the back watching some men shoot pool stood up. "Sure do, Judge, I'd appreciate a lift, if I can!"

"Well, come along, Walter, we'll enjoy this fall weather together."

As they walked toward the car, I heard the Judge ask, "I guess you've been staying out of trouble, Walter, seeing you haven't been in my courtroom in a while."

"Yes sir, I've been keeping my nose clean since . . ." And they drove off.

"That's Judge Landis, Leland. Guess you haven't seen him before. He's one of the real straight shooters. Wouldn't take any money from anybody that's in his court or otherwise. He's a judge in the county courts over in Marion. Oh, and he's a member of the Herrin Christian Church. Guess he was here for the services for the miners.

Did you go there yourself?"

"Yeah, I went over for a little while. Got there a little late, so I had to stand outside. Don't know how many people were inside, but there must have been a hundred or so outside. With the windows open, we could hear everything goin' on inside, it was real nice."

George put down his scissors and turned the chair so I could see his work. "Now you'll look nice for the girls you'll be dancing with tonight. Which roadhouse y'all going to?"

"I always go with Joe Petrie, so he decides where we're goin'."

"Oh, you hang with Joe Petrie? He's an interesting man, he is. People say he likes to get liquored up and use the women that hang out at the Easy Time. Any truth to that?"

"None I've seen, but maybe so."

I spent a few hours smoking and shooting pool with Caleb and some other boys. We all wore jeans and most had on BVDs for shirts. Caleb and I had on white shirts since we had been at the ceremony.

Caleb was about eighteen years old. He had finished Herrin High School last summer, then went to work in the mines. His family belonged to the Herrin Christian Church, had done so for many years, as he told the story. He was expected to go into mining as his father had and most of the other members of his immediate family. Like many other people in this area, he had only traveled as far away as St. Louis and only for one day—you didn't stay overnight in a big, sinful city like that. Working in the mines was most appropriate for his fair complexion, light brown hair, and blue eyes; obviously he hadn't spent much time in the sun.

Two other tables were also occupied with men playing pool; the one to the front was idle. Beside the sound of the pool balls hitting each other, the quiet talk of the men, and the occasional ping of tobacco juice as it landed in a spittoon, the room was fairly quiet and somewhat dark except for the lights over the occupied pool tables. A late September sun filled the barber area and the open doors at the front and back of the room encouraged the breeze, keeping the area fresh. Shooting pool was becoming my favorite place to spend time.

One of our group, Joe Bob, worked with me in the mines and he mentioned that he worked at Colp Tavern on Saturday nights and holidays. I asked about working conditions there. Joe Bob stood upright and applied the cube of chalk to the end of his cue stick. "Well it's pretty easy work until there's a problem: say a fight breaks out between some of the men, then you have to get your billy club and settle the men down. But that doesn't happen every night. I ain't never got hurt too bad myself, but sometimes they have to take a man to the hospital." He was a big, imposing man, strong arms on a lean body—the appearance of someone you didn't want to get upset with you. Atop his head was thick black hair with sideburns down to the bottom of his ears. His dark eyes were in the shadow of thick eyebrows, but his voice was soft; it was easy to listen to him.

"Now, if you really want to make some money, you can ask Mr. Mark Wallops about delivering the hooch—that's what we call the liquor around here. He works for Mr. Shelton. They also run the slot machines in the roadhouses. But you have to carry a gun for that work."

"No, I'll pass on the heavy work, but how do I get some work like you're doing?"

"Come on out to the tavern tonight and I'll introduce you to Mr. Goodfellow."

I started working as a roadhouse peacekeeper that night. Over the next month I was able to save some money so I had Joe show me how to drive a car.

The following Saturday night I went to work at the Colp Tavern at 9:00, but after a short while Mr. Goodfellow said the business was too slow that evening, so he told me to leave early. I caught a ride to the Black Forest Inn thinking maybe Bertha would have some time to talk with me. As I entered, I asked for a table in her area. This business was also lacking customers, so she shouldn't be too busy.

"So you've come back again this week. You're getting to be a regular customer, Mr. Leland." Her smile was getting to be more attractive to me each time I saw her. She was wearing the same clothes; I hoped she had more than one set of the same outfit.

"Well, I enjoy the beer and the conversation in this place, can you bring me a glass of the same dark beer as last week?"

"Coming right back!" Her voice was lyrical as she quickly turned and walked away.

As I watched her go, I felt my hands were getting a little sweaty, so I rubbed them on my pant legs. This was a new feeling for me; it had to be because of her presence, but I had been around girls in the past and hadn't been affected like this.

Bertha returned with the beer. "Would you like to have something to eat with your beer? Perhaps some sauerkraut, or soup? Anna is our cook and she makes delicious-tasting dishes."

"See, I had supper a few hours ago, but I could eat something light—what would you recommend?"

"Anna's Brokkolisuppe is quite delicious, it's a creamy broccoli soup. Or, we also have Kartoffelsuppe; it's made with potatoes, vegetables, and sausages." She laughed as she said it. "*Kartoffel* is the German word for potato, Americans usually think it's funny when I explain the meaning to them. Anyway, they're both good tasting!" I had to smile—her explanation was cute!

"You make them sound very good, but I haven't had either one so I don't know which I would choose. Why don't you bring me your favorite, I'm sure I'll like it."

Again, that lustrous smile as she turned to leave. I felt confused; she wasn't a really attractive woman—pleasant looking, yes—and her body was mostly hidden by her outfit, yet, she appeals to me in a different way than other women have. Getting to know her better each time we talked, I thought there must be something more about her that I wanted to find out. Then, what does she think about me? Am I just some man pestering her, one she's leading along for my tips? She just doesn't sound like that kind of a woman, at least I'm not thinking she is.

As I swallowed a gulp of beer, she returned with two bowls of soup, a plate of bread, and a container of butter.

"Each of the soups tasted good, so I decided to let you decide which you like the best. Don't worry, I'm not charging you for this if you promise to come back to see me next week." She smiled and winked at me; it seemed the room got warmer.

"Now for the broccoli, you can just eat it with your spoon, but the potato, you might want to soak the bread in it a little to soften the bread and to add the flavor of the soup to it. We always put butter on a slice of bread at our meals—oh, wait." She went to the kitchen and returned with silverware for me. "I don't know why I didn't think of these when I brought the soups, silly me." Her cheeks were red and she seemed a little flustered.

I tasted a spoon of broccoli soup; it reminded me of the vegetables Mrs. Wilson had fixed last Sunday. Then a spoon of potato soup; it was more like the vegetable soup Mrs. Goshen made in the wintertime in Kentucky.

"Here, let me butter the bread for you," Bertha said. She spread a thick layer of butter on it and handed it to me. "Just dip the corner in the soup for a second, then take a bite of it." She moved around to get closer to me; I could smell the sweat of her body nearby along with the lavender of her perfume. "Have you decided which is best?"

"You're right, they are both tasty to me." Her elbow kissed my shoulder; it took an effort to swallow each spoonful. "Why don't you sit down here?"

"Yes, but just a minute." She hurried to the kitchen again, then came back with another woman.

"Leland, this is Anna, my cousin. She's the cook who made the soups. Anna, this is Leland Vance."

I partially stood and nodded to her. "Nice to meet you, ma'am. You sure are a good cook, I've liked everything I've eaten here!"

"Well, aren't you nice to say that. I always like it when people enjoy my work. What else have you had?"

I had to stop to think what I had eaten when I came with Joe and Anthony.

Bertha was quick to respond. "He had the Rouladen with boiled potatoes and sauerkraut the first night—oh, and pickled eggs too."

Anna looked at Bertha, then looked at me. She smiled and nodded. "Well, enjoy," then excused herself to go back to the kitchen. Again, I felt unsure of what was happening.

I had more of the soups and bread, then finished the beer. Bertha went to get another beer for me without my asking. When she returned she sat at the table with me.

"Bertha, you said you work at a tailor shop. Can you fix a coat for me? It's got a torn pocket."

"I'm sure I can, I can fix most anything like that—can you bring it by the tailor shop?"

"I can. Tell me how you learned to sew, did you learn at the tailor shop?"

"My mother taught me when I was growing up. My father and my brothers were always tearing their clothes or wearing out the knees or elbows. Mother and I fixed them each time. And, we had to adjust the size of my dresses to fit my younger sister as she got my hand-me-downs." She was becoming animated; she obviously enjoyed talking about her family.

"So you had two brothers and a sister? Where are they now?"

Bertha's countenance changed as she thought about her words; I could see it wasn't a pleasant memory for her. She crossed her left arm on her chest and tapped her temple with the fingertips of her right hand as if it would help her to think. "Well, as I told you last week, my oldest brother and my father were killed in the war. The army informed Mother of each of them. My younger sister went to work as a nurse on the Russian front. No one has heard of her since. My brother and his wife went to Poland to try to find her, that's the last place they knew she worked. They stayed there in Poland when he found work at a factory. Later my mother joined them in Poland, that's where they live now."

"That must be tough for you. Do you still hear from your mother?"

"We do write, but the problems over there are not good for them. All three of them work continuously, so they don't have much time to write me. I hate that we are losing contact like this, that's one reason I like to keep busy here—then I don't have time to think about their situation." She looked very dejected; I wanted to do something to make her feel better, so I put my hand on hers. She immediately looked up at me and smiled.

"I'm sorry to tell you about my problems, thanks for listening," she said as she put her other hand lightly on mine. Finally, she managed a smile as she looked at me. I realized my armpits were dampening my shirt.

Her cousin Carl walked up to our table so Bertha introduced us. Then she got up. "I need to get back to work. Maybe I'll see you here next week?" Her voice sounded very hopeful—it made me feel good.

"You bet you will. I'm already looking forward to it."

Chapter 7

Late the next Saturday afternoon I took my coat to Rogers' Tailor Shop for mending. Bertha was there behind the counter. She was wearing a white blouse that was buttoned to the neck; it had short sleeves. Her hair was fixed the way she usually wore it at the tailor shop: straight with a loose curl going under at her neck. As I entered, she looked up from the till where she was counting the coins. I felt my mouth go dry as an old walnut shell, so I rubbed my tongue against the roof of my mouth to try to produce saliva, then licked my lips.

"Hello Bertha, good to see you. Like I told you the other night, I need to get my coat repaired. Will you take a look at it?" I put my coat on the counter.

This was the first time I had come into the shop; she obviously didn't expect to see me here. Her face turned white as she put her hands flat on the counter, then she reached out to take the coat. Her eyes were wide open as she glanced up at me. Her face gained a little color: her cheeks turned rosy. She cleared her throat as she examined the item.

"This tear here on the pocket? Sure, I can fix that in just a few minutes. Did you lose much money falling out of here?" Bertha joked as she smiled.

I smiled too, feeling foolish. "I wish I had some money to lose. Us miners don't have extra money, don't you know?" Now I was feeling a little confused; normally I felt in control of myself, but here I had trouble talking normally. When I tried to smile, I had to force my face muscles to move, and I noticed that Bertha seemed a little different acting as well.

"Yes, but you told me you're working another job now. How is that going?"

"Good, sure, I do it all right. With the extra money, I'm saving up to buy a car. Maybe in the next month I'll have enough for a down payment."

"You should talk with Herrin Motors next door. Mr. Kelly comes over to see Mr. Rogers and he seems like a nice person, I'll bet he'll give you a good deal. Want me to ask him for you?"

"No, I can do that! I just don't know how long it'll be before I have enough money saved up."

Bertha took the coat to the back to do the work, so I tried to pull myself together. I'd been alone with women before, so why was I acting like this now? I turned to look out at the street, straightened my back and shook my hands, then turned back to the counter. Clearing my voice helped me calm down a little more.

When Bertha returned a few minutes later with the repaired coat, I asked, "Bertha, what do you do on Sundays? I'm looking for something to do that's different, but I don't know much about this area—what do you suggest?"

"I'm going to take the interurban over to Carterville to see an old friend, would you like to ride along?" She smiled, raised her eyebrows, and cocked her head to one side.

"Sure, that sounds like something new. When you goin'?"

"We'll get on the train at 10:30 at the station on Cherry at 14th. My friend will give us a bite around noon and we'll come back in the late afternoon. Will that work for you?"

"Well, sounds like we'll have a fun day. I'm glad you're lettin' me go with ya!"

I took the jacket and paid for the work. As she looked up from the till, I noticed that very pleasant smile on her face. I couldn't think of any more conversation and I felt my face begin to flush, so I turned to leave. "So long now, I'll see you tomorrow."

When I arrived at the station the next morning, I had a cut on my cheek and a black eye.

"Oh, my goodness! What happened to you?" Bertha exclaimed. She had on a long brown cloth coat and black shoes. Her hair looked just as it did last evening, but combed more thoroughly, and she had placed a bobby pin at each temple to hold the hair off her face.

"There was a little fracas at the tavern last night. Nothing bad. I just turned around at the wrong time. One man was swinging a beer bottle at another man and I wound up gettin' in the way. I held the cut closed for a few minutes and the bleeding stopped. Then we put a piece of tape across it till this morning. The black eye will go away in a day or two. What do ya think, do I look too bad for you to be seen with me?"

"Good God, no! It will look like I'm going around with a fighter. Can we tell people that you got it in a fight with Jack Dempsey? We'll pretend that you were in St. Louis last night for the fight there!" She was obviously enjoying making up her story.

I smiled. "You can try, but I don't think anyone will believe you. You don't think I'm good enough to get in the ring with a professional fighter, do you?"

Bertha put her arm through mine and hung on tight. "Leland, I think you can do anything you set your mind to." She looked up at me and smiled. My mouth went dry again, and I couldn't think of anything to say in response.

The train ride to Carterville headed west through Herrin, then traveled through the Herrin Plain. In the cool morning the windows of the car were closed. We chatted as we watched the scenes go past. A few farms with cattle in the field and the morning mist lifting gently; some fields had rolled bales of hay; near a wooded area was an old barn that was partly collapsed, then a large pile of earth next to a deep hole in the ground.

"What's that dirt piled up for?" Bertha asked.

"It was a strip mine. Some coal company came in and pulled off the earth over some coal that was beneath it. Looks like they finished taking out the coal 'cause all the equipment's gone."

"Won't they put the earth back over the hole?"

"No, there's no money in doing that. The owner of the mining company is in another state, so he doesn't care what happens to this hole now that he has his money."

"I don't think it's right. It looks to me a deep hole like that could be dangerous. Children will want to play on the mountain of earth and they could fall into the hole. Don't you think that's dangerous?"

I shrugged but didn't reply.

"Well, I don't think someone should be allowed to take away something of value like this and not be responsible for the damage it's done to the way we live!"

As the train was approaching Carterville, Bertha changed to talking about her friend.

"I knew Mary in Germany, we went to school together. She's a few years older than me. In primary school, she was my mentor, she helped me with the class material. Her family was Prussian; they had money, so my grandfather didn't like them, but I loved Mary, she really helped me. When she finished secondary school, she and Hans got married; he had just finished university.

"You'll like Hans, he works for the mining companies too. He measures the ground where the companies want to start a mine. I think he's called a civil engineer or something like that. Mary was expecting a child when they left Germany. It was born in Murphysboro after they were living there, but the baby got diphtheria and died shortly after she was born. Then they had the two boys, then another girl but there were problems with the girl at birth. The child didn't make it and now Mary can't have any more children."

"That's too bad. I guess probably Mary wanted to have a daughter?"

"Of course. What about you, Leland, do you want to get married some day?"

"I guess, sure."

"Do you want children?"

"I think that comes with getting married for most people."

"Yes, but tell me, how many children would you like to have?" She smiled and leaned forward so she could look fully at my face, then raised her eyebrows.

"At least two. A girl for my wife and a boy for me." I was a little hesitant in my response. I wasn't sure where this conversation was going, so I felt this was a safe answer.

"I want to have more than two. I like the thought of a large family, maybe four or five youngsters. If you have many children, there's a better chance of many grandchildren and so on. I don't know my ancestors, of course, but I think I wouldn't be here without their having had children, so I want to do my part too." As we sat close together, I could feel the warmth of her body through my pant leg: I liked it.

From the station, we walked the few blocks to the Schobel house. They lived on a large, tree-lined street. Mary was standing at the door as we approached. She had black hair which was pulled to a bun on the back, a white-and-blue-striped blouse, and a blue skirt that ended just below her knees. Her shoes were similar to Bertha's: black with laces up over the ankles.

It was a two-story house with a large garden to the left side. On the right was a driveway heading to the garage in the back. One of the nicest houses I'd ever seen, nothing like Kentucky and even nicer than any of the houses in Herrin, at least the ones I had seen so far.

Bertha quickly mounted the steps to the porch. "Mary, it's so good to see you!" The two women had a long embrace.

"Mary, this is Leland Vance, a friend I met recently. Leland this is my friend, Mary Schobel."

I smiled and nodded. "Nice to meet you, Mrs. Schobel."

"Oh, please, call me Mary. We're all friends here in my house!"

"Sure, Mary. Nice to meet you." I smiled and nodded again. I felt a little more relaxed, but still stayed on my toes in this situation. I had never met someone like this—not at all what I had expected. It made me wonder about Bertha's background: was she raised in a house like this? would she be expecting her husband to provide a similar one for her?

Mary stood back and waved us into the entrance hall. It was wide and contained a stairway to the second floor. The walls were covered with wallpaper and there was finished wood on the floor, on the stairs, and around each doorway. I could smell German food cooking somewhere toward the back. I counted five doors off the hall.

"Let's go to the living room here." Mary motioned to the first door on the right. As I walked in I saw a large colorful carpet laid on the floor, almost covering it. There was a short couch and two padded chairs. A well-worn rocking chair was made of wood; it looked very comfortable. The wall to the front of the house had two windows and the side wall toward the driveway had a single window. All the windows had lace curtains on them. Three finished wood tables, each with an electric lamp, were next to pieces of furniture. I felt uncomfortable, as if I might cause damage to anything I touched.

The women were talking about Mary's boys. "And Stephan has taken up the violin. He just started so we don't know how it will work out. A woman from Carbondale comes on Saturday mornings to give him lessons."

Mary turned to talk to me. "What do you do for a living, Leland?"

"I work in the mines digging coal, mostly. I also help out at a tavern some. I like to keep busy."

"Are you new to the area, it sounds like you have a different accent."

"I'm from Kentucky. Just got here last summer."

Bertha asked, "Where's Hans? I'd like the two men to meet."

"I'm sorry, but Hans had to go to work today. I hate it when he works on Sundays. But a new mining company is coming to the area and they asked Hans to do some measurements on their property between Herrin and Marion. Today is the only day he had available. And the boys are at a marching event in Carbondale, so they won't be here either. It's just the three of us today. I was hoping to set up dinner in the dining room, but now I think the kitchen will be more cozy, if that's all right with you?"

"Of course it is. Don't go to any trouble for us!" Bertha said.

"Bertha, do you remember the Sunday afternoon marching exercises we had in the square? Everyone in town would spend their Sundays listening to the marching music and the men all marching back and forth. Hans met a teacher at the college in Carbondale who is also from Prussia and they thought it would be good to start something like that here. I think the discipline the men get is good for them. In some cities, even here in Illinois where there are many people of German descent, they have established that custom."

While the two women talked, I looked at the newspaper on the side table next to me. It was the latest *Illinois Miner*. I was reading, as best I could, an article about a mining accident in West Frankfort. The mine had been closed down for a few days while the federal inspectors did their work. When the miners returned to work in the morning, one of them had lighted a match which ignited gas coming from a trapdoor that had been left open. No one was killed; however, nine men were injured. The article noted that a St. Louis newspaper had written an erroneous article saying that fifty to sixty men were entombed in the mine, but that was incorrect: no one was killed and all survivors were able to walk about when they returned to the surface. I shook my head as I wondered if I would be involved in an accident.

Mary noticed my reaction to the article. "What are you reading about, Leland? You seem concerned by the article."

"It's telling about an explosion in a mine around here. These things always make me wonder if I'll be in one of the accidents someday."

"You're right to be worried, that will make you more cautious when you work down there," Bertha offered.

"That's why I'm glad Hans works on the top measuring. He says it's difficult work but it isn't dangerous, at least. Well, let's go to the kitchen for a bite."

As we walked into the kitchen, I thought the living room I had been in was as large as the first house I remembered living in. And the living room and hallway together were as large as the Goshen home, or all the houses I knew in Kentucky.

The kitchen was also a good size. It had a sink with running water, a large stove, and plenty of counter space, all of which were made of shiny metal. The room's walls were all painted gray. There was an enclosed back porch where many fresh vegetables were stored. I expected they had been taken from the garden recently.

"Please sit at the table while I dish up our dinner. I'm cooking a roast with potatoes and carrots for the men when they come home this evening, but it's thoroughly cooked already. I hope you like it."

There were also slices of a dark bread and some butter on the table, which the women ate along with the rest of the meal. After we finished eating and had a cup of coffee, the women talked while I walked around outdoors, looking at the garden and the neighborhood. In the late afternoon, everyone said their good-byes.

As we waited for the train, I asked Bertha, "When you were growing up in Germany, did you live in a house like the Schobels'?"

"Good God, no! Our house was in a row of houses in a part of town that was different from Mary's family. My family was not poor, but we didn't have much money. My father worked most all of the time to support us, so we didn't see much of him. I like to come to see Mary because we were so close when I was little; now, seeing her reminds me of those happy times."

I felt somewhat relieved. Being able to live like the Schobels was not something I could ever imagine doing.

Bertha and I enjoyed our trip back to Herrin. Bertha was again talking about the children, saying she was disappointed since she had wanted for me to meet Mary's two boys. The full stomach, a rocking train car, a short night of sleep, and Bertha's soft voice made it hard to stay awake.

When she saw me nodding off, she rubbed my shoulder. "Why don't you take a short nap until we get to the station? I don't mind at all."

When we got off the train, we each said we enjoyed the day. We had a gentle hug, which felt good. We promised each other to plan something for the next Sunday. I was getting to like her more as I got to know her better. After that, we found other things to do together on most Sunday afternoons.

Chapter 8

Just before Thanksgiving, I had saved enough money for a down payment on a car. Joe Petrie had given me some lessons so I could drive it on my own. I went to Herrin Motors next to Bertha's tailor shop for the purchase. Mr. Kelly said he had just recently received a Model A that a local customer had traded in on a new model. It took several hours to finish the deal because of the lengthy conversation and detailed instructions Mr. Kelly wanted to give me.

"Now Leland, I've taken a little more off the price than I should have because you're a friend of Miss Alles, next door. She's a real sweetheart she is. Why, if I wasn't married, I'd be calling on her. Say, why aren't you interested in her yourself?

"So, if you decide to trade up for your next car, I hope you'll remember me. Most of my business comes from previously satisfied customers. You get in now and I'll crank it for you."

I waited for Bertha to get off work, then invited her to take a drive with me. "You'll have to be patient with me, this is my first car, so it'll take a little time for me to get used to driving it." As we started off, the car jumped a little as I worked the clutch. Bertha grabbed the door handle tight.

"You're doing just fine!" Bertha lied as she smiled at me.

Shortly, we pulled to the curb in front of Mrs. Wilson's house. "Wait here a minute," I said as I jumped out of the car and ran into the house and came back a minute later, escorting Mrs. Wilson to the car.

"Mrs. Wilson, this is Bertha Alles, she'll join us for our ride. Bertha, this is my landlady, Mrs. Wilson. She was a teacher at Herrin High School and I promised to take her by there when I got my car." Bertha moved to the center of the seat so Mrs. Wilson could sit by the door.

"Here we go!" I exclaimed in excitement.

Mrs. Wilson was anxious to find out more about Bertha. "Darlin' where are you from, you sound like you have an accent."

"Yes, I'm from Germany, I moved here several years ago. I really love living here in Herrin."

"Well, welcome to our country. How is it you know Leland?"

"I work at the Rogers' Tailor Shop and Leland brought me his coat for repair. We just like to spend time together now."

"I must say your English is certainly good for a newcomer. Where did you learn to speak it?"

"In Germany, we all had to learn a foreign language in school, so I learnt English. Then, before the war, my parents sent me to America to live with my cousin—he owns the Black Forest Inn here in Herrin."

"Do you miss your parents?"

"Of course, I do miss them, but my father was killed in the war and my mother has moved to Silesia, well, Poland, to live with my brother. I hope to get over to see them sometime in the next few years."

We had arrived at the high school. I asked, "Do you want to get out and look around, Mrs. Wilson?"

"Goodness no! I can't walk very good and the ground is too uneven here. I just wanted to see the place, it's the first time I've been here in a few years. It still looks the same, though. We can go back now."

Back at the house, I helped Rosemary into the house, then returned to take Bertha back.

"That was very nice of you, Leland. She really loved to get out like this, you're our hero." Now she seemed comfortable sitting close to me, and I was getting more relaxed with driving the car.

On a warm Saturday afternoon in November, Bertha and I went fishing in Big Muddy River to the west of Herrin. There had been a hard frost earlier in the week, but the weather turned warm again for a few days—Indian Summer. It was the first time I had driven outside of town. Bertha had fixed a picnic lunch for us, using some leftovers from the Black Forest Inn—it was quite the feast. Some of the trees still had colorful leaves, but most were getting bare. Often, a gentle breeze would bring elm leaves down, giving a look of rain falling. While a few fish were biting, we were more interested in each other.

"Leland, what do you tell your friends about us?"

"Well, I tell them that we go different places together. I don't like to tell them too much, though. Why?"

"I was wondering if you think we're more than just friends. I think you like to be with me—I know I like to be with you, so are we more than friends, or what?"

I stubbed out my cigarette, scooted closer to her, and put my arm around her shoulders. "Yes, I think we're more than just friends." And I gave her a kiss.

"Good, that makes me really happy. I've thought we'd make a good couple, but I wasn't sure if you felt that way—you don't express yourself very much."

"Well, like I've said, back in Kentucky, when I grew up, people didn't talk much about their feelings. It weren't 'til I got here to Herrin and got around you folks that I found out it was all right to be talkin' much. And you really make it easy for me to talk. I guess I've still got a ways to go, though."

"No, you're doing fine. I'll be glad to help you speak better, if you want."

"What do you mean? What's wrong with the way I talk?"

"Nothing's wrong, I understand you fine, but things you say, like 'it weren't 'til,' isn't quite right. The correct English would be, 'it wasn't until'—see, it's just a small thing isn't it?"

I had to think about her suggestion: correcting me might help, but it would show that she knew more than I did, which I didn't like. But then it was Bertie, and it would help our getting along together. "Sure, all right. Since I don't live in Kentucky anymore, I guess I don't have to sound like I do."

Bertha gave me a knowing smile and kissed my cheek.

During the month of December, we spent many weekend evenings together, or going to gatherings of our friends. Anthony threw a party at the Rome Club with the help of Mr. Marlow, Vinny's Bar was celebrating the season most of the month, and the Black Forest Inn put up a Christmas tree early to spread the aroma of the pine for the customers. We enjoyed being together, laughing, reading books; she even taught me better social skills, which I sorely needed. What I really liked about her was that she made everything we did a fun experience.

I had been working more nights than usual at the Colp Tavern, which gave me some extra money. I used a little of it to buy a nice necklace for Bertha, which I gave to her before we went out to eat on Christmas Eve. When she showed it to other people that night, she told them it was a Christmas gift from her boyfriend and she squeezed my arm or kissed my cheek.

I felt very happy with my status here in Herrin. I had made many friends, had gotten a girlfriend, was making some good money. Yes, I felt I had come a long way from Kentucky in a short time. Mrs. Goshen would be proud of me: I was proud of myself! I expected that the next year would be even better.

Chapter 9

For the new year, I decided to make more money so I could afford a large apartment on my own, and running hooch was the only choice I could see that would make that possible. I realized the extra hours of evening work would leave me tired for the backbreaking work in the mine, so I asked Jethro if I could be trained to become a shotfirer, because that work would be easier. Jethro agreed to put me in that slot since Anthony Garagiola was leaving the mine soon.

I found Mark Wallops at the Colp Tavern on the second Saturday I worked there in January. I was waiting for him to arrive. When he came through the door, several men paused in their conversations to look his way. Mark was an easy man to pick out: he dressed like a gangster, wearing a white, long-sleeved shirt, dress pants held up by suspenders that buttoned on the inside of the waist. The pants were a herringbone pattern; they were loose around the legs with a large cuff resting on the shoe tops. The front pleat broke just below the knee, giving a look of "knee-sprung trousers." On his head was a gray Stetson hat with a small feather in the band. Over the shirt was a black leather jacket, open at the front. His choice of dress made sure no one mistook him for a local patron in any tavern or roadhouse.

Mark had obviously served in the Army, since the right side of his face had the uneven texture that indicated he had received mustard gas at some time. He had a pencil-sized mustache which accentuated his slightly large nose. His eyes were gray like mine and slanted down a little at the outside ends, giving him a sad look, I thought. As we talked he was all business with me, but at least we had a pleasant talk. He let me know that he was just a delivery man, he didn't do the "dirty work" that most gangsters performed for Charlie Birger or the Sheltons. Now, I felt confident that I wouldn't be associating with the gangster element in this job, so I would be keeping my commitment with Mrs. Goshen.

We agreed that I would be the protection whenever hooch was being delivered. Up until now Mark had been working alone, but the job was becoming too dangerous, so he welcomed my asking. Our first delivery was scheduled for the following Tuesday.

Mark Wallops arrived at 7:00 on Tuesday evening. He was driving his truck which had an enclosed bed. The weather was cold and cloudy with some snow starting to fall. This being my first time for a run like this, I felt a little unsure of myself. One time I had run moonshine in Kentucky when our truck had been chased by the police for a short distance; I remembered the thrill of the chase, but Mark assured me our work wouldn't be like that.

"We'll go over to Saline County to pick up the stuff. Mr. Birger has a farmer there with a still in his woods. He makes corn alcohol and adds toasted brown sugar to it, then puts it in quart jars. Sometimes Charlie even has federal labels for the jars. We'll deliver the stuff to the taverns and roadhouses. You take the goods in while I collect the money. Now, if we see Mr. Birger, be sure to be polite and call him 'Sir.' He'll take a liking to you if you show him you respect him, got it?"

"Sure do, sir, I can show lots of respect to anyone paying me money."

"Good! Now if we have any problems you reach down under the seat and pull up the machine gun down there. There's extra rounds down there too. I don't expect any trouble, but we've got to be ready."

"I ain't never used a machine gun before. Is it hard to work?"

"Naw, the thing doesn't have a safety, so just aim and pull the trigger. Make sure you hold it tight because it does have a kick when it goes off. And don't hold the trigger back too long, it uses up the bullets pretty fast—800 per minute, the man told me."

I pulled the gun up to look at it, but I was concerned at the thought of using it.

We traveled south out of Herrin, then east toward Harrisburg. A mile or so before reaching Harrisburg, we went south toward Ledford. Mark slowed the truck; it was a dark night and the roads weren't marked.

Mark leaned forward to get a better look out the front window. "I've been here many times and I still have trouble finding his place. Oh, here's his farmhouse—now we just need to go another half mile or so and take a trail on the left. Keep your eyes open for it down here."

Shortly I saw a break in the weeds on the left. I pointed out the front window. "Just ahead, there's a break in the brush."

"I see it now, yeah, that's it all right, I recognize that pine tree."

As we traveled along the two-rut road there was a field on the left which had the remnants of last summer's corn crop. On the right was a dense woods. At the end of the trail we came on some brush.

Mark instructed, "Get out and move those bushes on the right. The farmer puts them there to cover the way to his still."

While the bushes looked permanent in the dark, I found them easy to move. When the truck had passed, I moved them back and then jumped back on my seat. A few hundred yards further on we came to the still. The farmer was standing by it, waiting for us to arrive.

Mark introduced me. "He'll be helping out from now on. In time he may be coming without me. Mr. Birger tell you about this?"

The farmer was a crusty old "salt of the earth" individual. "Yeah, he told me about it. I don't like for so many people to know where I make this stuff, but if Charlie thinks it's hunky-dory, I can't say nothin' different. Just go ahead and load these crates and we'll get outta here."

Mark and I made quick work of loading the ten crates and then we were all on the way out. The farmer moved the brush aside and waved us on our way. The roads were mostly empty and somewhat snow covered. The air was crisp and clear; even with the truck's heater going, the windows would fog over at times. Mark drove slowly until he got his bearings on the main road, then we made good time getting back to Williamson County.

The first stop was at a tavern just before Marion. Mark pulled out a sheet and told me to carry in three crates, which I did. I sat them on the bar as Mark collected the money. Then we were off to a hotel in Marion which had a restaurant just inside. A case of six quarts was delivered to the bar. A policeman was standing in the lobby talking to an elderly couple and he saw us go through, but he didn't seem to notice what was happening, or he didn't care.

As we were driving north to Herrin we stopped at Toady's Roadhouse, which had a full parking lot. Mark instructed me to take in one case. I noticed that Mark pulled a pistol from beneath his seat and put it in his pocket so the handle was showing.

"Sometimes this crowd gets a little rowdy. Don't worry: if they do, I can handle it. You just take the booze behind the bar and set it on the floor, then come back out to watch the truck."

Inside the roadhouse it was very noisy. A band was playing loud in the back, people were dancing around the room, there were slot machines on the wall to the right; they were all being used. The bar was on the wall to the left, so I worked through the people standing around drinking as I carried the case carefully. A bartender waved me through and I set the case on the floor, then worked my way back and out through the door to the truck. Three men had gathered beside the truck and were laughing about something. I went to stand between them and the truck.

One of the men stumbled into me and I pushed back.

"Hey, what the hell you doing here?" the inebriated man slurred.

"Just standing by my vehicle, sir," I said, shaking my head.

"Well, I don't like be'n pushed around!"

The other men noticed that I had arrived and they also became belligerent.

About that time Mark walked out the door.

"What's going on here?" he said loudly, pulling back his coat.

One of the men noticed the pistol and grabbed the others. "We ain't doing nothin', sir! We just came out to get some air and admire your truck. It's a nice-looking vehicle! Come on, fellas, let's go back inside." And they all quickly stumbled toward the door.

We got back in the truck and started north again.

"You know, Leland, I'm from East St. Louis, lived there for thirty years or so, and when Mr. Birger asked me to come down here to help him out a couple of years ago, I thought this was going to be a backwoods kind of an area. But after I've got to know these people, I think they're real nice—nicer than the people up north. Sure, they get liquored up and they get a little crazy, but most of the time they're real nice."

"Yep, I agree. I'm from Kentucky and the folks are nice there, but here they want everyone to feel welcome and they can't do enough to help a stranger out. That's what I've found out so far."

Mark held the wheel with one hand and made his points by waving the other. "Even Mr. Birger, yeah, he'll kill anyone that looks at him wrong, but if you're down and out, he can't do enough for you. He's just got a good soul!" Mark was obviously sympathetic toward Charlie.

"I've never met the man, but I've heard lots of good things about him and lots of bad things too. He's hooked up with the Shelton boys, ain't he?"

"Yeah, they all got a good thing going with the slot machines, I guess. You saw some slots in the roadhouse back there, them's ones we put in 'bout a year ago. Big Jim said he just keeps getting more and more money when he does the slot machine collections. Course, Mr. Birger makes money off the women too. Guess you could say he's got every angle covered that men wants to do to sin!"

As we entered Herrin city limits, Mark slowed the truck. The snow had started again and it was falling in large flakes that obscured our view even more than the foggy windows. When we reached Monroe Street, we turned left and stopped in front of the European Hotel.

Again, Mark checked his sheet. "They just want three quarts here. I think they ordered too much for New Year's Eve celebrations, so they still have some left over. You better come back out quick and watch the truck. The crowd at the Commercial Hotel next door makes me a little uneasy."

I did as requested, but no problems came.

Next, we went west to McNeil's Addition and the Black Forest Inn. Bertha's cousin Carl was behind the bar. I set the case on the top of the bar.

"Hello, Leland. Are you working with Mark tonight?"

"I am, I just started this job today."

"Good to see you, how's cousin Bertha doing?"

"Yeah, she's doing good, I guess. We spent Sunday together."

"You're taking up pretty much all her time these days. Anna was saying how she misses having Bertha over since she met you."

Mark interrupted, "That'll be four dollars, Carl."

As Carl paid, I went out the door. When I approached the truck, I heard a noise at the rear. I went toward the sound. Rounding the back, I saw a man trying to get the gate open to get inside.

"Hey, what the hell you doin'?" I yelled at the man. "Get your ass away from this truck—now!"

The man jumped back at first, then screamed as he ran at me, swinging his fists. I blocked the first fist and swung through the second, hitting the man squarely in the left eye. The man rocked back and shuffled his feet to regain his balance before attacking again. He ran forward with his head down like a battering ram. I held my two arms together and brought them down on the man's back. We both went to the ground with me on top. I quickly brought my knees onto the man's shoulders to hold him down, then started hitting him in the kidneys. After two blows I realized the man had become very quiet, so I got up on my feet. Now, I heard Mark yelling at me from behind.

"What the hell's going on, Leland?"

"This man was trying to get in the back of the truck when I came out. I told him to get away but he attacked me instead, so I had to handle him."

"Let's get him up and see if he's alright. We don't want any trouble that'll bring the police."

We helped the man get to his feet. He was bleeding from the left eye and groaned as he held his back. He was able to stand on his own.

"You alright, mister?" Mark asked.

Saying nothing, the man slowly turned and stumbled away.

"See, that's why I need to have you with me on these trips. Seems like more and more of the time some men are getting to be drunkards and can't work, so they try to steal their liquor. Maybe I should carry the stuff in and leave you with the truck?"

"Sure, if that's what you want, I can do that too."

"Well, until you get to be known by these barkeeps, I think you should keep carrying. Come on, let's get over to Colp."

At the first roadhouse north of Carterville, our last stop, I took in two cases. I waited at the front window so I could see the truck from inside, since it was getting pretty cold outside. As I stood there, one of the women in the bar came up to me.

"You're the new helper on the delivery truck, aren't you?"

I nodded. She smelled of cheap perfume and liquor and looked like she had had a profitable evening. Her hair looked almost white and she had bags under her eyes. A bright red dress was open at the top, showing her bulging breasts.

"Well, since you work for Mr. Birger, I can give you a good deal any time you want it. I would even say right now would be a good time for it. Whadda ya think?" she almost cooed and tried to focus her eyes.

"Lady, I'm working."

That didn't deter the doxy. She rubbed her right breast on my arm and used her left hand to rub my stomach, still cooing, "Mr. Wallops can just wait for us to do our business, can't he?"

"Come on, Leland, let's get outta here." Mark headed for the door.

We were finished delivering for the night. When the truck stopped in front of Mrs. Wilson's, Mark handed me a five-dollar bill.

"Thanks for helping tonight. You handled that drunk at the Black Forest real well. You're just the kind of help I need."

We waved and I headed directly for bed. In five hours I would be starting another day at the mine.

Tuesday was another cold day as I headed for the Tidy Boy Diner for lunch. Snow covered the ground. As I entered, Anthony called out to me. He was sitting with his sister Maryanne at a table near the front window: they asked me to join them. He gave me a pat on the shoulder as he shook my hand, then Maryanne gave me a gentle hug. I was getting more accustomed to people doing that with me. She looked very pretty today; the conservative suit she wore was a good match for Anthony's.

After our greetings, Anthony started, "Maryanne and I were just walking around the area soliciting donations for the Easter celebration we have each year. Mr. Daniels, the owner, made a good donation, so we decided to have lunch here. What brings you in?"

"Well, no, I come here often for lunch. I really like their food. Maryanne, I have to say you look very pretty today." I assumed having her along might help with convincing some store owners to make a donation, especially as nice as she looked, and Bertha had informed me that women liked men to make positive comments on their looks. And she did look attractive: her curly hair of our previous meeting was now longer and shaped in waves going down from the top of her head. Her eyebrows were pronounced, probably some black mascara added to them, and also a little on her eyelids to complete the image.

She beamed in response. "Thank you, you look nice yourself." Her smile looked even prettier than it did when I would see her at Vinny's—still the captivating smile with full red lips. The reflected sun shining on the snow covering the street outside lightened her skin; it looked perfectly clear and smooth.

"We've been getting a lot of donations this year; it promises to be a good event, if the weather cooperates that day! I hope you'll come yourself, Leland," Anthony said.

"If you can make it, come by the shelter on the south side, I'll have my class of young dancers performing a dance recital there," Maryanne told me.

"So, you teach children to dance?"

"Yes, on Saturday mornings. I have about seven girls and boys who come each week. They'll be doing the Charleston on Easter. Do you have children, Leland?"

"No, I've never been married."

"Well, after the children perform, the band will be playing music for people to dance to. Maybe you could join in." Another pretty smile.

"I'm not much of a dancer myself, never did do much dancing."

"I can help you with that, I teach people of all ages to dance, I think it's good for everyone to dance, it's good exercise and it allows you to express yourself. And, since you're a friend of Tony's, I'll give you a special price!"

"Better watch out, Leland, this girl is a shrewd money manager." Anthony gave me a warning wink.

While we enjoyed our lunch, I noticed Maryanne was watching me closely as she listened to Anthony and me talk about mining and the people we worked with. Several times she asked me for more details on the people we were talking about. As we parted later, she gave me another hug and reminded me of the dance at the event; she said she hoped to see me there.

Chapter 10

On Sunday afternoons Bertha would visit Mrs. Wilson and me at the house on 14th Street. Usually, Bertha would bring a traditional German dish, which Rosemary loved. We would partake of a luscious meal, then study English.

Rosemary was talking to Bertha: "When you studied English in Germany, did you have a German teacher leading the class?"

"Yes, Mr. Hauptman was our teacher. He learnt English when he studied in England."

"That's what I thought. The English you use is similar to the way the British speak. For instance, the British say the past tense of the verb 'to learn' as 'learnt,' while here in America we say 'learned'—see the difference?" Bertha crossed her left arm on her chest and tapped her temple with the fingertips of her right hand as if that would help the information sink in. "Most everyone understands what you mean either way, so it's all right, the way you talk, but if you want to sound like an American you'd say 'learned.'"

"I see, what other idiosyncrasies do you have for me? I do want to sound like an American!" Now she put her elbows on the table and propped her jaw up with her hands. Her wide-open eyes gave Mrs. Wilson her full attention.

"Then I need to enlighten you on some of the cultural items you two have missed by not growing up in Little Egypt."

I interrupted, "I've heard people mention 'Little Egypt' before. What is that?"

"Well, sir, Little Egypt is what we call the southern third of this state. The early settlers came here along the Ohio River and saw the flat plains on the north shore with large mounds on it, Indian burial grounds, and thought they looked like the pyramids in Egypt, along the Nile River. The town where the Ohio River converges with the Mississippi River was named Cairo, to be similar to Egypt too. Many of the towns in this area are named after biblical towns, like Palestine, New Athens, Sparta, or Dongola. Oh, yeah, we're proud to be in Little Egypt!

"See, the people here are very religious. Every one of the families that have lived here a long time are very serious about their religion; they attend church every Sunday, they love their revival meetings each summer, and they accept the Bible just as it's written. If you don't agree with the way they do things, you best keep those feelings to yourself, to get along with these folks. Especially here in Williamson County, people with lots of education are not too respected, until you get accepted by them. Johnathon and I have our college degrees, but we were born and bred here, so the local people accepted us as one of them, but people who have degrees and come from somewhere else have a hard time fitting in with the locals."

I was beginning to get the feeling Rosemary thought she was still running a high school class with Bertha and me as the students.

"Now, with all the new people coming in here because of the coal mines, we're seeing some new thinking come with them. The Italian community is a good example. Those folks are mostly Catholics, so they worship God a little different. The locals don't like it that they aren't attending the Christian churches. I've been hearing about the ministers at the Baptist and Methodist churches preaching bad things about the 'demon' Catholic folks.

"Then there's this prohibition thing stirring up the locals. Those same preachers give sermons condemning alcohol and the members all nod their heads, but I've had some of those members to dinner here with Johnathon and me, and they loved to drink right along with us!

"These Egyptians are strange creatures, I'll say. They're real nice and friendly to everyone, until someone or something comes in here from the outside that gets their dander up. Then they seem to just get set off. They all stick together against that problem like all get out! Take that Carterville riot a few years back—it wasn't just the miners on strike that got involved, the whole community of Egypt was ready to fight Ole Man Brush and the people he brought in here.

"Now, you two are outsiders to these people here, so my advice to you is to keep most of your opinions to yourself, if you can. Then you'll get along with them just fine."

One Sunday afternoon while Rosemary was napping, I told Bertha I had bought tickets to the Hippodrome vaudeville stage show for the following Saturday night. She objected at first, saying she could fix a nice meal at her place and we would have the evening together.

"Bertha, we won't have to be as penny-pinching as we have been. I took on more work with Mr. Wallops, so I'll have more money for us. I'm thinking I might be needing a bigger apartment in a few months, so the extra money will be saved for that. But my first pay will be spent on something we will both enjoy!"

"So now I'm going out with Mr. Big Money!" She feigned a smirk, then, "I like the sound of that, but I didn't know you were looking to move to a larger place—what's wrong with this place here?" Now her face was more serious.

"It's hunky-dory for me, but if I got a bigger place there would be more room for someone else." The sentence trailed off as I looked at the ceiling.

"I didn't know you were going to get someone else to live with you. Is it anyone I know?"

"I haven't decided just yet who it'll be. This is just 'in case.' I'll tell you more about it later."

Bertha looked at me and squeezed my hand: now she had a pleasant smile!

Chapter 11

The Hippodrome was in downtown Herrin. Mr. Marlow had the theater constructed in the fashion of Italian theaters. In the lobby were several marble statues of scantily clad women and many posters of the currently popular comedians, some of which had performed at this theater in the past year.

For the evening, Bertha was wearing a light blue chiffon dress that went to the floor. It had a silk band over the bodice and matching silk around each side pocket. Above the bodice, the dress had a shiny gauze material over the shoulders and a half sleeve on each arm. She was wearing a black silk coat until we reached our seats. I had been able to afford a black suit and a white shirt with a black tie. However, a nice coat was beyond my pocketbook.

As Bertha and I arrived, people were going to their seats through the two sets of double doors. We were both excited to see a vaudeville show—something we had only heard about in the past. Looking around at the other patrons, I recognized some of them from the Italian events in the past. The attendees appeared to be a cross section of the Herrin community, but mostly the well-to-do folks. When I saw Anthony Garagiola, I waved, then Anthony came over.

"Good evening, my friends! It's so good to see you here at the show. This is going to be a good one, I hear," he said as he shook hands with me.

Bertha was bursting with excitement, but trying to contain herself. Anthony kissed both of her cheeks as he held her hands. She was beaming!

"I'm here as a guest of Mr. Marlow, he wants me to be seen around the people of our country. Have you heard that I'm going to be opening an Italian-style grocery store next month?"

"I did hear that at the mine. In fact, I've asked to take your place as a shotfirer and Jethro agreed. So congratulations on your new store and thanks for leaving the mines so I could get your job."

"Then we both have good news: congratulations to us!" Anthony was beaming as he looked at each of us.

The lights went down so Anthony returned to his seat as the show started. A pair of comedians started the evening's production, then the dancing girls came on stage. Next, another comedian made jokes which included some of the local people. Anthony was the butt of one of them, and he waved famously, standing briefly! As he sat down, Mr. Marlow put his arm around him and patted his shoulder, exhibiting a giant smile.

After the show, we went to the European Hotel for dinner. The dining room was very elegant; Bertha commented that it looked similar to one she had seen in Germany. All in all, it was a very happy evening for both of us.

I recalled from my lunch with Anthony and Maryanne that she had said she gave dance lessons, so the following Saturday afternoon, I went to Vinny's to see if Maryanne was around. Vinny called her out from the back. Her hair was still wavy and today she had on a quite colorful, short dress showing her firm legs. When she saw it was me waiting for her, she almost bounced toward me, offering her cheek for me to kiss. I made a quick peck on that cheek without touching her, then stepped back. I noticed her perfume as being different from the one she wore the day I met her or at Tidy Boy Diner.

"Maryanne, I need to learn to dance a polka. Do you know how to do that dance?"

"Oh, you want dance lessons"—her eyebrows rose and her eyes widened—"that's why you're here . . . sure, I can dance most anything, even the new Charleston." She glanced over at Vinny; now she had on her business face. "Tell me why you're wanting to learn the polka, it's not a common dance around here."

"See, I've been dating Bertha, a German girl, and I want to be able to dance a polka with her. Can you teach me how to do it?" She nodded a little, then said she would be happy to teach me the polka. We made the arrangements and this time we had a nice handshake as I left.

I went to Vinny's the next few Saturdays. There was a building behind the bar that had one room inside, about twenty feet by forty feet—one he rented out as a meeting room or small party room. Maryanne used it for her dance lessons. It had a wooden floor and windows high at each end. There was a table with a record player on it for our music and a davenport where we would sit to rest during our hour-long lesson.

At first, as she tried to get me to learn the steps, she made a mistake or two, which caused her to laugh at herself. Very soon, though, she had the steps down pat and was able to get me moving with her. At fifteen minutes we took our first break. I sat at one end of the couch, she sat in the middle, cross-legged as she faced me.

She had that smile on her face. "You were right the other day when you said you didn't have much dancing experience. I can tell we're starting from the beginning here."

"Yeah, I really don't know what I'm doing out there, guess I looked like a pig on ice. But you're really patient with me. And now my legs hurt already and we've just begun."

"Don't worry, you'll get the hang of this quickly and your legs will gain some stamina so you can go longer."

"But you aren't even breathing hard and you don't need a rest either—you must have good legs for dancing."

She stretched out one leg over the edge of the couch, holding her dress above mid-thigh with her hand. She ran her other hand down and back up the outstretched leg, moving her foot up and down as she did. "I don't remember a time when I wasn't dancing, either taking lessons or teaching others. I guess my legs show the exercise they've had. They aren't too muscular looking, are they?" She looked up at me with a coy smile as she said it.

"No, they look great to me!"

She took my hand and led me back to the dance floor.

At the next break, she asked me about Bertha. I told her where Bertha worked, how we met, but not too many items about our relationship.

"She's lucky to have you. I've dated many miners, but I haven't found one that is as smart as you or Tony. To me they're just boobs." She liked to use the latest slang words when she could. "You sound intelligent, someone who would be able to hold an interesting conversation." Then back to the dance floor. The lessons continued with many breaks for my legs and for conversations. Between the conversations and our movement together on the dance floor, we got to know each other more intimately.

At the end of the last lesson, "Maryanne, to be honest, I thought you were out of my league when we first met. You seemed to have a good grasp of conversation and you enjoyed meeting people, getting to be friendly with them, things I have trouble doing. I thought you were a little intimidating."

"What about now?"

"Well, since we've spent some time together"—I smiled and dropped my head forward—"I think you're a very friendly person, one I like to be with."

"Leland, if things don't work out between you and Bertha, well ..."

"Of course ... ah, I've got to go now, it's later than I realized."

I knew I needed to get out of the room quickly, so I gave her a hug and left.

Chapter 12

The next Sunday was March 27th, Easter Sunday. The Italian community planned their annual celebration as a social in the park. Anthony had invited Bertha and me to come as his guests. Since Anthony was one of the main organizers, we would be welcome to attend. Again this week, the weather was sunny and warm, so the people were happy to be out of their houses again after several days of rain during the week.

Many people were participating in games along a midway-type area, near the food and drinks. Since the park was located in the Italian neighborhood, there were two bocce ball courts. Each court had two teams of four players each with other teams waiting to play the winners. Many card tables were in use. The people were playing games of Pitch, Seven Up, and Poker.

This year many of the Italian eateries provided tables full of food for the guests, each with their advertisements regarding the food and the restaurant's location. Several judges walked along these tables tasting the food and talking about the presentations. Prizes were to be awarded at the end of the festivities for each category being judged.

In total, it was a grand day; people were smiling and talking all around. One exception was at a card table. I heard Caesar Garagiola talking loudly about the game he was involved in with some other players.

"You must have cheated on the last hand, you yellow bastard!" he exclaimed. "I haven't won any hand yet—you assholes are taking all my money and I'm not putting up with you rats any longer!"

Father Senese hurried over to talk with Caesar. "Calm down, Caesar, your temper is getting the best of you and the other people here are concerned with you. What are you saying to these men?"

"Father, I've been playing Pitch with them for almost an hour now and I haven't won yet! That can't be possible, unless they're cheating me!"

"Caesar, of course it can. You just don't have any luck today and the other men do. Come, let's go to get a beer and talk about this. You remember the last time you got upset like this at the DiGiovanni—no, sorry, at the DeJohn wedding? Perhaps you shouldn't blame other people for your bad luck?"

Caesar pulled away and stomped off, leaving the festivities, and the general mood returned to gaiety.

I watched Caesar's tantrum and turned to Bertie, shaking my head. "That man is going to get in a lot of trouble someday. He just can't control his ill temper."

"I see now what you mean when you've talked about him in the past. Yes, he definitely has a problem. One day he saw me return to the tailor shop after lunch and he followed me inside. He stood around asking me stupid questions for a few minutes, then asked if I was seeing anyone, he would like to ask me to go out sometime. I told him you were my boyfriend and he said he thought we were over because he saw you dancing with Maryanne at Vinny's Bar several times. I don't know who Maryanne is, maybe you'll want to tell me sometime, but I told Caesar that we were still together. His eyes got large and he turned and walked out. He hasn't been back, but when I pass him on the streets, I can feel him looking at me."

After Bertie's comment on Maryanne, I decided it would be best if we didn't go to the shelter on the south side of the park where

Maryanne was demonstrating her student's dancing skills. No need for her to see the two of us interacting.

As the afternoon wore on, there were speeches by the mayor and the state congressman each saying what a benefit the city had received from the Italian community and pointing out how they were each much better friends of the group than their opponents were in the coming election. Each speaker ended by thanking Anthony Garagiola for inviting them to this wonderful event. Then as the judges started making the awards to the winning eateries, people began to depart.

For the next few weeks, Anthony trained me in the skill of blasting. We talked about the danger of working with the dynamite and the best places to bore holes for it. I had been joining him for some of the blasting during the previous week and now I was getting to do it myself, under Anthony's watchful eyes. At first I was very nervous doing the work, but I had settled down by Friday. After the last shot Anthony declared me a real shotfirer!

"Thanks for teaching me this, my friend. I'm going to miss having you around here, but I know you'll do well at your new store. All my best to you and I'll be stopping by for some groceries soon. Well, Bertha and I will be coming—she's the one who does the grocery shopping."

"Either way, I'll love to see you guys. And, remember my wedding is coming up in June! I want you both at that event too."

Chapter 13

Saturday I was waiting to get a haircut in George Johnston's chair on Park Avenue, getting ready for my date with Bertha on Sunday.

George had a good selection of newspapers for the men to read while they waited for their time in his chair. Some men would just stop by to pass the time. Everyone was welcome and sometimes the conversations were very lively. It was a good place for the citizenry to learn the latest news of the community. At times, a man or two would drift to the back of the room to get in a game of pool while they waited their turn.

Caleb and I were recapping the activities in the mine for the week, including a fire that had started from a spark on the rails down there.

"The firemen at the mine were quick about getting to the fire, and, in getting it out," I commented. "In Kentucky we didn't have a full-time fire crew and several men got hurt when they had a fire start there."

"Do you know, Leland, is it just Madison Coal Company that has fire crews?" Caleb asked.

"I read an article in the *Illinois Miner* that said all coal companies are now required to have mine firemen. There was also some other things that the mining companies have to do now. It all makes it safer to work in mines," I said.

A cab driver who was sitting against the wall next to Caleb put in his comment, "It's about time the companies are required to do things like this. I've felt bad for my union brothers down in the mines every time I hear about mining accidents."

George paused with his current work to mention an article he had read in the *Chicago Tribune*: "The author covers the activities in the Springfield legislature. He listed all the new laws the mining companies are going to have to follow, for the safety of the miners."

The cab driver asked him, "What did the paper say about our governor? Is he going to go to jail for stealing our tax dollars? Seems to me that the taxes we pay just get taken off by some crooked politician and they take it to Chicago for the gang bosses there!"

Dan Blocker had come up from his counter in the back. "I don't know why we're even in the same state with Chicago! Herrin's closer to Memphis than it is to Chicago. We got more people in Little Egypt that fought for the South in the war than they did for the Union. We ought to draw a line across the north end of Egypt and make us a whole other state. We could be a part of Kentucky or a little state of our own."

"And I say good riddance to them crooks in Chicago!" the cab driver agreed.

George tried to be the peacemaker. "You gents do understand, don't you, that we don't have enough power here in Southern Illinois to separate from this state whether we like those crooks in Chicago or not. And remember, we all depend on the coal mines for our livelihood, whether we work in the mines or get our sales to miners. These mining companies sell an awful lot of coal up there, so we better just accept the fact. Criminals in Chicago keep us going here, whether we like it or not."

I offered a different view: "I don't know how much worse the people in the gangs in Chicago are than the people in the gangs around here. But at least the local gangsters help out the local people and from what I read about the gangsters in Chicago, they don't have any heart at all."

Most of the men in the room nodded and grunted their agreement.

After my shave and haircut were done, I paid George the seventy-five cents and went to the pool tables with Caleb.

By mid-April the weather warmed a little, but then the clouds rolled in from the south. There was a two-week period when it seemed that the sun never peeked through the clouds.

"This reminds me of springtime in Germany," Bertha said one Sunday afternoon at Mrs. Wilson's. "Gray clouds and sometimes rain, washing the country clean. I love this time. We would gather as a family and play games all afternoon. Card games. Memory games—those were really lots of fun. Sometimes my mother would read to us children. Grimms' fairy tales mostly. They were good for children of all ages. What did you do when you were little on Sundays like this, Leland?"

I had been hesitant to tell Bertha the real truth about my childhood before this, thinking it might scare her off, but now we had a good relationship, so I felt I could tell her all my secrets.

"When I was a little tyke, I don't remember much. My mother was sick with consumption most of the time up until she died. I was six then. My dad had died when I was four and I don't remember much about him other than he was drunk most of the time."

"Really? That doesn't sound good."

"It wasn't. Many nights he would come home yelling at my mother and me. He stank awful and looked real mad. Mom told me to hide under my bed, but I could still see him hitting her. He yelled things about not knowing why he let her live, then pointed at me and said awful things I didn't understand, but they made Mamma cry. She kept telling him 'No, that's not true!' but he wouldn't listen to her. After a while they both got tired and he would fall in the chair and go to sleep. In the morning he might eat some toast, if we had any bread, then he was off until the next time. I was actually glad when he died."

"How did he die?"

"He got into a fight with some other miners in a bar one night. The sheriff came the next day to tell my mother and me how he had been killed. They never did find the man who did it."

"What happened to you after your mother died? Where did you live then?"

"My aunt, my mother's sister, took me in. I lived with her for three years."

"And then?"

"She said I was too much for their family, so I was taken by some folks in the church. Different ones every so often."

"What does that mean, 'too much for their family'?"

"They already had three children to feed. Uncle Mike was a miner too and so they didn't have enough food for them. Sometimes we might go for a day or two with nothing to eat. I don't think things got any better for them after I left, though."

"How many different families did you live with?"

"Well, the first two only lasted for a few months each. I guess by that time my 'manners' weren't too good, or so they said. I got in a lot of trouble with other kids at school and such. Then I moved in with Abel Goshen's family. He was a friend at school. His mother seemed to know how to deal with me better than the other folks. I got along better at school, started to study and not cause as much trouble."

"Did Abel have a father?"

"No, there weren't no dad there."

"Remember, Leland, 'there wasn't any dad there,'" Bertie corrected me.

"Oh, yeah, thanks. Anyway, he left them a few years before I got there. He just run off with another woman one day."

"How did she get along then?"

"Abel's mom had a big garden and she canned the vegetables so we had food all winter. Her brother had some pigs on his land, and they traded vegetables for meat. Then, when we turned twelve, Abel and me—no, Abel and I—started working in the mines, so we had enough money. Things got real better then."

"Things got really better then," Bertie corrected me.

"Sorry. I really like Mrs. Goshen. Before I left Kentucky, she was the last person I talked to; she wished me luck, told me to stay away from bad people, gave me a hug, and cried about me leaving. I had to turn to get to the train because my eyes were tearing up.

"Oh, and I need to ask you for another favor. Would you help me with other things, like math? I'm not good at math and I need to be."

"Of course. Maybe we could make a game of it, so it would be fun for us to do. How far did you get with math in school?"

"I can add and subtract fine, and I know the times tables. It's dividing that I have the most problems with."

"Got it. Let's start by reviewing multiplication tables."

So, on our Sunday afternoons, math schooling was added for the early spring. One day in early April, I suggested that we take a trip.

"Alright, where are you thinking we should go?" Bertie asked.

"In Kentucky the mountains are just starting to bloom about this time. I'm starting to see flowers around here this week. Let's go over to the hills south of Carbondale. They won't be tall mountains like Kentucky or the ones you talk about in Germany. So, this Sunday we'll go on a picnic to the Ozark Hills."

"That sounds like fun! I'll make a picnic basket. My cousin has a nice cloth for us to spread under a tree when we get there, it'll be great. I'm ready to get outside again!"

Sunday turned out to be a beautiful day, the warmest of the year so far. We started out around 9:00. I wore loose slacks and a plaid shirt. Bertie was clothed in a paisley blouse and a brown skirt that covered her knees. She had dark brown shoes and stockings that went to her knees. She had a sweater on until the sun warmed her.

We traveled west on Route 13 to Carbondale, then south on U.S. Highway 51. After about twelve miles, we found a road that went west to Cobden. As we traveled along, the hillside became more wooded; most of the trees were beginning to bud.

"Here's something I learned at the Union Hall on Wednesday: The town of Cobden was named for an Englishman who was a Member of Parliament back in 1859. One of the men at the Hall works on the IC Railroad and he read that in their magazine."

"That's interesting, Leland, but somehow I don't feel like we're getting very high up in the air, do you?"

"No, I don't really think we are. Some of the views are really pretty, though."

"Yes, the area is pretty. There aren't many people around. Let's find a nice place to park where we can see for miles, can we?"

"I'll drive and you keep looking around at the sights. Tell me when you find a good view."

A little further on, the road curved around a large limestone slab protruding from the hillside. There was room to pull over and park near it, so we decided to climb to the top to check the view. The sun had warmed the rock and the trees behind it were budding just enough to give a nice aroma to the area. When we reached the top, the view to the south was commanding. The air was very clear: we could see for miles. We decided that this was the perfect spot for our picnic, so I went back down for the basket and the cloth, then made a quick return to Bertie. She was sitting on the ground looking around.

"I'm glad you suggested this trip, Leland. I love the outdoors. It just feels so good to be outside after all the cold weather we've been having."

"Yeah, I think spring is finally here."

"That pair of birds in the tree there are realizing it's springtime too. They've been doing a mating dance for several minutes now. Oh, look, they're mating."

I sat down close to her and put my arm around her shoulders. She leaned into my body and took my right hand in hers and gently kissed it. I used the hand to raise her chin so we could kiss. It was long and gentle—the first time we had enjoyed each other this way. Bertha lay back and pulled me down on her. After another long kiss, I was thinking about the future. "I've been thinking about us, Bertie. Would you want to get married soon?"

"Tell me, Leland, am I the one you were thinking about when you said you needed a larger place?"

"Of course it was you. I can't think about anyone else anymore. Everything just seems right when I'm with you."

Another gentle kiss.

"I feel the same way about you. I believe you'll be a man who will make a good father for our children." She was smiling as she looked into my eyes, and she ran her fingers through my hair: it felt delightful.

"So, is the answer yes?"

"Of course the answer is yes!"

After another kiss, she asked me, "Do you want to have sex with me right now? We're all alone and no one can see us up here."

I wasn't sure I was hearing her right—was she really asking me to have sex with her? I pulled back from her a little, still looking into her eyes. "Really, right now?"

"Oh, you Americans are so conservative with sex. In Germany we had a different attitude. We feel if a man and a woman care for each other and they both want to enjoy each other, then they should. I know I want us to and I could feel that you're getting ready, so why not?"

I rolled off her and started to undo my pants as she pulled up her skirt and took off her panties.

"I don't think it will happen today, but we can practice starting our family. Doesn't that sound good to you?" she said as she smiled.

Afterward, we talked about our future together.

I was being practical. "But then we need to decide on a wedding. Have you thought about that? I always expected that I would be married at a courthouse. We didn't have big weddings in Kentucky. What do you want?"

"I thought I would be married in a church with a group of my friends present. Well, I would have had family too, but now most of them are in Germany or they were killed in the war. And, I was a member of the Lutheran church over there and there aren't any around here. So much for a church wedding, I guess. Now, I just have my cousin and a few friends here that could attend a wedding, so maybe your idea is best. We could ask Carl if we could have a celebration at his inn after we get back."

The conversation continued over the picnic lunch. With full stomachs and our feelings of satisfaction, we enjoyed the view together until we were both taking a nap. A short time later the sound of a car going by on the road below awakened us. We packed up the picnic remains and walked back to our car.

Bertie, do you have a gold tooth in the back of your mouth? I thought I saw one while you were breathing hard here earlier."

"You really got me excited, so I was breathing hard! But, yes, I had an accident in Germany when I fell on a sharp rock one time and it knocked out a tooth. That's why I have a scar on my cheek. The doctor was able to make me a gold one to replace it. Fortunately, my grandfather paid for it. I don't even think about it anymore."

On the trip back we discussed possible living arrangements once we were married.

"I think I should continue working at the tailor shop for a while.

There's no need for me to stop working, at least until our first child is born. I've sometimes mentioned to Mr. Rogers that I could do some of the sewing work at home and he seemed fine with that. Then, we would have enough money to move into a house—a rented house, of course."

"I guess if you want to continue working, that's fine with me. But after we have children, I would want you to be able to spend your time raising them properly. And you can't depend on me to know what to do as a father. I didn't know of any families in Kentucky that had a man in the house all the time." I made a quick glance toward Bertie to check her reaction.

Bertie patted my knee. "Don't worry, you'll know what to do when the time comes. Just give him lots of love and attention, or her, I mean—well, whichever. You probably won't be around the children a lot, since you like to work so hard; but that's all right, I can take care of raising our children, just like my mother did with her children."

I felt relieved. "The Stotlar people have homes for rent. Let's talk to them next weekend."

Bertie's face beamed with happiness!

That night, as I lay in bed recalling the events of the day, I compared lovemaking with Bertie to the "experiences" I had had with the girls in Kentucky. While Bertie was involved in the act, looking into my eyes and running her fingers through my hair, the other girls I had been with were more intent on having the experience and then getting to the end, as if my feelings didn't matter. Looking back, I thought those girls were wanting to be able to tell their friends they had been with me, as if it were a milestone that would validate themselves. I just couldn't imagine Bertie being in that position at any point in her life.

I thought she would make a perfect companion for me. Marrying her would make my goal of being seen as part of a happy couple here in Herrin complete!

Chapter 14

Saturday afternoon Bertie and I were viewing a Stotlar rent house in McNeil's Addition, not far from the Black Forest Inn. It was a quiet street of new homes. There were two large trees on the lot shielding the house from the noontime sun and the backyard was open, making it perfect for a garden, which Bertie liked. The house had gray clapboard siding with a porch across the entire front of the house. There were wide steps leading up to the front porch; a small window above the porch roof was open for ventilation. Another house was being constructed on the lot to the north; the lot to the south was vacant except for some stakes standing in the ground, indicating that a home would be started there soon.

As we walked to the backyard, Bertie asked, "Do you like to garden, Leland?"

"I wouldn't say I liked to do it. I did help Mrs. Goshen with her garden when she needed help, but I was young then. Making a garden with you would be different, I suppose."

"Oh, yes. We could spend a lot of time there, but you would probably be too busy working to help with a garden. I would love teaching the children how to garden, though. I always loved to go to the garden with my mother, I learned so much from her."

We walked toward the back porch as a man wearing a suit came out the door. He looked like a typical salesman: neatly combed gray hair, no facial hair, and a smile that seemed fixed on his face. "Sorry I'm late. Lots of people are asking about a home at the office today. It took a little time to get away. Well, what do you think so far?"

"We like the backyard. Is the soil rich in the yard here? We're interested in a garden," Bertie asked.

"Most of the soil in Herrin is great for gardening. I haven't heard anyone complain about it yet!"

I nodded, trying to look like I understood these things.

"Come up here and we'll take a tour." We walked up the three steps and onto the wide porch. "You can see that the washing machine could be located out here in nice weather. And there is plenty of room for a table and chair, should you want to work up the vegetables from your garden. Some people put a bed out here for sleeping in the hot weather, but that's up to you, of course."

He paused, I suppose to give us time for questions, then continued the tour.

"Let's go inside. Here's the kitchen, checkered linoleum floor; you'll want to put curtains on the windows, I suppose. We've put this new Frigidaire refrigerator over in this corner. Now, this stove is a four-burner with a broiler below and an oven on the side. Both appliances are ivory colored; the latest style, you know. Naturally, the house has running water and sewers—nobody has outhouses in town anymore!" He gave a short laugh as he walked into the small bathroom. "Everything you need to keep clean." He used his full hand to indicate the sink, stool, and a small tub. There was only enough room for Bertie and me to peek our heads through the doorway.

The kitchen and bathroom were painted white. There were cabinets above and below the sink and countertop in the kitchen, a medicine cabinet over the sink in the bathroom.

"You can see there's plenty of room for the family to eat right here in the kitchen. We didn't look under the back porch, but there's plenty of area to store things under there, too. You know, like canned vegetables, things like that.

"Now, through here"—he walked into the next room—"we have the living area, plenty large for company." He pointed toward the ceiling. "Up here is a ventilating fan to pull hot air out of the house. You would want it closed other than the summer months to keep the warm air inside. And, in the winter, the gravity furnace under the house blows warm air through pipes and out these registers in the floor. Now, these two are the bedrooms. All the walls will be painted, but you might want to add wallpaper—we can talk about that later."

He waved us into the first bedroom, toward the front of the house. "Plenty of room for your double bed, a night stand and a wardrobe to hang clothes, and a chest for unmentionables." And again he gave a short laugh.

Waving us on, he went into the rear bedroom. "This room is the same size as the front room, one less window here, though. You mentioned earlier that you will be wanting a family, so this will be an excellent room for the children! Do either of you have any questions?"

Bertie asked, "You said thirty dollars a month, right?"

"That's correct, and you'll pay for the utilities on your own."

"And it'll be ready for us to move in at the start of June?"

"Sure will, we'll just need to sign the papers and you'll be all set. Can we go back to the office to do that now?"

Bertie looked at me, then said, "We'll need a little time first, this is the first place we are seeing."

Shortly, the salesman left us to go back to the office.

Bertie asked, "Leland, you haven't said much. What are you thinking?"

"This is a big step for me—us."

"Be truthful with me, Leland. Are you unsure about the house or about us getting married?"

"No, I want to get married, it's the house that bothers me."

"We don't have to take this one if you want to look around

awhile, or we could look at a larger apartment. I don't want you to think I'm pushing you, that's all." Bertie was making a pleading face as she looked in my eyes.

"I know you're right. Let's walk over to the Black Forest and get something to eat. I think I just need a little time here."

We were quiet on the walk over. Bertie seemed anxious to move forward with the house. I was trying to look at the neighborhood for signs that this was the right thing to do. I wanted to please her, but being the man of the house was something foreign to me; I hadn't lived in a house where a man took care of it.

Once we had ordered some food, Bertie began, "The salesman said this house will be ready on June 1st. We can wait for them to have another one. Maybe you'll be ready a little later. It just seems to me that we should plan to have our marriage about the same time that a house is ready. What do you think?" From her look, I could see she wanted me to respond, and I knew I had to make a decision. I had always been able to decide on important things in my life in the past. At those times, though, the decisions were always totally mine. Now, I will have to include Bertie in the decisions I would be making.

Bertie took my hand. "Leland, be truthful, do you love me?"

I knew this was the real point. Everyone else seemed to know when they were in love and what that meant. But I didn't feel love for anyone in my life before; at least, I didn't know I had. My dad didn't spend any time with me before he died; the little time he was around, he treated me like I was a bother to him. My mother was too sick most of our time together to teach me things. And all the other people I had lived with seemed to just put up with me, until Mrs. Goshen gave me help. Bertie was the first person who actually expressed that she loved me. She seemed to know what that meant. I wanted to feel that way too. Perhaps the best way to go forward was to just get married, move into the house, and my love for her would grow over time!

"Yes, yes I do. And, I want us to get married and live together."

"Go on."

"We can sign the papers on this house tomorrow. Can you be ready to go to the Justice of the Peace the first week of June?"

Bertie beamed. "Of course I can!"

Before we left the restaurant, Bertie arranged with her cousin Carl for a wedding party on Saturday evening, June 4th.

Our new house was ready on the 1st of June, so we started to move our things in. On Saturday we were married at the Justice of the Peace's office in the morning. All our friends came to the Black Forest Inn for the party that evening. Then we started our new life together.

Two weeks later, Saturday, June 18th, was the big event in the Italian community—Anthony's wedding to Josephine Colombo. The wedding took place in St. Mary's Catholic Church with a reception party at the Rome Club following. Not being Catholic ourselves, Bertie and I sat at the back of the church for the wedding, then we were some of the first people at the reception. The large hall of the Rome Club was finely decorated with bunches of flowers and streamers on all the walls, long tables with assorted Italian food at one side, the band from Vinny's in a corner with a dancing area before it, and many tables spread throughout the room.

As with most Italian parties, everyone was having a great time, dancing and drinking until late into the evening. Maryanne looked lovely as we passed several times on the dance floor. Even the children were included in the festivities and they too were allowed to stay late. Some of the city officials attended, a few partaking of the liquor, but some stayed across the room from it. I had a great time, and Bertie did as well. Later, she said the exception was when she knew Caesar was watching her. While it made her uncomfortable, she didn't mention it to me at the time. She told me about it when we got home, but we were both exhausted and went right to bed and to sleep.

Chapter 15

The months of July and August were spent setting up our new home and preparing a garden in the back. Bertie planted some lettuce and carrots that would grow quickly and be ready in the fall. She thought it would be too late to plant anything that would bear fruit, but we did get some strawberry plants in the ground for the following year.

Also, she encouraged me to keep trying to get her pregnant.

"I want to start having children soon, don't you?"

"I do. And I think we will have them when the time comes for us."

"I know you're right, of course, it's just that my mother had her first child before she was twenty, so I feel like I'm getting a late start, that's all." She was trying to sound hopeful.

After a few months, there were some nights I would rather have gone to sleep instead. My feeling was, if there were going to be children, it would happen in time. But pleasing her was important to me, and having children will give me a different status with my friends; they will know I am a "family man."

On a Saturday in late August a new family moved into the house just completed on the north side of our home. By afternoon it appeared that the move-in of the furniture was complete, so Bertie and I walked over to introduce ourselves. The new family consisted of

Hershel Morrow, his wife Cynthia, and their son Charles.

I helped Hershel move some of the living-room furniture into place.

"Hershel, what do you do for a living?"

"I'm a typesetter at the *Herrin News*. The news you read every day is what I create; that is, I put the letters together for the printing machines to run; I don't write the articles, of course."

"Now that's interesting. I've never met a typesetter before. How did you learn to do that?" As we sat down on the sofa we had just placed, I could hear the women talking in the kitchen.

"I was raised in Baltimore and my old man was a typesetter for the *Baltimore Sun*. He showed me how to do it. But he was a mean bastard, so I decided to move away. I saw an ad in a Chicago paper for the *Herrin News*, so I answered it, and here I am."

"You've just got the one boy, no other children?"

"Just Charles, we named him after my father. And he's turning out to be just like him—mean to the bone. I guess it runs in the family. Now, what about you, Leland. What do you do?"

"I work in the mines, Madison Number 12, over at Colp. Some nights I catch some extra work helping out at the Colp Tavern, things like that. Bertha there works at Rogers' Tailor Shop, behind the counter."

"Do you and Bertha have any children?"

"Not yet, we've only been married a few months, but we will have one soon, we hope."

"Oh, they're great when they're little, but as they grow up they seem to change. Charles was a sweet little boy, but now that he's nine, that boy is a handful. Some nights when I get home I have to beat him for another thing he's tried. I guess boys have to learn on their own how to behave."

Because Hershel was getting animated about his son, I wanted to change the subject. "Are you folks going to have a garden out back? We're setting one up in our backyard, getting ready for a good harvest next year."

"Yes, well, Cynthia wants to have a garden. I don't have the time or the energy after I get home from work, so I leave that up to her. She really likes to have fresh vegetables for our meals. She's a real good homemaker, she is."

"You said typesetting is hard work—isn't the type just little pieces of metal? What's hard about it?"

"Well, all right, the typesetting is just part of the job"—Hershel's voice began to rise—"I also set up the printing machine and load the paper into it. A roll of paper can weigh a hundred pounds, and that ain't easy to move around. Then, I have to move the printed papers over to the loading dock so they can be shipped out. Is that enough work for you?" By now he was almost shouting.

"No, I wasn't trying to question why you're tired, I was just trying to understand all the things a typesetter does, that's all."

From the kitchen, the women heard Hershel's loud voice. They walked into the living room. "Leland, why don't we leave these people to their work"—she turned to Cynthia—"we know how much work it is to move into a new home and we don't want to interrupt. We just wanted to meet you all."

Cynthia appeared embarrassed by Hershel's outbreak, but she tried to cover it over: "Well, it was real nice of you two to come over to introduce yourselves. We love to have company, so come back anytime." And she looked nervously at Hershel.

"Yeah, we love company!" Hershel said too loudly.

Neither of us talked on our walk back home. Once inside, Bertie sounded flabbergasted.

"Cynthia seemed like a nice woman, but I think she is terrified of Hershel! When she heard him getting loud in the living room, her hands started to shake, like she was really nervous. I could see she needed to get to him, so I told her we needed to get back over here, we had things to do."

"My guess is that he beats the boy regularly. He might beat on her as well," I said as I shook my head.

"These aren't the kind of neighbors I wanted, but then we don't have any choice there, do we?"

"The house on the other side is about to finish, maybe we'll have better luck there," I said, trying to be hopeful.

The company shut down the mine early on Friday, September 2nd, for federal inspections over the Labor Day weekend. We miners had extra time off, which is good for our health, but bad on our pocketbooks. Our pay is based on the number of tons of coal sent out on railroad cars. The shutdown meant no coal would be shipped so no pay was earned. Many of the miners joined me on Monday at the Herrin Union Hall for coffee and conversation.

Matthew Lewis sat down at my table with exciting news. "Did you hear about the mine explosion over at Harco Saturday?" Accidents like this always spooked Matthew. He had recently married a woman with two children; her former husband was killed in a mine accident three years earlier. While Matthew was only twenty-one, he did have a receding hairline, which made him look a little older, but his young age and the new family did give him concern at times like this. He said his wife would go into a deep state of sorrow over the news that men had died in a mining accident, bringing back terrible memories to her, and he didn't know how to give her support.

"I don't even know where Harco is," I responded, taking another drink of coffee.

"It's over northwest of Harrisburg, about ten miles from Harrisburg. That's pretty close to us, ain't it? Must be about twenty miles." He ran his fingers over his light brown mustache as he studied the newspaper on the table before him, a worried look on his face; the fingers of his free hand were drumming on the table.

"Now, slow down and give me the details. Was anyone killed?"

"There sure was! Eleven men were killed right there. Six more were injured but they should be all right shortly."

"Does anyone know what caused the explosion?"

"The *Marion Semi-Weekly Leader* paper here says 'the driller set off a dynamite charge which penetrated an old walled room providing means of escape of black damp, which, it is believed, killed the miners.' Ain't that awful?" Matthew looked up at me with a furrowed brow and questioning brown eyes.

"It is awful and I'll take it as a lesson to remember whenever I go to set off a charge of dynamite. Does it say how deep they were?"

"Let's see. Yup, they were 445 feet down and back 1,000 feet from the shaft."

"Will there be a memorial service?"

"Doesn't say, it's too early for one to be set yet. I 'spect it'll be over in Harrisburg, though, if there is one.

"Oh, Leland, listen to this: 'The mine was considered a safe one and which had been closed down most of the summer for repair work.' Then it says, 'The crew of seventeen miners were engaged in working a new coal bed near an old shaft, which had been walled in, when the driller exploded a charge of dynamite which crushed the old vein walls, and entombed himself and fellow workers, according to reports from the mine.' I hate to hear these stories, don't you?"

"They can give me shakes. But, now that I'm working with the dynamite, I have to remain calm, so I try to put these things out of my mind. What does your wife say about these newspaper reports?"

"Oh, I don't show them to her; I don't even take the newspapers home if there are stories like these. I can see her sorrow when she hears other people talk about mine accidents. She told the people at our church she thought she was going to have to do something drastic for her and the kids until I came into her life. I think the mining companies should take care of the families of miners killed in mining accidents, don't you?"

"Sure do, I think everyone does. It would be easy and inexpensive if they would just use another company, someone like the Foresters of America, to give us insurance for times like this. The Italians have gotten together as a group to join up with the Foresters. Now, they have insurance benefits."

"I guess we could ask the union to do it for us, huh?" Matthew pondered.

"Sure could, but that would be higher union dues and most miners don't want to pay that amount."

We were quiet for several minutes.

"Well, Matthew, if you hear about a service for the men, let me know, will you?"

"You can count on me!"

I wondered how long he would last as a coal miner—his small frame and nervous personality didn't match well with work below the ground.

By this time the news of the accident was spreading around the room. Otis Clark started to get loud about their plight and the things he wanted to do to the leadership of the local mining companies. Many of the people were encouraging him along. He enjoyed the attention and played to his audience with his quips on management. His rotund body was bouncing as he talked. He was bald on top, with muttonchops for sideburns, which made him look like a Dickens character in a book Bertie had me reading. His arms flew as he described the imaginary cutting off of their heads.

"Goddammit, it just ain't right, us giving up our lives so some men that ain't around here get all the money and they don't care one iota about us'ns. I'm usually a nice guy, but it's times like this when I want to get a gun and shoot the whole bunch."

The men who were with him up to this point began to cool down.

No one in this room wanted anyone killed because of an accident in another area. They all understood that mining was dangerous work and they didn't know any of the miners at Harco; most had never even been over there. As Otis saw that the men were backing down, he lowered his voice until the issue was dropped by the room.

I continued to ride with Mark on Tuesdays and work for Mr. Goodfellow at the Colp Tavern. The extra fifteen dollars each week, plus the money from mining and Bertie's work, provided us with a good living. We were able to get all the things we needed for the house, and by the end of the year, talked of getting a better car.

Some evenings I came home with a puffy eye or a cut on an arm, but none of it was serious. On the nights I worked late, Bertie didn't bother me for sex when I came home.

One Friday evening in December, Bertie had a little news: "Leland, Emory, the man from the car dealer next door, was telling me about a new car he's been working on. He says he should have it ready for sale next week and it's a really good deal for a buyer— maybe you should go over there to check it out."

"How did you happen to hear about it from Mr. Emory?"

"Well, first, it's Mr. Emory MacIntosh, his first name is Emory. He's a mechanic working in the repair garage at Herrin Motors where you bought your car from Mr. Kelly. He brings the mechanics' coveralls over to me to be washed. Sometimes he has extra time, so he stays to talk with me a little, that's all. I've known him since I started working for Mr. Rogers. And if I know what you're thinking, he's married and has a family!"

"That's not what I was thinking, but now that you mention it, just how much time does he spend with you?" Our voices were rising.

"What's that supposed to mean? Are you asking me if we do more than talk?" She stood up to face me.

"Alright, yes! Just what is going on there?"

"You're saying you don't trust me? You actually think I might have a relationship with another man? You're crazy!" Bertie screamed.

"I didn't until now!" I yelled back.

"And what about you? I remember a few months ago, asking you to tell me about what Caesar said, that you were seeing his sister, Mary-whatever-her-name-is, when you were seeing me, but you wouldn't answer that question. What about that?"

"See, I'll tell you. I knew that I was going to ask you to marry me and you would probably say yes, so I wanted to learn how to dance the polka for you without you knowing it. I heard from Anthony that his sister Maryanne gave dance lessons at Vinny's so I went over there on a few Saturday afternoons for lessons. That's all we did, just dance lessons."

"Well, that's all I do with Emory—that's Mr. MacIntosh—we just talk a little at the end of the day, nothing more!"

"Just talking with him alone in the back of the tailor shop is enough! When other people hear that's going on, they are going to assume there's more to it than just talking and goddammit, I won't have it!" I started toward her with a raised, clenched fist, which caused Bertie to cower back with her arms raised to shield herself, then I stopped. "I'm tired of this, I'm getting out of here!" And I turned and walked out the door, got in my car, and sped off.

Entering Vinny's through the side door, I took a seat at a table nearby. The bar wasn't too full—it was too early for most of the usual crowd. It took a minute for Maryanne to see me, but when she did, she came right over.

"There's my dance student, how's it going?" she said with a smile and sparkling eyes.

"Not good. Bring me a beer"—sternly.

"Aw, trouble at home, or at work? No, let me guess. It's too late for you to be coming from the mine, so I'm gonna guess the problem is at home—am I right?"

"I'm not in a mood for this conversation. Just bring me a damn beer."

"Alright, I can see you're in a bad mood, but I'm not sure it's a beer you're looking for." She walked to the bar swinging her hips so her skirt moved a little extra.

As I sat waiting, I began to settle down. Thinking about the conversation, I could see similarities with people talking, no yelling, back in Kentucky, accusing each other of transgressions that might or might not have happened, my mother and father included. I became aware that at twenty-three years old, I still didn't understand why people did the things they did to each other. More exactly, I didn't understand Bertie, though we had been living with each other for many months now. I shook my head, clenched my fist, and smacked the table.

"Hey, take it easy on that table. What did it do to you?" Maryanne asked as she started to set the beer down, then raised it back up. "Is it safe to give this to you? Or, are you going to hit it too?" She acted like she was horrified.

Realizing what I was doing, I leaned back and smirked. "Yeah, it's safe—well I'm not going to hit it, but I will be drinking it! Go ahead and set it down."

As I looked up at Maryanne, she smiled warmly at me, put the beer on the table while bending and resting her other hand on my shoulder.

"Is there anything else I can do for you?" she whispered in my ear.

I shook my head. "I wish there was."

"Oh sweetie, I could do lots for you, but it wouldn't help with your problem, it'd only make it worse—and neither of us wants that, do we?"

I took a long drink, setting the glass down hard. My mind was confused, so I said nothing.

Maryanne rose up slowly. "Well, if you think of anything, you know I'm here for you."

As the alcohol sedation began to take effect, I thought the argument was a bad thing, one that would have an impact on both of us. I regretted the fear I saw in Bertie's eyes when I started toward her. Leaving her alone wasn't a good thing, but it may have been best considering the mood I was in. I thought of what that kind of anger had done to me one night in Kentucky, and it just couldn't be repeated!

I finished the first beer quickly and ordered another.

As Maryanne set the second one down, she asked, "Feel like talking yet?"

"Oh, it isn't a big thing, just a little discussion I had with my wife that wasn't going the right way. Happens to all married couples, right?"

"Since I work in a place where people come when that happens, I'd say it happens to all married couples and to some, it happens quite a lot. But then, most of the customers here are Italian, so I may be biased in my observation."

"I guess this is the first real argument we've had and we've been married for six months now. Is that too soon for this to happen?"

"Sweety, I'm not married, so I don't have any real experience, but I'm sure you two are just normal people. Go home, make up, and go to bed to show her how much you love her. That's my advice. You're a real nice guy and I really like you. Now finish your beer and go back home, all right?"

I did just that. Bertie was glad to see me and we had a long talk to work things out, went to bed and expressed our love for each other, then a long night's sleep.

In the morning, I went to Herrin Motors to talk with Mr. Kelly about the car Bertie had mentioned to me. Arrangements were made and Mr. Kelly said he thought it would be ready for the trade before Christmas. I called the new car our Christmas present to each other.

I felt it had been a very good year. I hoped the next one would be just as good.

Chapter 16

The second week of January Mark Wallops and I were going to Harrisburg to get a load of whiskey.

"We're going to make a little different trip tonight, Leland. Mr. Birger wants us to go to the depot in Harrisburg to pick up some cheap moonshine there. Then we're going to the roadhouse in Energy to drop it off. Reverend Glotfelty is going to be waiting there with some Herrin police officers. Charlie's been told that they intend to bust up the whiskey and the slot machines inside. Charlie says, 'let 'em, we got plenty more and this will help settle down the do-gooders.'"

The moonshine was being shipped by train from Kentucky and dropped at the railroad station in Harrisburg. Charlie Birger was supposed to be there waiting for us, but when we arrived the porter told us Mr. Birger had been arrested and he was being held in the Saline County Jail. However, the police had neglected to take the cases with them, so Mark paid the station agent a "pick-up fee" and we loaded the cases in the delivery truck. Then, we headed back toward Williamson County.

On the return trip the conversation turned to Kentucky. I was comparing the present trip to the moonshine run we had been on in the mountains, the one where the feds had stopped our truck in an ambush and thrown me in jail for the night.

"The next day the two federal officers sat me down for a talk. They wanted to make me understand that moonshining in the mountains didn't hold a good future for me. They thought that I would have a better chance at life if I got out of the area. So they gave me some money and a train ticket to Louisville. You never know what's going to happen next in this life, but that day I will always remember as one of the best for me! Coming here to Herrin is just what those damn revenuers said it would be."

"You don't miss your kin?"

"Naw, I didn't really have any blood relatives there and the only ones I was close to still write with me, saying they're happy for me, that I would have gone to jail for sure, if I had stayed."

"No little woman that misses you back there?"

"The only women I had anything to do with were just young girls. I guess there was one of them that did tell me I got her pregnant, just before I left. She hasn't tried to get in touch with me since then, so I guess she didn't care about me enough. Some of the people there ain't never going to leave."

As we arrived at the Energy Roadhouse, the Reverend P. R. Glotfelty, the Methodist minister from Herrin, and two Herrin police officers were waiting for us. Talk was that the Reverend had become a member of the Klan and was taking an active role in ending the liquor and gambling activities in the county. Mark slowed the truck to park at the roadhouse. As the police officers got out of their cars, he stopped in the lot and backed up to the front door.

"Evening, Officers," Mark greeted the men.

"What ya got in the truck here, Mark?"

"Well James, I'm sure you know what I got in there. I'm just doing the job Mr. Birger pays me to do, just like you're doing the job you're paid to do."

Rev. Glotfelty interrupted, "Officer, we don't need to be doing any small talk tonight. We all know who we are and what our jobs are, so let's get on with it. These men are breaking the law, now you have work to do. Why don't we just get it finished and we can all go home?" His voice sounded like he was giving a sermon on Sunday morning, warning his flock of the evils of Satan.

"Yes sir, Reverend, we'll just do that. Mark, would you open up your truck and hand out the liquor you got in there?"

Mark opened the back and I jumped inside, handing out the moonshine to the officer. Each time, Officer Oliver handed the bottle to his partner, who threw it against the brick front of the roadhouse, smashing it. The moonshine was making a puddle there and running across the parking lot.

When the last bottle was broken, I jumped out of the truck. "That's all there is."

Rev. Glotfelty still had a strict look on his face. He waved at the door. "Let's finish the job, men," he said sternly to the officers. Everyone went into the building, which was empty except for the manager, Samuel Dewmaine.

The Reverend continued, "You officers will want to arrest Mr. Dewmaine here. You can see that he is running an illegal liquor and gambling house. You will also want to destroy those slot machines over there against the wall. Now, get about your duties, please!"

Officer Tracy had brought in a sledgehammer. He began to smash the slot machines as Officer Oliver put handcuffs on Mr. Dewmaine and took him to the car. As he passed Mark, Sam handed him the keys to the roadhouse.

"Lock it up, will you Mark?"

As the last slot was smashed, Officer Tracy began working on the bottles of liquor at the bar. When the liquor and beer had been destroyed, we all emptied out of the roadhouse. The police cars took off as Mark locked up the building, then we got into the truck.

"What's going to happen to Sam?" I asked.

"He'll spend the night in the Herrin jail and Big Jim will come by tomorrow with bail money and then they'll go over to see the judge for the fine. Big Jim will pay that too. The roadhouse will stay closed over the weekend, then we'll restock it and get more slot machines to put in there. This way, the Reverend looks good, the police look good, and the dry people will be satisfied that they took a step toward making the city clean again."

"Where do the slot machines come from?"

"I have to go to St. Louis to pick them up on Friday. You want to make a little money and go with me? I could use some help lifting them and it's always good to have company on a long trip like that."

"Sure I would, you pay better than mining does and I don't work this Friday. I'm guessing the work will be a lot easier—you expect we'll have any trouble?"

"Naw, and this will give you a chance to meet some of the Shelton gang. They own the slot machines, so we're getting them from those boys. Going up there and back won't be a problem 'cause nobody will know what's in the truck."

On Friday we went to Carbondale, then turned north and then west to use the hard roads to get to East St. Louis, in St. Clair County. By 11:00, we were loading the machines in the truck.

After the last one was loaded, Mark suggested, "Let's go over to Minnie's Place for lunch. She's got good food and the girls are pleasant to look at."

Minnie's was already crowded at noon when we arrived. I looked around the room in amazement. There were so many men in there you couldn't stir 'em with a stick. Against one wall were several couches with attractive, scantily clad women lounging on them. Directly ahead was a small band playing without anyone paying attention to them. On the wall opposite the couches was a bar, fully occupied by male patrons who were watching a couple of almost-nude women dancing on pedestals behind the bartender, seemingly to the band's music.

I raised my voice for Mark to hear me. "I guess I'm in the big city now. I've never seen this many people at a girly show this early in the afternoon!"

"We're only a few blocks from the Mississippi, and the ships come in at all times of day. Some of these sailors have been on the ship for weeks, so they want to get some 'relief' right away. And these women want to get some of their money!"

Mark waved to Minnie to get some service.

"You men want to see a couple of women, Mr. Mark?"

"No, Minnie, today we're here for some of your good food. You got a table for us?"

"Sure, come on into the next room. I serve lunch in there."

While the first room was decorated somewhat ornately, the second looked more austere. It was filled with tables and had a buffet on one wall.

"It's thirty-five cents for all-you-can-eat and drinks are extra. Take this table here." Minnie wiped off the table, then walked away.

We put our hats on the table and walked over to the buffet to fill our plates. As we returned, Mark waved at a man at another table. The man got up and approached us as we sat down.

Mark introduced the man to me. "Carl, this is my helper today, Leland Vance—well, he helps me a lot when I deliver hooch for Charlie. Leland, this is Carl Shelton, his brother is Earl."

I stood up to shake Carl's hand. "Pleased to meet you, Mr. Shelton."

"No, no, just call me Carl, we ain't formal around here. We're not like that goddamned Jew, Charley Birger! We're just honest God-fearing people here," he said as he winked and smiled. "Well mighty nice to make your acquaintance, Leland." Carl turned and walked back to his table.

I was about to take the first bite of my food when a woman behind me said, "Vhat you fellows vant to drink today?"

When she started to talk, I began to jump up from my seat! As I turned around, I saw the woman speaking, so I sat back down.

"Did I scare you, hon?" she asked me.

"Yes and no. You sound just like my wife and I thought it was her talking. You even have a slight German accent like her." I shook my head as I looked at her. She was about five feet, five inches tall, had short black hair curled all over her head. Somewhat plump, her looks weren't similar to Bertie's at all. A little too much makeup covered her face and neck, and her dress was a little too short for her body, I thought.

"You don't suppose I have this accent because I'm from Germany, do you? Now tell me vhat you're drinking!"

Both of us ordered beers and she left to get them. When she returned with the drinks, I asked for her name.

"My name is Gertrude, but everyone calls me Gertie, vhy do you ask?"

"My wife's name is Bertha, but I call her Bertie, so that's similar too."

"Isn't that great! If you got the time and five dollars we can go upstairs and you can see if I'm like her in bed too." She gave me a stern smile and raised her eyebrows for a few seconds, then turned and walked away.

"Wow, she's some woman! She's not like Bertie in any way other than her voice. Gertie, she said." I was still recovering.

"That's what she said. It's not a surprise she's German, there's lots of them around here. There's a big brewery across the river and they all run it."

We finished our meal and started back. At the edge of town we stopped at a filling station for gas. On the inside there was a map on the wall of East St. Louis.

Mark pointed out where we were and which streets we had traveled.

"In case you have to come back here without me, you need to know how to get around."

I didn't think that would be happening, but I did take it in. This day was an experience I was glad to have, but I didn't want to get too involved with these gangsters. I thought of my promise to Mrs. Goshen to stay away from these people and I preferred the quiet life I was making in Herrin, where people were friendly and helped each other. It's best I stay away from the Sheltons and this life.

On the road going back to Herrin, Mark talked incessantly about the things he missed in the big city: baseball and various restaurants, and some of the women he had been associated with, none of them on any kind of permanent basis. He liked the easy life, didn't want any children, didn't want to be tied down to one woman; he said he just liked living by himself and working for the Birger and Shelton gangs. He thought gangsters had a creed they all lived by and he liked it.

I told him I didn't think I would want to get married until I met Bertha, but now I felt being married was a great way to live. Then Mark opened up with his real story.

"Well, I was married at one time, just for a few months. I met a girl in a bar and we had a fling together. After a couple of weeks she started staying with me regular. It was great, she was always ready for us to have sex, we both really loved doing it. For the next month or two it was always lots of drinking and sex, then she told me she was pregnant, was I going to marry her. Of course, marrying her would be the right thing to do, so I said yes, even though I didn't really know her. Well, I was working the evening shift at the brewery in St. Louis, four to midnight, see. We'd go out drinking after I got home at 12:30 or so, we were having a great time for a while. Then, one morning I got up and found her on the kitchen floor bleeding real bad between her legs. I took her to the hospital and they said the baby was lost. The doctor took me aside and asked if I thought she might have caused the miscarriage. That really surprised me, but I told him 'No,' because I didn't think she would have done it."

Mark was watching the road as he drove, but he kept glancing over my way, regular like. I think he was trying to read how I was taking this story he was telling.

"After a couple weeks, she was back to her old self and we got back to the fun times. Then I noticed that she was always in her nightgown when I got home like she had been in bed for a while. I asked her about it and she gave me a story about not feeling like she had enough energy since the incident. But she had plenty of energy when we got in bed, so I began to wonder what was going on. I took a sick day from work one evening and watched the apartment from across the street. Sure 'nough, about 7:00 another man went into the apartment and I could see through the window when they went into the bedroom. About 8:30 the man left the apartment. I was thinking what I would do next—should I beat up on her, or just kick her out. Then at 9:00, just as I was going to go in, another man went in the building and to my apartment. Soon, I could see them go into the bedroom. Around 11:00 he left. I waited for a little while to see if anyone else went in, then I went in myself. She was waiting for me, like nothing had happened. I just asked, normal like, what she had been doing.

"'Oh, just waiting on you to get here so we could go out to a bar. You ready?' she said.

"She was just normal acting, I couldn't believe her sitting there like nothing happened. Then I told her what I'd seen, the two men come into my apartment. She lit a cigarette, real causal, and said, 'Yeah, that's what I been doing, to be truthful.'

"I told her to pack her things and get out. If she left quiet like and didn't object to a divorce, I wouldn't do anything bad to her, so she just got up and grabbed her things and left." He shook his head, like it was still fresh in his mind, like he still couldn't believe what had happened.

"A few months later I was sitting in a bar talking to a guy who was some kind of doctor. We got to talking about women and he told me that some women can't get enough sex to satisfy them. They'll have more than one man in one day, they're called nymphomaniacs. I guess that's what this woman was, I just wasn't satisfying her, so she found other men to fill her needs. I wouldn't never trust another woman again. I hope you and Bertha work out like you want."

"See, I don't think Bertha is anything like that. Sure, she likes to have sex with me, but she says it's mainly to get a kid, and I believe her." I did wonder, though, does a man ever know what his wife is doing when he's not around? I guess I'll just have to trust her unless she makes me think otherwise. Then, well, I hate to think what I would do if I found out different. My aunt told me one time she thought that was what happened between my mom and dad, that he thought she had taken up with another man. She said he questioned whether I was really his child—that was why he treated Mom so bad.

I went on, "But I do think I knew a woman like you're talking about when I was in Kentucky. She was living with a friend of mine outside of Mule Shoe. Jimmy worked a different shift from me, so one night when he was working she came into the bar. I was with two other men and she let it be known to us that she was available if one of us wanted to go out with her. I didn't say anything 'cause I knew who she was, but I didn't think she knew me, or that I was a friend of Jimmy's. One of the other men did go out to his car with her for a while. He came back later and said they had a real good time.

"The next day I felt I had to tell Jimmy what happened. I was surprised when he said he didn't care, he was just letting her live with him for the sex. He figured she'd leave him soon and, sure 'nuf, that's what happened."

"So, tell me Leland, just what were you like in Kentucky? You've mentioned a little about being in prison for killing a man—is that the only time you were in jail?"

"Oh, no. No, I don't talk much about what happened while I was in Kentucky. If people knew too much, they wouldn't think good about me, so I just talk about the decent things I did there. Yeah, I did have my share of bar fights that put me in jail a few times. One night I was with a fellow who was delivering moonshine up to Pennsylvania when the revenuers stopped us. They put us in jail for thirty days that time."

Mark smiled at me. "Sounds like you were a real badass."

"The last thing I'll say is the time Jimmy and me went to Booneville to rob a hardware store. It sold guns and ammo and we needed a rifle to shoot squirrels and rabbits for food. Well, the sheriff found us in the store before we got anything lifted. He took us and put us in jail for a week. But, Jimmy and me had a good time in there together! That time being in jail wasn't too bad."

Mark had an idea. "Why don't you talk with Charlie or the Sheltons about doing more work for them? It sounds like you already have what they're looking for in a gangster."

"No, I don't want to get back into that life, if I can help it. Being in jail isn't any fun and I like the way things are going now. Bertie doesn't like me working with you as it is. But, she does like the money I'm making, so she goes along with it."

"I agree, Leland. Those guys get crazy once in a while and ask their men to do things I wouldn't do myself. We got a good job delivering, so why change, right?"

Mark talked a lot more about his experiences with the Sheltons to kill the remaining time on the road. When we arrived at his place, he pulled the truck inside the garage and locked the door. He thanked me for helping, paid me, and we parted.

Chapter 17

February brought some warmer weather during the first week. The house to the south had been completed for several weeks and a new family was moving in. We went over to meet them and welcome them to the neighborhood. We were hopeful these would be nicer people than the Morrows turned out to be.

A man met us on the porch as we walked up.

"Well, hello." He smiled broadly as he said it. "So nice to meet you, come in, let me introduce you to my wife, Heather." He held the door back for us to go through.

Bertie entered first and held her hands together as she smiled at Heather and nodded.

"Hello, I'm Bertha and this is my husband Leland Vance. We just wanted to say 'Hello' and welcome you to the neighborhood."

"Well, that's right nice of you all. Our daughter Sara is staying with some of her Sunday school friends today and tomorrow, or I'd introduce her to you as well. And, this is my husband Howard."

We shook hands and nodded.

"Mighty nice to meet you," Howard said, "and sorry for the mess in here. We hope to get it cleaned up real soon."

I nodded. "Oh, we understand. We just moved in last summer."

"Leland, what do you do for a living, if I might ask?"

"I'm a miner, Madison Coal over in Colp."

"Lots of miners around Herrin, ain't there! That's real good for the community these days. Why, Herrin is really growing because of the coal, I'll say. I'm a salesman myself. I sell the Good Book and other religious paraphernalia around Little Egypt. Bible study guides, hymn books, religious fans, stuff like that. It keeps me real busy—I travel all over the area, even into Indiana some."

The women were chatting together and moved away from us so their conversation didn't interrupt.

"Do you stay out overnight, or can you get back here by night-time?" I asked.

"Oh, no, I have to stay out on the road most weeks. Well, I try to schedule sales calls in this area on Mondays and Fridays so I'm only out on Tuesday, Wednesday nights. I like to be with the family as much as I can. Have you met the Hosocks? They live over here"—Howard pointed toward the house further down the street—"and they're old friends of ours. We were glad to get this house so we could be neighbors. We both go to Herrin Christian Church. Do you folks go to church?" The salesman finally gave up control of the conversation.

"No, we don't attend anywhere. We haven't felt the need to do that yet," I said firmly.

"Well, if you decide you want to find the Lord, we'd be glad to introduce you to our church family. We've been active with the church's work with the combating of Satan these days—demon alcohol and gambling. If you'd like to help our city, we can get you involved that way too."

I had heard enough. "We don't want to keep you from your moving-in work here. Looks like you have a lot to do, so Bertha and I need to let you get to it." I shook Howard's hand and motioned to Bertha.

Both Howard and Heather were overly nice as they said good-bye.

Bertie was the first to speak. "I thought we had an ideal couple at first, but when Howard started to talk about his religion, I knew we were not going to hit it off anymore. Heather seems real nice, though. I might be able to get along with her. She said she will have a garden when the weather warms up, so we may have some things in common."

"I hope you do. I'm just as sure that Howard and I won't be friendly, though. He's one of the do-gooders that Mark and I have to put up with more and more. Well, you two women can talk in the back about women things while I read the paper."

On Saturday, I sat in the barber chair with George Johnston, my news provider.

"I was reading in the *Chicago Tribune* about the gangs up there. One of the groups is called the Chicago Outfit; this Italian named Johnny Torrio is the head of it and he sounds like a real monster. I hope they don't come this far south. We've got the Shelton and Birger gangs here already. Say, don't you work for them some of the time?"

"Yeah, I help deliver the booze sometimes." I didn't want to tell the barber too much, thinking George would wind up telling everyone about it.

"Say, did you hear about the police breaking down the roadhouse down in Energy? That happened a week ago Tuesday night. They put that Dewmaine in jail, 'course he got out right away. I heard Charley Birger paid his fine and got him out. They'll probably open it back up real soon, don't you think?"

"Could be, you seem to have all the news, so I'll agree with you on it. I heard the Reverend Glotfelty wants it closed, though."

"The Reverend wants all the liquor establishments closed in all Williamson County. Just between you and me, the Reverend has joined up with the Klan. Them folks is getting pretty much in control of the county and most everywhere around here. They're against drinking and gambling and even against the Catholics."

"The Catholics too. That's all the Italians are, is Catholics. He's going to cause trouble if he tries to go up against them!" I thought of my friends in the Italian community.

"He surely is! But they're saying that there's lots more Protestants here than there are Catholics, so he's going to win. You know, most of the city officials and the police are all Protestants. Even the judges are." George knew most everything about everybody.

"I sure hate to hear this. We've got a nice quiet community here, I've noticed since I moved here two years ago that everyone gets along just fine. Hope the Reverend isn't going to ruin that."

After a pause, George changed the subject. "How're you and the missus getting along? The honeymoon still going on?"

"Don't think you can call it that after being married six months or so. But yeah, we're still having a good time."

I noticed Mr. Kelly walking up Park Avenue, passing the barbershop. "There goes Mr. Kelly now. I'm going to trade cars next week; he's got a good deal for me, at least that's what he's been saying—well, that's what he's been saying for some time now."

"Oh, you can trust Mr. Kelly to give you a good deal, he's a good egg. I can't afford his prices, but everyone I've talked to that deals with him says he's as honest as the day is long!"

"And what do they say about the repair work there, if something goes wrong with the car?"

"I hear that their lead mechanic, Emory MacIntosh, is real good. He goes to my church, so I know he's a real gentleman; has a good family, too."

"That's good to hear. You don't want to have trouble with your car, but they're machines so things do go wrong sometimes."

I paid George and went back to shoot pool with Caleb for the afternoon. My game was improving with all the practice I had been getting.

Caleb opened the conversation. "Are you hearing anything about a strike coming up, Leland?"

"Yeah, there's an article in the *Illinois Miner* that says we probably will have a strike across the nation starting in the spring, maybe April."

"Did it say if it'll be a long one?" Caleb sounded worried. At his young age, this strike was a first for him.

"No, nobody knows that ahead of the strike. The article said the union felt the companies would go along with a pay increase and improve the safety conditions down there in the mines. As long as Mr. Lewis doesn't get greedy with the money, it should be over pretty quick."

"Criminy, I sure hope it is. We don't need no violent strikes like this country has had in the past."

"Around here, if there's a problem, it'll be on the company's side. I think the union people here are generally happy with their pay now. You might want to save some money if you can, just in case the strike is a long one. Or, see if you can get some work here in the city to make a little money."

"Well, I live with my folks, so I got a room, but my daddy works in the mines too, so he's real concerned about a strike, but he has a brother who has a farm just a little north of here. He says we can help with the plantin' for a while. As long as it isn't a long strike, we'll be just fine."

Chapter 18

In March it had been cloudy for weeks—not a peek of sunshine. The winter hadn't been exceptionally cold, but the lack of sunshine left the impression, even when outside, that one was still in the house. The population was weary of these conditions and beginning to feel that it was time for a change. Many talked about things they did like going to the motion pictures to see shows such as Robin Hood *or* Manslaughter. *And, for most, the good times continued at the restaurants, social clubs, "soft-drink parlors," and roadhouses. Except for the "dry" part of the community: they were entertained by religious meetings and the growing influence of the Klan.*

In general, all the people living in the county were loyal to union causes. The rising miners' wages were lifting the whole community toward a comfortable middle-class stature. Williamson County people were loyal to the American culture; that is, they weren't interested in the communist or socialist propaganda that was rampant in other parts of the Union. They were strongly in favor of the miners' need for higher wages, and it appeared that John L. Lewis of United Mine Workers was going to call a strike soon.

Friday evening Bertha was cleaning off the table after supper. "Leland, we've been married for over six months now and we've been trying to get a baby almost all the time, but nothing is happening.

I'm starting to wonder if there's something wrong with one of us—what do you think? I mean, of course, it's probably me, but how do we know what the problem is?"

"You're asking the wrong person that question. I don't have any idea how everything works in that area. I just know I do my part when I give you my stuff. What happens after that, well, you know."

"Yes, well, I know that my mother didn't have any trouble making children and she was younger than me when she had her first. And her mother had many children, too," Bertie stated firmly.

"My parents just had me, but I heard that my dad may have gotten another woman 'with child' before he married my mother. To be honest with you, just before I left Kentucky, a young woman I had been with told me I had gotten her pregnant. That was the day before I was thrown in jail, then the next day I was sent out of town so quickly, I forgot about what she said."

"And she never contacted you after that?"

"No, I haven't heard anything, but that isn't unusual over there. People living in the mountains don't want to leave there and she would have known that I wouldn't be coming back, so it wouldn't have worked out for her to try to get me back. Lots of girls get pregnant in the mountains and never get married, that's just the way it is."

Bertie got a worried look on her face. "Then, maybe I should go to the doctor for a check. Perhaps there is something wrong inside me." She was starting to cry.

I went to her and held her in my arms. "Go ahead and go to the doctor if you want. I know how much a baby means to you, and I want to have one too, just not as bad as you. Let's keep trying, though." As I held her, I could sense her grief and I wanted to help her any way I could. Perhaps I was beginning to feel love for another person after all, maybe this is what love for another feels like, so I held her even tighter.

"Oh, Leland, I'm so thankful to have you. Maybe tonight we can try a different way to be in bed?"

The following weeks we tried every way we could think of, but still no baby was conceived. Bertie was becoming dismayed. I also noticed she didn't laugh as often as she usually had.

We had to go to Carbondale for a specialist. After a thorough examination, he reported that he couldn't see why she would have a problem, so we might have me checked, he suggested.

I told him my story about the pregnant girl in Kentucky, so the doctor threw up his hands.

"Just keep trying" was his advice. And we did.

April was the beginning of the miners' strike and it brought a typical spring to Williamson County: warmer weather, rain showers, greening lawns, smiling faces. Gardens were being planted, home construction got underway in earnest, and the wildflowers were in bloom.

One Saturday, I decided to get a shave and a haircut from my barber. I had a spring in my step; I felt life was favoring me! Three good jobs, a pretty wife, a nice car—more than I had ever dreamed of as a child. Sure, the strike had begun, but everyone, including me, thought it would be a short one. Even with the loss of wages in the area, people were still in a good mood and I was one of those people. The miners were drinking liquor more often so Mark and I were making more hauls of hooch to the soft-drink parlors, and Mark was sharing a little more of Charlie Birger's pay with me because I was on strike. Even the way I spoke was changing: I was losing my Kentucky accent with Bertha's help. Lately, I noticed that the men I worked with were trying to imitate my better diction. They seemed to give me more respect just because of the way I talked. My studies with Bertie were paying off, and we both loved learning together.

As I walked through the door, I noticed one man in the chair and Mr. Potter, from the mines, sitting in a waiting chair. Several men were playing pool in the rear section.

"Mornin', Leland. Have a seat, there. We were just talking about the strike ending. Mr. Earnest Moreland here thinks it will be over soon. Have you heard anything from the union people?"

"Naw, no one's been saying that, that I've heard anyway, but I don't always get over to the hall, like some."

"Like I was telling George here, I was working up a home construction loan for one of the miners and he told me he heard it was going to be a short strike, that the union would be getting a nice increase. You think there's any truth in that?" Earnest Moreland wanted my opinion.

"Couldn't say, you're asking the wrong person." I was hesitant to make any definite statement and I felt that was the intent of the loan officer's probing, so I started reading the Chicago paper.

George was finishing up with Mr. Moreland's haircut. "What's a new home cost to build these days, Earnest?"

"Oh, that depends on the size. Most people are moving up from a two-bedroom to a three-bedroom nowadays. We like for them to own the lot when they come in, so the construction costs run around fifteen, sixteen hundred. If you can catch Stotlar Lumber in a good mood, it won't be no more than that. Course, that's going to mean about eighteen or twenty dollars a month for a mortgage payment," Earnest said with importance in his voice.

George whistled. "Boy-o-boy, I didn't know things were going up like that around here!"

"Oh, yeah, Herrin is becoming a place where people want to move to; the lots are reasonable and it's in the center of the mining. We're getting good railroads being built, the interurban takes the miners to work, or people shopping, and lots of hard roads are coming in. The big banks in Chicago and St. Louis are always asking if they can loan us money because they know the people here are honest, hard workers who pay their bills on time."

"Don't the people in those cities pay too?" George asked.

"Oh no, there's a lot of deadbeats in those places. And the crime is going up too. You know, the gangsters are taking over Chicago! There's shootings there all the time. Sure, we've got a little liquor problem, all the ministers keep crowing about it, but a working man's got to have a little sedation to calm his nerves, is what I say. And, men will be men and want to gamble now and then. As long as it doesn't bother me, I say live and let live!"

Mr. Moreland paid George and headed for the door, as George shook out the apron for the next customer, Mr. Potter.

"Earnest, there's a problem with your attitude," Mr. Potter said stoutly. "The forces of evil are around us, now more than ever, and we can't allow them to get a foothold in our community. That's why the forces of good are coming back to help us."

Mr. Moreland didn't slow down as he walked out the door. George placed Mr. Moreland's cup back on the shelf and got Mr. Potter's down.

"Guess you want your regular cut, Mr. Potter. Leland, when the strike's over, you thinking about buying a house yourself? You and the missus will probably be starting a family soon, won't you?" I thought George was attempting to defuse Mr. Potter by changing the subject. He didn't want an obviously radical man ruining the pleasant atmosphere of his shop. Mr. Potter's recent KKK ranting was getting noisier these days.

I ignored the question. "This Chicago paper makes the gangster activity sound like they just expect lawlessness to keep going on. The police don't control it at all. I don't understand these people!"

Mr. Potter continued his sermon from the barber chair, so I laid down the paper, got up, and walked to the soda counter in the pool-playing area. A young man served me an orange drink.

"Where's the boss?" I asked him.

The boy proudly stated, "He's doin' somthin'. He left me in charge."

I watched the men shooting pool until Mr. Potter left. I wasn't going to allow my good feelings to be taken down by a teetotaler. Soon, George called for me.

"Sorry for the outburst from Mr. Potter. I think he's one of the new Klan members they've been signing up. Most all the ministers are members now and they're trying to get people to join up with them."

"Oh, that's nothing new to me. We get the same kind of arguments at the hall among the miners. I just try to stay away from those people who are radical, one way or the other. Like Mr. Moreland said, 'Live and let live' sounds like good advice to me."

"Say, Leland, you've been coming in here for many months now. I'd like to put a cup up on my shelf with your name on it! How's that sound to you?"

"I saw that shelf on the wall back there. What does it take for me to have one of my own?"

"No, nothing"—George shook his head—"... well, maybe a little extra when you pay once in a while, if you want. I just like to get my best customers a cup of their own—that way you always know there'll be shaving soap here for you when you come in, not that I don't have plenty anyways. But it's a little pride we barbers take around here. If you're a good barber, you'll have lots of good customers, like you, who have their own cup, you see. I've got fifteen now, so you'll be number sixteen. Pretty good, huh?"

"Sure, go ahead, I'd like that."

George completed the shave, and started cutting my hair. "You follow the St. Louis Cardinals, Leland?"

"Well, I have been, a little. It's new to me, though."

"The season's just starting and that Rogers Hornsby is doing real good again this year. His batting average was .397 last year and he hit twenty-one home runs. They say he'll do even better this year."

We continued to discuss baseball, with George giving me a quick lesson on the intricacies of the game, as he understood them. Then, I paid and left a generous tip, and George promised to have my cup the next time I came in.

As I went toward the back, I noticed that Dan Blocker was standing behind the counter adjusting a radio box on the shelf behind him.

"What ya got there, Dan?"

"Oh, hi, Leland. It's one of the new radios that picks up signals from far away. Just got it this morning from over at Herrin Electrical Supply. Mr. James sold it to me. He's up on the roof puttin' up the antenna. He thinks we'll be able to pick up St. Louis stations, maybe Chicago at night. Wouldn't that be a hoot?"

"Was it expensive?"

"Of course, seventy-five dollars, but they give me a discount 'cause I'm going to put a sign here advertising I bought it at their store. And I got the money from playing the slots at the Polecat Roadhouse last week."

Mr. James came into the hall through the back door. "Are you getting anything, Dan? Tune it to 835 kilocycles. That's the Paducha station. They should be transmitting now."

There was a lot of static until the dial indicated 835, then music could be heard. It was the voice of Marion Harris singing "Mississippi Choo Choo." Dan had that record and he played it many evenings for the people in the pool hall.

"Well, ain't that somthin'?" Dan crowed. "Now we can have some different entertainment in here."

Mr. Jim gave more information: "This station has been on the air doing testing like this. They play records and have some local people perform. You should be able to get a St. Louis station soon. All the big towns are starting to get broadcast stations. I haven't been able to hear the Chicago station yet, but some people tell me they've heard it at night."

I shook my head. Another miracle I would have to try to understand. Life was starting to move too fast for me.

Chapter 19

The UMW had called for a nationwide strike for higher wages of all coal mine workers to begin on April 1, and those loyal miners in Williamson County were in unison in their dedication to the cause. Most of the coal companies operating in the area were planning to stop working operations in the hope that the strike would be short and the negotiations would result in an agreeable contract. In fact, almost all of the coal mining companies nationwide had reached an agreement to take the miners' wages back to what they had been on the previous contract. It was well understood throughout Illinois that Williamson and Franklin counties had about sixty percent of the miners in the state. That meant that the vote in Illinois would be determined by the miners in those two counties. The UMW negotiators had been so successful in the past, the miners nationwide were willing to continue to strike until a good contract was reached again. They placed their confidence in their union.

Before the strike had been called, the Southern Illinois Coal Company, a new mining company, had planned to remove a vein of coal to the southeast of the city of Herrin that was near the surface. The coal markets had become rather tight, so prices were up, and the company was in need of a large sale to meet their financial obligations. The sale of this vein's coal would provide that money. To get the coal to market, the company only needed to remove the earth covering it, up to ten feet of it, and then load the coal into railroad cars: there was a spur that had been built onto the property and several shipments had been made prior to the strike. As the strike started, two steam shovels—a large one for removing the earth and a smaller one for removing coal—were in need of repair, so no more earth could be removed until they were fixed. From December until April 1st, about fifty union men had been employed at that site.

Mr. Claude McDowell, the new mine superintendent on the site, called for a meeting with the UMW representative for the local district. He asked for an exception to the general strike conditions so he could use five union workers to do repair work on the cranes he had been using for this strip-mining operation. Mr. Hughes, the union representative, agreed to contact the UMW for the exception, which he got a few days later. But he instructed Mr. McDowell to contact Hugh Willis, the president of the local Association of Union Workers, to be sure the local union was also in agreement, which Mr. McDowell did.

All the other mines in the country were closed for the strike, so the union workers were idle. This was not the usual mode for these men to be in, so it worked on their minds. At the start, many union men would congregate at the Union Hall, looking for news about the strike, hearing what the other men were doing or just getting out of their houses. Some of the striking workers would make bold statements about the owners, threatening bad things for them if they didn't give in to the union, but that was mostly just men letting off steam in these trying times. For the most part, the men would congregate to keep up with each other's lives, or to arrange fishing trips to the local ponds—anything to keep busy.

Chapter 20

On the first Saturday night in late June, I was working at the Colp Tavern, standing at the bar, watching for trouble. One of the bar's girls approached a man leaning on the bar a couple of seats away; I could hear their conversation. She asked him to buy her a drink, which he did.

"I've seen you here before. You live around here?"

"No, I live in Peoria. My work takes me all over the state and this week I'm in Williamson County."

"Why?"

"Why am I here, or why do I travel at all?"

"Yeah, why are you here?"

"See, I inspect mines and most of them are in Williamson and Franklin counties."

"Where do you stay when you're here?" Her smile and the toss of her head were intended to induce a nice feeling in him; his smile indicated it did.

"This trip I'm staying at the Liberty Hotel, over on Monroe Street in Herrin."

"Oh, I heard that place has real pretty rooms and soft beds. Would you like to show me your room there?"

"Sure, I'd like to do that. When would you be able to go over there?"

"I guess I could go now, if my boss says it's alright." She looked up at him and smiled as she waved to her boss to come over.

The salesman smiled back at her. "Before you go asking him, tell me how much this is going to cost me."

"Oh mister, I don't do it for money, I ain't that kind of girl"—she paused for effect—"but my mother's real sick and I do need some money for her doctor bills." Her voice trailed off with that.

By this time the man she'd waved at had arrived and started listening to the conversation.

The salesman put his arm around the girl's shoulder and whispered in her ear, "Just how many doctor bills does she have?"

To which she responded coyly, "Twenty dollars' worth."

The salesman jumped back and yelled, "Twenty dollars! Hey, I just want to rent your body, not buy it!"

Her boss grabbed the salesman by the bicep very hard and jerked him around. "Listen mister, you can't proposition my girl and then not pay. You took her time and bought her a drink, so now you're going to pay her!" the man yelled.

"Like hell I am!" The salesman tried to get loose from the man's grip, but couldn't. Then he pushed the man hard, but that didn't work either.

I worked my way down the bar toward the commotion. As I arrived the boss made a fist and smashed the salesman in the face, bending him over the bar's top. As he came back up, he appeared to be going to hit the boss with his fist, so I tried to get between them to stop the fighting. Unfortunately, the man had grabbed a beer bottle and smashed the bottom off it in the second or two he was bent over the bar. The sharp edges of the beer bottle caught my outstretched left arm. The pain was immediate. I made a fist with my right hand and hit the man hard. This time the man went over the bar and landed on the floor behind it, out cold. The artery in my arm wasn't cut but I was bleeding badly. The girl screamed and jumped away from the bar. Her boss grabbed her and took her away from the action.

John Patman grabbed a bar towel from under the counter and hurried around the bar to help me. He tied the towel around my arm to try to slow the bleeding. Then he called Joe Bob over to help.

"Joe Bob, this isn't going to stop the bleeding. He needs to get stitches in this right away. Take him in my car over to Herrin Hospital."

It was a short trip, so we made quick time of it. Joe Bob helped me get through the door of the hospital, then he returned to work.

I went inside and grabbed the closest chair as my strength began to ebb. Soon enough, a nurse came over to look at me. She pulled the towel off the cut and the bleeding immediately got worse. The sight of the wound and the loss of blood were starting to make me feel weak. She saw my eyes lose focus, so she called for help. That's when I passed out . . .

I could faintly hear people talking at first, then the voices got louder and I could make out what they were saying. I tried to open my eyes once, but that didn't work until the second try. I was in bed in a hospital room. The lights were dim and I could tell it was dark outside. I kept my eyes open, though they seemed to hurt a little. Soon a nurse came in.

"There's our big brawling boy now!" the nurse said lightheartedly. "Are you ready to answer some questions?"

My mouth felt dry, my tongue felt swollen. And my arm hurt badly. I looked at her with a blank stare.

"Uh-huh, I see you're still not quite here yet. Do you remember what happened to you, why you're here?"

The fog lifted a little. I remembered my arm was bleeding and the sight of it was awful. My mind momentarily went blank, then I remembered the glass bottle cutting my arm. Again, a fog seemed to cloud my vision and I drifted off.

The next time I became aware that there were sounds around me, I opened my eyes again. No one was in the room except me. I lay with my eyes open for a few seconds, then tried to move, but that produced pain in my arm, so I moaned. Now the pretty nurse came back into the room.

"So you're back again, are you? Feel like talking yet?" She was smiling and straightening my bedsheets.

"What do you want to know?"

"Silly boy, you came in here last night and sat in the entryway in a chair. You had a deep cut in your arm and you were bleeding badly. That's all I know, other than your name is Leland Vance. Why don't you fill in the details for me, Leland."

"How do you know my name?"

"Last summer I was with some friends at the Easy Time Bar when you came up to us with your friend Joe Petrie. He introduced us. I think you said you had just come to Herrin from Kentucky."

The clouds in my brain parted a little. "Sorry, I don't remember your name. I do remember meeting you that night, though." Yes, she was the blonde nurse with the sunken chin.

"I'm Penny, and I need to know what happened to you before you got here last night. Do you remember anything yet?"

"I was working at Colp Tavern, trying to keep the customers from killing each other. Two men got in a fight and one had a broken beer bottle. He took a swing at the other man and my arm got in the way. John Patman asked someone else to drive me here—I'm not sure who that was, though."

"It doesn't matter who did the driving. The doctor who stitched you up said you'll be all right in a few days. You'll need to come back next Wednesday to have him take the stitches out. And you won't be able to do much with that arm until it heals correctly. I guess you aren't doing any mining work right now anyway."

"Not mining work, no. But I am working at some of the soft-drink establishments, most evenings."

"Well, take it easy there. Now, I need some information for the hospital entry form. We'll get your vital signs later, when you can stand up. But tell me what other things have happened to you, like a heart attack, or an operation. Have you had any diseases, like mumps, chicken pox, scarlet fever, maybe?"

"I hardly ever get sick. When I was younger I did have measles."

"How long ago was that?"

"I'd been working in the mines for a while, so I guess I was about thirteen, or so."

"What do you remember about it?" Penny was beginning to write down my words on the hospital form.

"I was very sick, Abel was too. We must have given it to each other, or we got it from someone else at the same time, they said. When the doctor came he looked us over and told Mrs. Goshen to keep putting cold water on us because we were both burning up with the fever. I don't remember much because I think I slept for several days. Finally, the fever broke and I slowly got better."

Penny continued writing for several minutes, then looked at me and smiled. "Is that it? Any other problems you've had over the years?"

"That's all I remember having, and I don't remember much of that."

"I'll tell the doctor what you've said. He may want to talk to you more about it when you come in to have the stitches removed."

"Next Wednesday, did you say?"

"That's right, I'll give you a reminder card when you leave."

"When can I go?"

"As soon as you feel you can walk. It'll probably be a few hours. Do you think your friend will be back to take you home?"

"Maybe." My eyes shut from the exertion of remembering things and I went back to sleep.

The next time I awoke, Joe Bob was laughing with a new nurse: it was easy to recognize his soft voice. When they noticed that I was waking up, Joe Bob started telling me the same story. I waved him off with my arm and began to get out of bed. It was a chore, but I made it with Joe Bob's help.

The nurse recorded my height and weight in the hall, then handed me a reminder card.

Joe Bob was still laughing. "I've got your car outside. Can you drive yet?"

"Sure, I can—this hurt my arm, not my mind."

Joe Bob told me, "I went by your place last night and told Bertha what happened so she wouldn't worry."

The nurse gave a sack of items to me and we were off.

I stayed at home the remainder of the day. Bertie was glad to have the chance to take care of her man! She applied Sloan's Liniment to my arm to relieve the aching and made sure the pillows were placed correctly to allow me to rest.

Chapter 21

On Monday morning Caleb Avery was at the hall when I arrived. Caleb was animated and telling the other men what he had heard.

". . . men from Chicago to do our work. Listen, Leland, I was just saying that Harry Fisher, one of our steam shovel repair workers, said he heard Claude McDowell talking with his accountant about bringing men from Chicago to work at our jobs digging coal. Criminy, ain't that something?"

I asked, "Did you tell Hugh Willis about this? He needs to hear it!"

"I'll tell him when he gets here, he comes in every day, doesn't he?"

"Sure, he'll be here in a little while. Now, you're sure about what he heard, right. We don't want to stir up these men, you know what could happen if they was just talking about something else out there."

"I guess you're right, I didn't ask Harry too much about what he heard. I'll see if I can catch him tonight. Can you come over to my place too?"

"No, I'll be busy with Bertie tonight. But be sure of the facts here. If what he says is true, we'll have big trouble on our hands! These miners, well the whole town, won't stand for strikebreakers coming in here."

It was Friday morning when Caleb came back with the news: Harry Fisher had confirmed Claude McDowell was conspiring to bring in scabs. He tried to find Mr. Willis to give him the news, but Hugh Willis was out of town on union business until Monday.

I said firmly, "Caleb, you don't want to give out this information on your own. We've been on strike for almost two months now and the miners are getting uneasy about this whole thing. Just a small spark might set them off, so you tell Mr. Willis on Monday and let him decide what to do next!"

The repair work on the cranes took five men almost eight weeks. After the union workers had completed the work of repairing the one large and one of the two smaller cranes, they were dismissed by the company on Tuesday. Again, McDowell contacted the UMW to get approval to remove the earth over more of the coal, and the union agreed.

Mr. Willis finally showed up at the Union Hall Tuesday morning. Caleb and I asked him to meet with us alone.

"I've got a meeting with Fox Hughes, my boss, in a few minutes, so we'll have to meet after that. We're getting together with Mr. McDowell to talk about the removal of the earth over the coal."

"That's what we need to tell you about. McDowell's planning to bring in scabs to the mine, is what Harry heard," Caleb told him in as quiet a voice as his emotions would allow. Several other miners around him stopped talking to hear more.

"Now, let's keep our wits about us. I'll ask him directly at our meeting about it. I'll tell you this afternoon what he says," Mr. Willis assured us. And he hurried off.

Other miners nearby began asking Caleb and me what was going on.

"What are you talking about, scabs coming in here?"

"That better not be what we heard you say!"

I held up my hand. "Now settle down, men. We don't know for

sure what they intend to do at the mine. This is just a rumor right now. Mr. Willis will get us the facts in a little while and then we'll know for sure, so just settle down, will you?"

Now the entire hall had heard what was being said. The undertone grew louder.

"I knew we couldn't trust those bastards!"

"The union better not put up with any shenanigans from those company assholes!"

"The people of Williamson County won't stand for strikebreakers to come in here. We stopped them in Carterville a few years ago and we'll stop them again here!" said a truck driver who regularly joined in the activities at the hall.

I got on a chair and yelled for their attention. "Now, we all have to keep our heads from going the wrong way with this. We don't know for sure what McDowell's plans are and Mr. Willis told us he'll find out this morning when he talks to him in a meeting. We'll know for sure then, so let's not get carried away yet. Let's have some coffee and wait here for him to come back."

That helped to settle the group a little; the tone of the room became more civilized.

Mr. Willis didn't return that afternoon, but he did send word that he wanted to have a meeting at the Union Hall the next morning, that things were going to be all right.

That evening at dinner I was telling Bertie about the day's activities.

"Caleb and I finally talked with Mr. Willis about the news I told you Caleb heard from Harry Fisher. Bertie, I don't like the mood of the men in that room today. These union people—and I mean all the people in Williamson County—are on edge. It's been a long strike and they're getting the feeling that it's not going to end any time soon. Every business is starting to feel the drop in money coming in because of the strike, and it'll just get worse over time if the strike continues."

"Mr. Rogers has mentioned that too. We don't have as much business as we usually do."

"At least you're still working now and I have work for the liquor businesses. I suppose, if things get worse here, I could go up to East St. Louis to get work with the Shelton guys." I shrugged my shoulders and shook my head. Even I didn't like that idea.

"Now let's not talk about that yet. I don't want you to even think about it. We need to keep thinking good thoughts, stay focused on getting through this time, that better times are coming. That's what I learned to do in Germany—well, even until I got settled in here. And we'll make it through this tight spot as well. We'll lean on each other. We'll just spend more time working on your math skills and read these books we bought."

"I guess you're right. It's just so easy to get caught up in that mob thinking I heard at the hall today. First a few people got excited and then, soon enough, the whole room was getting to yelling, saying they would be ready to handle any scabs at the mine."

After dinner, we spent the evening reading our books, then went to bed together. For me, it wasn't so much lovemaking as it was doing the action that should produce a child. For Bertha, she said she felt closer to me as we were making love.

Chapter 22

Wednesday morning the Union Hall was crowded: miners and men from various unions had heard the rumors and wanted to know if there was going to be trouble. Even miners from other towns were present. The mood wasn't good.

Mr. Willis stood on a box at the middle of one wall.

"All right, men, I have good news for us today. I was at a meeting with Mr. Hughes and Mr. McDowell yesterday. The steam shovels have been repaired and our five brothers who have been doing the work were released yesterday afternoon. Next, Mr. McDowell asked for permission to continue working to remove earth from on top of the coal using Steam Shovelers' Union workers—card-carrying union people. He said it would give his company a leg up on the competition when the strike ends because they would be ready to load coal before their competition, which Mr. Lester needs due to some loans he has. We agreed that he could continue to remove earth, but no coal was to be removed. All in all, it was a good meeting. I did ask him directly if he intended to bring in strikebreakers and he said 'No.' I feel that he is a man of his word, so we can all settle down again and just wait a little longer for the strike to end."

The miners began to smile more and more as they understood the news Hugh was giving. As he finished, they started to pat each other on the shoulders and talk in more civilized tones. Caleb Avery and Harry Fisher both shook my hand and thanked me for keeping them from getting wrapped up in the general melee. Then I left to walk to the hospital.

The doctor began by examining my file, then my arm.

"The wound looks to be healing well, I guess we can remove the stitches now. Do you want me to put you to sleep for this? There won't be a lot of pain, but some people don't want to feel anything."

"No, I can handle pain," I said in an offhanded manner.

The doctor called the nurse over to assist. "I never did hear how you wound up getting cut Friday night. Did you say the wrong thing to your wife?" The doctor glanced up and winked.

"No, I was at work and put my arm where it shouldn't have been. The sharp glass on a broken beer bottle made the cut."

"They'll do that. The cut was pretty deep, you're lucky it didn't cut an artery, or bruise a bone."

He had finished removing the stitches and left the cleanup to the nurse as he continued to look at my file. Then the nurse left the room.

"Now, we need to talk about your medical history. I see in your file that you told the night nurse you had a case of the measles when you were younger?"

"That's right, but I don't remember much about it."

"And that's why I want to examine you further. How's your hearing? Both ears about the same?"

"Yes, I hear just fine."

"Can I take a look?" The doctor got up and bent over to look in each of my ears. He sat back down again and grabbed the stethoscope that was hanging around his neck.

"Take off your shirt, please. I'd like to listen to your heart."

The doctor had me breathe in and out slowly, holding the stethoscope to my chest and then my back.

Next, he opened the file to review the nurse's writing again. "She wrote that you said you had been cooled down by the person helping you at the time. Do you remember what she said to you after you were well again?"

"Just that I had been real sick, that I was red and hot all over my body, so she was trying to get the fever down. It took over a week for me to begin to feel good enough to go back to work in the mines."

"I see. Here's why I'm concerned. Your ears look fine, but you do have a slight heart murmur. You told the nurse you work in coal mines, so your heart must be doing fine. There is sometimes another problem men get when they have a high fever, such as those caused by measles, scarlet fever, or some other diseases. You said you were around thirteen at the time you suffered from the measles; are you sure of your age then?"

I nodded. "I was at least thirteen, best I remember."

The doctor got up and closed the door as he talked. "I'm going to assume you had reached puberty then? You had hair on your legs, in your groin area, under your armpits?"

I cleared my throat and swallowed. "Yes, I'm sure that's true—why?" I scratched my neck and took a sideways glance at the doctor.

"Well, men who have reached puberty and then get a fever that affects their whole body sometimes get what is referred to as the measles 'going down on them,' meaning that their testicles receive the impact of the excessive heat." He paused and looked directly at me.

"I don't understand what you're saying."

"In those cases, and I don't know if it happened to you, the testicles become sterile, meaning you won't be able to have any children."

I recalled the girl in Kentucky. "Oh, no . . ." Then I thought better of commenting any further. I really hadn't heard any more about that girl, so was she really going to have a child, or not?

"Were you going to say something?"

"No, that's fine. I just need to think about what you've said a little more. Is there any testing you can do to tell if I'm that way?"

"Not really, we don't have the ability to do that kind of testing here. Well, unless you have any other questions, we're through here. Just put on your shirt and see the nurse out front."

I left the hospital with a sore arm and a lot of questions. The main one was what to tell Bertie about the doctor's comments. I was so sure I had gotten the girl in Kentucky pregnant, yet there was a slight doubt about it. And, if what the doctor is telling me is true, am I really a man? Will I ever be able to be a father? Reaching the hall again, I decided that I would keep this new information to myself for now. I don't want Bertie to think any less of me and I sure as hell don't want to get her upset over all this.

Chapter 23

*T*he next day, the Southern Illinois Coal Company brought in crane operators, some qualified mechanics, two cooks, and along with them were ten other men who were going to provide security for the company's property. A total of fifty men were on hand at the strip mine. They came from Chicago on railroad sleeper cars which remained on the property so the men would have a place to live. The new workers built a tank which was filled with water, and the warehouse was filled with adequate food to feed the group for a few weeks. During the first week, the new security people constructed a fence around some of the property and used the dirt removed from over the coal to build a protective berm.

Some of the union miners started going to Mr. Ed Crenshaw's farm, where they could observe the goings-on at the strip mine. Ed had sold the property to Mr. Lester the previous year, so his house was only a few hundred yards from the mine. The men reported back to Mr. Willis on everything they observed. Mr. Willis started calling meetings each morning at the hall to keep the men informed.

Starting on the day they arrived, the new guards were going out onto county roads to tell the local people that the roads would be shut down during the strike so the people should find other ways to travel. These cars were stopped at gunpoint and the people inside were harassed; some of them were robbed. On the second day, in one instance, a car loaded with children was stopped as they returned home from church. Another car *with two young men was stopped at gunpoint. Those men were hit with pistols and told to stay away from the mine.*

The following Monday at 1:00 in the morning, a car with four men was stopped by the guards, who then took them to the mine office. Once there, they were harassed by the guards and Claude McDowell. After a few hours, they were released.

All of these events were being reported back to Mr. Willis and subsequently to the union men at the morning meetings. Hugh would always report the facts and ask the men to hold their anger. Each day, that request was met with more hostility as the men's anger continued to rise.

I was at the Monday morning meeting and before it began, Otis Clark was telling everyone, in a loud, angry voice, that he had received a visit from the loan officer at his bank. The man was questioning him on his promise to repay a construction loan he had with the bank. The banker said he had been at a meeting held by the Chamber of Local Businessmen and they were warned that the mining companies were going to break the unions with this strike. Now, he wanted to know if Otis would be able to repay the loan on the lower pay scale that would be in effect after the strike. Otis was getting the union people in a vicious mood.

Hugh Willis lost control of the daily meeting before it got started.

"How long are we going to allow those scabs to work in Williamson County?"

"Why does Claude McDowell feel he needs guards at the mine, anyway?"

"Why have they built the dirt piles around the mine? Are they trying to keep us from seeing what they're doing in there?"

The men yelled loudly, pointing their fingers at some unseen evil and shaking their fists at Hugh.

"And if they are, just what are they doing—digging coal?"

"Why are the men from the Steam Shovelers' Union working in a mine on strike by our union?"

Hugh Willis agreed to have Mr. Fox Hughes call John Lewis to see if the Steam Shovelers' Union was even a legitimate union, one recognized by the UMW. The next day a telegram was received back from the union office stating that the Steam Shovelers' Union was not recognized and that the people working at the mine should be treated as scabs!

The telegram's information got to the *Herrin News* as quickly as it got to the Union Hall. The afternoon paper spread the news to the community: "The Scabs Are to be Forcefully Removed from the Area!" But the union people had already heard the news. The area around the Union Hall became a beehive of activity. Cars were pulling to a stop in the street, its occupants brandishing pistols and rifles, and they were yelling at men standing nearby to join them in a search for other weapons and ammunition. After loading more men in the vehicle, it would speed off as another pulled up. Other men were running on the street toward the hardware stores, where they forcefully took guns and ammunition. Some men went to the homes of friends to borrow weapons. A few of the cars went over to Marion to strip those stores of their pistols and rifles. As word spread in the local communities that guns were being absconded, people began to hide theirs so they wouldn't be taken.

I was working with Mark Wallops that evening. As we passed the Union Hall around 11:00, it was obvious that something was happening. Guns were being fired in the air, a crowd stood on the street yelling at some demons, and lights showed brightly inside.

"What the hell is going on here?" Mark wondered.

"Mr. McDowell over at the strip mine between here and Marion has brought in scab workers to break the union and these people are getting ready for a fight. This one might be worse than the one over in Carterville a few years back. They've been getting their neck hair up all week now, threatening to go out to the mine and start shooting scabs, but today there was word from Mr. Lewis that they need to take action. I guess that's what's happening now."

After the night's work was over I drove to the Union Hall. Inside, I heard planning among several men on their actions the next day.

"We just get some of the scabs to run off and McDowell brings in more men. We've got to put a stop to any more people being brought in tomorrow!"

"Old Billy said they come down from Chicago on the Illinois Central to Carbondale. Then some of the guards go on over from here to pick 'em up."

"All right then, let's take a few cars over toward Carbondale tomorrow. We'll be ready for them when they cross into Williamson County. One car can sit at the railroad station to see if these guards pick up some men. That car will follow the guard's cars until the county line, then pull around it and fire a shot in the air. That will be the signal for the others to start shooting at the scabs. We'll make 'em wish they was still in Chicago!" I thought I could see in the men's eyes that they were serious about the killings.

"Are you men talking about killing these men from Chicago, or are you just going to run them off?" I asked one of them.

"Were you here when Hugh told us that Mr. Lewis said to get rid of the scabs? He didn't say to scare them away. He meant that we should kill the bastards! And, YES, that's just what we intend to do!"

A cold chill ran down my back. I wasn't talking to the same miners I had been talking to the day before or any day before that. These men were feeding off each other in their hatred of the men at the strip mine. I got up from that table and moved to one where Otis was yelling at the other men.

"Hugh's right, men, the mining companies are out to break us. My loan officer told me the Chamber over in Marion was telling all the businessmen in their group to cut off the miners' union people. They think this strike is going to break the union and then they'll all have cheap coal after that. Well, we stopped them in Carterville and we'll just damned well do it again. The only thing I ask is that you men let me do the killing of McDowell. He told Hugh that they wouldn't be taking out any coal with the scabs so the union would agree to let them work. We were just stupid enough to think that he was an honest man—now look what he done. He made a fool of union people and I want to be the one who takes him out! I got a house I'm building and that man is trying to take it away from me and my family."

I got up again and walked around the room. No one was drinking, so alcohol wasn't the problem, but I just couldn't understand why the men were talking so violently. It was obvious they hated being lied to and having the strikebreakers doing their work, but that wasn't a reason to kill these men. After all, the men hadn't killed any of them. Next, I thought back to what Mrs. Wilson had said about the people of Egypt, how she said, "They all stick together against a problem like all get out!"

And, that's what I saw in the faces of these men, from the wild look in their eyes and the rapid, loud talk of their voices; anyone could tell these people weren't listening to reason. I tried to think of something I could say or do to settle them down, then I decided that would be fruitless. I went to my car to go home.

Chapter 24

I got up early the next morning to have breakfast with Bertie. I told her of the previous evening's happenings at the union hall.

"Please tell me you won't get involved in that," Bertie pleaded. "It sounds like the entire town is going crazy! There's no telling what they'll do. Emory came over to drop off their wash last evening and he seemed really scared. He said the men at the car dealership were all worried—both because they were counting on the union people to get more money from the strike and then would be able to buy more cars, and because the mining companies are causing trouble with the union. I talked him down a little, but he was really wrapped up in this. After I got here but before you got home, I heard lots of guns being fired—more than usual."

"Well, you can be sure I won't get involved in the shootings. But these people in Herrin are all strong backers of all the union people and things just might explode if the right conditions happen. They seem to know they can count on each other afterward."

"What are you going to do?" Bertha asked.

"I'm going to the Union Hall to see if I can talk some sense into some of the men. It probably won't do any good, but I feel like I have to try."

I arrived at the Union Hall at around 10:00. Mr. Willis was talking with some of the men.

"I talked to Sheriff Thaxton last night. He is going to be all right with us protecting ourselves. If anything happens on Route 13 coming from Carbondale later, he'll be the one to investigate it as long as it happens in Williamson County. Just you men remember this on election day, that's all he asked."

I saw Caleb sitting at a table with a cup of coffee in his hand. I went to get one for myself and joined Caleb.

"I just got here, what's going on?"

"I haven't been here long either. I heard a group of men went toward Carbondale to get some of the scabs that are coming in today."

"I was here around midnight and they were talking about that. They made it sound like they intended to kill some of them—is that what you heard?"

"Pretty much. I didn't like the look in their eyes, either. Criminy, some of them looked like hungry animals, you know?"

"Or scared animals backed into a corner. One night in Kentucky I was on a mountainside tending to a still. I heard something, some kind of animal behind me, so I went to look with the lantern. There was a draw in the rocks and a varmint was pulling in a dead mouse getting ready to eat it. I didn't get too close because it just might want to kill me if he thought I was going to take his meal. His eyes looked like some of the men here last night."

"If Mr. Willis is right about them wanting to break the union, these men might just be in that same condition. I'll tell you what: I don't intend to get between these men and the scabs, not the way they looked this morning."

"Caleb, that's good thinking. I'm right there with you. I just wish we could do or say something to make them see what they're doing isn't right."

"I gave up on that this morning and you should too." Caleb sounded dead serious.

"Come on, let's go over to the pool hall and shoot some pool. We can get a hot dog there for lunch."

After noon we heard a commotion at the Union Hall. As we rushed over, we saw more cars were filling the street. Several of the men were very animated, talking loudly and quickly!

"Gordon Henderson was out at Ed Crenshaw's farm, taking Ed some berries he had picked. Shots started coming from the mine—it's a fur piece north of the mine, so it's a long shot. Crenshaw said there must have been forty or fifty shots fired and he took cover right away, but Gordy didn't make it. After the shooting stopped Ed went out to see if he could help Gordy, but he was dead, shot through the heart." The man speaking hung his head as he took off his hat. Many around him did the same.

I looked at Caleb. "It's started," I said softly.

Before the group could gather their thoughts, some of the cars from Carbondale came speeding up. The occupants were screaming at the people on the street, "We did it! We shot several of the scabs coming in and probably killed some of the guards from the mine!"

Their enthusiasm was short-lived when they heard about Gordon Henderson.

"Then let's go out to the mine and kill us some more guards for Gordie!" several of them screamed.

I watched eight or ten cars go tearing out toward the mine. Some of the men inside were reloading their weapons. As the car engines roared, many people came running from nearby to see what the latest developments were. Gordon Henderson was well liked by the people of Herrin and they were devastated by the news. Some yelled and swore they weren't going to take this treatment from outsiders—the gangsters from Chicago!

Caleb and I went inside the hall where we found it had filled with people; many of them I had never seen before. From the talk I heard, miners had come from adjoining counties to support the brothers of the Herrin Local; they had all heard the news from Mr.

Lewis on treating the scabs. And, they had brought their guns and ammunition, ready for anything.

By 2:00 some cars returned from the mine with the latest development. The Lester mine locomotive was driven out of the compound to take out some cars of coal. Miners all along the track began shooting up the engine, so it returned to the mine area. As the guards returned fire, four union people were wounded. Some of the wounded were from the nearby towns of Johnston City and Ziegler.

The crowd continued to grow along with the animosity. I could see that cornered animal look in the eyes of more, if not most, of the people. I didn't know Gordon Henderson personally, but Caleb did and he was quite shaken. After working hours, the wives and children were coming to join their men at the hall. Mr. Willis arrived with Mrs. Henderson, Gordon's mother. I went to a far corner to watch as the people went to her pouring out their hearts in tears.

With tears in her eyes, she commanded the men, "Please get the men who did this to my son! Make them pay for taking him away from me!" Those around her shuffled their feet and nodded their understanding. After a while the sadness turned to hatred for the scabs who did this to one of their people, their Gordy.

At 6:30 Mr. Fox Hughes, vice president of the union subdistrict, came into the hall. He stood on the box at the wall and asked for attention. As the room quieted he gave a short speech.

"I have been in contact with Colonel Sam Hunter of the Illinois National Guard. He has spoken with Mr. Lester about our situation. Mr. Lester has agreed to shut the mine down if we will agree to a ceasefire." He had to pause at this point.

"That's the bastard that said he wouldn't use strikebreakers to mine coal!"

"He's a lying son-of-a-bitch, we don't trust him."

"Tell him to stick his deal up his ass!"

"Of course he wants to stop the shooting after he's killed some of our people, the asshole!"

Mr. Fox tried several times to calm the crowd, but they just became more virulent, so he left in disbelief. And many of the crowd left as well, taking their guns to the mine.

Bertha came by after the tailor shop closed. We took Caleb to a restaurant for a sandwich and potato salad. We each had a beer as we talked of the events so far.

"Leland, why don't you come home and get a night's sleep," Bertha pleaded.

"No, I feel that I should be with the men of the union. You saw how many people are here to support us. I wouldn't feel right leaving now."

We decided to drive out to the mine area to see the happenings without getting too close, just to be safe. We drove south of Herrin, then turned east. Going north toward Crenshaw Crossing, we could see forty or fifty cars parked in the field next to the mine, perhaps four hundred to five hundred people on the piles of earth surrounding the mine itself. There was a constant stream of more people joining in. It was getting dark, so we returned to the city. Caleb was dropped at his house; Bertha and I went home.

Chapter 25

Several times throughout the night we were awakened by the sounds of blasts going off in the distance. By the time the sunlight began to light the day, the blasts had stopped and the town was quiet.

While Bertha slept I decided to drive to the mine area to see what had happened during the night. I turned south on Park, then east on the public road that would take me south of the mine. Going north just beyond the CB&Q railroad crossing, the road became congested with people. They were still in their wild state of the night before, perhaps even worse, I thought. As I approached the mine property entrance, I saw several people—men, women, and children—coming out the gate carrying pieces of material. They were telling others how they had taken items for souvenirs to remember this day.

I asked a man sitting by the side of the road what had happened. He looked like a man I had seen working around Herrin, but not at the Union Hall.

"It was a hell of a night," he said, looking vacantly ahead without seeming to recognize that I was nearby. "We showed those scab sons-a-bitches. That Lester bastard got what he deserved, the whole place is blown to bits!" He began to look around the area, then at me. "Two or three of our boys were hit by the guards' gunfire before our bombs got to 'em. Then they stopped shooting. A little while ago they raised a white flag and begged us to stop. Otis told them to come on out, that we'd take them to Herrin so they could leave. I watched them line up in twos with McDowell in the lead. They went up the road toward Crenshaw Crossing a little while ago."

While he was talking I could hear gunshots off in the distance. I got back in my car and headed further north. It was slow going because many people were lining the road, standing and talking or walking ahead of me; others were coming back toward the mine. At Crenshaw Crossing I went west toward the powerhouse. The mass of people continued as did the remote gunfire, though it was getting louder.

Approaching Moakes Crossing, a road to the south, I saw a group of people around a body on the ground. Some of the people were kicking the body and cussing at it. I continued west. To my right about fifty yards, I saw a man moving stealthily along a fence line heading east. The man dropped to the ground often, as if he was trying to avoid being seen. A little further on, I saw another man running fast, following the first one. Some men with guns were following him and began to shoot at the man. I could see that one of the bullets hit the man when blood flew out of the front of him as he fell to the ground. The men with the guns caught up with him and they began to fire at him on the ground. After each of them had shot him, they seemed to congratulate each other with slaps on their shoulders.

As I neared the woods to the north of the powerhouse, the gunfire was getting very loud. Some of it was in the nearby woods, some further north, at Harrison's Woods. The crowd was now more at the entry to both of the wooded areas, fewer on the road. But the people I saw were still in the mode of celebration—celebration of the killings that were going on around them.

I continued further north. When I reached the grade school a crowd was to the east, by the Herrin Cemetery. I thought there were at least two hundred people gathered in a circle. The road was blocked, so I stopped my car and walked forward. In the center of the crowd were six men being tied together with a rope around their necks. The crowd—all ages of men, women, and children—were yelling at the men.

Even the children were yelling!

"Scabs!"

"Bastards!"

Someone to my right yelled out, "The sheriff is coming!"

Three shots were fired near the center of the crowd and the captives began falling or being pulled down. More pistol shots. The men on the ground groaned in pain. Quickly, their moans stopped. One of the men in the crowd started to reload his pistol but he didn't have enough bullets. A boy stepped forward from the crowd and pulled some bullets from his pocket and handed them to the man. After reloading, he held the gun to each man's chest and fired. The men were quiet for several seconds, then two of them began to breathe again.

"I'll fix 'em!" A man drew a pocket knife, opened it and slit the throat of each of the men on the ground. The crowd yelled their approval. Then many of them began to leave. I had to put my hands to my stomach, it was roiling so badly.

In a few minutes a new man arrived by car. He saw that some of the men on the ground were still alive and asking for a drink. The man ran to a nearby house and brought back a small pail of water.

One man in the crowd had a rifle, which he pointed at the newcomer, warning him to get away. Then a young woman carrying a baby stepped forward and put her foot on one of the breathing men. As she shifted her weight onto him, the blood poured out of his wounds. "I'll see you in hell!" she yelled!

Next, one of the men came up to the pile and urinated on each of the faces.

I had seen all I could stand. The rabble was still going on with their celebration of the ending of the lives of the strikebreakers. My stomach was near puking. I needed a drink, something stronger than water, to calm my nerves. I was glad I hadn't invited Bertha to come with me. When I got back to my car, I had to bend over at the grass nearby and tried to vomit, but all I could do was cough several times.

When I got back to Herrin it was 9:30, so I stopped at a soft drink parlor on Cherry Street.

"Will you give me some whiskey, please?" My face was white and my brow was wet though it wasn't hot yet.

"It's a little early for this, isn't it?" the barman said as he poured the drink.

I sat on a stool. I held my head in my hands with my elbows on the bar. My body shook as I recalled the scene at the cemetery.

"I've been out by the mine just now. I need to settle down. I've seen something I never want to see again."

"I heard bombs going off all night," the barman said. "Was it coming from that strip mine south of here?"

I nodded.

"Yesterday, all the people were talking about what they were going to do to the scabs. So they finally did it, eh?" he asked.

I straightened up and looked out the door, nodding again. My body shuddered once. I turned back to the bar and swallowed the drink, then motioned for another.

"How bad was it out there? You look like you've seen the end of the world!"

"That's just how I feel. Like I've seen my fellow citizens at their lowest point. I don't ever want to see something like this again!"

I finished my second drink and stared outside. The sounds of the people I had heard that morning kept reverberating in my head. Not the people lying on the ground, gasping for water, but the wild screams and sickening laughter of people out of their minds in a wild orgy of terror.

In a few minutes my neck and shoulder muscles began to relax and I realized how tense my body had become. I had a quick recollection of my efforts to change the course of events the previous day and decided I wouldn't have been able to make any difference to them in anything I tried to do.

These people, the miners of the entire area and many of the local residents, had been pushed to the brink by the mine owners in their efforts to break the unions. Over the past few years the people in all of Little Egypt had come to believe that their lives were going to be better than their parents because the mining companies had been paying better and making the mining jobs safer. And that was a result of the miners sticking together as a union and demanding the improved conditions. Yesterday, they came to the realization that Mr. Lester and his company intended to break the trust between the companies and the union. As a matter of self-preservation they took matters into their own hands and weapons. They saw outsiders coming into their territory with the intent to do them harm, and no one was going to protect them from it. It was going to be up to them, acting as a group, to win this battle; then, when their people started dying by the hands of the outsiders, they became a mob that wanted revenge. When even more of their people were killed, they turned into an orgy of death.

I came back to the present when cars started going by on Cherry Street, honking their horns and shooting their weapons in the air. At first it was only a few, but the number grew rapidly.

I walked up the street to see the events. It was like a holiday in the city. All the parking places were being taken and people were double-parking so they could talk to other revelers about the morning's events. I walked over to Park Avenue and the scene was the same.

Some of the people were saying that the bodies of the dead were being taken to the Dillard Building, placed in an empty storeroom, so some people headed that way. Others told of the injured, both strikebreakers and union people being treated at the Herrin Hospital. They talked of going to see the dead bodies as if it would be a fun thing to do. They were laughing about it as they walked into a restaurant to eat lunch. Still the honking car horns and gunfire continued.

The sun was shining, some puffy clouds dotted the sky—it was a beautiful summer day!

The victory celebration continued into the evening, but with less horn honking and gunfire as the day wore on. I walked around on the streets. Several times I heard people talking to newspaper reporters who had just arrived in town. Visitors from nearby cities had come to join in the revelry and to view the bodies of the strikebreakers. People on the streets joked about the condition and the wounds of the corpses.

Bertha and I had a quiet dinner at home, though we didn't eat much. We were both too disgusted to want to talk. We went for a walk in our neighborhood during the evening, then tried to read but went to bed early.

In the morning I decided to get a haircut and shave, thinking a fresh look might just take away some of the scum of yesterday. George was just getting his area opened as I walked in.

"Well, there's my favorite customer! How you doing today, Leland?"

"I'll be doing better after your shave and haircut. I need to get rid of the stench of yesterday."

"Oh, that was real bad, wasn't it? I saw some men acting like I never thought I would see in all my life; it was really bad, what I could see from here. I even closed early, just in case it got any worse. Were you out at the mine?"

I told George my activities of the previous day. From my choice of words George could tell that I was still embroiled in the tragedy.

"Weren't nobody getting a haircut in the afternoon yesterday, so

I stood out on the street to talk with some of the folks. Mr. Richie came by from Dillard's Warehouse where they put the bodies for viewing. He said it was just awful in there. People were abusing the dead, sticking their fingers in the wounds, putting a cigar in the mouth of one body, and the police weren't doing nothing to stop the shenanigans. Folks were even taking their children in for a look-see and making fun of the scabs, calling them names and like that."

"Are the bodies still over there?"

"Naw, they been moved over to the Albert Storme Funeral Home. Getting them ready for burial, I suppose. Ain't none of them got names on them, just numbers. Guess that's the way they'll be buried."

I was looking out the front window at the activity, or lack of it, on the street.

"Park Avenue looks a lot different today than it did yesterday. No horns honking or gunfire. Will this town ever be able to return to the way it was?" I wondered.

"That's a good question. People will settle down, but now they'll remember what happened for the rest of their lives. As high as they were on killing yesterday, they'll probably be suffering from a hangover kind of low today, especially those that actually did the killings."

"Next, we'll be reading about this in the newspapers." I could visualize the headlines in the *Chicago Tribune*.

"Some were saying they expect the Illinois National Guard to be coming in to restore order. I think it's too late for that, they should have come in here yesterday.

"Is anyone fessing up to the killings, that you've heard?" George asked.

"No, and the union people are saying that everyone should keep their mouths shut on that."

"Some say, and I ain't sayin' who, but some say Sheriff Thaxton stayed away on purpose and he kept the Guard from interfering, too," George said wisely.

"Why's that?"

"Don't know for sure, but he's the County Sheriff and the mining people were outsiders coming in here to cause trouble. He sure didn't have enough people working for him so that he could take control of the situation, so I suppose he let the miners and the owners fight it out themselves. When the rowdies started robbing the hardware stores of guns and ammunition, the Herrin Police could have got involved, but they didn't. Seems to me like the whole community just decided to stick together and get the outsiders who were threatening to take away our livelihood here."

"You think anyone will go to jail for this?"

"A grand jury is the next step after things get sorted out, and with nobody talking, that's going to take a while."

The haircut was finished and we gave up on trying to solve all Williamson County's problems, so I headed for the Union Hall.

Harry Fisher and Caleb Avery were already at a table with coffee. I joined them.

Harry had gone to the mine on Wednesday evening so he was talking about the events of the night. He looked haggard, like he needed to get some sleep. His green eyes were drawn, his elbows rested on the table, and one hand, then the other, was used to support his head as he talked. His dark brown hair was ruffled; it needed to be combed.

"The guards started shooting at us first. Four men were standing in the wrong place and the guards shot all of them and they didn't even have guns with them. That set off the other men on the earth piles. We all started shooting back for several minutes. There were several hundred men circling the guards in the mine area, so we had a lot more guns than they did. After a while the firing stopped. Some more men came along to help and they brought dynamite. They gave two of the men sticks and I told them where to put it under the new building that held the food and the tank being used to hold their water, since I had been working there when those were being built. They sneaked through the fence where they couldn't be seen. Pretty shortly they came hurrying back and right after that we heard explosions and stuff was flying in the air. Word was passed that the guards were without food and water now." Harry was getting animated over the action as he recalled it. He sat straighter and his voice was rising.

"They was beneath the iron railroad cars, so we couldn't get clear shots at any of them, but every once in a while someone tried. Several times a stick of dynamite was tossed over the railroad cars with the hope that someone would be killed. We figured they had to be getting low on ammunition since we had blowed up the storage house, so we were going to wait for sunup and then make an attack on them.

"As it started to get light, the guards showed a white flag and yelled out they wanted to surrender. Otis started talking with them and got them to come out by promising them safe passage to Herrin. He smiled and waved his arms to encourage them to respond—you know how Otis can be, waving his arms as he talks. They came out peacefully all right. Otis had them line up in twos and started them marching toward Herrin. I went with them to Crenshaw Crossing. The men by the guards were awful mean to them, hitting them with their guns as they walked. When we got to the store at Crenshaw, Joe Petrie went in and called Hugh Willis to let him know what's what.

"While we waited, Otis hit McDowell with his gun several times and he kept yelling at the crowd that we needed to hang the whole of the scabs. When Joe came back out he said Hugh wanted the scabs to be treated like POWs. Otis yelled at him to shut up and smashed his gun over McDowell's head, knocking him to the ground. Some men got him up and they marched on.

"When they got to the road going south, Otis and another man dragged McDowell's body a little way down the road and then Otis shot him twice. Most of the crowd cheered, then some of them started going back to the mine saying they wanted to get souvenirs. I went forward with the rest to the woods by the powerhouse. As we got there Hugh Willis came by in his car. He stood up in the car and yelled out that the men should be killed in the woods, not on the open road—too many eyes were around to see the happenings. So they did. I went partway, but I was getting tired from being up all night, so I stopped at the edge of the woods.

"As the miners were talking about hanging them but said they didn't have enough rope for that, the scabs starting running into the woods. There was a barbed-wire fence they had to get across and it slowed them down enough so that the miners started shooting them down. Many of the men got across the fence and were running while the men were shooting at them.

"One of the miners was laughing and saying it was just like shooting at jackrabbits. That's when I turned around and got a ride back here. I was so tired I went home to get some sleep, but that didn't work out well, I kept waking up and thinking about what had happened."

I told them about my trip the previous morning.

Caleb sounded disappointed. "Leland, after you dropped me off Wednesday, I stayed home and didn't come back until yesterday afternoon. Criminy, I missed all the action."

"Be glad you did," I told him. "You'll be able to sleep better than Harry and I will, for sure."

Hugh Willis stopped by our table just as he had been at all the tables of men in the room. He looked haggard and weary; he probably hadn't gotten any sleep for some time. "Now you men got to be careful. We want to be sure not to tell anyone what happened out at the mine or on the road back this way. If anyone asks you, you didn't see anything of importance. Maybe you saw some people shooting but it was dark that night and you couldn't see who was shooting. And in the morning you didn't see anything at all! Right?"

The three of us nodded.

I was feeling the stink of the entire event start to cover me again, so after Hugh Willis left, I got up and left the building.

Chapter 26

As we finished supper, I told her, "Bertie, it's just depressing to go to the Union Hall anymore. The men there are trying to act like nothing happened last week, men that were in a frenzy to kill—they couldn't wait to spill blood. They're saying that because the men they killed were from someplace else, they deserved what they got. I just don't understand."

"But Leland, you told me one time the people in Kentucky killed other people too. Doesn't that bother you?"

"The way I was raised we didn't kill our neighbors, but the federal agents that came to our mountains and tried to take away our livelihood, they weren't any different than the outsiders here. But in Kentucky, we didn't talk about killing those people like we were proud of it, like these people at the hall are. They talk to me like I'm one of them and I'm not. I suppose it's because I work in the mines with them."

"I know what you mean. The people who come into the tailor shop don't want to look me in the eye, but they will Mr. Rogers. I'm an outsider to them and he isn't, I guess that's the difference. Like they think he'll understand what happened and I won't. They're probably right in that—I don't understand."

"They sure do stick together around here. The union men are getting their alibis together as to where they were or what they were doing that day. Some men are ready to lie to protect the ones that did the shootings. Hugh Willis asked me but I said I didn't know any of the men except Otis Clark and they have plenty of people ready to lie for him. Just as well."

Bertie went to bed at the regular time. I had been sleeping on a cot on the back porch for the past week because I couldn't get a solid night's sleep; I kept waking up from the bad memories and I didn't want to wake Bertie.

The following week Mark Wallops and I were delivering liquor to the Energy Roadhouse. I got the cases out of the back of the truck while Mark went in to collect the payment. As I entered, the place was quiet except for the music from the slot machines. All the people were staring at a man who was pointing a pistol at Mark, demanding money. He had a wild look in his eyes and the gun shook in his hand.

"I said give me all your money, mister! You too, behind the bar, dig all your money out of the till!"

I walked slowly toward the man with the cases in front of me.

"Stay back, you! Don't come any closer or I'll shoot!"

I continued walking slowly until I was about three feet from the man. I was staring intently at the man's eyes as I walked, which made the man more nervous.

"I mean it! Stay back!" the man shouted.

I shoved the crates of whiskey forward. They were aimed at the gun and they hit it. The man's face lit up in surprise when he saw the cases flying at him. He got one shot off as the cases hit the gun. By the time he was able to fire, the gun was pointed at the floor. I jumped forward and hit the man in the face with my fist, knocking him back. I charged into the man, grabbing the gun and swinging it into the air. Another shot was fired into the ceiling.

"Drop the gun, you bastard!" I yelled.

I hit the man once more. This one took him off his feet. He fell backward, bringing me down on top of him. The gun went off again.

The man beneath me groaned and went limp, then shook several times.

I slowly moved off the man. As I stood up, I saw there was blood coming from his side. The man's eyes were staring vacantly at the ceiling. The gun was on the floor beside him.

Mark quickly moved to me and put his arm around my shoulders to steady me. I was shaken by the whole event, especially the fact that I had been on top of the man when he died.

Sam Dewmaine went to the phone and called the police. When he came back he grabbed my hand and shook it vigorously. Then the room began to buzz with conversation and activity.

"We all owe you for this," he exclaimed. "That man was out of his mind! He was telling everyone to give him all their money, waving the gun real nervous like. When Mark walked in he went crazy and started screaming at us. You did the right thing, attacking him. I'm sure some of us would have gotten shot if you hadn't done this."

Another man moved a chair over for me to sit down. I didn't understand why at first, but when I sat, I realized I was shaking all over.

Sam Dewmaine poured a strong shot of whiskey and handed it to me.

"Drink that to settle your nerves, you deserve it!"

In a few minutes the police arrived. Mr. Dewmaine gave them a rundown of the event. They listened intently, then questioned several of the men that had been there throughout. One officer went through the man's pockets and his identification while the other talked to me.

"You're the man that saved the day here? Tell me how it happened."

"Yep, I was bringing in the delivery when I saw that man"—I pointed at the dead man—"holding a gun on my partner. I attacked him and held the gun so he couldn't shoot anyone. As he fell to the floor, he tried to point the gun at me, but I held it away. It was pointed at his side when he pulled the trigger."

The police looked at the bar area, surveying the bottles there.

"You say you were delivering liquor here when this happened?"

"That's right, we come every week."

"You know distributing liquor is illegal, don't you?"

I nodded, then Mark jumped in, "We deliver for Charlie Birger. You can check with him if you want."

"No, that won't be needed. We know what you people do around here. But you should know that there are people who say they're going to put a stop to your business. Have you heard about them?"

"Sure, we've heard some things. We'll deal with them when they show up, if they do," Mark said.

The policeman turned to talk with his partner. When he came back he said, "This looks like a case of self-defense. Everyone seems to think that you were protecting them from this man, so we'll let you go for tonight. If the prosecutor has a different idea tomorrow, we'll have to take you in for questioning, but you're free to go tonight."

The men from the morgue had arrived and removed the body, so the officers left with them.

Back in our delivery truck, I confessed, "That wasn't the exact truth I was telling back there."

"What are you saying?"

"When I went to the floor with that man, I got the gun away from him. I pointed it into his side and pulled the trigger. I killed him!"

"All right, you pulled the trigger instead of him, but he's dead either way, right? That was a man threatening the lives of everyone in that bar and he needed to be killed. You're just the man that did the right thing."

"Sure, I know that's right, I just felt like I did in Kentucky. Since I left there, I've tried to be a good citizen and I thought I had done a good job of that, but then this crazy man got in the way and I lost my temper. Well, the way we told the story, at least I sounded like the good man."

I lost more sleep that night, worrying about the possibility of the return of the old Leland.

Chapter 27

Bertha was already at work by the time I got up in the morning. I ate part of a piece of toast and drank some coffee, then went to the Union Hall. Caleb was there when I arrived; we both had the day off.

"You look like hell!" Caleb exclaimed. "What happened to you? You're usually Mr. Clean when you come in here."

"Please don't give me a hard time, I don't need it right now. You're right, I didn't get much sleep last night. A bad thing happened on our deliveries."

"It must have, tell me about it."

I held up an open palm, then got up to get more coffee. When I returned, I related the events of the previous night for Caleb, deleting the part where I was the one firing the shot.

"Criminy! It's a good thing you were there to rub that guy out! Did you tell Bertha about it yet?"

"No, not yet. I don't think she'll take it too good. She hates firearms, doesn't want me to carry one. She doesn't like for me to be working with the gangsters either, though I don't consider Mark Wallops to be one of them. We're just delivery people."

"So, are you going to tell her what happened?"

"I thought I'd check the newspaper to see if they covered the story. If I'm not charged with a killing, there may not be anything in the papers. If there isn't, I probably won't say anything to her about it."

"Keeping secrets from her now? I guess the honeymoon's over then," Caleb joked.

"Actually, this isn't the first one, but I'll leave it at that."

I thought about the commandment: *Thou shalt not lie*. I thought about that one as it related to my talk with the doctor. I justified it by telling myself that I really wasn't lying if I just didn't say anything. And she didn't need to know every detail of my work; that would just get her upset—no need for that. And, the other part: well, I just thought we could go on a little longer the way things were now. I could tell her the truth later, she might decide to do something radical—leave me for someone else, or want to adopt an orphan. What would my friends think of me then?

Caleb started talking about the St. Louis Cardinals, his favorite team. I smiled and nodded on the right occasions, pretending to be interested. I was also listening to the men at the next table talking about the aftermath of the massacre.

Harry Fisher was saying, "The out-of-town newspapers are really putting the heat on Delos Duty to make some arrests. The police are asking a lot of questions. Are you guys worried?"

Joe Petrie shook his head. "They ain't goin' to get any of us. We might have shot a scab or two, I ain't sayin' I done any shootin' myself, but even if some of us gets arrested, they won't be able to prove anything. We'll get off scot-free." He gave a little laugh. "Damn it all, if the authorities won't help protect us from outsiders taking our jobs away from us, we have to do it ourselves!"

I glanced around the room. Otis Clark was entertaining a table of men with some jokes. He didn't seem worried at all. Joe Petrie was rumored to have shot scabs at the fence in the woods and Otis was said to have killed Claude McDowell, yet neither man's conscience seemed to bother him.

"They even beat the Cincinnati Reds three out of four last week!"

Caleb was making a point about the Cardinals.

"Yeah, I heard that," I lied. "Let me ask you, Caleb, what are you thinking about the killings last week? Are you concerned about this city?"

"How do you mean?"

"No, I'm talking about the articles in the newspapers, well, the out-of-town papers, calling this 'Bloody Williamson'?"

Caleb leaned forward and lowered his voice a little. "Oh, that. It isn't good. I heard my neighbors talking about that awful day, like it's going to make Herrin look real bad. It guess it will, but if some people are thrown in jail or hanged for it, maybe we'll be all right again."

"What does that mean, 'be all right again'?"

"Well, I heard Donny Hurst went to Springfield on Friday to buy cleaning materials for his business. When he went to register at the hotel, they gave him trouble because he put down his residence here in Herrin on the registration slip. People all over know what happened here."

"Yeah, it's bad all right, when you look at it the way they do. And you think some convictions will help?" I wondered.

"That's what people are saying."

As I rose from my chair, I told Caleb I was going to go home to try to get more sleep. My body was beginning to feel fatigued. On the way home I picked up two out-of-town newspapers and the *Herrin News*. Nothing was reported on the killing the previous night.

Bertie arrived around 6:00 and quickly fixed some soup. We supped on the soup, bread with margarine, and beer while we caught up on each other's day.

"Mr. Rogers says our business is beginning to pick up again. It's been pretty slow since the murders. People don't seem to know how to feel about the goings-on here in Herrin."

"It's for good reason. I read in the papers what people are saying in other parts of the country, they call us all murderers. Even if we didn't participate, we are guilty for not arresting the people who did. One paper said we are the black spot on the state of Illinois."

"Then, they don't understand us. Only a few people did killings and we want the murderers arrested, don't we?"

I had to struggle with the answer. "Yes, I want justice, but what about Lester. He started the killing by bringing in outsiders who shot miners before the miners shot the scabs. No paper is saying Lester should be arrested and I don't understand why."

She crossed her left arm on her chest and tapped her temple with the fingertips of her right hand. "That's true, I hadn't thought about that."

"People on the outside don't see the whole story, but they're quick to blame the people of Williamson County. That's just not fair."

"Enough of this stuff, let's talk about something good. August 6th will be Abel Schobel's birthday and we've been invited to the party! He will be ten years old and Mary is having a party to celebrate. Can we go?"

"Yes, that sounds like a good idea. Let's plan on it."

Chapter 28

It was another hot night. I was trying to sleep on the cot on the porch. A half-moon gave a glow to the backyards of the neighborhood. A few nocturnal animals could be heard rooting around looking for food. A hoot owl was off in the distance and some frogs were croaking. A cicada was singing his loud sound. But the memories of the massacre were still haunting me, so sleep was fitful. Around 1:00 I heard a different noise, like the breaking of a branch. I sat up and looked around, then I saw a person moving two doors to the south. It appeared to be a man walking through the plants in the yard. He was coming toward the back of the Renn house. He went up to the back porch and embraced a woman. That's when I realized Heather Renn was on the porch waiting for him—Charles Hosock.

The two people kissed, then entered the house in silence. I thought this was an interesting turn of events, one that said a lot about my neighbors. I lay back on the cot and tried to go to sleep. I closed my eyes, but the dead bodies were still there.

After about an hour, I heard some movement again, so I got up on my elbows to peer over the porch railing and watched the couple saying good-bye on the porch next door. The man had just reached his house when the kitchen light came on at the Renn house. Young Sara was at the door. "Mom, is Dad home?"

"Shh, be quiet, Sara, people are sleeping. Let's go back inside."

"I thought I heard Dad moaning a few minutes ago—is he here? Mom, why don't you have a nightgown on under your robe?" Sara asked.

Mother and daughter went inside and the light went off. I tried again and finally drifted off.

On Sunday we were at the Schobel party. Several other families were also attending the celebration. I met Hans Schobel, and we talked briefly about mining and the strike.

"I'm hearing that it will all be over by the end of the month. Negotiations are progressing well for the bituminous mines," Hans said.

"That's good news, I'm anxious to get back to work!"

"I am also. With the strike going on, the mining companies aren't buying new land, so I've been without work as well."

That was all we had in common, so we drifted apart.

"Leland, come look," Bertie requested, "they've got a new phone now." It was a large wooden box hanging on a wall in the hallway. A microphone stuck out from the front and the receiver was hanging on the side. "Maybe we could order one for our house? Mary said it took over a month for them to get it after they ordered it. Let's think about it after this awful strike is over."

"Sure, after the strike is over."

"Then I could call Mary any time I want, wouldn't that be great? I got her number written down, look." Bertha opened her address book to show me the number.

One of the other guests was also a miner on strike. We talked about other striking miners we both knew and talked about a mining accident that had happened near Springfield early in the year, both of us cursing the dangers of working underground.

As the party wound down, we left for Herrin. Bertha said with a smile, "I love going to see them. They are such a happy family." She slid across the seat to get closer to me, even though the weather was very warm. She rested her hand on my thigh and sighed. I could feel her happiness. Our mutual affections continued through the evening and on to bed. For a while I forgot about Herrin's problems.

Heading west on Route 13, the delivery truck was about to enter Marion for the stops there.

"We've got company," Mark said, "they've been behind us for about a mile now."

"Can you see who's in the car?" I asked as I looked out the side mirror.

"No, but I can guess. The Reverend Stickney at a Marion church was said to be preaching about the evils of liquor last Sunday. He was stirring up the congregation to take action against the sinners delivering demon alcohol, or something like that. I'm guessing the men back there were listening to the Reverend."

"Are we delivering at the hotel here?"

"No, they're not taking deliveries anymore. We're going to be dropping their delivery off at the Energy Roadhouse and the hotel manager will send someone over to pick it up there. The Reverend's putting pressure on them to stop selling liquor, so this is how they're getting around him."

Mark moved the truck into the parking area of the roadhouse on the west side of Marion. As we got out, the trailing car pulled in as well, parking just behind our truck. Mark and I both went to the rear, I entered to get the delivery: two bottles of whiskey. As I came out, two of the men from the car approached. A third man stood beside their car. Mark started toward the roadhouse door.

"What ya got there?" one of the men asked.

I didn't respond, just turned toward the door of the roadhouse.

The other man slapped the bottles from my hands, smashing them on the ground.

I became furious! I reached out and grabbed the man's shirt front with one hand and hit him in the face with the other. The man fell back to the ground—his nose was bleeding profusely! As I stepped toward him, the man beside the car pulled a shotgun out through the door and held it to my chest.

"That's enough, sinner! Now step back and you two get in your truck and get out of here. I can pull the trigger right now and blow a hole clean through you if I want, just to stop you from hitting an innocent man."

Mark hurried back. "All right, all right, we don't want no trouble here, either. We'll just get on our way, yes sir!" He grabbed my arm and pulled me toward the truck's door.

"And don't be bringing the devil's brew back to Marion again. We'll be watching for ya, ya hear?"

Our delivery truck pulled out, heading for Energy Roadhouse.

As we drove along, I said, "You know, when that man knocked those bottles out of my hand, it made me mad, like I haven't been mad in a long time. If the other man hadn't put a gun in my chest, I might have killed him!"

"But you didn't! That's a good thing, right?"

I didn't respond; my thoughts were on the remembrance of how I had felt in Kentucky a few years back when I had beaten a man to death. For several years now, I had been able to control myself and I knew I had to keep from getting that angry again. As the rage comes on, it takes over my mind completely; it's like my brain gets locked up or goes dormant as my muscles do their work. When I was arrested in Kentucky, I was asked why I beat the man so bad, but I couldn't remember anything about what happened after the rage took over. I knew I couldn't allow that to happen to me again—I have come too far from that person and I don't want to go back.

We finished the deliveries and went home early. Bertha was still up when I arrived.

"You're home early, is something wrong?"

"No, it was a quiet night," I lied. It was getting easier to do that these days.

Chapter 29

Union Hall was buzzing when I entered, but there weren't many people here. I easily saw Caleb sitting at a table alone.

"What's going on, Caleb?"

"The sheriff came through here earlier and arrested some of the men for the murders, like we've been expecting. Harry said some of the men listed on the indictments went on over to the jail in Marion when they heard the sheriff was looking for them. Otis Clark was one of them. Harry was glad his name wasn't on the list!"

"Did anyone say how many were being arrested?" I asked.

"Fifty men now, but they say there'll be more later, about ten was taken out of here. Joe Bob said he heard that several of the men on the list already left town, trying to escape to a better climate."

"Poor Otis, he just started building a new house for his family before the strike started. I wonder what will happen with that," I pondered.

"He'll probably get out on bail soon and he can still work on it."

"What about the warrants for Mr. Lester or any of the men he brought in to work at the mine?" I asked hopefully.

"That's what some of us asked the sheriff when he was here. He said no warrants have been set for them.

"Some were saying some of the men won't be allowed to post bail to get out. We're all getting on a list of people who will donate to a fund to get the others out. If you want to give some money, you can tell Fox. He's organizing the whole thing," Caleb said as he nodded toward Mr. Hughes.

I walked over to the table where Mr. Hughes was sitting. "I'd like to donate to the fund to help out the men in Marion."

"Now that's mighty nice of you, Leland"—I was surprised Mr. Hughes knew my name—"to help out your union brothers. Those men will appreciate what you're doing." Mr. Hughes' expression as he shook my hand reminded me of the face I saw on a mortician at a funeral parlor one time. I hoped that wouldn't be an indication of the fate of my brothers.

When the strike ended the end of August, one of the first items Bertha wanted was a telephone. She ordered it the day the strike ended; she said she wanted one that would sit on a table! A few weeks later was the day the installation was scheduled. I was at home on the day it was installed.

The telephone installer needed to connect the wires from the telephone pole at the street to the house first, then he came into the house to install the telephone on the table in the living room.

I asked, "How long have you been doing this work? You seem to know what you're doing here."

"I've been installing phones for over a year. I started over in Marion, but there are so many new homes here in Herrin, I've been working here most of the time."

"I guess we'll be able to talk to Carterville real good? That's what my wife wants the phone for, talking with her friend over there."

"Sure, this will work for that. They should be able to talk good, unless the trees get in the wires along the way. Sometimes it gets hard to talk when that happens."

"Why, I don't understand."

"Well, especially in the springtime, the trees grow quickly and the new branches go out over the wires. They're full of moisture so when they come in contact with both wires they tend to short-out the circuit. Most of the time it's just temporary, the people can still talk, it's just hard to understand each other. I try to drive along the wire lines at least once a week in the spring to cut back those limbs.

"Then in the summer, the wires get hot and they stretch out. If the wind blows real hard they bang together and that makes talking hard too."

As he finished the installation, he picked up the handset and held it for me to listen also.

"I've got to call the operator to check it out. I'll make a little static on the line while we talk so you will know what it sounds like."

The operator answered the signal and the installer told her where he was calling from, then, "Doris, will you talk a minute while I show Mr. Vance some static?"

Doris kept a one-sided conversation going while the installer ran his knife blade across the two wires to short-out the connection. He did it quickly several times so I could hear how Doris' voice was interrupted.

"See, you can still hear, it's just hard to understand the other person. We call that static on the line. We hope it doesn't happen too often, but let me know if it gets too bad. I can usually fix the problem real quick."

When Bertie came home she sat on the couch and looked at the phone like she had never seen one before. She gingerly touched it first, then went to the kitchen to get her address book with Mary Schobel's number. She laid the book next to the phone and lifted the handset to her ear. She smiled at me, then said the number into the phone. In a minute she broke out laughing!

"Mary, it's me, Bertie!" She was talking very loudly, her eyes were wide open, and she had a wide smile. She was so animated that her hair bounced as she talked. As they continued to talk, her voice gradually came back to a normal level. The conversation lasted for several minutes, then she said good-bye.

"Leland, this is so great! Now I can talk with Mary anytime! I really love this phone." She was still looking at it with the same big smile all over her face. For a little while she called the few other people she knew who had phones already, so she could give them her number.

I became bored, so I relaxed with my latest book.

Chapter 30

For me, work with Mark Wallops was increasing. In early September, on one of our deliveries, Mark said, "Charlie wants us to go to East St. Louis tomorrow to bring back one of his cars. Can you get the time off work in the mines to come with me?"

"Sure can, I'm scheduled to be off tomorrow. Why's his car in East St. Louis?"

"With Charlie we don't ask those kinds of questions. With the Shelton gang we don't ask questions, either. They pay us good money to do their jobs, so we just do them."

"Got it. Then, yes, let's go to East St. Louis tomorrow!"

I had breakfast with Bertie and told her I would see her in the evening, that I was going to make a run with Mark Wallops.

"Since you're working in the mines again, can't you do less work with Mr. Wallops? I really don't like you being with those gangsters."

"Sure, I can tell him I want to work less, but then he'll just find another man to do the work and drop me altogether. Can we afford to have a telephone and this nice house then? No, we can't. Think about the budget for our family that you've been teaching me—we need this money for our plans."

"I know you're right. It's just that once we have a baby, I don't want to have someone come to the door one night and tell me you've been killed! Although, I'm beginning to wonder if we'll ever have any children."

"All right, when a baby comes, I'll quit this work." I didn't feel good about saying it, but it did leave Bertie with an answer she wanted to hear. I needed to find a better time to tell her the truth, I thought.

We took our regular route through Carbondale, then north on Route 51 and west on the hard road toward Belleville, then north to our destination: a garage in Glen Carbon, Illinois, in Madison County. We arrived just before noon and took possession of the car from the garage owner, Tom Hugely.

"There's paperwork for the car under the front seat. Try not to need it 'cause it ain't too good. We had to use a different artist this time. Oh, and Charlie said he wants you to stop at Minnie's and pick up two women on your way back," Tom instructed.

"Leland, follow me down to Minnie's. We'll be making a lot of turns to get there, so don't get lost," Mark said.

Almost an hour later, we arrived at Minnie's Place. We went in for lunch and found the crowd and noise was even worse than the last time we were there. Minnie showed us to a table in the dining room. We got our food and were returning to our table when Gertie asked for our drink order.

When Gertie left, Mark waved Minnie over to the table.

He asked her, "Charlie Birger sent us here to get two women to take back to Harrisburg. You know anything about this?"

"So, you're the ones taking two of my best producers, are you? I wouldn't let them go, but Charlie talked them into going down there with him. He sure can charm the young ones, I'll give him that."

"We'll be done eating in a few minutes—are they ready to go?"

"Sure, they're ready, been ready all morning. You'd think they were getting ready to go to Paris, as giddy as they are. I'll send them out to you right away."

"Leland, you can take them in your car with you. You know how to talk to women better than I do."

"Sure, there won't be anything to it, I'll be glad to."

We finished eating and went to our cars. Immediately after we walked out the front door, the two girls came after us. I held the back door of my car open for them and they literally jumped in, both of them giggling and talking. They wore short skirts and blouses that displayed plenty of breasts. One girl's hair was blonde and especially curly, while the other one's was long and brown and curled under at the end. I guessed they were around eighteen years old. The curly-haired one had large eyes and a small mouth with gum in it that she chewed constantly. She seemed to be the leader of the two.

Both cars had their tanks topped off at the usual gas station and we were on our way back. The curly-haired girl asked, "Have you been to Harrisburg before?"

"Why, yes I have, it's a pretty town, lots of trees."

"We've never been out of St. Louis, so we think this is going to be something!"

The second girl added, "Charlie said there are lots of men there, coal miners with lots of money, is that right?" She had a deeper voice and a pleasant smile—not too big.

"Well, I don't live there so I don't know for sure, but if Charlie says it, then it's got to be true,"

I assured them.

Curly-haired asked, "What's your name, mister?"

"Leland Vance. I do odd jobs for Charlie. Beside working in a mine."

"I'm Charlene and this is Mable. So you're a miner, are you? What's that like?" she asked.

"Most of the time I dig the coal. At times I set off explosives, I'm a shotfirer."

Both girls giggled. "You fire shots, do you." And they looked at each other and giggled some more. "I bet you're really good at firing shots, a big handsome man like you." More giggling. "If you'd like to fire a shot with me, I'll give you a special price." And then they both laughed. Mable's laugh had a deeper sound, almost like she was laughing to participate, though she did seem to be merry. Charlene's laugh had a higher pitch, and she seemed to really enjoy laughing because it seemed to come from deeper in her chest; it was almost contagious. I enjoyed hearing her laugh.

"No thanks, I married, so I'm well taken care of there."

The girls continued to talk with each other. At times they would ask me about something in their view as it passed and comment on the differences from the big city they had just left.

As we traveled across Route 13, their conversation began to die out. Charlene leaned over the back of my seat. "What do you do for fun around here?" She was chewing gum fast and blew bubbles often.

"Well, see, I work a lot of the time. Then I have my friends I socialize with some. How about you, what do you like to do?"

She started picking at the shirt on my shoulder. "I like to dance and drink with people too, when I have time off." Up close, I could see her green eyes were young looking, very clear; her skin was smooth and clear too. She had bright red fingernail polish, probably fresh this morning. The bright red matched her lipstick.

"Tell me, if you don't mind, how did you get started in this business?"

"Oh, I don't mind, it just kind of happened one day. See, I had been with a lot of guys in my neighborhood and I really liked having sex with them. Then one of them asked me if I wanted to get a real job and get paid for doing what I had been doing without getting paid and I said, sure. So he got me over to Minnie and she's been real good to me since."

"And Charlie, how did you and Charlie decide that you should come to Harrisburg?"

"Well, Charlie thought I was real good in bed with him, so he wanted me to come on over to his place. He said, with my talents I could make some real good money. I guess I really turned him on, you know?" She stopped picking my shirt and started twisting her hair and looking at the road ahead as she talked.

"Are you leaving any family behind, there in St. Louis?"

"Naw, my daddy left us when I was little and my mom has a new boyfriend all the time. I think she likes men too, guess that's where I got it. But she don't spend any time with me, hasn't for years now. I suppose Minnie is the next best person to me like a mother. And, I got Mable here. We're good friends, that's why we're both going down here."

"So, how does a girl like you get to be so good with the men?"

"Oh, I like to look at the men's expressions as they watch me undress or when I touch them, you know—I can read a lot from the way they look. Then, the women at Minnie's taught me some new tricks they knew about things they do when they're with men. Anyway, I think it's great to have a good time and get paid for it!"

Mable moved forward and put her arms over the seat back. "I like it too. Making money just laying in bed. The only problem is the men who aren't so nice. It isn't fun then! Minnie had men around who helped us if we got in trouble, I hope Charlie has men there to keep us safe too."

As we approached Harrisburg, the girls sat back in their seat to take in the city. It surely wasn't anything like the city they had just left. Looking in the mirror, I could see by their looks they were a little disappointed with it.

At the appointed place in Harrisburg, the car and the girls were turned over to Charlie's lieutenant. Again, I held the door open for the girls to exit. As Charlene got out of the car, she held my hand and kissed me on the cheek.

"When you get tired of your wife, why don't you come over to see little ole me?" she whispered in my ear.

    "I just might do that. Will the special price still be good?"

    "For a gentleman like you, I'll even give you the first one for free."

    "I'll keep that in mind, the next time I'm in Harrisburg."

Chapter 31

Bertha had fixed some leftover stew for dinner. She had a concern she shared.

"When I walked home tonight, it was just getting dark. As I turned the corner off Park onto Madison, I saw Caesar standing ahead of me at the entrance to the alley that goes behind the tailor shop. When I got close to him, he nodded and winked at me, said 'Good evening' in a way that sounded a little grotesque, you know what I mean? It made me feel uncomfortable."

"What did you do?"

"Nothing, really. I kind of smiled and nodded and just kept walking. That man makes me feel like he's got something bad on his mind. And this isn't the first time he's been there. I told you about the time he came into the shop to talk to me, you remember?"

"I do. I'll look into this. You've got to feel safe when you walk on the streets of Herrin."

"Please just talk to him, will you? I don't want any gangsters involved, all right?"

"You have my word on it."

The following day I went to George's shop for a shave and haircut. Fewer men were sitting and waiting on the barber, or in the back shooting pool, since most everyone had returned to work in the mines.

Mr. Moreland, the loan officer at Herrin Savings and Loan, was also waiting his turn.

"Looks like our state's attorney isn't too sure he can get a conviction on the men that's been arrested, Leland. Our manager was over from Marion the other day. He said he heard Delos Duty told the newspaper that he didn't think he could find a jury that would convict any of these men. He's under a lot of pressure to make arrests and have trials, so he has to do that, but he doesn't expect convictions. He said, with the trial being held in Marion, there won't be a jury to be found that isn't connected with the miners in some way. He won't be able to convince them their fellow miners are guilty, it just won't happen."

"Then why are they going to spend taxpayers' money if there won't be any convictions?"

Earnest Moreland chuckled. "That's another thing I was reading in the letter I received from the Chamber over in Marion." He leaned back in his chair and stared vacantly at the ceiling, as if he were looking at the letter in his mind. "The State Chamber is requesting each city's Chamber in the state to send them money, then the Chamber will pay the cost of the trial, since Williamson County doesn't have the funding. The letter said the state has to provide justice here, which means they want men convicted and hanged for murder. They think that will restore the credibility of the state as Williamson County will be following the Constitution and the laws of the state."

"Earnest, since they want justice, why aren't they arresting Mr. Lester? I just don't understand why he gets off here. He's just as guilty of murder as the union people are."

He sat up straight again and turned to look at me.

"For the same reason the Chamber is pushing for the convictions of the miners: all the big-money people want to protect each other, it's as simple as that. I'm caught right in the middle of this—I work for the big-money man, yet I have to live in this community with my friends and customers. I see both sides and, yes, I think like you do. Hanging a few miners for protecting their livelihood isn't right if the man who started the whole thing isn't hanged as well. But, that's all I'm going to say on this."

George was determined to lighten the mood. "Did you fellas hear the radio Dan put in the back a few weeks ago? It was picking up stations in St. Louis and Louisville yesterday. The signals come in on the ether, Mr. James told him. The antenna on the roof grabs the signals and the radio changes them to sound coming out the speakers."

"Things are changing fast, aren't they," Earnest declared.

"Sure are. I heard a Sunday school group in Paducha singing 'Amazing Grace' yesterday afternoon. It was hard to make out, but I bet it sounded real pretty."

When my haircut was over, I headed for the Union Hall. Caleb was working in the mine, but I found Joe Bob at one of the tables.

"What's going on today, any more arrests been made?" I asked Joe Bob.

"People are saying there may be two hundred fifty people arrested before it's over. They're also saying that eight of the first fifty arrested won't be out on bail. The rest will have their bail set later this week. Otis is one of the ones that won't get out, so his house will have to sit for now."

"I feel bad for Otis and his family."

"Me too. Some of the men in the carpenters' union are talking about helping, but I don't know what they're going to do." Joe Bob was concerned.

Just then Harry Fisher joined us. "Did you guys hear about the carpenters helping out Otis? They've said they'll finish his house for him. They're going to use union money to buy the materials and they'll work for free! Isn't that great for Otis and his family?"

"I like to hear those kind of stories," I said, smiling. I leaned back in my chair and rubbed my hands together.

"Me too," Joe Bob added. "It just gives you faith in the goodness of some people!"

"Yeah, and I also heard that some of the wives of the men in jail are cooking meals for all of them and the jailers are letting them serve it at the jail. They let the men out of their cells to eat at one big table together. That's mighty nice of those officers.

"And another thing: the United Mine Workers Union is going to provide a lawyer for the trial. A Mr. A. W. Kerr, or something like that, will be coming here. They say he's really good at this kind of work." Harry smiled and nodded at us, happy with the news he brought.

I felt this was the first good news I had had in a while. I decided to take Bertie home after she finished work. I walked in the front door of the tailor shop just before it was time for it to close. Not saying a word, I rang the bell on the counter. After a minute or two, Bertie came to the door from the workroom in the back. Her hair was strewn and she was adjusting her skirt as she entered; she looked like it was a busy day of work.

"Oh! Hi, Leland, why are you here?" she asked, glancing into the back room.

"I thought I would give you a ride home, since you said you were concerned about Caesar."

"That's nice of you, give me just a minute to finish up back there and I'll be right back."

As she turned from the counter, I thought I heard the back door of the store close.

Heading for the back, Bertha said, "We're having trouble with the wind blowing the back door." In a few moments she came back through with her purse and coat and we were off. As we drove along Madison past the alley, there was no sign of Caesar. I felt troubled about the tailor shop's back door, knowing that Caesar was active in the area. Each night the next week, when I was available, I sat in my car on Madison Street and watched for Caesar, but to no avail.

Chapter 32

October was a cool month. Usually, the cool weather encouraged the men to drink a little more as their bodies took on extra calories to prepare for winter, but this year the miners were paying off their bills from the strike, so they didn't have extra money for alcohol. But the month was getting warmer for Mark and me; the preachers in the local churches were encouraging their members to start taking action with the liquor and gambling in their cities. It was becoming more common for cars of the saintly men to meet the delivery truck at the drinking establishments. Charlie Birger was getting upset because his income was coming up short from alcohol sales. Slot-machine collections were also down, but it was mostly the Shelton brothers hurting from that shortcoming.

"Leland, I'm getting worried that we're going to get caught in the middle here pretty soon. Charlie is saying that we need to strike back at the do-gooders that are hurting the alcohol business. I don't want to do no shooting of those men, but we got to do something, or Charlie's going to replace us. There's so many gangsters coming into Williamson County these days, he won't have any trouble finding someone to fill our shoes."

"I don't have any ideas how we can change things, do you?"

"No, we can't take out any of the ministers and if we got one or two of the saints, that'd just cause more of them to follow, so that's no good." Mark was shaking his head as he talked.

"I heard he was paying off the police in Harrisburg. He's using the policemen to help him control the saints. The people in Harrisburg think the world of Charlie because he gives a lot to the poor people, food and stuff like that. But he's also a killer. Isn't that true?" I asked.

"Oh yes! People say he will just kill a man and think nothing of it. Then, turn around and send a load of groceries to a family in need."

"And the young girls, is he helping them when he has us bring them from East St. Louis to Harrisburg?"

"He seems to think he is. They're making more money here than they were up there, so he thinks he's helping them along."

"I think that's a really sick way of looking at things," I said, expressing my disgust.

"I didn't say I agree with his way of doing things, I'm just telling you how he is. The people in Harrisburg overlook the bad things because he helps them out at times. He pays some of the salary the policemen make and he brings a lot of money to the community. They say he uses the services of some of the lawyers when he gets arrested, which is often, so they like him too. And he likes to wear nice clothes, so he also gives the clothing stores business, which they like."

I asked, "How did he get in with the Shelton brothers?"

"The Sheltons used to live around here a few years ago. The three brothers and Charlie started selling liquor together in a roadhouse north of Herrin. Then they started buying liquor cheap other places and selling it to the other taverns. After a while they were putting slot machines into the local roadhouses and selling them booze as well.

"A little later, the Sheltons moved back to East St. Louis and let Charlie run things around here. The Sheltons are killers too, but just not as crazy as Charlie Birger."

"Why doesn't Charlie just pay off the local police in Herrin and Marion to get the religious people off our back? If it works in Harrisburg, it should work here too," I asked.

"He's got to some of them, but the ministers control a lot of the votes at election time. The mayor and the sheriff here are both anti-prohibition, but they're elected offices, so they get a little nervous around elections. Then, there's the Marion Law Enforcement League that's being organized. They demand the police close down the selling of liquor in Williamson County and they carry a big influence with the businessmen around here. The good thing is the saints won't try to shoot us, they'll just stop us from delivering to the taverns and roadhouses."

The night ended without any problems from the religious people of the county.

In November the weather began to get cold. There was frost on the windshield as I cranked my car in the mornings. I swore I needed to trade it in for one with an electric starter. It would have to be one with windshield wipers and a heater too!

George's barbershop was abuzz with stories of the prisoners in Marion. "The Illinois Miners' Union furnished fans and a local Herrin union group donated a Victrola and a supply of records. Other friends brought delicacies to give them relief from prison fare. All in all, they weren't being treated that badly," Mr. Potter was saying.

Joe Bob walked up from the back where he had been playing pool. "That Mr. Kerr is really giving the trial hell about the real issue here. He wants to use the trial to make talk about the big-money people in this country trying to break the unions. That's what people need to understand."

We all agreed with Joe Bob on this one.

Caleb joined the group. "The rest of the country needs to understand that we were invaded by outsiders that were trying to take away our jobs. Mr. Kerr is just the man to make that happen!"

More agreement all around.

I began to get angry. "That goddamned Lester should be one of the people on trial over there in Marion! Why don't they do anything about him, that's what I want to know." I was becoming more and more convinced that the killings in June were justified and that the mine owner was the real cause of the killings on both sides. It all just made the criminal justice system look like it was run by big-money people and the working people of the country didn't matter.

The next day, November 8th, was the first day of the trial; Judge Hartwell was presiding. Jury selection and other formalities took until December 8th. Judge Hartwell then set December 13th as the day opening statements would be heard. I was working in the mine that day, so I went to the Union Hall when I finished.

Caleb and Harry were discussing the trial. Since neither had gotten inside the courtroom, they were summarizing the comments they had picked up from others in the courtroom hallway or on the sidewalk outside.

"Otis Clark, Bert Grace, Peter Hiller, and Joe Carnaghi were in good spirits, but Leva Mann was definitely concerned by the goings-on," Caleb related. "I wish I could get in tomorrow, but I have to work in the mine."

"Some of the people coming out said Mr. Kerr told the jury just exactly the same things we were reading in the newspaper," Harry said. "A man said the jury looked like they listened to him closer than they listened to Mr. Duty, the state's attorney. That's a good thing for us!"

I offered, "The *Herrin News* said most of the jurors are common folks—miners, farmers, like that. Maybe they'll be good to our friends, you think?"

"Sure, Delos Duty told the reporter awhile back that he didn't think he could get a conviction. The miners are too well liked around here. They're all somebody's neighbor or they go to church together. I know I couldn't convict any of them, they're good people," Harry said confidently.

I kept going, "We just need to see Mr. Lester on trial here! The folks on that jury would want to see him hang!"

The next morning I went to George's for some conversation. Mr. Moreland was in the barber's chair when I arrived, so I took a seat to read the newspapers and listen to their conversation.

"Williamson County is really taking a bashing in the state and national papers, isn't it," George was saying to Mr. Moreland. "An article in the *Herrin News* questions where the money will be coming from to pay for a trial. The state's broke and Williamson County isn't far from it now that we don't have coal wages coming back to normal yet."

"Of course the state's not broke, it's just that the Governor cut off Attorney General Brundage's budget," Mr. Moreland said wisely.

"The *Tribune* says the Governor's a crook, that he stole money from the state when he was treasurer. I don't understand how he got elected if he's a crook." George was concerned.

"We'll never know the true answer to that question, George. Illinois politics is the worst in the country, in my opinion. This whole thing might never have happened if the Governor was in the capitol instead of being at a trial in Lake County. Colonel Hunter asked both the Governor and Brundage for permission to bring in the Guard before the union went out to the mine, but they wouldn't give it."

I stopped reading the papers. "All the news in these papers is about the actions of the union people and there isn't one mention of the men the guards killed, which started the whole thing off. That isn't right!"

George shook his head. "I agree, that isn't right."

Mr. Moreland, who had been a schoolteacher at one time, had an explanation: "We have to remember that the newspapers are paid by advertisements and that money comes from big businesses, like the mining companies. The Mining Association wants to break the UMW, so they are paying the papers to put out their story. That's the way it is and that's the way it will always be.

"Take my business, for example: We rely on business owners to work as our partners by investing their profits with us, so we have capital to loan for mortgages, buying cars—the big-purchase items. But the coal-mining business here in Williamson County is owned by people in other parts of the country, not here in Southern Illinois. So we have to borrow money from the banks where the 'big money' is, to loan to our local miners. Now, when the mines aren't producing coal, everything stops. Our banking partners don't have money to loan and we don't have a local demand for money to borrow. So, unlike the rest of the country, our local banking business has no relationship with the businesses that generate payrolls here."

I scratched my head; this was hard for me to understand.

"You might remember a little while back, when we were talking about the price of houses in this area. This will change that whole situation if we don't see some men convicted. The way the papers are talking about 'Bloody Williamson' will make us all look bad. And that will drive prices down, on houses especially, because outsiders won't want to move here. So, Leland, if you were thinking about buying a house, I'd wait a little while—the prices might be moving your way."

"No problem, there. Bertha and I aren't ready to take that step yet."

My stomach was beginning to sour, so I got up and went to the back to watch a pool match. I hadn't been this depressed since I lived in Kentucky. I began to mull over ways to improve my lot.

Chapter 33

Over the next few weeks my personal hygiene began to deteriorate as I became depressed about the trial. Bertha was watching closely, trying to figure out what I was thinking or what was influencing my actions. Even our lively conversations at supper had degenerated to small talk neither of us was interested in holding. On several occasions she had made offhand remarks, then one evening she brought it up with me directly.

"Leland, what's going on with you, why aren't you keeping yourself as neat as you used to?" She stood in front of the refrigerator with her arms crossed.

"I'm just not in a mood to worry about how I look," I replied. "What's wrong with my growing a beard, anyway?"

"Nothing, it's just that it's not like you. You seem to be acting different lately, that's all. I'm just curious to see if anything's going on that you want to talk about." Bertie was becoming a little louder, trying to coax the information out of me.

Now I was getting louder too. "I know what you mean by that. You think I'm doing something you don't approve of, don't you? Well, I'm just being me, so quit trying to get inside my mind!"

"You're taking this trial too personally. You're not the one sitting in jail over in Marion, and you didn't do any of the killings of those men. Now, you should just get over it!"

"Sure, that's easy for you to say, sitting in the tailor shop. But I work with these men, they're my friends, so I can't forget the fix they're in and it bothers me. Why can't you understand that?"

"Because you said at that time the men were acting like animals, that you didn't approve of what they were doing. Now you suddenly take their side—what happened to make you change your thinking?"

"I realized that the whole system in this country is working against them and I hate it!"

"Oh, grow up, you know how the system works and you can't change anything about it, so just accept it!"

"I can't accept it, that's why I want to do something about it," I yelled and got up and left the house in a rage.

I sat fuming at a table in the bar at Vinny's. I could see Maryanne out of the corner of my eye, watching me. Since I didn't really want to talk yet, I was glad she was taking her time to come over. Then Vinny said something to her and pointed at me. Finally, she walked to my table.

"Leland, is that you behind that scrub of a beard? I didn't recognize you."

I didn't look at her or seem to be aware that she had said something.

"Having trouble with your boss or your wife?"

I looked down at the table, then pulled myself upright and rubbed my hands together.

"Just bring me a damn beer." I said it without looking at her directly.

Maryanne turned around and went to place the order. Then she waited on people at other tables, wiped off a table or two, glancing sideways at me several times. I was staring straight ahead, acting like I was in another realm. After a few minutes she walked back to the bar, picked up my glass of beer, and brought it to my table.

"You know, it seems like you only come in here when you're

having problems. Since Tony doesn't work in the mines anymore, I hardly ever see you around. Why is that?"

I took a slow draw on the beer, then said, "I've been busy working at the mine and working at liquor deliveries."

"But here you are. Seems if you're that busy, you'd want to be home with your wife when you're not working, not coming here."

"I was home with her, but I didn't like her conversation, so I came over here to talk with you."

"I don't believe that, but it does sound nice." She smiled at me and put a hand on my shoulder.

I finished my beer in one last gulp. "Bring me another, will you?" I was beginning to settle down a little.

When she returned she sat in the chair next to me. "Why did you say that, that you came to talk with me? You've never said anything like that to me before."

"Now you sound just like my wife—'why did you say that, what the hell do you mean?'—that's why I came over here. I want to have a damn drink and relax, can't you let me do that?"

She put a hand on my arm. "Sorry, I didn't mean to upset you. Do you want to talk to me or not?"

I didn't have an immediate response; Maryanne started to get up, but I held her arm to restrain her, so she sat back down.

"Of course, I like talking with you, you're very sweet with me and you're very easy to look at. I sometimes wish we had gotten together before I met Bertha, I think we could have had a good time together. Don't you?"

"Yes, Leland, I would have liked that too, but that's all in the past. Now, I'd just like to be your good friend, someone you can talk to when you need to. Is that what you're saying, because that's fine with me."

"All right, now tell me how you're doing, what's going on in your life."

Maryanne put on a weak smile and looked into my eyes. "There's a new man in my life, now that you've asked. He recently came to Herrin from Italy." She was shaking her head.

"You don't sound too happy about it, why's that?"

"When my parents went to Italy last summer, they met Vito and they decided that he would be a good husband for me. So, when they got back here, they told me I should pick him as a husband myself. At first he sounded good, but when he got here, he turned out to be a typical Italian man. Now I'm thinking that marrying him is a wrong choice."

What do you mean by 'a typical Italian man'?"

"See, in Italy the men are the masters of their house. They make demands on their wives, but they think they can behave any way they want, even have other women for their sexual needs. But the wife can't complain or he will make her know not to complain again. So many of the men are that way, it's just accepted as normal. Some of the men here are the same way with their wives, but I won't be one of them."

"How can you be sure he'll be that way here?"

"Since he's been here for a while now, he goes on sales trips around Little Egypt, selling to stores. He stays out on these trips during the week. When he gets back here, I see him talking with other men in the bar. He tells them about his travels, then they slap him on the shoulder and laugh. Sometimes they glance at me, then quickly look away. I think he's telling them about the women he sees out there—a woman can tell these things."

"But, you live in America now, not in Italy. You can make your own decisions, not do what your parents tell you to do."

"I know, that sounds good, but I live in this Italian community and all the people here are so happy for me; if I don't go through with it, everyone will be disappointed in me, they'll say I am the one who's to be blamed."

I put my hand on her thigh as I leaned in closer in sympathy. "What's more important, their feelings or your happiness?"

She lowered her voice and put her hand on mine, and slowly shook her head, gazing in my eyes. "You don't live here with these people, so you don't understand."

"I know I want you to be happy, you deserve to be." I rubbed her thigh, squeezing gently.

"Oh, Leland, you're such a good man. Why didn't we have this conversation years ago?"

We were both quiet as we looked into each other's eyes.

"Now what are we going to do?" she asked, but her expression was hopeful.

"When do you get off work?"

"I can take a break now, it's really slow tonight. I'll tell Vinny I have a headache coming on and I need a break—he won't mind. Why don't you go out the front door, then come around and meet me at the dance studio in the back?"

When I arrived at the studio the door was open and it was dark inside.

"What took you so long?" She giggled in the darkness. She took my hand and led me to the couch.

That was our first night of lovemaking.

When I got home, Bertha was already in bed. I slept on the cot on the porch. It was a good night's sleep, the first I had had in a while. In the morning I was ready to clean up my appearance.

Chapter 34

Over the Christmas season, we went to the Black Forest Inn several times to enjoy their seasonal fare, which reminded Bertie of Germany. We also went to Carterville to see the Schobels' decorations, also reminding Bertie of Germany. On our return from Carterville, Bertie mused, "I hope we have children soon. In Germany my family always made an occasion of having St. Nicholas arrive with presents for us children. It was one of the best times of the year! I do so want a family."

She gave me a warm smile, and I smiled back, just not as warmly. I just couldn't bring myself to tell her the truth—she was in such a good mood, but my main concern was what she would think of me if she knew I couldn't father the children she wanted. I thought we were so happy together and my life was going so good, I just didn't want anything to change.

The next weekend the Renn family had a small party for their neighbors. Attending the party were the Morrows, neighbors to the north of our house, and Charles and Nicole Hosock, who lived to the south of the Renn house. I remembered Charles as the night visitor to Heather when Howard was away.

Heather had made Christmas cookies for the party. She also prepared the eggnog—without liquor, of course—which was the drink for the evening.

Howard was in a good mood. "This has been my best year ever! My business is doing fine, I must say. I hope you're doing just as good, Leland."

"Well, I don't think I'd say it's my best year ever, but yes, it's been a good year overall. Where do you get your best business in Little Egypt?"

"The accounting people in Chicago tell me I have the best receipts from over the Harrisburg way. From there on over to the Indiana line, then down along the Wabash River. That's where I spend a lot of my time, of course."

"I haven't spent much time in Harrisburg myself. Do you like that town?" I asked.

"Well, you know it's the home of the big gangster Charlie Birger. He's really loved by the people, even the religious people I deal with. Sure, he's a gambler and deals in liquor, but he also gives his money freely to God's poor people. There's a lot of foreigners living outside of that town. Eastern European, people from Kentucky, most all of the men are miners. They say Charlie attracts gamblers to the area, because of his gambling establishments, but that's where he gets the money he gives to the poor. Of course, I don't respect anyone who makes a living off of demon alcohol myself, being a good Christian.

"Say, I don't hear you talking about your religious affiliations—do you have any yourself?"

"No, I guess you could say I'm lacking there. I'm just happy with who I am."

Howard appeared to get my message. "Well all right, let's see what these gentlemen are discussing." Howard turned to join the other two men.

I glanced at Bertie, who raised one eyebrow and smiled at me, obviously just enduring her conversation.

Charles turned from the other men to talk with me. We had

talked before, but just introductions on the street in front of his house.

"I'm in the grocery business. We sell wholesale to the local grocery stores," he said. "And you're a miner, isn't that what you told me?"

"That's right, I work at the Number 12 mine over in Colp."

"You know, we have many community groups here in town. Have you given any thought to joining any of them? I know you're fairly new here and so joining a civic organization would be a good way for you to meet people, people who think like you. And, belonging to one of our groups would make you more acceptable to the other people here; you'd be one of us, so to speak."

"I'm a member of the miners' union, so I have many friends there."

"Sure, and that's good, I agree. I'm in several Grocery Association groups, sort of like a union. But I also belong to the Herrin Conservative Party. We work toward the election of people who think like us—conservative people. Do you have any leanings in that area?"

"I don't want to get into those things. You see, we miners had a rather bad summer and it's still going on over in Marion, so I don't like to discuss those kinds of thoughts right now. After the trial is over and we hear the outcome, I might be able to have this kind of discussion," I said firmly.

"Of course, I understand completely," Charles said, nodding his head vigorously. "You folks are going through some tough times. Well, maybe we can talk about this sometime later."

Charles turned toward Howard, to rejoin that conversation.

Next, Hershel joined me. "I guess you and Bertha think we're loud neighbors, don't you?"

"Not at all, Hershel. With our windows closed in the cold weather, we don't hear anything from your house."

"Oh, that's good. Sometimes I have to get a little loud to get Charles' attention and I hoped it wouldn't be disturbing you all."

"No, but tell me how things are going at the *Herrin News?*"

The neighbors all exchanged pleasantries for the remainder of the evening, then wished each other a Merry Christmas and a Happy New Year to end the evening.

The Morrows joined us for the short walk back.

"Leland, I heard Charles mention the Herrin Conservative Party to you. You need to be aware that those people are members of the 'Invisible Empire' group. Did you know that?"

"I don't know what you mean by 'Invisible Empire'—should I?"

"No, most people aren't aware either. It's the Klan."

The next day, I went to see Mark, who sold me a .38 snub-nosed pistol. One that would fit inside the front of my pants in a holster that wouldn't be visible to others.

Bertie stomped her feet as she came in the front door. "This damned cold weather freezes my feet as I walk home, Leland."

"Do you want me to come to pick you up after work?"

"Oh no, that would be a waste of money. I can walk the few blocks all right, although there are more men lying on the streets these days. I don't know where they come from, but they are just disgusting! Some of them make awful comments as I walk by them. They must have so much alcohol in them that it keeps them from freezing."

"Something should be done about them." I said it while shaking my head.

"You know what you do is a part of the problem. Emory said the number of speakeasies and bars in Herrin is bigger than it is in Chicago. And, I see more of them starting around here every day, it seems. That's most of the problem."

I had noticed her mention of Emory, but I let it pass. I just didn't like the way she talked about him, but I couldn't put my finger on the reason why. Bertie had taken off her coat and moved to the kitchen to drink some of the coffee I had made to try to warm up a little.

"Leland, your friend Mark came into the tailor shop today to get a shirt repaired. He introduced himself so I would know who he was. He dresses nicely, doesn't he?"

"I guess so, why?"

"Oh, nothing, it's just that I think he wants to make himself appear successful, like he is someone important, you know. He must have a lot of self-esteem. Sometimes people want to look important to cover their shortcomings; perhaps he is one of those, what do you think?"

"Well, he has told me some things about himself that would prove you're right. But, I think he just wants to fit in with the gangsters he deals with, so he dresses like them."

"Now, you do realize I'm not opening any new bars in the work I do. Neither does Mark open any bars. We just deliver the alcohol to the people who do. And they wouldn't be opening these places unless the people around here were wanting to buy the stuff." I sat down at the table to join her.

"Yesterday Mr. Rogers got a police officer to come to the front of our place to remove a drunk who had fallen and couldn't get up again. What is Herrin coming to?" Bertie removed her heavy sweater and placed it across her lap.

"Howard Renn would tell you it's Satan in his glory." I tried to sound grandiose as I talked. "He would want you to take up a sword and slay those men who are doing the Devil's work by opening up those taverns! He'd also say we should drive the gambling out of Herrin."

"Mr. Rogers has said some of those things as well. He's a member of the Rotary Club and when he comes back from a meeting, sometimes he rants about Herrin's problems with the drinking and gambling. One day he said Charles Hosock is a member of the Rotary."

"Sometimes I wonder just how religious these two families are down the street here. They talk about how committed they are to their faith, but how they act is sometimes different, I can tell you."

"What about you, you socialize with them and then deliver alcohol later the same day."

"No. When I talk with them I don't give them any idea I agree with their preaching ways. I stand my ground, I just don't mention my night work. Hell, I would, if they asked. They just haven't asked."

"Isn't that the same as lying to them? If you don't tell them something when you know it would cause them to not like you?"

"No, I don't think so." I began to think how I could turn the conversation to the truth I hadn't told Bertie yet. It's just that, well, I wouldn't look like a man any longer, even though I wasn't in that regard and she wouldn't be happy to hear this news.

"I'm going to go take off these smelly clothes and put on a warm robe. Then, I'll get us something to eat," she said as she walked toward the bedroom.

While I didn't like lying, I was realizing I wouldn't ever be able to get the truth out to her and it made me feel all the worse. I had worked so hard to get my life to this point, I just couldn't tear it down, and that might happen if I told her the truth.

Chapter 35

I was reading in the latest edition of the *Herrin News* that the trial of the five men had resumed the first week of January in Judge D. T. Hartwell's court. Delos Duty was the state's attorney prosecuting and Mr. A. W. Kerr was still in charge of defense. A lengthy trial, it was losing the avid interest of the community. Mr. Duty was taking the jury step-by-step through the events and providing many witnesses that stated the guilt of each of the accused. Talking about Otis Clark, he brought in Mr. Harrison and then his son—men who said they saw Otis shooting men in their woods that morning. They definitely identified Otis and Bert Grace as two of the shooters. Mr. Kerr cross-examined both of them, but couldn't find a crack in their testimony. He brought to question their eyesight and the distance they stood from the men doing the shooting, whoever they might have been.

Mr. Kerr was following the exact plan he had outlined in his opening statements. The latest newspaper articles reported that the prosecution had made a solid case as to the guilt of the defendants. Mr. Kerr was working to prove that the state's witnesses were wrong, first by challenging their testimony, then by bringing in witnesses for the defense who testified that each of these men was at a different location on the day of the murders.

So, when it was the defense's turn, Mr. Kerr brought up witnesses who testified that Otis Clark was eating breakfast in Herrin the morning of the shooting, so he couldn't have been at Harrison's Woods. A similar excuse was given for Bert Grace: he couldn't possibly have been out there that day. Mr. Duty's cross couldn't shake their testimony, the article stated. The reporter wrote how he thought the jury was more interested in hearing the defense witnesses' testimony as the trial progressed.

I continued with my conviction that it should be Mr. Lester who was on trial, but I understood that the rich people around the man would not let that happen. My understanding of this travesty was influencing my outlook on the very essence of the workings of the community around me. I could plainly see that the people with the money decided who should be arrested and who should get off. Each week the newspapers were demanding the lives of the accused, while their articles ignored the guilt of Mr. Lester. In fact, the Illinois Chamber was working toward the elimination of the miners' union, setting back the progress of the past several years. These facts were only too obvious to me.

I started my day off with a shave at George's. Several of the men with mugs on the wall were sitting, waiting also. In the cold weather the door remained shut except for the occasional patron as he entered; otherwise the air was filled with cigarette smoke. Dan Blocker had an exhaust fan in the ceiling of the pool hall area, but it didn't help in moving the air up front, so the men here were regularly rubbing their eyes.

I stopped reading when I heard Jacob Potter make a statement: ". . . if these bars and taverns were shut down. It's demon alcohol that's perverting the minds of the good citizens of our city. Just look at the drunks on the sidewalks each morning. That shouldn't be allowed!"

I countered, "And what would you have the community do to stop the sale of alcohol?"

"I'd close all of those establishments tomorrow. Send the owners to jail for breaking the Volstead Act. We should have everyone held responsible for following the law!"

George stopped the haircut and began to fidget nervously.

"Well, I think it was a stupid law, one enacted by the people who want everyone to sit in churches every day and pay their tithes so the leaders of those places can live on easy street. No, that isn't how the world works these days." My voice continued to rise as I stood up. "Men who work hard need to have a place to relax before they go home to their wives and children, and the social clubs you mentioned provide just that."

The other man sitting in the area voiced his agreement.

"You can yell at me all you want, but the law is on my side here. I know you're one of the gang members who provides this alcohol and you're just trying to protect your income, that's all."

I had rolled up the newspaper and started using it to slap my hand for emphasis.

"And that shows just what shit your laws are. Herrin's people depend on coal mining. Our families depend on mining jobs. Yet the law allows one man to try to break the peace of the community by trying to reduce our pay. And what does he get for his action? Nothing! But the events he created led to the massacre of his men and now our union brothers are at risk of their lives because of him"—I pointed the newspaper directly at Potter—"so you can stick your laws up your ass." My rage was getting too strong, so I went to the pool area before I did something I would regret.

Jacob Potter was still yelling something at me at the front as I ordered a beer from Dan Blocker.

"Leland, you know I can't sell beer here," Dan said weakly.

"Don't worry, I'll drink it in the back where I'll be away from that asshole, Jacob Potter. If anyone comes in, I'll put it under a pool table." I reached across the counter and patted Dan's shoulder and gave him a wink.

Dan dug deep in the cooler, under the soft drinks, and pulled out a beer for me.

After about an hour George called to the back. By this time I had settled down and was enjoying a conversation with some of the pool players. When I got to the barber's area, Jacob had left. With Jacob gone, the conversation centered on Governor Small's decision to send investigators to Williamson County. No one in the capital of Springfield was accepting the words they were getting from "Bloody Williamson" on the affairs of June 21 and 22. While Sheriff Thaxton responded to all the state's inquiries, the information forthcoming was not at all helpful to them—just what the Sheriff intended.

"Thursday, the 18th of January, 1923, will go down in history," Caleb stated with a solemn tone. "This is the day the jury will decide the fate of the five men who are accused of murdering the strike-breakers last June." He tried to sound like a newspaper reporter covering the trial.

"Come on, give us your verdict," Harry encouraged him.

Number 12 was closed for another state inspection; so many men were in the Union Hall and talking excitedly about the trial. It had gone to the jury the previous day and everyone expected a decision would be heard shortly.

"Leland, what do you think the outcome will be?" Caleb asked.

As I finished my sandwich, I said, "I think the real answer is guilty. I'm talking about the trial that should have taken place with that bastard Mr. Lester at the defendants' table." I finished my beer and wiped off my mouth with my sleeve.

"Sure, we all agree with you on that, but what about today's verdict?"

"Can't say, I don't want to jinx the boys over there. Let's just say we hope for the best and let it go at that. The jury is taking its time deciding, so maybe we'll hear good news."

Most of the men had decided to stay at the hall until the verdict was announced. Some talked of causing trouble if any of the men were found guilty, but the union officials tried to head off that attitude. There was a constant undertone of the tobacco juice landing in the coffee cans used as spittoons. I had told Bertie I would be staying at the hall with the other men until the verdict was announced. Some of the wives prepared a potluck dinner for the men staying and coffee was available throughout the night.

In the morning many of the men drifted to nearby restaurants for breakfast. Throughout the morning, the men remaining in the hall were subdued; their nerves had reached a point of null on the whole event. Again at lunchtime, some men went out for a bite, but never far from the hall.

About 2:00 there was a commotion at the door as Harry rushed in with the news: "My wife called from the square in Marion. All the defendants were declared 'not guilty,' they're all going free!"

The hall erupted with cheers; everyone was jumping up and yelling. After a short while, the celebration moved to a nearby tavern for most of the miners; the teetotalers in the group went home. I stayed a short time, then left. Again, my anger began to rise. I continued to question the whole system, one that tries the men who are protecting their own security, the well-being of their family, but doesn't prosecute the man who caused the problem.

Instead of going home, I headed for Vinny's and the one person who I was coming to depend on for understanding since my argument with Bertie over the trial.

"Everyone says your friends got off free"—Maryanne put her hand on my shoulder—"guess that makes you feel pretty good?" She set my beer on the table.

"Good for these men, but not good for the people who run our legal system. I'm still upset about them not trying Mr. Lester, the asshole who started the whole thing."

"And you should be upset about that, it's just not right, I agree. On the other hand, there isn't really anything you can do about it, is there?"

"No, not at all, unfortunately. Not anything or anyone will impact the system we have. But there are things I can do for myself." I didn't look up at her, I just continued to tap the table with my thumb.

"Like what?"

I turned my head toward the side of the room, away from Maryanne. "Just things. If some people can get off from the responsibility of killings, why can't everyone get off, like the men over in Marion?" Then I turned back to Maryanne with a soulful look in my eyes, wanting to be understood.

"Sweetie, you're hurting now, I get that. I wish I could take you to bed for a good rubdown and help you understand how to get through this, but the evening is young and I have to work. Can you come back after midnight and we'll get together then?"

The noise level in the bar had been rising, I began to realize. "Sure. Can you bring me another beer?"

Later, as I went out the door, I knew I shouldn't come back.

Chapter 36

Delivery of the illegal liquor was becoming more and more exciting for Mark and me. Quite often now, men were being sent out by the local church leaders, men who were also reported to be members of the Klan, to try to intercept our deliveries. We might be met at a roadhouse or tavern and confronted by five to ten men with guns. These times Mark would not stop when he saw them. Other times the men might cut a truck tire while we were inside the establishment. Even though it was effective in slowing down deliveries, other methods were devised to keep the product flowing, like changing our schedules or even changing nights of delivery.

I was getting more anxious than Mark for a real confrontation with the men outside the roadhouses. "Let's show them they aren't going to scare us off. I can handle two or three of them if you hold a gun on the others!"

But Mark still believed my plan would only make matters worse in the long run. "We need to keep doing what we've been doing so they can't ask for more help from the Klan. We're making the deliveries so you and I are getting paid and that's all that counts."

Working in the mine was becoming a problem for me because of the time I was dedicating to liquor deliveries. Bertha was beginning to notice the difference in mining hours and she wasn't happy.

"Leland, do you recall when we talked about you working for the

Birger gang? How you said it wasn't going to be permanent? Well, it looks to me like you're working more for the gang than you are in the mines. When our first baby comes along, are you going to be able to get back to working the number of hours you were before?"

"Of course I will. Jethro, my supervisor, said I'm one of the best miners at Number 12, if not in all of Madison Coal Company mines. He wants me to work more hours now, but he understands that I can make more money at the other job." I put my arm around her. "Don't worry your pretty little head, it's going to work out just fine. What was it you said, 'We just have to believe everything will work out and then it will.'"

I went to sit in the living room; Bertha came over to the couch and sat next to me, giving me a kiss on my cheek and holding on to my arm. She smiled as she sighed in satisfaction, like she believed I would listen to her without question.

On February 12th the second trial started. A few additional miners were charged with murdering Antonio Molkovich, a cook at the strip mine. During this trial the Union Hall was much more placid. Testimony of the witnesses would be about the same, so the men expected the same results. Indeed, the prosecution did present the same witnesses for the most part, and the defense followed the same strategy in blaming Mr. Lester and Mr. McDowell for the entire affair.

After about a month, the case was given to the jury. This time, the deliberation was much shorter, but the outcome was the same— all defendants were said to be "not guilty." Judge Hartwell agreed with State's Attorney Duty that all further plans to prosecute any other miners would be a waste of time, that all outstanding charges should be dropped. This would be done in the interest of getting the community back to a normal status. They believed that all members of the community needed to put this horrible event behind them and get on with their lives.

In the morning of the next day the regular group was gathered for coffee at the Union Hall. Caleb was still playing the reporter: "Tell me, Mr. Vance, what do you think of the outcome of the trials?"

I was in no mood to play Caleb's game. "Here's what I know: the whole justice system in this country is at fault—first for the enactment of the Volstead Act which is making most of the men in this country break the law most every week, second the lack of prosecution of the man responsible for the Herrin Massacre, and last is for the crooked police and bureaucrats who take money from the gangs, then allow those gangsters to commit crimes without prosecution.

"I can take you to gambling establishments here in Herrin and all over the area that operate without any threat of prosecution. Men have been killed from fights at these establishments and most of the time no one goes to jail.

"Stolen cars and prostitution are rampant around here, but nobody seems to care, except the religious do-gooders. And they are just as guilty of breaking the law by stealing money and booze from the taverns, carrying guns, and making threats of violence in public places.

"I regularly see gangsters from other parts of the country coming into this area to do their various evil activities. I tell you that we are called 'Bloody Williamson' for a good reason and I don't see how that's going to change!"

Several men at nearby tables clapped and cheered for me, which I didn't want; in fact it disgusted me so much that I got up from the table shaking my head, going to get more coffee.

Harry started with me as I returned to the table. "Leland, we do have laws here and many people who follow them. Now, the Good Book says we shouldn't kill other people and things like that—you know what I mean here—so if we all choose to ignore these ideas, we lose our direction as a society, don't we?"

"I'm just saying that we've already lost those ideas, because the people we elect to defend them aren't interested in doing their jobs. So the people who do follow the law are just going to fall further behind the others, it's just a fact of life. So why should I not deliver booze, which is breaking the law, if no one is going to arrest me? Or, why shouldn't men around here become drunks if no one is going to arrest them? Please tell me!"

Conversations at nearby tables were underway with the men there arguing their points on the subject, with no conclusions being drawn.

Harry and Caleb changed the subject of conversation to the St. Louis Cardinals and their chances of winning the World Series. I sat quietly, still fuming at the lack of prosecution of Mr. Lester.

By the end of March, winter was receding and spring was beginning to take hold. New rains were washing away the grime that was left over from the previous months' snows. On Saturday Bertie was anxious to plant some early lettuce, onions, and garlic. She decided to wait a few more weeks for the carrots. The ground was warm enough to put a shovel in it a little way down, but still too cold for most plants. After breakfast she suggested that I should help to turn over some of the topsoil so she could put down some seeds.

"Bertha, let me see if I understand you. I work in the coal mines during the week, digging coal, and now, on my day off, you want me to dig some more?" I said it as I tried to make a serious frown. "After I break my back down there, bring home the money to keep you in this beautiful home, you still want me to dig for you on Saturday? What a slave driver you are!" Then I broke into a smile.

She knew I was only kidding with her. "But you're my man, the one who said you will support me in my endeavors, aren't you? Now I need your help, and remember, you will get to enjoy the harvest of the delicious food we get from our efforts!" She put her hand on my shoulder and kissed my cheek, then gave me a hug. "I love you so much. You're so nice to me. And, someday in the near future, you'll be a great father—I just know we'll have a child soon!"

"I love you too." Still, I wondered when I would begin to feel real affection for her. I did really like being with her, it was just that I didn't think I felt the same way toward her as she seemed to feel for me. As I talked with other men, they would sometimes say they didn't know how they would be able to get along if they lost their wife, that life would lose its meaning then. I certainly didn't feel that way with Bertie, but maybe I hadn't lived with her long enough yet. And, why does she think we'll have a child soon?

"Listen, why don't we go on a date tonight? We can dress up a little and go to the Black Forest Inn. Enough with staying in the house all the time; we both need to have a little fun, don't you think?"

"Oh, Leland, that sounds great! Yes, I'd love to do that, let's do!"

As soon as she cleared the table, Bertie grabbed her coat as she rushed out the back door. I was still in my pajamas, so I had to put on my clothes and collect the right shovel, then I went out to join her. Bertie was talking happily with Heather Renn about each other's plans for gardening. I started working with the shovel, but the ground wasn't going to allow me to go too deep. Still, I was able to get an area of adequate size turned by the time Bertie joined me.

"That's great, the ground looks like it's ready—were you able to go very deep?" She put her garden trowel in to test the depth. "Yes, this should do it. By the time the plant roots get down this deep, it'll be soft even further down.

"Can you taste the lettuce and onions, honey?"

As she evened the soil, made a shallow groove in it, then poured in the seeds, she asked me, "Heather was just telling me about a store over in Marion that sells nice scarves. Can you drive me over there this afternoon so I'll have something nice to wear tonight?"

"I'm sure I can, I haven't been shopping in Marion for a while; I'll even buy you ice cream while we're there."

"Well, I'm sure I don't know what I did to deserve you, you're so nice to me!"

As we drove south out of Herrin that afternoon, we passed the Energy Roadhouse. Bertie was looking forward, chatting about the dress she would be wearing in the evening, so she didn't notice two drunks fighting in the parking lot of the roadhouse. I could only shake my head.

"What are you thinking about, honey?"

"No, nothing."

"Well, you sure were thinking about something or you wouldn't have been shaking your head. Now what was it?"

"I guess I was thinking about the shirt I would be wearing tonight, but then I changed my mind because it wouldn't look good with my coat."

That worked. Bertie started off with several minutes of chatting on my clothes. Better that than to hear her talk about the number of drunken men going about the city these days.

Our evening at the Black Forest was enjoyed by both of us. Good German food, good German wine, and then a piece of German chocolate cake for us to share. Bertie was starting to fall asleep before we arrived back home. We both slept soundly.

Chapter 37

Toward the end of April, I called Anthony to arrange a lunch with him. Sitting in the restaurant at the Rome Club, I was reading the *Herrin News* while I waited for Anthony to join me. An article about a new Fusion Party in Herrin caught my eye. The journalist said the party members wanted to have a choice for voters in the next election, just a slate of good men who would lead the city regardless of their party affiliation. Maybe there will be some progress made here after all, I thought.

Anthony came into the room, smiling and waving at everyone he passed. Everyone seemed to know him and was glad to see him. As he got to the table he grabbed my outstretched hand with both of his. "Hello, my friend! It's great to see you again!" He looked fresh and clean, like he had new clothes and his weekly bath had been this morning.

"It's great to see you as well. It's been too long for us to be apart. How have you been?"

"Couldn't be better. My store is doing good, my new wife is doing great! I don't want to say too many good things, though, because I might jinx my good luck. How's Bertie doing?"

"Good, good, yes, we're doing very good as well."

"Maryanne tells me you get to Vinny's once in a while. She likes it when you come in to see them. Did you know she's getting married this summer?"

"She did tell me that. Are you happy with the man she's marrying?"

"Well, yes, he's a good Italian man, so we think he will be a good husband, eventually. You know, he has to learn the language and our customs here. But I know it will all work out in the end."

A waitress arrived and took our orders.

"What about you, are you working on any new projects for Herrin? Like you did with the Columbus Day event?" I asked.

"Yes, actually, I'm heading a committee to raise money for a new Catholic church for this city. We're outgrowing the one we have now, so we need to get going on a new one. That's what I'm raising money to build. Father Senese wants to have a building that would be similar to a Lombardic church in Italy. It will still take a year or two to raise the money, but we're sure, over time, we can bring in enough."

"It looks like Vinny is doing good business these days. Maryanne says they are always busy. Things must be doing good in the Italian community?"

"Things have been good since the strike is over. We do have some concerns about what might be coming up for us, though. We're hearing that the Protestant ministers are saying bad things about us, that the Catholics are causing most of the drinking problems in the city. They seem to think that every Catholic family has a still in their house and that they're selling booze to everyone. On Monday, a family—mother, father, and two children—stood outside my store and yelled at the people coming and going. Why do they do that? I don't understand those people."

"What were they saying?"

"Oh, things like 'Why don't you go back where you came from, you stinking wops'—things like that.

"I'm also having trouble getting deliveries from McCormack Grocery Supply. They like my business, but they say the religious leaders are giving them a hard time because they sell to me."

"This article I was just reading said most of the Protestant leaders are joining the Klan, or have already joined it." I pointed at the article.

"I believe it. One of the Italians over in Marion said there was a Klan rally at a field south of the city last weekend with several thousand people attending. Those occasions are when they bring in new members—burning a cross, white hoods and all that."

The waitress returned with our food. As we ate, the conversation moved to mining work—who was still there, what was happening in the mines, and our many happy memories.

As the temperatures began to rise in the early summer, I started to sleep on the porch again. Many nights Bertie would lure me, one way or another, to go to bed with her first. She said she still dreamed of having children, that she believed we would have one this year, she just felt it. On the other hand, she became more distant with me at times. She still went through the usual, casual conversations and acted normally around the house, but I detected a change in her attitude.

Then, one day in early June she broke the news. She cooked a special meal for our Sunday dinner, which was around noon in Herrin. After the meal was over she told me she had good news. She led me into the living room and sat next to me on the couch, obviously very excited.

"Leland, it's finally happened, the good news we've been waiting on. We're going to be parents!" Bertie was almost yelling as she bounced on the couch. "Aren't you really happy? Isn't that great?" She leaned over to put her arms around me and gave me a kiss on the cheek. Then she leaned back to look at me with her beaming smile.

"What's going on, why aren't you smiling too, what are you thinking?"

"This is a big surprise. I just don't know what to say, how to think about this."

"I know, I'm having a hard time myself. After all these months of trying! Well, we need to start thinking about making a baby's room in that back bedroom there."

I interrupted her. "Have you been to the doctor yet? Are you sure you have a baby in there?"

"Oh, honey, you're new at this. I know when I'm pregnant, I don't need a doctor to tell me. I didn't have a regular month last time, and I'm two weeks past now, so, yes, I'm sure."

Bertie started talking about her plans for the child's room as she walked into the back bedroom. I knew my legs were too weak to try to get up, so I continued to sit on the couch. I was completely confused; was I sterile or had a miracle happened? She had always said we should be patient, that this day would come, so had it actually happened? And if she is pregnant, how should I act? I hadn't been around men who were expecting to become fathers, so I wasn't sure just what I should say or do.

I realized she was asking from the bedroom, "Why don't you come in here and we can talk about the color. What one do you think would be nicest?"

"Coming." I tried to get up, but my legs were still not responding very well. Finally, I pushed my body up with my arms and then the legs started to work again.

"Honey, your face is white! Are you feeling sick? I didn't ask you how you felt before I broke this news on you. Are you all right?"

"Yes, that is, I think I am. This has never happened to me before, hearing I'm going to be a father. So many things are going to change for us."

"You're right, that's what I've been saying: we need to start planning for those changes."

During the afternoon we talked about coming changes like a

name for the baby, how long Bertie should continue to work, what furniture we would need to buy and how soon. We even talked about how much longer I should be working at my delivery job.

Several times during the evening, Bertie tried to reach Mary Schobel to give her the good news, but there was no answer at the Carterville home.

"They must be out with the boys this evening, maybe over in Carbondale. I'll try again tomorrow night. Mary will be glad to hear our news, Leland."

Chapter 38

Monday morning was another day that I didn't work in the mines. I headed to the Union Hall to meet up with my friends. I wasn't sure how to react to Bertie's news, so I decided to keep it quiet for a few days. Caleb was working at Number 12, but Joe Bob was there reading a newspaper as he drank some coffee.

"Morning, Leland." Joe Bob just gave a glance at me and went back to reading. "The *Herrin Semi-Weekly Herald* here is talking about the number of drunks on our streets these days. The reporter is requesting the police to get them off the streets and into jail. He goes on about closing some of the illegal taverns in the city too. That wouldn't be good for us, would it?"

"No, it wouldn't. Last week one of the Herrin officers took a man to city court for drunken behavior, but Judge Bowen gave him a light fine and sent him home. So what good would it be for the police to arrest men for drunkenness? My concern is the drunks on the streets when Bertie walks home in the evenings."

Joe Bob put down the newspaper. He looked at me as he raised his bushy eyebrows and suggested, "Maybe you should pick her up each evening?"

"I suggested that to her one evening, but she wouldn't hear of it. She likes to walk and it isn't that far, but she did say the drunken men say bad things to her as she goes by."

"You know, if we both went down that street and cleared out the drunks a few evenings before she walked home, they would soon learn not to be on the street anymore. Just crack a few heads, break a few arms—nothing too serious. What do you think?" His soft voice didn't match with the violence he was suggesting.

"Maybe I'll stand on the street this evening and do just that. You don't need to help out, I can handle it myself."

"Sure, well, good luck with that, I've got to go over to Colp to help out Mr. Goodfellow. I'll see you tomorrow."

Very few people were still in the hall and most of those who were had voiced their disdain for liquor in the past, so I decided to walk over to the pool hall for a while. About a quarter hour before Bertie's quitting time, I walked up the street from the pool hall, passing the tailor shop, then Herrin Auto Sales, then to the corner of Madison Street. Before I started west on Madison I glanced back south, noticing Mr. Rogers depart his tailor shop and walk south, leaving Bertie alone in the shop to do the closing. I started west on Madison and walked past the alley going behind buildings I had just passed going north from the pool hall. No men were lying about the streets this evening, not even in the next block.

I walked across Madison and back east to the alley going north, stopping a few steps into that alley north of Madison. It was darker there so it would be hard for anyone to see me in the bright daylight. I was thinking perhaps Caesar might make an appearance if I waited a little while.

Soon Emory MacIntosh entered the alley from the back of Herrin Auto Sales, carrying the bag of dirty clothes. I thought the dirty uniforms must be heavy, since he walked with a little bit of a list to his right. He went to the back door of the tailor shop and entered. I glanced around the corner of the building to see west on Madison—still no one was lying on the street.

After several more minutes, I glanced again with the same results.

Now I was beginning to wonder why Emory hadn't come back out of the tailor shop. This was just the kind of thing I had warned Bertie about; it was not good for the two of them to be talking in there alone. I started walking south across Madison and into the alley— still no Emory after almost ten minutes now and I was getting more upset with Bertie. As I reached the doorway I was expecting it to be open, but it was shut and the light inside was off. I was feeling the rage boil inside me—this was not what I had expected at all!

I turned the knob and pushed the door open. The room was dimly lit but I could easily make out the bodies lying on a pile of clothes on the floor. Emory was on top of Bertha; his pants were down at his ankles and his shirt pulled up so his chest was on her bare breasts. I ran into the room and over to the couple on the floor. Bertie shrieked as she saw me coming. Emory pulled back off her and stood up, pulling up his pants as he turned to get away. I grabbed Emory and put one arm around the top of his shoulders, holding him tightly. With my other arm I put my hand around Emory's face and grabbed his chin. A quick pull on the chin turned Emory's head around, past the point of its natural movement. I heard the neck snap, then Emory's body shook before it went limp. I let go of the body and turned toward Bertie.

She was still screaming as she was getting up. When she saw me approaching with a look of malice in my eyes, she started talking quickly.

"Leland, stop! We can talk this out. Just stop for a minute, will you?" I continued walking slowly, glaring at her. "Yes, I have been having sex with Emory, but you have to understand. You and I have been trying to have a baby for a long time and it just didn't work. So, now, I did have sex with Emory and I did get pregnant! Don't you see, you're the problem, you're the one who is sterile! Not me! Can't you just let me have a baby? No one will have to know it's not yours. We can be a happy family with just one child, can't we? This doesn't have to mean you're not a man, can't you see that?"

"I'm not a man? I'm not a man? Well, can 'not a man' do this?" I hit her jaw with my fist. Her head turned with the blow and she collapsed to the floor, unconscious. I looked around the room. On a work table I saw a reel of cord. I cut off a length of it and used it to tie her hands behind her, then pulled her legs up and tied them behind her too. I grabbed a shirt off the floor and tore off the sleeves, using one sleeve to stuff as much as I could in her mouth and the other to tie around her head, covering her mouth. I stuffed the remains of the shirt in my pocket.

I went out the back door and south down the alley to my car parked on Monroe. Driving up the alley, I stopped behind the tailor shop. I went inside and carried each of the bodies out to the car and placed them in the back seat—Emory on the floor and Bertha on the seat cushion. I threw her purse in on top of her. Driving north in the alley I turned right to go over to, and up, Park, then west on Herrin Avenue, heading for Colp. I drove the car at a normal speed, my mind in a rage but outwardly calm; I wasn't thinking about what had just happened, I was just driving the car.

I reached the Number 9 mine, which had been vacant for several years. No machinery remained, just the opening of the shaft going down into the ground, and it was covered by heavy ties of wood. I lifted several of the ties off the opening. Going back to the car, I pulled Emory out and over to the opening of the mine shaft. First, I emptied his pockets and looked for any rings or a necklace, but there weren't any of those. In the next instant, the body disappeared through the opening. I went around the area, picking up limbs and other trash that had accumulated there, throwing it down the opening. Now I had made sure the two of them weren't going to lie together for eternity.

When I had finished that task, I returned to the car.

Bertha was next. I pulled her out of the car and over next to the opening. She was now sobbing as she realized what was about to happen. I cut her bindings and removed the sleeves. She was begging me, "Please, Leland, let me live. What about our baby? You aren't going to kill the baby, are you?"

I was yelling to be heard over her screams. "But the baby isn't mine, is it? It isn't mine!"

"No, it's not yours because you can't make a baby. We know that now, so why don't we go on together? No one has to know about your problem!"

"My problem? You're saying I'm not a man?" My anger rose again! "You let this man make a cuckold of me by impregnating you and now you think I should just forget what you did and accept his child as mine? Never!"

Straddling her, I pulled the gun out of my pants and put it to the back of her head. Looking away, I heard the gun go off several times. Next, I took off her ring and necklace, then helped her body go down the shaft; the cords and cloth went down after her. I replaced the wooden ties to cover the opening again, went to my car, sat on the seat, and looked at my calm hands. There was still blood splatter from the shot to her head, so I grabbed the remains of the shirt from my pocket and wiped off the blood, then threw the cloth down the shaft as well. Picking up the items I had removed from her body, I put them in Bertha's purse. I sat still in the car for a while, till my nerves settled down some.

I was still swearing at her in my mind as I drove back to Herrin, but I tried not to do anything that would attract attention. I went to a restaurant on Park for some soup and a beer, then met up with Mark for our evening run of deliveries. My shaking had stopped, but I still didn't want to talk.

"How ya doing, Leland?"

"Fine, sure." I didn't look at Mark, but continually looked around at the surroundings.

"Since this is an odd night for deliveries, we shouldn't have any problems." Mark glanced at me as he continued to drive.

"Then let's get to it." I was talking in a monotone and looking out the windows.

"You all right there?"

"I just don't feel like talking, if you don't mind."

"Sure, no problems here."

It was a quiet night, both for the deliveries and for conversation. In the morning, I left for Number 12 a little early. I traveled north on Division to a pond on the east side of the street, not far from Number 9. Joe Petrie, being a fisherman, had said this one was quite deep. Taking Bertha's purse out of the back seat, I grabbed a large rock nearby to put inside it, and threw it into the pond. It immediately went down and the bubbles from it came up for several seconds.

Working in the mines doesn't allow for much conversation between the miners, and I was able to avoid talking with the other miners altogether that day.

As I parked on the street in front of my house that evening, I saw Mr. Rogers getting out of his car parked just ahead.

"Evening, Leland, how you doing?"

"Tired, been working in the mine all day. What's going on?"

"I'm looking for Bertha. She wasn't at work today and she doesn't answer the door. Have you seen her?"

I paused, putting my hand to my jaw, and looked down like I was thinking. "No, she wasn't in the kitchen this morning when I left for work. I guessed she was still in bed and I didn't want to wake her up too early."

"This isn't like her. Maybe you should go inside and see if she's in there?"

"Of course, hold on a minute. Or, you can come in with me, if you want?"

We both walked into the house. Mr. Rogers waited in the living room while I looked through the other rooms.

"No, she isn't here. That's strange, I don't know where she could possibly be."

"Could she be at a neighbor's house? Maybe she has a friend she could be visiting?"

"Wait here, I'll check with the neighbors, maybe they've seen her, at least."

I went to each of the immediate neighbors' houses to inquire. Returning, I shook my head at Mr. Rogers.

"I'll call her friend over in Carterville." I went to the kitchen and found her address book on the counter, then went to the phone and called the Schobel house. After a brief conversation, I hung up the receiver.

"No, she isn't there. Mary said they haven't talked in a while." My voice trailed off as I looked at the floor.

Mr. Rogers sat on the couch next to me. "Mr. Kelly at Herrin Auto said Mr. Emory MacIntosh wasn't at work today either. Have you heard her mention Emory?"

"She has told me that he brings the dirty uniforms to your shop for cleaning, why?"

"Well, there's been some talk that he spends a little too much time with her when he makes the deliveries. A little gossip, that's all, I'm sure."

"No, I haven't heard anything about this. Should I be concerned?"

"Well, not yet. Mr. Kelly went to the MacIntosh house around noon. Mrs. MacIntosh was very concerned about Emory. He didn't come home last night. By morning she had gone to the police station to ask if they could help find him. She said they're working on it, but nothing yet."

Mr. Rogers stood up and turned toward me. "Are you going to be all right, Leland?"

My head snapped up to look at Mr. Rogers, then I stood next to him. "Oh, I guess so. I-I don't know what to think about this, though."

There was a knock at the door. "Police!"

I walked over and opened the door to let the officer enter.

"I'm Officer Oliver. Are you Leland Vance?"

Mr. Rogers interrupted, "Yes, Officer, we've just been looking for Bertha Vance, Leland's wife. She works at my shop, I'm the one who called you for help."

"Have you been able to locate Bertha?"

Mr. Rogers responded, "Well, not yet. She isn't here and doesn't appear to have been here all day. She's not at any of the neighbors' houses, nor at the home of her good friend."

"Can I look through the house for a minute?" Officer Oliver asked me.

"Yeah, sure."

The officer walked slowly through each of the rooms. Opening drawers in the bedroom and the kitchen. He walked out the back door and looked under the back porch, then returned to the living room.

"Nothing seems to be out of place here. Can you look at her clothes, see if any of them are missing?"

I shrugged my shoulders. "Sure, I can look, but I don't have a good idea of all her clothes—I just don't look too closely at those." I walked into the bedroom and opened the wardrobe door, rifling through the ones hanging there. Walking to the chest, I opened her drawers and moved several items, then turned to the officer standing in the doorway.

"I think everything is here. If any items are missing, I suppose she might be wearing them."

The officer asked, "What about last night, did she come home after work?"

"I work evenings delivering things, so I wasn't back until late. I just go sleep on the porch those nights, so I don't disturb her. I guess I don't know if she came home at all."

"All right then, that's more or less what Mrs. MacIntosh said about Emory's clothes. I guess we'll keep looking for these two people."

Mr. Rogers and Officer Oliver said their good-byes to me and left in their cars. I felt relieved, but I knew I had to finish off the disappearance to keep the spotlight off me.

Thinking back, I could remember everything I had done with the two people much better than the first time I had gone into a rage and killed a man. But it all seemed like a dream; I didn't stop to think about anything after I saw the two of them on the floor of the tailor shop. My mind seemed to go into another realm while my muscles did the necessary work, helping Emory go into the mine shaft, then putting the gun to the back of Bertie's head while it went off and finally helping her go through the opening too. Only after the bodies were gone and I sat in my car did I begin to think about what had happened. Now I walked through each of the rooms several times trying to think if I had overlooked any details, but I couldn't come up with anything more I could do just now. Sitting on the couch, I tried to imagine what would happen next if the two lovers had gone away together: a letter from a remote city, word sent back from the lovers through someone else. I walked to the kitchen and opened the address book again, writing down Mary Schobel's telephone number on a sheet of paper and putting it in my pocket.

Opening the refrigerator, I grabbed some cheese to eat with bread and drank a beer, then went to meet up with Mark for our night's work. I told him Bertie was missing, along with Emory, nothing more. He was concerned, he said. I noticed he watched me closely all evening.

Chapter 39

During the following week I was given updates from the police a couple of times, mostly just saying that they hadn't been able to find any leads on my wife or Mr. MacIntosh. I tried to sound anguished about her disappearance, telling the police of my concern for her safety. I stopped by the tailor shop to see Mr. Rogers, who informed me that other people had been telling him of the evening visits which lasted for some extended periods. He expressed his regret in having to give me this news!

On Friday, Mark and I were again headed for East St. Louis for more slot machines. After loading the truck, we headed for Minnie's.

Minnie wasn't her usual ebullient self. "Pretty quiet in here today, boys. The Mississippi River is flooding further south, so the barges aren't getting through. Which means we don't have as many customers, so you can have your pick of the tables."

Mark chose one near the food and we went to fill our trays. On returning, Gertie came to take our drink order.

"Gertie, we'll have two beers. Say, after we finish eating, I'd like to do a little business with you. Can you get off for a few minutes a little later?" I asked.

"A few minutes or an hour doesn't matter to me, but the price is still the same: five dollars." She responded causally.

I chuckled. "No, that's not what I want—I need for you to make a telephone call for me. It'll just take a few minutes, but I'll still pay you the five dollars."

"Sounds like you got some perverted ideas here. You wantin' me to do somethin' odd or what?"

"No, nothing odd, just make a phone call from a quiet place; that's all I want, honest."

"Sure, I'll do that, but you better not be trying to pull something weird."

After she left, Mark's curiosity got the best of him. "Leland, you're doing some strange things lately, since Bertha went missing. You got anything you can tell me?"

"I could, but it would be best for both of us if I didn't. I can say that if anyone asks you about me, you just say that I'm acting as normal as a man would act who just lost his wife. I know I'm not Carl Shelton or Charlie Birger, but it's best for you to not ask too many questions, then we'll get along just fine."

"That's the way it'll be then—you got your secrets and I got mine. No need for us to let that interfere with our business activities, is there?

"I guess you'll want to go with Gertie without me, then?"

"Right, we won't be gone long; I don't know where there's a telephone in a quiet place around here, but Gertie should know where we can go."

We finished our meal, then I went to find Gertie.

"Minnie said we could use the phone in her office, but if it's long distance, you got to leave her the money!" Gertie said as we went up the stairs.

Minnie's office was at the end of the hall. Six doors lined the hall and most of them were open. Through the one that was closed, I heard a woman's muffled scream from inside. I stopped and tried to listen closer.

"Better keep moving, buster. What's going on in there ain't none of your business," Gertie warned me in a low tone. "We got all kinds of customers here and some of them ain't very nice. The woman will just get a little more money from that guy or he won't be able to walk well later. We got mean security men here who take care of that."

She knocked on Minnie's office door, then opened it and went inside. The phone was on the desk and the wire from it went to a box on the wall near the floor. Gertie closed the door, then turned to me. "Now, what's your plan here?"

"Just a minute." I went to the box on the wall near the floor and pulled out my pocketknife. The blade I opened was missing a tip; it was flat so it would act as a screwdriver. I worked on the screw on the cover of the connection box to take it off. Inside were the wires I wanted. Standing up, I took a sheet of paper out of my pocket and handed it to Gertie.

"I hope you can read English—can you?"

"Sure I can, what do you take me for?" she responded indignantly.

I picked up the handset. When the operator answered, I asked for a long-distance operator. "I'd like to call Carterville, Illinois; the number is two-six-seven."

While the connection was being made, I gave Gertie her instructions: "When someone answers make sure it's Mary. She should be home alone at this time. Read the first line and wait for her response, then read the second line. As you read it, I'll be making static on the line so it'll be hard for her to hear. After she says something, you read the last line." After a few minutes I could hear the phone ringing at the Carterville end so I handed her the phone.

Gertie started to read the lines: "Mary, is that you, it's Bertie, can you hear me?"

She paused to hear the response.

"I'm all right, I'm with Emory MacIntosh in St. Louis, but we won't be here long. Please tell Leland I'm sorry." Now I began to make the connection between the wires to create a static sound.

"Mary, I can't hear you very well, this connection is really bad. Please take care. I'll miss you."

I reached up to take the phone away from Gertie and place it back on the telephone stand.

"Thank you, Gertie. Did you hear her say anything important?" I asked as I put the cover back on the telephone box.

"She definitely thought I was Bertie. No, she just asked where I was and what was going on with me—well Bertie, not me."

"Oh, that's great. Now, here's your five dollars, and another five for Minnie should cover the cost of the call. All I ask is that you don't tell anyone what we just did—can you do that?"

"You bet I can. This is easy work; any time you want to make another call like that you look up ole Gertie, I'm your girl."

I thanked her several times so I would be talking as we passed the closed door in the hall. I found Mark and we returned to Herrin. After making the slot-machine deliveries to a roadhouse north of the city, I returned to my house.

A little later, I was eating a cheese and salami sandwich when there was a knock on the door.

Standing on the porch was Officer Oliver. He took off his hat as I waved him inside. "I've got good news and bad news for you. Your wife has called her friend over in Carterville from a phone in St. Louis. Bertha told her that she was with Emory MacIntosh, that they were going away together. She wanted you to know that she's sorry. That's all she said. I guess the good news is she's alive, but the bad news is she won't be back to you. I'm sorry to have to tell you this."

I looked down at the floor and shook my head. "You know, I got to thinking after she didn't come home, maybe she did act a little odd the past few weeks. Not anything I can put in words, just that she acted a little distant, that's all. Well, it doesn't matter now, does it?"

"No, I guess it doesn't. Well, I've got to go over to tell Emory's wife the news, so I'll be going."

As I finished my sandwich, I tried to think through the events; I couldn't leave any loose ends which might come back to bite me. Just as long as no one looked into the mine shaft at Madison Coal Number 9, I should be safe.

Chapter 40

Over the following few weeks, Mrs. MacIntosh, Emory's wife, kept up a barrage of attacks on the idea that her husband would have left with Bertha. No one outside her immediate family believed her, but she kept insisting that Emory was happy with his family life; sure, he could have had an affair outside the marriage, but that didn't mean he would want to leave his wife and three children for another woman.

I brought a couple of boxes from the mine to put Bertha's clothing in, so I could donate them to a local church. I filled the boxes right away, but I couldn't bring myself to carry them away just then. I went out to buy new bedsheets and changed around the furniture in the room—anything to try to remove the memories of her. Many nights I would awaken with thoughts of her screaming at me.

I tried to continue to project an image of a man who was sad to have lost his wife, but I did sometimes acknowledge that it could be possible that she had left me for another man. Over time, the community seemed to accept the fact those two had left the area together. I didn't feel good about this, in that I had tried to live the good life Mrs. Goshen had implored of me. This one act was exactly what she meant when she'd asked me to leave my old life behind, but I didn't. I tried to justify what I had done by putting the blame on Bertie. Sometimes, that helped.

Mark and my delivery business was getting very busy as the year progressed. Even though some were being closed, roadhouses and taverns were opening on a constant basis and they needed product to sell. Charlie Birger had arranged a deal with the Shelton gang to be the sole supplier of liquor of all types to every establishment in Egypt. Charlie was arranging for more and more police and judges to accept his payoffs, especially in Williamson County. The two gangs also controlled all the gambling and prostitution, as well as the distribution of drugs, mainly morphine. Word among the gangsters close to Charlie was that he was using the morphine himself, and he was losing control of his actions.

One of the establishments we delivered to regularly was a roadhouse east of Marion, along Route 13. One of the bartenders was Cecil Knighton, a friend of Charlie's. One night our delivery to that roadhouse, known as Shady Rest, was interrupted as we arrived. Charlie Birger was leaving Shady Rest to walk across the highway, where there was a whorehouse he owned. As he crossed the street, Cecil Knighton came out of Shady Rest, yelling at Charlie that he was a Jew son-of-a-bitch. Just as Charlie reached the building he began talking to a man standing at the entry door. The man reached back into the room and brought something to Charlie. Cecil saw what was happening and pulled out a pistol. He began shooting toward Charlie, but at about fifty feet the inebriated man was off target. Charlie grabbed the shotgun from the man coming from the building, turned and fired two shots at Cecil. Both rounds hit their target. Cecil fell over backward. He didn't move again.

We stayed in our truck throughout, watching the action. Men scurried about trying to get Cecil to respond. By the amount of blood on the gravel parking lot, it appeared the man had to be dead. Within a few minutes a police car arrived. Charlie handed over the weapon as he sat on the porch. Once the officers had a good explanation of the event from the witnesses, they decided to leave Charlie to his misery after killing his friend.

As the excitement of the event ended, Mark entered Shady Rest and I got the delivery together. When I entered, Mark was getting the details of the first part of the argument. He was being told the two men had gotten into an argument over one of the prostitutes in the room. She had been playing the two men to see which of them would be paying her the most money to go across the street to enjoy her favors. At first it was in good fun, but as the men continued to drink, things began to turn nasty. Cecil showed the pistol in his belt to Charlie, who didn't have any gun on him. As Charlie started for the door, Cecil continued haranguing him, then followed him outside.

They said Cecil Knighton was a young man, someone who liked to think that he had the moxie to make it as a big-time gangster. He dressed better than most bartenders, and he was always careful with the style of his hair; he probably thought he could enhance his reputation by killing Charlie Birger.

At each of the remaining stops that night, we recounted the details of the event to rapt listeners. A killing by Charlie Birger was big news to everyone.

Late in December on a Monday morning, I headed for George's to get a haircut. It was the first time I had been in since Bertie had disappeared so I wasn't sure what George would say. I prepared myself, just in case, but George was most graceful.

"Well, there's one of my best customers," George beamed. "You've been sorely missed, my friend. How are you getting by?"

"All right, sure. I noticed I needed to get a haircut, so I thought my friend George would be just the ticket for these long hairs." I started to feel a little more at ease as I talked.

"Those Klan folk are getting rather rambunctious, aren't they?" George queried.

"How's that, I haven't heard much about them lately."

"Oh, yes, they got a new man to head up the closing of the road-houses and they hit a bunch of them last night. A Mr. Young was brought in by the Klan people over in Marion to work at shutting down the liquor establishments in Williamson County. Several hundred men were deputized over in Carbondale so the people around here wouldn't know about it. They carried a federal search warrant when they went out overnight and arrested several hundred people for running liquor establishments in violation of the Volstead Act. Some of those arrested were saying they were beat on pretty bad by the men doing the arresting. Some even said money was taken from the tills by them as well.

"Everyone was taken to Benton for arraignment, so the judges here wouldn't set them free with a small fine, as usual. I'm surprised you didn't hear anything about it."

"Well, I haven't been working at the Colp Tavern for a few weeks now; I've been trying to get things together again, you know?"

"Oh, sure I do. So, how has it been going for you?"

After the shave and haircut, I headed to the back for some pool and conversation. I decided it was time for me to get back into living normally again, although it was getting to be a bit of a misnomer, since the visions of Bertha at the end kept recurring in my sleep.

Maryanne would be working on Monday if her schedule was still the same, and it was. I sat at my usual table away from most of the activity.

She came over as soon as I sat down.

"So you're still alive, I see. Where've you been?"

"I've been recuperating. Didn't you hear my wife left me?"

"I did hear that, but the way you've been with me lately"—and here she emphasized the "me"—"I didn't think you'd care if she went away. I even wondered if you told her to get out?" Maryanne was having a little fun at my expense. She sat against the back of a nearby chair and crossed her legs. Her skirt was a little shorter tonight, more in fashion with the rising hemlines of the day.

"Could have been you asked her for a divorce so you could marry me, that's what I wondered." She showed a sly smile and winked at me.

"Don't flatter yourself. You're the kind of girl a normal man might leave his wife for, but I'm not normal. Beside, you're about to get married, so you wouldn't be available for me, would you? Or is that marriage still going to take place?" I returned her jaunty attitude in kind.

"Oh, yes, it's still on. Everyone is so happy for me! I just wish I felt the same way."

"Still not excited about it, eh?"

"No, I think he spends too much good time on the road and not enough good time with me. This will be his second week away, selling goods to the stores around Egypt. It'd be good to have a man in the house when the Klan comes to call." With that she got up and went for my beer.

When she returned, I asked what she meant about the Klan.

"I guess you haven't heard about the raids the Klan people are making around here. They have federal warrants, which they are using to break into people's houses. Then they steal their money and other valuables, beat up on the man, and break open any wine barrels they find. They don't arrest him, because the man is so badly beaten, questions would be asked about that.

"They're raiding the taverns all over the county, I'm told, but they're raiding the homes of the Italian families. We're wondering if they'll start raping our young girls next!"

"Sounds like I should call Mark tomorrow before we go out. We may not have any deliveries to make if the liquor houses have been closed. How is Vinny staying open?"

"He got a call from another tavern, telling him what was

happening, so he had time to get most of the liquor hidden before the raiders got here. They broke up what he had showing, which was the cheap stuff he couldn't sell anyway, so he's all right for now."

"What about you, do you need me to comfort you after you get off work?"

"Not tonight—with the Christmas parties and the extra customers, I won't be able to stand up at the end of the evening."

"That's just what I had in mind."

"No thanks, maybe next time."

She left for other customers, so I went to the phone to call Mark.

"Yeah, come on over tomorrow night, we've got work to do, but things are likely to be different from now on."

While I was able to enjoy some quiet over the Christmas week, I was having some trouble sleeping because of the thoughts of the dead. The man in Kentucky wasn't so much of a problem because I couldn't remember that fight well and I wasn't there when he died. The man in the Energy bar bothered me a little, as did Emory. But the big problem was Bertie. Her screams and begging were a fresh memory that I just couldn't deal with without the aid of whiskey. I made up my mind that I would start fresh with the new year—at least that was my goal.

Chapter 41

The action started again the first weekend of January. Raids were conducted by the Klan on the fifth and the seventh. Charlie Birger and the Shelton gang were getting concerned with the decreased income from the taverns and roadhouses and they wanted action taken to stop the raids. The newly elected Williamson County Sheriff George Calligan was sympathetic to their pleas, but since the people performing the raids had federal warrants, he couldn't get involved. The men being arrested were taken to another county, one that would take real action against them. Customers were also becoming more scarce since they didn't want to get caught up in the raids. Even the brothels were losing customers.

To Mark and me, this meant that we were kept busy delivering liquor to the establishments that had been raided and then reopened, sometimes more than once. One night, January 7th, we were going to deliver to a roadhouse north of Carterville, but Mark pulled past the parking lot when he saw a large number of cars sitting around the building. Men were getting out with rifles and pistols in their hands.

"Looks like a raid is starting here. We better keep on going. We'll come back later."

Our next stop was at the Colp Tavern. While we were inside, an obviously excited man entered, calling to Mr. Goodfellow, "You better shut 'er down here. The feds are raiding again, you'll probably be next." With that, he turned and ran out the door.

Mark and I picked up the liquor we were just delivering and ran back to the truck. Lights from the oncoming vehicles could be seen heading north on Division Street as we pulled out of the parking lot. We went slowly north for a bit, then returned south on the same street. Again the cars surrounded the building and men were exiting their cars with weapons in hand. The truck continued south to the roadhouse we had passed earlier. We pulled in and entered the building.

Mark recognized the man behind the bar. "I guess I don't need to ask how it's going, looking at all the broken glass."

"Naw, we got hit a few minutes ago. Mr. Skelcher was taken in, so I'm just cleaning up the place to help out."

"Is there any money in the register to pay for the liquor we got outside?"

"Course not, the men took all the money. They took Jack Skelcher and Carl Shelton in too. You want to bet that money never gets turned in when they get to the courthouse?"

"Course it won't. That's how they're payin' the deputies, I reckon. Well, if you don't have money, we'll just come back tomorrow night."

As we headed back to Herrin, Mark was disgusted. "I'm not going to be able to give you full pay again, Leland. We need to make deliveries to get paid."

"I understand. Well, maybe we'll get more luck tomorrow night."

Mark dropped me off at my house. Going inside, as I turned on the lights, I thought I heard someone in the kitchen. Envisaging Bertie sitting at the table drinking coffee, I started that way, then stopped. *What am I thinking, she isn't here anymore!* A cold chill ran down my back and the hair stood up on my arms. I took a shot of whiskey and went to bed, but I didn't sleep well.

My days of work in the mines were gradually slowing down.

Matthew Lewis noticed my lessening of days worked.

"I don't see much of you in the mine these days, Leland. Ain't you feeling well?"

"No, I feel fine, it's just that I've been working more at night lately, so I don't ask to be given as many days down there. I've been spending more time working with the explosives, trying to make sure I know what I'm doing with the TNT. You know, how much it takes to create the right amount of damage—things like that."

"Yeah, jiminy, that sounds like something you need to be sure of."

I nodded, then went to get more coffee. When I returned, Matthew changed the subject of conversation.

"I seen here in the *Marion Evening Post* about the number of taverns and roadhouses we've got here in Williamson County. Guess you must deliver a lot of the liquor those places sell?"

"Oh, I suppose that's right, don't rightly know for sure."

"The paper says we've got more illegal liquor establishments, on a per capita basis, whatever that is, here in Herrin than they got in Chicago. You think that's true?" Matthew asked.

"Again, Matthew, I don't have any idea. I've never been to Chicago, so I can't even imagine what their situation is, but I can say I don't really care what's happening in Chicago."

"No, I don't either, but I will say I don't like what Herrin is coming to. I see more drunks on the street these days than I ever have. Several of the ladies in our church are in financial difficulties these days because their husbands are spending too much money on liquor. It just makes us sad, you know?"

"Well, I've got to say, no one is twisting their arms to go out and spend their money on liquor. It's a decision they make on their own. I have to wonder if their family situation is what's causing them to go out to drink in the first place."

"We don't know what goes on inside the house of those people, that's true, but for the last few years, they were happy families, as far as I knew." Matthew had a downtrodden look.

"Come on, Matthew, no one knows for sure what happens inside a house when the door closes. I've got a neighbor who seems to be a hardworking, dedicated family man until he goes in the house at night. In the summertime, we can hear the man yelling at his son and then the boy starts screaming, like he's being beaten. One day we saw the boy starting a fire in a trash can near the back of the house after one of those beatings. The mother came out to talk to him, so he put the fire out. I'm just saying things aren't always what they seem from the outside." I tried to justify my delivery work, believing I was actually getting back at the people who wrote laws that didn't work for the general population and those people who protected the rich against the working people.

"Still, our minister at Herrin Christian says if we closed down the liquor establishments, we wouldn't have as many problems here as we do. You think he's right?"

"No, I don't." I didn't like the way this conversation was going, so I tried to change the subject. "Say, the paper there's got an article about a mine explosion. Did you read about it?"

"Sure did. Methane gas was leaking into one of the entries. It got to two naked lights and that caused the explosion. Thirty-two men died down in the mine and fourteen were injured, one of them died later, thirty-three died altogether."

"This is one of the reasons I want to get out of the mines. I always feel it's just a matter of time until my number is called." I shook my head and looked out the window.

"You're right to feel that way. Jiminy, I still have to be careful talking to the wife about these accidents, 'cause she lost her first husband in one of them. I'm pondering taking one of the courses by mail where they teach you how to be an accountant, then I can get an office job."

At the end of January, I went to have coffee with Anthony Garagiola. We caught up on each other's day, then turned to the atmosphere of the community.

"Leland, all the Italians here in Herrin are becoming terrified of these Klan people. They're raiding our homes and beating the families with their pistols. They're even taking any money they can find in the homes and destroying any wine or other liquor. Who do these people think they are?"

"From what I'm hearing, they are all of the people who run Williamson County and many of the judges and police officers. So, they have the full backing of the authorities around here. They've hired this Glenn Young as their main enforcer. He's the one who's calling for the raids that you just mentioned. It's most of the local Protestant ministers all over the county who are organizing the people over in Marion—the ones that run the County Board, the Law Enforcement League, ones like that, and they're all members of the Klan. Tony, I know you and the other Italians are getting tormented by the Klan and I feel sorry for you, but you just need to bear down for now."

"Well, enough about my problems. Tell me how you're doing without Bertha. Do you miss her? Have you heard any more from her?"

"Of course I miss her. I wake up each morning thinking about her, but there's nothing I can do about it, is there? I just go on with my work each day."

"Have you taken any time to think about your loss? She meant a lot to you and her leaving must make you sad, right?"

"Well sure, like I said, I miss her company. We spent lots of time together doing things, so I miss that."

"It seems to me, if your wife leaves you, even if it's with another man, you have a loss in your life, similar to losing her if she were to die. Of course, she didn't, but it's still a loss to you, someone gone that you loved. So you should make an effort to grieve over her, even if you don't like the way she left. You see what I mean?"

"Tony, I appreciate your concern, but I'm all right. I've gotten over her and moved on with my life."

"I'm just concerned about my friend, Leland. I want to be sure you're doing good and not holding back your feelings." Anthony patted my arm.

"Then you should relax. I'm doing just fine. Now, should we have a piece of pie with this coffee?"

Chapter 42

Mark had a gleam in his eye as I got in the truck. "You made mention several times now that you're interested in getting back at the officials that are ruining our state, isn't that right?"

"Sure am. Those bastards need to understand they represent the majority of us, not just the people with money!"

"So would you be interested in hurting a big banker? Would that be the kind of trouble you want to make for them?"

"I guess so. What do you have in mind?"

"See, earlier this week I was up in East St. Louis, like I told you. Carl, Carl Shelton, told me about a friend of his who robs banks for him. They usually walk in through the front door with guns shown and tell the people to give them the money, but then the people see them and call the police right away. It's too dangerous, doing it that way. So, now they want to go to the bank at night and blow the door off the safe to get to the money, valuables, notes, whatever. They just need a person who can blow the door off—is that something you can do for them?"

"Hell yes, that sounds about like blowing a hole in a mine wall to get to the coal. I haven't blown a door off a safe, though."

"Course not, most nobody has, but you think you can do it, don't you? Can you get a little dynamite out of the mine to use?"

"Yeah, well, not dynamite, but that wouldn't be a problem. When are they talking about doing this?"

"Carl said they're waiting to hear when the particular bank has a lot of money in the safe, then they'll go after it. Probably next Thursday, just before payday. I'll call Carl and tell him you'll do it, then?"

The next Thursday afternoon I was headed to East St. Louis. In my bag were a change of dark clothes, several sticks of dynamite, some blasting caps, a can of nitroglycerin, some fuse lead, and my pistol, a .38 snub-nose. When I arrived at the nightclub, I went in to meet Carl Shelton and Arturo Visconi, the man organizing the bank robbery.

I approached the table as the two men stood. They were both dressed in suits and ties; they each looked like any other business-man out for "an evening on the town" might look. I had tried to dress nicely, wearing a white, long-sleeved shirt and slacks; I had no idea these men would be dressed so nicely.

"Leland, meet Art Visconi. Art, this here is Leland Vance. Leland works in the coal mines in Southern Illinois, he sets off the dynamite charges that blow up the coal—ain't that right, Leland?"

After the greeting, we sat at the table, which was off in a corner of the restaurant.

"That's right, I've been doing that for about a year now. I think I'm pretty good at it, too."

Art asked me, "Is blowing up rocks or coal anything like blowing open the door of a safe, I have to ask?"

"Well, the door of a safe will be a little different; we'll use nitro-glycerin for that, I have some with me."

"Sure, but now, do you know how to use it or not, I'm asking you?"

"Yes, we use it in the mines for little jobs, setting off bigger ex-plosives, mostly. I have the blasting caps I can use to set off the nitroglycerin—no problem for me."

Arturo smiled with satisfaction. "Now, that's just what I wanted to hear. We plan to go on the job tonight. After we eat, we're goin' over to the Arlington Hotel to go over the plan. Leland, you can get a room there at the hotel if you want one, but we won't be back there until about four in the morning. You'll get your five thousand dollars then, if we're successful at the bank. If not, we all go home empty handed, but that ain't gonna happen!"

Carl stood to wave at two men who had just entered the room. At least they weren't dressed as nicely as I was, and they looked shabbier in general—longer hair and needing a shave.

"Leland, this is Art's brother Pete and this is Gerry Kennedy. They'll be working this job with you."

"Where you from?" Pete asked.

"Herrin, down south."

"Goddamn, you're from Herrin! I've heard about that place. Did you get in on the killing of those scabs a couple of years ago?" Pete couldn't hide his excitement.

"No, I didn't. I've done several killings, but not that one there. It was a real massacre, though. Some of the men I worked with were in on the killings."

I noticed from his look that Art could see his two helpers were getting a little too excited. "Now look, we won't be doing no killin' tonight. We want to get into the bank, blow off the door and take everything we can, and get out. We need to be far away before anyone knows what we did, understand?"

The three of us nodded our heads. Carl smiled; he was glad we understood. He waved the waitress over and we got quiet until she had taken our orders and left.

Carl asked me, "Tell us about that damn massacre. We all read about it in the newspapers, but they didn't go into a lot of detail. Were you at the mine that day?"

I entertained the men for most of the meal with my descriptions of the event. I could see they were anxious to hear about the killings, so I added many details about all the blood and gore. The others, except Carl, were loving my story. It was nearing ten o'clock as I wound it up.

"Now tell me about Charlie Birger. What do you know about him?" Carl looked directly at me without any emotion in his voice.

"Well, I've been around his joints in Williamson County, but I don't have direct contact with the man. I work with Mark Wallops. He does all the talking with Charlie, or with the men around him, so I don't have to have any contact with him."

"Sure, but what do you hear about him? They say he dresses like a cowboy at times—you ever seen him do that?"

"No, like I said, I don't see him much at all, but I've heard people say he likes to dress like Tom Mix, in the moving picture shows."

"Is he using drugs, have you heard?"

I was getting weary that Carl was pumping me a little too much for information, but I did try to help out since I would be wanting to get into more of these bank jobs, if I could.

"Damn Carl, I'd really like to help you out here, I just don't have no information on the man that you haven't already heard. I'm thinking you know the man better'n I do."

"Oh, that's all right, just keep your ear to the ground, down there. We know he's been stealing money from us and we want to know how he's doing it. If you hear anything I should know about that bastard, give me a call, will you?"

"Sure will," I promised.

With the meal over, the four of us bank robbers left for the hotel. We sat at a table in Art's room as he went over the plans for the robbery.

"Gerry, you'll be the one driving, so you stay outside in the car. We'll be going up to Glen Carbon to the state bank there. A delivery was made there today for the miners payroll that will be given out tomorrow. Our person at the bank said there was also a delivery of some government notes that we can get, too. We'll take in three big bags to put everything in, then carry them to the car. I want us to be in the bank and out in about fifteen minutes, so everybody needs to get their jobs done quickly."

"Just like the Nash gang, right, Art?" Pete was talking about the Nash gang from Texas that was holding up many banks. He had read about them in the newspapers; I had too.

"Just like them, that's right. Now Leland, about the nitro. How long will it take you to rig it up?"

"I need about five minutes at the most. What about the noise of the explosion? Won't people hear it in the area?"

"That's one of the reasons we picked this job—the bank's in the center of town and there ain't nobody around at that time of night 'cept drunks and whores, and they ain't goin' to be calling the police, that's for sure."

"That sounds keen, looks like you've thought of everything. Say, I need to go get the stuff outta my car, I'll be right back."

I went to my car to get my bag. When I came back we all changed into dark clothes for the job. Then we took a break, slouching back in our chairs, resting.

"Now Leland, like I told the others, when the safe is opened, I'll grab the money and put it in your bag. When I tell you, take the bag to the car and stay there. Pete and I will finish getting the rest of the stuff in the safe and we'll bring it to the car right away. Gerry has the maps of the streets we'll take on the way back here, just in case the police are tipped about the job. After we get back, you'll get your part of the money and you can scram back to Herrin. Just don't make any mistakes going back there, we don't want you getting stopped by the police along the way. Got it?"

"Sure, it sounds like you've got this planned out to a 'T,' just the way I like it. Don't worry about me, I know how to drive without attracting any stray eyes."

We lounged in the room for another hour, then headed for Glen Carbon. Gerry parked in the alley behind the bank and waited while the others of us went to the front of the bank. Art broke a window in the front door and let us inside. He had been in the bank the week earlier, so he knew where the safe was located: in the back right corner of the main room.

I opened the can of nitroglycerin and plied a strip of it along the edge of the safe's door. Next, I attached the blasting cap and fuse. I waved the other men over behind the tellers' counter to get them out of the way of the blast. After lighting the fuse I rushed over with them. The blast was loud—so loud it hurt our ears—but we quickly recovered and went to the safe. The door had been set cleanly on the floor next to the safe.

"Damn, that was nice!" Pete exclaimed.

"Come on, let's get going!" Art pulled back the door and started putting the money in the first bag. After it was filled, I grabbed the straps and lugged it to the car.

"Goddamn, that was a loud blast in there!" Gerry exclaimed as he helped me get the bag in the trunk of the Studebaker. "It's a good thing there aren't people living around here, or they would have been shaken up too."

Within a few minutes Art and Pete came to the car with their bags, then loaded them in the trunk with the first one. We all got into the car and took off for the Arlington Hotel. Pete followed the map, driving under the speed limit to avoid attention. An hour later we got to our destination. The full bags were heavy and we were tired, so it took two men to carry each one up to Art's room. We emptied the bags on the floor.

Art surveyed the treasure. "There's several hundred thousand here, if we can get the bonds cashed!"

He dug out my five thousand dollars and handed it to me, then gave me another five thousand. "Here's a tip for your work—you did good, real good!" We shook hands and I left for Herrin.

The ride back was uneventful. On entering my house, I went to the bedroom to put the money in a valise in my wardrobe where I was collecting all my extra money—my escape money, should it be needed. Next, I had a few shots of whiskey, then went to bed. After getting some sleep, I went shopping for some new clothes, including a fedora hat like the one Carl Shelton wore. I wanted to look like the successful businessman I thought I was. But, I told myself, I still wasn't one of the moneyed people I had come to hate.

Chapter 43

At my next occasion with Mark we discussed my trip to Glen Carbon.

Mark told me, "I read in the St. Louis newspaper that most of the banks are changing out their safes to ones that can't be opened the way you did the other night. They see how the Nash gang is getting at their money too easy and they intend to stop it."

"Art called me last night. He says he knows of a bank in Belleville that has an old-style safe. He wants us to plan on hitting it this Thursday. My problem is getting enough time in at Number 12 so I can keep that work. These long days with little sleep are plumb wearing me out."

"Yeah, I suppose you're doing all the work around the house these days too, now that Bertha has gone."

"Well good riddance to her, I say. Yeah, I do have to do all the chores around the house too. I don't do a very good job of it, but it'll get by. Still, I've been needing a few shots of whiskey to get to sleep nights."

Mark gave me a searching look. "You said a few weeks back that you'd tell me later the rest of the story of her going away. Is this a good time?"

"No, I've still got to get it straight in my head, then we'll talk." I somehow felt that if no one else knew she was dead, it was like it really didn't happen; then I could seal it off in the back of my mind until I just forgot about it.

We had arrived at the Energy Roadhouse for a delivery. As Mark went inside, I went to the back of the truck. An inebriated man approached me. "Look, mister, I need a drink but they threw me outta there. Can you give a friend a little drink?" The man was wavering and his eyes were completely out of focus.

I got a little loud: "I can give you a strong rap to your head if you don't get away from here!"

"No, please, just a little."

I pulled my gun from my pants as I grabbed the man's collar. I brought the butt of the gun's handle hard against the man's head, drawing blood and sending the man sprawling backward and to the ground. He was out cold. I felt like kicking him a time or two, but that passed quickly, so I calmly put my gun back in my pants and proceeded to take the delivery inside. When we came back out, Mark noticed the man lying on the ground.

"What happened to that guy, I wonder. He must have passed out in a drunken stupor."

"It looks that way, doesn't it."

We both got in the truck and departed.

Caleb was at the Union Hall. He was reading the latest issue of *Illinois Miner*.

"I seen here where some miners think the Klan has done some real good for Williamson County. They think the cleanup campaign is really helping. Then, another says the Klan is just as bad as the men serving the drinks. You know, Leland, the president of the Herrin Law and Order League asked the Department of Justice to investigate the county officials' complicity with bootleggers. I read that in the *Herrin Semi-Weekly Herald*. What ya think about all this?"

"Caleb, I don't see there is a right or wrong around here anymore.

With the mine owners being able to kill our brothers and then not be brought to trial, while our brothers are tried for murdering the mine owners' men that caused the problems, well, that isn't right. Next, the Klan do-gooders raid the taverns and steal the liquor, then take the stuff up north to sell to taverns there, and they steal the money in the taverns and don't get arrested for it. And, they beat up on families when they raid individuals' homes. Well, this world has just gone crazy, as I see it."

"But, Leland, what about the local officials here in Herrin, like the leaders of the Herrin Law and Order League. Or the County Board of Supervisors in Marion, that asked the state in Springfield to help in upholding prohibition. Doesn't that count as a good thing if they're for it?"

"Caleb, those men are all in the Klan, they run the Klan here in Williamson County. You just go to one of the cross-burning events they hold and you'll see those men wearing their white hoods and trying to get other men to join them. Then, they tell those men to go steal liquor and take it away from here to sell other places. Or, they rob the tavern owners, or, well, I'll just stop there."

Caleb continued reading the paper as I talked. "I see the leader of the raiders, Glenn Young, was shot up over in Okawville last night. He and his wife was taken to the Belleville Hospital. They both are expected to live, it says here. Ain't that a good thing, Leland?"

"I sure enough think it is. Would have been better if they killed him, though. Does it say who did the shooting?"

"No, just says a car passed up their car and shot it up as it went by. You got any idea who might-a done it?"

"Don't know for sure, but both the Sheltons and Charlie Birger would want Young dead. Could have been one of those gangs."

Most everyone at Vinny's was excitedly talking about Glenn Young being shot. Many of the raids on Italian families had been led by Young himself. He was also the one who did most of the trouble inside their houses. No, no one was sad he was in a hospital tonight.

Maryanne asked me if I wanted a beer.

"No, I think I'll be drinking whiskey tonight. We need to celebrate the shooting last night. And make it a double, will you?"

"Sure, I can get you anything you want. I'd like to know, though, what happened that you only drink whiskey these days. Used to be, you only drank beer."

"Well, I guess that's for me to know and you to find out!" I gave her a wink and nodded.

The room was crowded, but most of the men were standing around the bar, talking about their experiences with, or things they had heard about, Glenn Young, so Maryanne had time to spend at my table. When she brought my second whiskey, she sat near me to talk.

"You know, Maryanne, I have that big house I'm living in all by myself. I was wondering if you would want to come over to spend some time with me?"

"Oh sure, just traipse on over there with everyone watching and forget about the marriage I'm going to be doing! You crazy, or what?"

"How about this. You come over after you get off work. You tell everyone you're going to spend the night with a friend—someone they don't know, say. Then, you can go back early in the morning with a good story they'll all believe."

"No, I ain't spending the night with you, it'd be too risky. Not that I don't think Vito's having a good time on the road with other women, but he's a man—he can get away with that. So, if he can, I guess I can too. What's the American saying? 'What's good for the goose is good for the gander!' I might just as well have some good times myself. But, no, I'm not spending the night with you."

"Well now, I'm thinking we could still make something work. What will you be doing tomorrow during the day? I'll be off work, so I can stay home. Maybe you could get over my way for a while without being missed? I thought we had a real good time that night in your dance studio—why don't we try again?"

Maryanne was quiet for a few moments, then she smiled. "Maybe I could get over there around 9:00? I got a doctor's appointment in Carbondale at 1:00 and I'll just say I'm going over there a little early to do some shopping. Yeah, that could work."

"That's my girl! We can spend a couple of bliss-filled hours together. That sounds great to me. We can get to know each other real good in that amount of time."

"Leland, why do you stay in that big house all by yourself, anyway? Wouldn't it be cheaper for you to move into an apartment?"

"I just feel safer in the house. The neighbors watch who comes and goes on the street, so no one will want to try to break in so much as they might if I was in an apartment, see?"

"Oh, you got lots of money you're hiding in there, have you? I don't think you make that much delivering alcohol, and the mines sure don't pay you lots either. What else do you have to do that makes you money?"

"Like I said, that's for me to know and you to find out!" I gave out a small chuckle. "Will you bring me another drink, my glass seems to be empty."

"I'll bring you one more, then you better go home. You don't want a hangover tomorrow morning, it might slow you down in bed." Maryanne winked at me, then turned to walk toward the bar shaking her rear to entice me.

I took her advice. In the morning Maryanne arrived at my house about 9:20. I had cleaned myself and drank lots of coffee so my performance wouldn't disappoint her, and I didn't. Afterward, Maryanne went to the bathroom.

When she came back, she admonished me. "Leland, sweetie, you got to do a better job of keeping this place clean! That bathroom stinks like you can't hit the toilet when you piss in there."

"Yeah, well, I do have a problem when I've been drinking and it's dark, I know, I know."

"Well, the sinks are filthy too. Do you ever clean the house? You know, it's just not healthy to live like this." She shook her head and came over to the bed to give me a good-bye kiss. She was in a good mood when she left for Carbondale.

On Thursday I arrived at the Two Brothers Restaurant in Belleville. We had a meal at 9:00 in a private room Arturo had reserved. We discussed the work just as we had with the Glen Carbon job previously. Art had included the details, maps, and assignments for each of the people. His main concern was that the bank was in a more populated area of the city and just a few blocks from the police station. Carl hadn't been able to bribe the officers in this city, he told the group.

"So we have to be sure we get everything right, understand?"

Everyone nodded in agreement. I was confident we would be just as successful here as we were in Glen Carbon and I would be taking home five thousand dollars in just a little while.

Just after 1:00, we went to the Studebaker for the short trip to the bank, which was located in the business district. It was at the corner of Washington and Church streets. Just a few doors away was a tavern that had closed, but some men were standing in front of it talking. Art approached them and pulled out his gun as he walked. The men saw he meant business, so they began walking in the other direction. Art walked slowly back to the bank to give them time to leave the area, then he put his gun through the window of the front door.

Once inside, we headed for the safe in the back of the main room. As we reached it, we saw that it was a new one, one which we couldn't blow the door off.

"Goddamn it!" Art shouted. "Look at the back of it, Leland; can you blow it open some other way?"

I looked it over. The outside of the safe was one unit except for the door, and that was of a more secure design.

"I can put dynamite under it and set it off, but it'll just raise the entire safe in the air without blowing it open. That won't do us any good, so, no, I can't see how it can be opened."

Art was downtrodden. "Let's just look through the teller positions. See if you can find any of them with money laying there. I don't think there will be, but I hate to think we won't even get gas money tonight."

But we didn't find anything. The crew had to admit defeat on this job. I was disappointed that I had spent the time and money for no return. Art assured us he would find a safe he could get into in the next few weeks. Back at the restaurant we glumly took to our individual cars and I departed for Herrin. On my arrival at my house, I needed several shots of whiskey to soothe my nerves. It had been a long, unsuccessful trip, and the dead had been with me most nights recently.

Chapter 44

I had a plan. I needed to take a woman with me to Maryanne's wedding; after all, Maryanne would have her husband with her, so I needed to have a woman with me, preferably one that was very nice looking. I set out toward Shady Rest the next Saturday evening. It was the place where Mark and I had seen Charlie kill Cecil Knighton. When I entered the roadhouse we had seen Cecil leave, chasing Charlie, I was hoping Charlene would be working there: she would make the perfect woman on my arm at the wedding.

It was around 9:00 when I arrived at the roadhouse on the north side of the road. The place was crowded and noisy. A band played in the back and the slots were all being used on the right side of the room. I sat at the bar and ordered a whiskey. One of the young girls came up to sit next to me; she smiled coyly and said hello.

"You sure are a pretty young thing, but tonight I'm looking for Charlene—you know if she's here?"

"I do know, but are you going to buy me a drink so I'll tell you?"

"I can do that. Tell the man back there what you want and I'll pay. Now where's Charlene?"

She waited until I had paid, then she said, "Wait here, I'll go get her."

In a few minutes Charlene came over.

"Well, look who's here. I thought you had forgotten about me!"

She hugged my arm and smiled. She smelled of strong perfume, but she didn't appear to have been drinking much. Of course, she still displayed lots of her breasts.

"I couldn't forget a girl as pretty as you are. I've just been too busy working to get by here earlier. Won't you let me buy you a drink?"

"You sure can, I'd like that." She sat next to me after she moved her chair as close to mine as it would go. Her blonde hair was still curly and she still wore red nail polish and lipstick.

"So, tell me how you're doing here in Harrisburg, or wherever we are. You doing all right?"

"Sure am. These miners got lots of money, just like you said, and they love to spend it on little ole me." She put her hand on my thigh and rubbed it gently.

"You ever get to go back to East St. Louis to see Minnie?"

"No, I ain't never been back since I got here. You remember Mable? Well, she got beat up pretty bad by one of the gamblers one night last month. She went back home to get better. I don't think she'll be back here again."

"That's a shame, pretty-looking girl like her. Was she making good money too? She probably needed it to pay her doctor bills?"

"Oh, no. Charlie paid for everything. He even had one of his men drive her up there. He said he got the money from the gambler, then sent him on his way. Told him not to come back here, ever. He was real nice."

"Charlene, there's another reason I came to see you. First, let me ask: do you ever have a weekend when you get the day off?"

"Sure do. I can have any day off I want. Charlie says I can even take several days off if I want to go back home. Why?"

"I need a special favor. A friend of mine is getting married and I need to take a girl to the wedding. I was thinking you would be perfect for the occasion. We'll go to Herrin for the day, have a great time at the wedding and reception, then spend the night there. It's going to be an Italian wedding, so everyone has lots of fun at those. What do you think?"

"Wait, you told me you were married. What about your wife?"

"Oh, no, she isn't around anymore, that won't be a problem. The woman I'm thinking about is the bride. She's the one I'm trying to impress with you on my arm!"

"Now this is sounding screwy, but I like it. Sure, you can count on me!"

One of the other women working the room came over to Charlene and whispered to her. Charlene turned to me. "What you plannin' for tonight, we going across the street later, or what? One of my other customers wants me to join him, but I'd like to stay with you." Charlene gave my thigh an extra rub as she gave me her best smile.

"I'd like that too, since I drove all the way from Herrin just to see you."

Charlene turned to tell the other woman, but she was already headed back to the gentleman who made the inquiry. I watched the woman walk across the room to a table further in the back. She leaned over to tell him, then sat down at the table with him. Charlene was watching also.

"Oh, that's ole Howie who asked. He'll wait for me—well, that is if I get back at all. I'm thinkin' we might make a night of it, since I told you I wouldn't charge you for the first one." Her voice was dripping with honey.

I looked in her eyes as often as I could, but I kept thinking this Howie guy looked a little familiar, I just couldn't see his full face the way he was sitting.

Charlene noticed that I had become distracted. "Hey I'm still here—why ain't you looking at me, anyway?"

"Oh, I'm sorry, but that man who asked about you looks a little familiar. Howie, you said his name is?"

"Yeah, he comes in here every week or two and asks for me, mostly. He pays real good and doesn't treat me bad, so I like him."

"Did he say where he's from?"

"No, most people don't like to talk about that stuff. He told me once he was a traveling salesman, sells religious stuff, I think. Which is kinda funny, him selling religious stuff, then coming in here to be with me. He don't ask me to do nothing odd, you know. Says he wants me to do stuff he couldn't ask his wife to do, 'cause she's real religious."

Then I knew who the man was: my neighbor, Howard Renn!

"That's it!" I exclaimed as I slapped the bar. "That man is my neighbor in Herrin. I knew he looked familiar."

"Leland, please don't say anything to him, I don't want him to be embarrassed and not come in here anymore. He's one of my best customers!"

"No, I won't talk to him tonight. It's just that when he talks to me at home, he's so religious acting, asking me to go to church with him and like that. Then, the wife he's worried about offending, she has their other neighbor, a good friend of his, come to her bed during the nights when he's over here with you. What a crazy world!"

"It is, and we see the worst side of it in a place like this. Men show their true self in here, that's for sure."

I considered the best way for me to use this new information, or if I was going to use it at all. Then I again thought about how really confusing this world had become. I decided to just order us another drink before taking Charlene to bed.

A little later we drove to a hotel in Harrisburg where we spent the night. At breakfast we set down the plan for the wedding.

Chapter 45

Arturo's plan was to have the three men from East St. Louis come to Herrin, then travel as a group to Harrisburg, and from there go over to Equality, Illinois, in Gallatin County. He had scouted out a bank there and was assured it had an old-style safe. He was told it would contain an extra sum of money on that night, so we would be helping ourselves to it.

When we met up in Herrin, Art told me that Gerry wouldn't be able to join us on this trip so he would give me the job of driving and would give me a larger cut in the proceeds, which was good news to me! At our dinner in Harrisburg, Art again covered the details of the job. Each man got his assignment. He encouraged me to use the least possible amount of nitro because the bank was located nearer to the populated area—Equality was a small town.

Darkness was just setting in when we arrived at Equality. Slowly driving around the town, we located the bank and the police station. We went to one of Charlie Birger's roadhouses outside of town on Route 13 to kill some time. At 1:30 the three of us paid our bill and left the tavern. Arriving at the bank, we couldn't see anyone around the area. Even the police station was dark.

I parked the Studebaker at the front of the bank and we went in through the front door, as usual. Again, the safe was at the rear of the main room and it did have the old-style door. I worked quickly to rig the nitro and cap. In less than five minutes I was setting off the charge. It worked. The explosion was loud, but not as loud as the one at the first bank in Glen Carbon.

When the first bag was filled, I took it to the car, throwing it in the trunk. As I turned away from the car, I heard men's voices, so I ran back inside.

"Art, men are coming this way. We better hurry and get out of here!" I said in a loud whisper.

"We're going as fast as we can. Here, you take out this bag and we'll be right there."

I took the bag and threw it in the trunk, then closed it quietly. I stepped on the starter and got the car ready to go.

As the other two came out of the bank, a car with three men in it pulled up across the street. I could see police uniforms on the men as they stopped their car. Art and Pete jumped inside and I gunned the engine. The Studebaker shot forward just as the policemen realized what was happening.

They drew their pistols, then turned to get back into their car to follow the Studebaker. I was driving as fast as I could! Corners were navigated on two wheels, but the police knew the town too well. They arrived at an intersection from the south just as we arrived from the east. Shots came from the police car as we passed. Several bullets hit the car with a tinkling sound. Art and Pete were firing back. I kept the car going as fast as it would go. The Studebaker was too fast for the police car, so we outran it quickly.

"Is anyone hit?" Art asked.

"I'm fine!" I yelled as I kept the car going fast and watched in the rearview mirror for the police car.

"I've been hit!" Pete groaned from the back seat. "It went through my stomach, I think. I'm bleeding pretty bad."

"Leland, look for a side road up ahead. Looks like we outran the police back there. We need to find a place to look at Pete!"

After a few minutes, we approached a side road that looked safe. I turned north on it and quickly entered a wooded area. Pete was groaning in the back. The road wound through the trees, then into a clearing. Ahead was a deserted farmhouse, so I pulled up to it. We carried Pete to the front porch and laid him on it.

"I'm getting cold," Pete moaned. His breathing was getting slower.

I sat back against the side of the house as Art tried to stop the bleeding. After a few minutes, Pete let out a slow groan and stopped breathing altogether. Art began sobbing as he lowered his head on Pete's chest. He was mumbling to Pete's body, hitting the wooden porch floor. As Art's sobbing began to subside, I put my hand on his shoulder.

"There's nothing more you can do for him now. You did all you could."

Art shook his head. "I always knew this could happen to one of us, maybe both of us. I wish it had been me instead of him, that's all."

"Of course you do. But look, you did all you could for him. Now we have to try to figure out what we do next. The police are still looking for us, so we need to get back to our next move—can you do that?"

"Yeah, I know there's nothing more I can do for Pete. Can we get him in the car?"

"Sure, we can do that. But, let's think about what that will do for us. Where are we taking him? To your house? To a morgue?"

Art was quiet for several minutes. I knew we should respect the dead, that they needed a proper end to their lives, but that was when I believed everyone tried to be respectful of each other. Over the last year that concept had changed in my mind—now I needed to survive in a cruel world, one that gives the most to the people who fight for it.

I could see Art was thinking about the next step, so I waited.

"There really isn't anyplace I can take him, is there?" Art said pathetically. He seemed to think some more.

"It will only cause problems for me to take him anyplace else." Art was forlorn. He wanted to do the right thing for his brother, to get him a proper burial, but he knew that couldn't happen any longer. "I just don't know what to do, Leland—you have any ideas?"

"Other than burial, some people are cremated; you know about that, I'm sure. At this time, we only have his body—any other part of him is already gone, I guess. So, would you be able to have him cremated? We could do that, couldn't we. Would you be able to know that your brother was cremated when he died?"

"I guess that would be all right. People are cremated all the time. That way I wouldn't have to explain how he got shot up, would I?"

"That's the best part: no explanations needed. You just tell the folks back home he died and you had him cremated. You can even take some ashes back to show them. And, no one will be able to identify his body, so it can't be traced back to you."

"Yeah, sounds good, but I don't know how to cremate a body, do you?"

"I do. We just need a hot fire, like the ones we used to build for the stills when we made moonshine. We have gas in the car we can use to get a good fire going around his body. You can just go over into the woods and sit a spell, I'll take care of the rest—can you do that?"

"Damn, Leland, would you? I don't think I can handle any more right now." Art got up and slouched over to the wooded area.

After he was out of sight, I pulled the body into the farmhouse. I went to the back side of the house and collected handfuls of limbs and leaves several times. A small pyre was laid out inside the house and then I placed the body on it. Next, I took Pete's shirt and pulled off a sleeve. I went to the car and fed the sleeve down into the gas tank to soak up some gasoline, which I took back into the house before squeezing out the gas over the body. Several trips to the car provided enough gas to cover the wood under his body and some more around the walls of the farmhouse. A single match started the fire.

Going outside, I called out for Art. A few seconds later, Art came out of the woods. We got into the car and started off.

"Thanks for doing this," Art said sadly. "I couldn't have handled it without you, that's for sure."

We drove silently for a while. Knowing the police would be looking for us on the main roads, we circled north at the next main crossroad, then headed west.

Art sat upright and looked out the back window. "What about his ashes for my mother?" he asked. "We didn't get any back there."

I was ready. "Art, can you tell the difference, just by looking, between the ashes of a body and the ashes of a tree?"

"No, I guess I couldn't."

"Well, we'll get your ashes for you back in Herrin. You'll just tell your mother the ashes you have are the ones you got at the place you had him cremated, she'll never know the difference."

Art was quiet for the remainder of the trip back to Herrin.

It was getting light as we entered the city. I drove the Studebaker with bullet holes in it to Mark Wallops' house.

"Mark, can we put this car in your garage for a few days? We need to keep it hidden until the heat is off over the bank robbery we pulled last night."

"Sure, I'll pull the truck out and you drive it in."

After the change, Mark drove the two of us and the money to my place. The three of us carried the money bags into my house and Mark left.

"Leland, it was goddamned nice of you to handle Pete like you did. I'm going to give you half of the take for that. Let's count it out."

The total was just under twenty thousand dollars—not nearly as much as the Glen Carbon job! I was disappointed in the amount, but happy I was getting half. This was the most money I had ever had, much more than I ever imagined I would be able to have. The unfortunate part was the greater amount of whiskey it took to help me sleep when Pete's new demons joined Bertha's and the others.

I read the newspapers the next day. There was one small article about a fire in a remote farmhouse outside Equality; nothing was included about a body being in the ashes.

Over the next two days Art spent most of his time at Mark's garage working on covering the bullet holes enough to get the car back to East St. Louis. In the evening of the second day he left on the trip back. Art stated this would be his last trip—he thought he needed to find another line of work.

Chapter 46

June 28th was set as the date for the wedding of Maryanne Garagiola and Vituro Alphansi at the Roman Catholic Church; Reverend Emirgildo Senese would be officiating. The Rome Club, where the reception was being held, had been decorated in grand style. Maryanne was the darling of the Italian community throughout Egypt, and Anthony said he expected the attendance would be large. Many non-Italians had also responded as attending; most knew her from Vinny's.

Saturday started out as a beautiful day; rain the previous week had washed the area and prompted more blooms from the flowers in many yards. I headed for Shady Rest early—I wanted to be sure I could get back with Charlene in plenty of time. I picked her up at the whorehouse across from the bar where we had met earlier. She was wearing a stunning dress she had purchased with some money I had given her. It had a short hemline and the shoulderless top dropped fully between her breasts. It was dark green with colorful designs covering it. The green dress highlighted her verdant eyes perfectly! I knew she would be talked about as much at the wedding as the bride would be—exactly what I wanted.

On the way back we chatted about our expectations for the afternoon: who I expected would be there, how to talk with certain individuals, and especially, how she should perform in front of Maryanne.

If she fawned on me sufficiently, I anticipated that Maryanne might become jealous, which was my intent. She wouldn't be able to show it in front of her husband, but I would be able to feel her emotion and that's all I needed.

Father Senese did an extraordinary performance at the ceremony; he knew he needed to impress his flock with his wedding officiating skills. The father of the bride would surely show his appreciation monetarily and, who knows, perhaps some other brides would be inspired to have him perform for their weddings in the future. I decided this was just another way men manipulated others to receive benefits for themselves.

When we arrived at the Rome Club, the place was already packed with people. A band was playing, people were dancing on the crowded dance floor, there were long lines at the three bars set up around the room, and everyone seemed to be talking at the same time, so the noise level was very high. After a while, the bride and groom appeared and moved to the position assigned for their receiving of guests. I had anticipated where the spot would be so Charlene and I were one of the early couples to greet the happy newlyweds.

First we came to Anthony and his wife. When I introduced Charlene as my date, Tony's eyes looked her over enviously as he talked about how happy he was to meet her. His wife had to nudge him at one point. Tony congratulated me on my obvious interest in getting back to life, referring to his earlier concern over my mental state. Charlene smiled and squeezed my arm, intimating "There's nothing wrong with Leland's health that I can find." She winked at me, then giggled openly.

Next, we moved in front of Maryanne. I introduced Charlene as my date, someone I had been seeing lately. Charlene gazed at me and said suggestively, "Yeah, we've been seeing a lot of each other lately!" Then she kissed my neck without paying attention to Maryanne. I pretended to struggle to get my gaze back to Maryanne.

Maryanne introduced her new husband to me without looking at Charlene. "Leland, this is my husband, Vituro Alphansi. Vito, this is Leland Vance, an old family friend." I could see that she ignored Charlene for the introduction, so I did it, smiling broadly since I realized I had gotten to Maryanne just as I intended.

I found a seat for Charlene, then went for whiskeys for the two of us. A little later the newlyweds had their first dance, then others began to dance with each of them. Whenever Maryanne appeared to be turned in our direction, Charlene played her role of the affectionate girlfriend, at which Maryanne would then be sure to look in another direction. So I would whisper in Charlene's ear, telling her to laugh, which she did—that contagious laugh of hers that I really did enjoy. The laugh was also catching the attention of other people around us and they had to smile along with me. I was enjoying myself immensely. Finally, I had a chance to ask Maryanne for a dance.

"You look great, darling. The married life must be treating you well!"

"You bastard, what are you thinking bringing that harlot to my wedding? More people are talking about her than they are about me!"

"Why, whatever do you mean? I just wanted to have a date for your festive event—what's wrong with that?"

"And where did you find her, some whorehouse over in Harrisburg?"

"She's just a friend of a friend. Can't I take someone on a date? After all, my wife's been gone for over a year now. Isn't that long enough for me to be the grieving, abandoned husband." I feigned a sorrowful look. "I'm well aware that you're not going to be sleeping alone tonight, so why should I?"

Maryanne put her mouth close to my ear and said in a low register, "Now you look here, I know she's a prostitute and those girls carry diseases, which you'll probably get too, so I'm never going to have sex with you again." She pushed me back as she turned and walked away, leaving me standing on the floor alone. I laughed to myself as I walked back to Charlene.

"Well, this has worked out better than I could have expected. She's really pissed at me."

"I guess that's what every girl wants—to get another girl pissed at the man they're both interested in. I'm glad you asked me to help you out, this is fun!" Charlene giggled as she squeezed my hand.

"It has been fun! Now let's go over to the Ly-Mar Hotel for a nap. We've got dinner reservations at the restaurant at the Continental Hotel, then we're going to the Hippodrome for a vaudeville show. After that, back to the Ly-Mar Hotel for the night. Are you ready?"

During the vaudeville show Charlene was enraptured with the fancy costumes worn by the girls on the stage. She had several comments regarding their poise and dancing skills. "I'd like to be on the stage like that one day!"

At an intermission, I went to the bar for two whiskeys. Returning to Charlene I offered her one of them, which she turned down. After I finished mine, I started on the one I had brought for her. "You sure drink a lot of whiskey, don't you?" she mused.

"No, I don't think so. Besides, it helps me sleep through the night."

In the morning, Charlene was shaking my shoulder to wake me. "Leland, what are you saying? You were almost yelling, 'But it isn't mine, it isn't mine!' What does that mean?"

I lifted my head off the pillow. "What? I wasn't saying anything, I was asleep till you woke me. Why did you do that anyway? Now, let me get some more sleep." When I did finally wake up, we got dressed and went to breakfast downstairs, then back to Shady Rest. Our lighthearted conversation never returned to my fitful sleep.

Chapter 47

On a Saturday afternoon in the middle of July, I was at George's barbershop for a haircut and an update on the local news. George was quite excited about the local activities.

"Were you able to attend that big wedding a few weeks ago, Leland?"

"Sure was. It was a doozy, that one."

"That's what everyone is saying. It just might have been the biggest event in Herrin since the massacre. I know that's not a good comparison, of course, but we had more people come to town for that wedding than we've had for a long time, that's for sure. And then the newlyweds went on a honeymoon trip to Italy—it's just like a fairy tale, isn't it?"

"Sure is, I guess she'll be very happy to be married to him!" I lied. "Did you have a lot of business, men getting haircuts for the event?"

"Oh, yeah, I cut a lot of hair that week. I had to stay open late to accommodate my customers. I couldn't let my folks down."

"I suspect those kinds of events help the local businesses all over, don't they."

"Sure do, say did you hear about the goings-on over in Marion this week?" George sounded like he had big news.

"Guess I didn't, I've been too busy to read the newspapers. What happened?"

"On Monday Mr. Glenn Young was over at the courthouse to post bond. He was charged with carrying concealed weapons, and he showed up with three carloads of his henchmen. They all had weapons: pistols, rifles, and a portable machine gun. Of course, Young had on his pearl-handled automatics. The charges against him were filed by Ora Thomas, so Young got real upset; did you know those two were mortal enemies? Well, he went crazy about it and started yelling in the courthouse room. Then, they went onto the street and kept yelling back at the people inside. People on the square were running for cover 'cause they were sure the shooting would start, but it didn't.

"Then on Tuesday, they showed up on the square again. The same three cars full of men with weapons started circling the square, cussing at the people inside. Well, Sheriff Galligan leaned out his window and shouted something at Young. Then Young yelled back at him. 'Come out here and say that, you dirty crook!' or something like that. They cussed at each other for a few minutes, then Young and his gang left."

"I wish I could have been there to see it!" I lied. Lying was becoming quite easy for me these days.

"Well, the paper said the people on the square were running for cover when they saw Young and his gang with their guns. You might not have seen too much of the action if you were there."

George's news continued: "Mr. Porter was here earlier, and he said the Klan folks are planning a big picnic at the county fairgrounds for late August. They expect a big turnout for that."

"Will they be wearing robes and burning crosses over there?"

"Maybe, but no, I doubt it. This is just going to be a show of strength, he said. He claims the Klan has over a thousand members just in Marion, and close to that here in Herrin. There's a group over in Carterville, too. Now, another man, I won't say who, says they're getting tired of that Mr. Young. There's some talk of getting him kicked out of here. That's why he's been spending so much time up in the St. Louis area, the man said."

"Well, I say good riddance to him, and the sooner the better."

"The man said Mr. Sam Stearns—he's on the county board, or some group over in Marion—is the Exalted Cyclops of the Marion Chapter of the Klan and he wants to see Mr. Young get out of Williamson County. He said they think he's causing more trouble than he's doing good."

With the haircut complete, I headed to the back to play some pool.

The following Tuesday I was riding with Mark on our delivery run when Mark asked, "What would you think of organizing a bank robbery of our own, Leland?"

"That sounds interesting, what have you got in mind?"

"I was up in East St. Louis on Saturday, talking with Carl Shelton. He said the bank over in Shawneetown would have lots of money in it for a riverboat festival the last weekend in August. The bank has one of the old safes, the kind you can blow the door off of, so we should be able to pull off the job real easy."

"What did he say about the police over there? Has he got to them with some of his money?"

"That's the good part, he says he can get them out in the countryside whenever we tell him we'll be doing the job. He said the cops don't like Charlie Birger; he's been spending a lot of time with a lady over there lately, along with some of his gang, so they want to get back at him. Charlie's put some of the money in the game there at the bank, Carl says he put in twenty thousand dollars. Carl thinks it would be a real slap at Charlie if we took some of his money!"

I thought this through. The Klan party at the fairgrounds might tie up the local law enforcement, so we only needed to get through Saline County peacefully. Next, we would need a speedy automobile.

"How are you thinking we would get over there and back, we'd need a speedy car."

"Carl said he could get Gerry Kennedy to do the driving for us. Gerry bought the Studebaker Art was using off him. That should do, don't you think?"

"It sure will! Hell, yeah, count me in on this one!"

"Damn, this is going to be great, my first bank job in a long time! I'll tell Carl we'll do it and make sure Gerry is along too."

The evening of August 28th was scheduled for the robbery. I had prepared several bags to carry the money out to the car. I emptied the money out of the valise I had in the bedroom—the one I kept my money in for "getaways." I put the explosives and my new automatic pistol in it, just in case things went wrong. Gerry Kennedy arrived in Herrin in the late afternoon and the three of us rode in the Studebaker over to Harrisburg for a late supper at one of Charlie's roadhouses. We thought it would be fun to eat at his place before taking his money from the bank. About midnight, we left for Shawneetown.

Carl had given us some good information. As we drove around Shawneetown, we couldn't see any cops at all. The town appeared to be sound asleep. Carl had prepared a small map of the inside of the bank, so we parked on a side street, broke a glass in a nearby window, and entered the bank, going directly to the safe. The information had been correct: it was an old-style bank safe. Shawneetown was considered to be out-of-the-way for most bank robbers; since it was at the end of Illinois Route 13 and there was no easy way to get over the Ohio River, it wouldn't appeal to them.

I quickly rigged the explosive and set it off. We pulled off the door and loaded the bags. Mark took his bag to the car first, then Gerry took his bag out. I emptied the remains of the safe into my bag. As I stood up, I heard someone yelling outside. It was a strange voice yelling for the men to put their hands in the air! I quietly walked over to the window to peer out. A man in a uniform held a gun on Mark and Gerry. Was it possible Carl hadn't gotten to all the police in the city? I reached into my bag and pulled out my gun.

"Drop your gun!" I yelled out the window.

The man spun around to point his gun at me, but I fired first. The man didn't have time to pull his trigger; he dropped the gun and clutched his chest as he fell to the ground. I grabbed the bags on the floor and fled out the window to the car. Mark was kneeling to inspect the man on the ground as I arrived. Gerry was getting in the driver's seat and starting the car.

"Come on, Mark!" he yelled. "We've got to get out of here fast!"

I threw my bags in the trunk along with the other two bags, then jumped in the back seat, holding my gun. Mark got in the front seat and we were off. Gerry drove the car fast to the edge of town.

I was the first to regain my composure. "Gerry, slow down. We've got away from the town and the police aren't going to be following us. We need to just go at a normal speed so we don't attract attention."

My calm voice caused the other two men to begin to relax. Within a few miles, we began to talk about the event.

"Who was that man back there at the bank?" I asked.

"He said he was the bank guard. He thought someone might be interested in getting at the money in the safe this weekend, so he was glad he stayed up to catch us," Mark said.

"Oh, so he wasn't a cop at all." I realized Carl's information was indeed correct.

"No, Carl told me he had paid off the police, so they wouldn't be around," Gerry confirmed. "It's a good thing you were ready to handle him, Leland, or we would be up to our ass in trouble right now."

"Well, I guess he's killing number five for me. I'll probably need to drink a little more whiskey each night from now on. I sleep better that way." I stared out the side window to try to ease my mind. I noticed Mark turn and look at me with a quizzical glance.

The ride through Harrisburg and the rest of Saline County went quietly until we passed Charlie's Shady Rest roadhouse. We threw some epithets at the building about our thoughts on Charlie, and the money we had taken from him; it was good for a little levity. Through Williamson County we went, passing the Williamson County Fairgrounds in Marion. Again, a few shouts at the Klan people milling around in the early morning hours, then on to Herrin.

We toted the bags of money into my house just before the sun began to light the sky. After counting it on the living-room floor, we split the forty-four thousand dollars three ways. Mark and Gerry took fourteen thousand each. They laughed about giving me a tip for shooting the guard. After a few shots of whiskey, Mark left for his house, and Gerry went to sleep on my sofa. I had another drink before going to bed. This night a new demon visited my sleep. When I awoke, I didn't feel well rested but I did feel the aftereffects of the alcohol.

After sleeping a little longer, I decided to count the "getaway" money I had been collecting. Sitting on my bedroom floor I counted it out, spreading it across the floor in separate piles. The total came to over thirty-five thousand—more than I'd expected. Glancing up, I realized the window was open: anyone could look in and see my money—that wouldn't do! I quickly closed the window and lowered the shade. My mind began to race. I needed to find a safe place to store this money!

Since it wouldn't all fit inside the valise I had been using, I decided to buy another one and split the money between the two. Then, I could hide one in one location and the other someplace else, but where? Could I even trust Gerry in the next room? I decided to make coffee and get Gerry on the road. I knew once my head cleared I would be better able to think things through.

I made coffee and toast with cheese for the two of us, then got Gerry on his way. Washing myself and putting on clean clothes got me into a better frame of mind. A hearty lunch at the Tidy Boy Diner also helped. Next, I purchased a second valise. Back at home I split the money between the two bags and put my gun in one of them, which I slid under my bed. The second one I carried around the house looking for a safe location. Then I noticed the floor register for the warm air in winter! All I would need to do would be to loosen the screws and lift off the metal grate, place the valise in the furnace pipe, and close the grate again. Grabbing a screwdriver from my toolbox, I made quick work of hiding the bag. Perfect! Now I could relax from the thought of someone stealing my money.

Chapter 48

The Labor Day break gave me a chance to catch up on my rest. I also realized that I had been drinking too much whiskey, that it had not really helped my sleeping soundly. So, not imbibing at bedtime was my new goal. I had also heard that Maryanne had returned from Italy; she and her husband were now living in an apartment near the Southeast Elementary School, not far from Vinny's. My need to see her gave me another reason to stay off the alcohol.

I was able to work all three days of the next few weeks and felt good about myself. I did wake up several times each night, but I got back to sleep every time. Just a walk around the house, a glance out the windows, relieve my full bladder, then the demons would shrink away and I could return to sleep.

The next week the National Guard was back on the streets of Herrin. Mark explained, "Carl and Earl were supposed to go on trial for the killing of Caesar Cagle awhile back, but the state's attorney dropped the charges because his only witness had disappeared. So the Sheltons wanted to get their Dodge back, the one that was being held for evidence. When they went over to Smith's garage— he's a big wheel in the Klan—to pick it up, a gunfight broke out. After the shooting was over, they took some of the people who were wounded on both sides of the firefight to the hospital. Klan men began to gather nearby, so Sheriff Galligan called for the National Guard. They got here just in time to stop another Klan attack on the hospital."

"How long do you think they'll stay this time?"

"No tellin' for sure. I expect they'll stay till the Klan settles down again. And, it looks like that might be awhile, since there are as many Klan walking on the streets to keep peace as there are Guards. That Glenn Young just won't back down!"

With the Guard in town, the Klan raids would stop for a while. I thought it would be a good time for another visit with Maryanne.

"Welcome back! I've missed you. How was Italy?"

"It's hard to stay mad at you, Leland. But, I can't forget what you pulled at my wedding, you bastard!" She slapped me on the arm in a playful fashion.

"Oh, come on now. It was just all in fun, you know that. But, it was a beautiful wedding, the grandest I've ever seen. Was your honeymoon just as great?"

"I really enjoyed myself. Italy has many beautiful sites, lots of old buildings, a lot of history. I even got to see the original cathedral, the one Tony is raising money for here. It will be something if we can raise enough."

"And how was Vituro, was he good to you?"

"Was he good? Yes, he was nice to me the whole time. Maybe you and I can talk about it later?"

"We sure can. But tell me where you're living now."

"Mr. Marlow recently built some apartment buildings near here. We're living in one of those. No need for us to get a house; since Vito is constantly on the road, he wouldn't have time to take care of it."

"Sure, that makes sense. Is he back on the road already?"

"Of course. We have to have money coming in for him to live the lifestyle he enjoys. Even if I have to keep working to pay the bills."

"Doesn't sound like you're too happy with this arrangement." I reached over to touch her hand. "Is there anything I can do to help?"

She pulled her hand back, then straightened her back. "What are you drinking, a whiskey?"

"No, I'm back on beer again. Will you bring me one, please."

Maryanne turned and walked to the bar. I was a little upset; I cursed Vito in my mind, vowing not to let him hurt Maryanne.

When she brought the glass of beer, she set it on the table in front of me and turned, walking away. I took my time to finish the glass, then sat and waited for her to return. After she finished talking to another table of people, she walked back over to me.

"Are you ready for another one?" she asked.

"That would be nice, yes, please." I could tell by her attitude that she wasn't ready to resume our previous arrangements. Either she was genuinely upset with me, or Vito had gotten into her head. She just needed a little time to come back around.

As she set my beer on the table, she placed her hips on the back of a chair at the next table, crossed her legs, and composed a long look at me, like she was trying to think what to say. Finally, she brought it out.

"Look, Leland, I'm a married woman now and true to my Catholic faith. I have a big family and lots of friends here in Herrin. I don't want to do anything that would ruin any of that, so you need to leave me alone. Sure, you're welcome to come in here to drink, and we can talk, but that's all that's going to happen. Can you be happy with that?"

"Of course I can. I don't want to suggest that you do anything you don't want to do. Just seeing you and talking with you is plenty for me."

"Good! I'm glad you understand."

"You can count on me. We've been friends too long for me to want to do anything that would ruin our relationship."

She smiled at me and squeezed my arm as she got up to walk away.

That night the demons were especially violent to me. At one point, I had to have a shot of whiskey to get back to sleep. The next evening, when I got home from my delivery job, I sat at the kitchen table to have my bedtime drink. As the alcohol soothed my nerves, I felt the room begin to change, like each item—the table, the stove, the refrigerator—became calm. It was as if they were perfectly formed, almost angelic, very white or pristine. I felt good so I poured another drink. Memories began to come into my head, thoughts of the people in Kentucky: Abel, Mrs. Goshen, Jimmy. Then, my friends here in Herrin: Mr. Huntsman, Mrs. Wilson, Bertha, all my work friends. It felt like all these people helped me gain this good life. Then I heard Bertie's voice. She wasn't happy with my ideas here. Next, I heard Mrs. Goshen telling me to stay away from bad people. I realized I was crying, so I got up and walked through the house several times, then went to bed. It wasn't a good night—none of the nights were good for a while.

Sometime later, I went back to Vinny's to have a drink and talk with Maryanne again. I noticed her makeup was thicker than usual. She had a sour look as she came to my table.

"What can I get you, a shot of whiskey?" Her voice was drawn when she placed a hand on the table and looked at me.

"I'd like a brandy tonight. I'm trying to move up in the world." I smiled as I said it. "You do serve brandy here, don't you?"

"Sure do," Maryanne said briskly and turned to go to the bar.

When she returned, she set my drink on the table in front of me and turned to leave.

"Do you have a minute?" I asked.

Maryanne turned and stepped back toward me. "That depends—what do you want?"

"I'd just like to talk with you, you seem out of sorts tonight. Is it something I said?"

"No, I'm just not in a good mood tonight. This isn't about you."
She seemed downtrodden.

"If it would help to talk about it, I'm here for you. You know how
I feel about you, so I want to help any way I can."

"Oh, I know, and I appreciate what you're saying. I'm a little busy
right now, though. Can you stay until it slows down?"

"I can do that. Take your time, I'll wait for you."

Several times she brought over another brandy when my glass
was empty. Later, the crowd began to thin out in the room. The
few customers remaining were seated at the bar talking to Vinny.
Maryanne returned to my table and sat down. She started right in.

"Vito and I have only been married a few months and he's already acting like he's still in Italy. He comes and goes when he wants
and he treats me like he owns me. I have to do everything he says
or he takes out his anger on me. Leland, this marriage is starting to
look like a mistake, but I don't know what to do."

Tears were filling her eyes as she stared at the table. She was talking in a low, tormented voice, not wanting anyone else to hear.

"What does your family think about him now?"

"Oh, they don't want to talk about him or me. They understand
how Italian men are, so they just assume we'll work things out, even
if that means I'll have to go along with his ways, and I can't do that."

"Is he still out on the road, selling to customers?"

"Yes, and it's getting worse. Now he leaves on Monday or
Tuesday, then he's gone for ten or eleven days before he comes back.
I see lipstick stains on his shirts, but I've learned not to mention
those to him. He does bring home lots of money and he lets me buy
things; he even brings me gifts when he returns, but so what? I have
to share my husband with other women? No, not me."

"Does Anthony know what he's doing?"

"Yeah, I told him a few weeks ago and he did talk to Vito. Then
I paid for telling Tony, because after Tony left, Vito yelled at me

and knocked me around in the apartment. He said he doesn't want me to talk to anyone about us, or he'll make me regret it. So, now, I don't feel I can talk with my family or my old friends. I don't know if you can tell, but he hit me in the face before he left this time. I put makeup over it to hide the bruise."

"Is there anything I can do to help?"

"No, of course not. But it does help to be able to talk to you about this. I feel better just knowing you care to hear me talk. Thanks for listening."

"I'm glad to do this, but I want to do more. What else can I do? You just tell me anything and I'll do it for you!"

"I know you would, and I do appreciate your offering. But I don't know how to change my situation, at least not yet." She leaned back in her chair as she wiped her tears. A little smile cracked on her face.

I reached over to hold her hand. She squeezed mine so tight I knew she was hurting emotionally, but I didn't know what else I could do.

"You know you're welcome to come to my house anytime, if you need to get away from your place. It might give you some release to get him out of your head for a while."

"Yes, and I know you mean well, but that just won't help right now." She got up and turned to walk away. I could see that her former, erect posture was wilting. Even her step was changing to more of a shuffle. I could feel her sadness in my heart. Perhaps two whiskeys would be needed when I got home.

As I got up to leave Vinny's, I was a little unsure on my feet because of the alcohol I had consumed, but when I got outside, the fresh air revitalized me, sobered me up. I drove north on Park Avenue until I got to West Herrin, where I turned left. Within a block I realized this road would take me to the mine, not home, where I wanted to go. I turned left on 14th to get to my house. *What was I thinking to come up here instead of going home?* I asked myself.

Chapter 49

By the middle of September, the National Guard troops had left Herrin again. I went to the Union Hall to catch up with my friends. Harry Fisher was sitting with Caleb Avery and Joe Petrie. I got a cup of coffee and joined my friends.

"Fishin' was real good out at the pond near Number 9 last night. I'm thinkin' I just might go over there again tomorrow night. Any of you want to join me?" Joe was a serious fisherman. Being a resident of the area for his entire life, he knew all the good places to fish.

"Is that the one on the east side of Division or on the west?" I asked.

"The one on the east; it's the one that's really deep, so the fish seem to like it," Joe said in a knowing manner.

I hoped it was deep enough so no one would be able to pull up a purse I had dumped there over a year ago.

"Well, I'm not a fisherman myself. What about you, Caleb, you do any fishing?" I asked.

"Criminy no, I have to stay around the house on Sunday to help the Cardinals win games. We got the World Series to think about these days!"

Harry joined him. "I'd like to think we can get them there, but it doesn't look good. The Washington Nationals are really playing good ball right now."

I couldn't help with the conversation on baseball. "Joe, what's going on these days on the killings of the scabs a couple of years ago? Is that all over and done?"

"Don't know much about it myself. After the two trials things seemed to just die away. You do know, don't you, that Otis Clark got his house finished by the union carpenters; they even paid for the material they used. When Otis got out of jail, the house was almost completed—that were really nice of them guys!"

"I did read in the papers that the mine owner, Mr. Lester, tried another mine down south someplace, and it broke the man. Couldn't have happened any better!" Caleb said happily.

While I was happy to hear that news, it still didn't make me feel any better about the men that had died because of that man's decisions at the strip mine that summer. Just knowing he was still walking on this earth gave me a bad feeling.

"How 'bout the election coming up in November? Any of you guys like one of the candidates?" Caleb volunteered.

Harry shook his head. "I think all the men running are members of the Klan. I don't like any of them."

"Even the ones they say are members of the new Fusion Party?" I asked.

"The Fusion Party is just a smoke screen for the Klan. That party says it's just looking for the best person for the job, but everyone they endorse is a member of their Invisible Empire. It's all a setup for them."

"At church last Sunday, Reverend Glotfelty said we should support the candidates of the Fusion Party because they all want what's best for Herrin," Caleb said.

"Ain't he one of the Klan members too?" Joe asked.

"He didn't say that," Caleb replied, "but the *Herrin Semi-Weekly Herald* is also backing the Fusion candidates."

"Wake up, Caleb," Harry scolded, "that paper is owned and run by men who are members of the Klan. Now, with all the influential people backing the Fusion candidates, we'll probably see them get elected in November. Most of the idiots around here just read what the papers put out and don't know how to think for themselves. It's a shame, I say."

Harry and Caleb went back to their discussion of Cardinals baseball, so Joe got up to leave. Shortly after, I left for the pool hall. A few of the local players I had shot pool with previously were at the table in the back.

"Hey, Leland, you here to take some more of our money?"

"No, I don't play to get money from anyone, I just play it for sport; you fellows just like to give your money to me for the privilege of playing with me," I retorted. My game was good enough for me to win against most of the players who frequented this pool hall. "Is the usual nickel a point still good for you boys?"

"Let's do it."

I could see right away I was not playing my best game when I took my first shot. My hands were not as steady as they had been. After I finished my turn, I went over to Dan to buy a drink.

"You got anything stronger than beer?" I asked Dan.

"Naw, beer's all I have. Do you want one?"

"I guess it'll have to do." I opened the bottle and took a long draw. It helped to steady my hands at first, but the shaking returned shortly.

The first and second games went quickly, so I paid off the other two and headed for home. Entirely disgusted with myself, I poured a whiskey to drink while I fixed myself a sandwich, but by the time my plate was ready the alcohol had taken effect and I wasn't hungry any longer. By nine o'clock I had read and reread all my newspapers and magazines, so I went to bed. I immediately went to sleep, but in a few hours I was awake again. Lying there, I thought about Bertha, first what she had meant to me, the good times we had had together, then how I had withheld the information that I was sterile. I knew, if we had talked it out, things would have ended differently.

After a short while of trying to get back to sleep, I got up and went to relieve my bladder. One more whiskey helped me get back to sleep for a short time. That was pretty much how Sunday passed: lots of naps with a shot of whiskey in between. On Monday morning, I called the mine office to report that I was too sick to make it in. The manager took the phone to tell me I was getting on thin ice with all the sick calls I had been making. I pleaded that my grief over the loss of my wife was the cause of the problem, that I would surely get over it at some point, if the manager could bear with me a little longer. This excuse bought me a little more time.

I can't say I remember much about October or November. I did work at the mine on my scheduled days, but the shotfiring wasn't one of the tasks I was assigned to do again. The hard work of throwing a pick ax against the hard coal did help to work the alcohol through my system. I tried several times to stop drinking the hard stuff, but each time my body demanded just a little fix, which never was just one.

Sometimes I thought I was getting free of the stuff, so I would go to the hall to talk with my friends, but they didn't seem to have the time to spend with me. Caleb tried to convince me to join him at his church; he said it would be good for me, help me to be with more people. I know he meant well, but I told him it just wasn't for me.

My work with Mark was slowing down as well. He would give me some work on occasion, but he said he was training another man to help him too. I missed the time we used to share, but I was glad I didn't have to work the extra hours.

One night in early December, I decided to go to Vinny's for a night out. At that point I was trying, once more, to get off the hard liquor, so I had just been drinking beer for a few days—it seemed to help. I knew I needed to get out with other people too, just to get away from the temptations in the house.

"You look like hell!" Maryanne chided me. It had been a few weeks since she had seen me and the alcohol was taking its toll. "I know the lighting isn't good in here, but, honey, your skin looks pallid. Are you all right?"

"Yeah, I'm all right. I've decided to cut back on the alcohol, though. I haven't been eating right. It's because of the drinking I don't get enough to eat. My friends tell me I need to quit, but I know I'll be all right if I just switch back to beer."

"Tony said he saw you on the street the other day. He said he didn't hardly recognize you, you've lost so much weight."

"I have lost some of the fat I used to carry, but that's not a bad thing, is it? Don't you think I look better now?"

She raised her eyebrows and shook her head in disbelief. "Well, no, but that's just my opinion. But I'm here to sell you a drink, so what are you having tonight? A soda pop, perhaps?"

"No, just bring me a beer. I'll nurse it for a while. Maybe you'll have time to talk later?"

"Sure, if the business is slow, I'll join you."

Around an hour later the flow of customers had slowed, so she was able to sit with me.

"Tell me about yourself, why have you decided to quit the alcohol?"

She was interested in me, but didn't seem to want to get too close, so she sat on the opposite side of the table. She said she had seen alcoholics in the past and they didn't usually manage to recover, so she wanted to be careful with me. It was depressing.

"I came to realize I was just hurting myself with the excessive drinking, that it was affecting my work at the mine. I can't be a shotfirer and a drunk—they don't go together for long. I've always been afraid of getting hurt in a mining accident and that kept me on my toes down there. Lately, I've noticed my worry went away when

I still felt the alcohol the next day. So, I'm going to quit drinking the hard stuff." I paused, looking in her eyes. "Now, what about you, what's going on in your life?"

"Yeah, things are getting better, I think. Vito has stopped demanding as much of me, I guess Tony got through to him. He still travels constantly, but he does make good money out there. I still find lipstick stains on his collar when I wash his clothes. Last week, I found a lipstick stain on his underwear! So, he's still enjoying himself out there." She looked back at the bar to avoid my eyes. When she turned back, she looked at her hands, which she was rubbing together.

"That doesn't sound good. But, are you able to talk with your friends, is he still keeping you isolated?"

"No, he's gotten better about that, as well. It just makes me feel bad, knowing other people know he's cheating on me and I have to go along with it."

"What are you thinking about your marriage, are you going to stay with him?"

"There's something else I haven't told you about that. He said he's been writing with his father about the family business in Italy." She was mostly looking at her hands, only glancing at me on occasion as she talked. "Dad is getting too old, so he wants Vito to come back over there to take over. He will give the business to Vito and go to the countryside to live the rest of his life. Vito wants me to go with him, if he decides to take the offer."

"And you're considering it?" I couldn't hide my surprise.

"Well, I still have some of my friends over there, the girls I went to elementary school with. When we were there on our honeymoon, I got to see some of them." Now she looked directly at me with her head cocked to one side, almost a pleading look in her eyes, as if she wanted me to understand. "They complain about their husbands, just like I do about Vito, so I guess his philandering would be common there. I wouldn't like it, but I would be just like the other women."

"I've got to say, I hurts me to hear you talking about leaving here. I feel like we've become close; I think of you as a good friend, one I don't want to see leave. But, if that's what you think is the best, I'm happy for you." I reached across the table to hold her arm.

Tears came to her eyes; she wiped them. "As I understand, we won't go until later next year, if we go at all. So we can still have our talks together until then, can't we?" It was a weak smile.

"Sure we can, we'll just have to plan on it."

"There's one other change I'm thinking about. I may be going to work over at the Rome Club next year. The men here are talking about me, and I don't like being here anymore. Vinny said he understands. Of course, he can find a replacement for me easy enough. You can meet me at the Rome Club, can't you?"

"Sure I can. It's even closer than coming down here. Be sure to let me know when you make the change and I'll follow you anyplace you decide to go."

A new group of men came into the bar, so Maryanne got up to go serve them. "Leland, I feel the same way about you. Thanks for being my friend." She smiled and squeezed my arm before she walked away.

I told myself I would have to be a better person—I had to stay away from the alcohol! Maryanne needed me to be sober and I needed her friendship. After Thanksgiving I decided I should spend more time out of the house, so I went out to eat at local restaurants that didn't serve alcohol; that way I would get good nourishment but not be tempted with liquor. Some of my friends noted my attempts to dry out, so they invited me to their homes for a meal with them. Their encouragement and camaraderie helped me immensely. My hands became steadier and I was able to put together complete sentences.

My efforts continued during the Christmas season, and I spent some time at Vinny's eating good Italian food that Maryanne served me. She even taught me to like sweetened iced tea. I had thoughts that maybe, sometime in the future, she might decide to leave Vito. Then we could make a life together. Just that remote possibility spurred my need to stay away from demon alcohol.

Chapter 50

The third Monday of January, the weather cleared for a few days; the sun was shining and the temperatures warmed above freezing. Those of us working came up from underground to a meeting. Jethro called us together, but before he started he came over to me and looked me in the eyes. "You've been doing a lot better lately, Leland. Now, I need you to help with a new job we got here, so keep up your good work with staying away from the drinking, can you?"

I nodded and said, "Yes, Sir!" He patted my shoulder; I was glad to see my efforts to sober up were being recognized.

Jethro told us what he had been instructed to accomplish by the head office. "Now look, men, we need to reopen Number 9 and go deeper. I know it's going to be a hard fight to go further down than one hundred feet in the ground of a worked-out mine, but the engineers in St. Louis believe there is another vein of coal down there. We've gotten one hundred fifty down at the Number 7 mine and we can go deeper in Number 9 too. Some of the newer mines have gone down four and five hundred feet, so I know you men can get us down the three hundred feet they're asking us to go. We'll need to watch out for rotten timbers in the tunnels we dug before and keep checking for gas as we go down, but we can do it. What do you say?"

The miners gave the boss a hard look and then glanced at the sky or the ground, shaking their heads. The ones in the back were standing, leaning against the huge tractor's metal track while the men closer to the boss were crouching down, putting one knee on the ground. All of them wore cloth jackets and work jeans with boots. Some had flannel shirts, some wore wool shirts, but they were all gray from the coal dust of many years—these were seasoned miners.

I was the first to talk. "Sure we've done it before, but that was a new mine, not one that's been shut down for over two years. Do those engineers understand what happens in a mine after standing closed for that long? We don't even know what might have happened down there. I say it's too dangerous to do. Don't you guys agree?" I thought I'd give it a try, but I knew we were going to open the shaft anyway. My secret was about to be exposed; hopefully, the bodies wouldn't be able to be identified by this time.

Joe Petrie spoke next. "Well, look, Leland, we don't know what we're up against yet. We could at least try to make a go of it. What say we send a few guys down to have a look-see before we decide to do this?"

Seeing the other miners nodding their heads as they looked at Joe, Jethro knew he needed to give them a little room. "Sure, alright, we can go down this afternoon for a look-see. Just remember as you're down there that the owners want this to go forward in the next week, so any problems you see we need to find a way to fix them. We're the best miners around these parts and we need to show the owners we can make it down as far as they want. That's what they pay us to do."

Joe took two steps forward and went on, "I know this group can do this, we all been down in mines that are deeper than one hundred feet, so that ain't a problem. We just need to go with the engineer's plan and things will work out all right. At least, that's what I think."

The disheveled group nodded and voiced their support of him.

Jethro sensed the time was right. "Look, men, seven of us will take two trucks over to 9 and the rest will stay here loading coal. A crane is set up over there, so we can get right to it.

"Now, let's take our lunch break and then get over to Number 9. Otis, you and Joe will go down in the bucket so bring your lights with you. Come back here in fifteen minutes. We'll take the trucks over to Colp and Number 9."

As the truck stopped at Number 9, the sun had warmed the air so the men pulled off their outer jackets and got the rig over to the pit opening. The crane's arm extended over the center of the shaft. A second truck pulled up with the cables and bucket and additional men to help. Everyone knew their job and we did it quickly with some lighthearted banter. This was easy work compared to moving coal, so we were happy to be working in the sunlight.

Otis and Joe attached their lights to their helmets, then secured the helmets to their heads. Other men hooked the bucket to the cable and then began the raising process. As the bucket was positioned in the opening, the two men jumped in it. Jethro was signaling to Ben, who was running the controls of the crane, as he slowly lowered the two down into the opening. Jethro yelled his instructions as the cable was fed out and the men descended. The idle hands collected around the opening to watch the action.

"Ten feet, twenty feet, thirty, forty, fifty feet, slow down now, we're going too fast. Can you men see anything down below you?" Jethro kept waving his hand to urge Ben to keep the unrolling of the cable going.

"It's plenty dark on down there. I think we can see something, though. It doesn't look like the bottom, it's too uneven," Joe yelled from below.

At around eighty-five feet the bucket seemed to hit on something.

"Hold up here!" Joe yelled up. Then it was quiet for a few seconds.

Jethro noticed some side movements to the cable. "What have you got?"

Joe was talking to Otis: "There's some fill here, dirt and timbers.

Looks like this is about ninety feet down. This isn't right."

"I can't figure it out either," Otis said, rubbing the arm he had hit against the side of the bucket on impact with the bottom.

Joe yelled up the shaft, "Better pull us back up, Jethro, there's something wrong down here."

Jethro called out instructions for the men to be raised back up out of the hole. Once the two men were on the surface, they told the others what they had seen.

"Jethro, you need to see what's down there!" Joe exclaimed as he jumped out of the bucket. "Looks like there's a leg sticking out of the trash. I think there's a body down there!"

Jethro's eyebrows lowered as he listened to Joe, then he shook his head. Jethro jumped in the bucket with Otis and went down. I moved to the edge of the shaft opening to better hear what they were saying down below. As they reached the bottom, Otis showed Jethro what they thought was the leg.

"Yeah, I guess it could be a leg. If it is a body, it's been here an awful long time by the looks of it.

Yep, we got a problem here. Let's go back to the top and get the sheriff over here for a look-see."

As Jethro set foot on the ground again, he told one of the men in the second truck to go to the sheriff's office to get them over to the mine.

When the sheriff's deputy, Pete Miller, arrived it was getting late in the afternoon, but he wanted to get the body lifted out of the mine. He knocked the dust off his hat as he walked over to the group of men near the opening of the shaft. "What you got here, Jethro? A body, you think? Why would a body be in a mine shaft, anyway?"

"That's what we been asking ourselves, Pete. Sure, we've taken miners' bodies out of mines plenty times. But this ain't a mining accident, nohow."

"Well, bring it up and we'll see what it is."

"Pete, don't you want to go down to see what we got?" Jethro asked.

"Naw, sounds like it's a body in the ground. Don't know what good it'd do for me to see that. I need to get it over to the mortician right away. We need to know if this was an accident or something more," the deputy said as he spit on the ground. I was getting more anxious as the events were unrolling.

Jethro gave the instructions for his men to go down and put the body on the lift. A short while later the deputy was able to inspect the remains in the lights that had been set up. By this time the county hearse had arrived and the body was put in it. Now that the men were all quietly watching the body being moved, their earlier chatter had quieted. I had been able to keep anyone else from knowing what I had done to Bertie and now I was seeing her body again; my stomach was not doing good!

Jethro told the men to shut down the site for the day. Everyone was to start again in the morning. As the body was being moved, I went away from the men and bent over with dry heaves. I tried to hide this so the others wouldn't see me.

"This is just a little setback, men. We'll still be bringing up the remaining fill tomorrow. We've got to get to the bottom like we started to do earlier. I know this isn't sitting good with any of you, but we've got to put it behind us and keep working on the mine. Let's get together here at sunup."

As the sun came up bright the next day, the men started to bring up more of the fill. The first two lifts were just dirt and branches. Then Joe called from below that he needed to have Jethro come down again—another body was found! Again, my stomach began to tighten.

"Joe, just put it on the lift like you did with the one last night. I don't need to see it down there."

He turned to tell one of the men to go get the sheriff again.

Not long after the body was on the ground, Deputy Pete arrived.

"Jethro, this is getting old. How many bodies do you have down there, anyway?"

He made a quick inspection of the body. "Looks like this one's been in the ground a long time just like the first one. The main difference is that this one looks larger than the first one. Doc said last night that the first body was a woman. He thinks she was killed by a bullet in the back of the head—maybe three or four years ago. This body's pretty rotten too."

Again, the body was put in the hearse as soon as it arrived. The miners stood back and watched the hearse as it drove away. Some removed their hats, but none of them said anything.

I was able to watch the happenings with the others this time.

Deputy Pete pulled off his hat as he peered down into the open mine shaft. "Jethro, you can't keep bringing up bodies out of your mine here. It's going to make Williamson County look bad again. We've already had more murders here than we need. You have any idea who these people could be?"

"Don't know, Pete. All I can say is they weren't down there when we closed this mine down in '21. Over the last two, three years anybody could have put bodies in here and covered them up.

"I don't like to mention any people in particular, but with all the gang killings we've seen in the past couple of years, some of their dead people could have wound up here," Jethro said.

Pete sat on the running board of his car and shook his head. "There weren't anything on the woman from yesterday. Don't suppose we'll ever know who she was. This one will probably be the same. Let's hope there aren't any more. Guess I'll wait here with you for a little while."

"Pete, the last body was laying on the bottom of the shaft. We'll go down now to look in the side opening to see if there's any more down there."

When they came back up, Jethro told everyone, "Well, looks like you got your wish, Pete. No more bodies. Anything else you need from us here today?"

"Naw, I'll just get on over to the hospital to see what the doc's found out about this latest body. Thanks for your help here." And he drove off.

Jethro told the rest of us how it had gone below, then, "All right then, we'll get the equipment ready for tomorrow. I'll be calling some more miners for this work and you all can get back to work at the Number 12. Be ready to go for the 6:30 shift."

Chapter 51

At the Easy Time roadhouse Jethro was telling Jessie and me about the next crew of miners that would be arriving to work the Number 9 mine. They each had a beer or two when Sheriff Gallagher came in. He got a beer at the bar and joined us at our table.

"Doc inspected today's body just now. He said the man died of a broken neck. There weren't no identification on him either, so we won't know who he is, just like the woman. Since they were buried at different levels, it looks to me like they were killed at different times. Maybe they weren't even related killings—we'll never know, I suspect."

Jethro said, "Well, it sure spooked some of the men today. Most of 'em seen some bad things before. I guess most miners have been around mines where men have got killed while mining. But we know that comes with the job. Finding a dead woman in a mine is something else, though. And both of them being killed and dumped down there ain't good. That's why I'm putting the new men in that mine tomorrow."

I leaned back in my chair and rubbed my head, pushing my hat forward. "Jethro, you said this may have something to do with the gang wars we got around here. You got any idea which gang would do something like that? Or, what about the Klan folk—that Glenn

Young could have done something like this." I desperately needed to deflect any possibility of anyone recognizing the real events that had occurred.

"I'm not sure this was gang related," Sheriff Gallagher interjected; then he paused, and, shaking his head, he continued, "but I just don't know how else this could have happened, two bodies throwed down a mine opening and then covered up. If you folks hadn't gone back into working on the mine, we never would have found them. Suppose that's what the killers wanted—nobody finds 'em. Oh, and something else. The doc said the woman was carrying a baby. Maybe a month or two along."

Jessie finished his beer in one big gulp. "I've heard enough about dead people for today. I'll probably have trouble sleeping tonight. Guess I'll go over to the meeting of the Flaming Circle to get my mind off this. You men goin' to be there?"

Jethro rubbed his face with both hands. "I'd like to go to the meeting with you two, but my wife belongs to the Herrin Christian Church and all them are strong Klan folk. She reminds me every day that I shouldn't be coming to a place like this, but she still wants me to bring home a bottle of whiskey when she runs out. She thinks because she drinks it in the house where nobody else sees her, it's all right—but I'm a sinner because I drink it with you. Donny Hurst, that runs the dry cleaners, is a friend and he tells me his wife, who is also a member of the Christian church, does the same thing. She even has a cigarette on occasion. I just don't know what this world is comin' to."

"Neither do I, Jethro." I stood up. "Come on, Jessie, let's get a bite at the bar over at the Rome Club before we go into the meeting. We've got to be good Knights of the Flaming Circle to keep those Klan folks in check and the liquor flowing."

We got into my car for the ride to the hall. After a plate of spaghetti, we went into the meeting. Many of the loyal Knights were already there and the room was very noisy. In a short time, the sheriff and the Herrin mayor walked in to applause and loud cheering.

Barry Chester, the Grand Knight, called to the mayor to come up to speak.

"I want to thank you all for coming tonight. We have a rather large group in the Circle; surely not as many people as our enemy the Klan claim they have, but we have right on our side!" The men cheered loudly. "Now, as your mayor I must keep the peace between all groups in this city and ensure that law and order predominates, and I will keep my promise to make that happen. So any of you fellows that decides to do any harm to any of the Klan folks, just make sure that you don't get caught!" More loud cheering. "All us Klan haters, whether we're wops, Micks, Huns, spics, or whatever, or even Jews or Japs, we all need to have a little nip now and then. Those Klan people want to take this pleasure away from us and make us into teetotalers like they claim they are. Although, I for one don't believe they are all as sanctimonious as they say." Another chance for the people in the room to yell. "And before I finish, I want to thank all you businessmen who make your weekly contribution to our cause. Remember, it's your generosity that helps us keep the politicians with us so we can continue our happy lifestyle. And thank you all for coming tonight!" More cheering!

The Grand Knight then asked Sheriff Galligan to say a few words.

"The mayor is right when he says 'don't get caught' because if you make a mistake, I'll be the one catching you. I don't want to do that but if you're careless or not thinking about what your actions may cause, you may be going to jail. So be smart. And speaking of that we still have several of our circles that some of you might enjoy placing in the front yard of a Klan's house. Just wrap them in a cloth and set them on fire. And, yes, thanks to all of you who donate to the cause."

The crowd stayed awhile to drink and talk, but I went home to resist any temptations from the demon alcohol.

On January 29th, I went to watch the funeral parade of S. Glenn Young going through the streets of Herrin. The mine, as well as all businesses, was closed for the day. Glenn Young had been killed in a gunfight with Ora Thomas on the 24th. Ora's funeral was held on the 27th; it was a much smaller event. This one attracted Klan members from all over the area; total attendance was estimated to be over five thousand people at the church and on the streets. The procession wound through the streets of Herrin, then to the Herrin Cemetery, where the body was placed in a mausoleum. Klan members stood guard at the mausoleum for weeks afterward as a show of honor and to protect it from desecration.

Afterward, I went to the Union Hall, as did many miners who weren't Klan members.

Joe Bob wondered, "Is this the end of Herrin's problems with the fighting between the Klan and the gangs?"

Caleb gave his usual optimistic view. "I believe it is! Those two were bitter enemies. They each started many of the problems we've had over the sale of alcohol. Their deaths should put that warfare to an end."

"Leland, you've been doing great staying dry these past few months—how long has it been now?" Harry asked.

"About six weeks, I guess. I try not to think about it that way, though. I just concentrate on one day at a time."

"And that's a good way to do it, I hear. Well, I'm proud of you! Keep it up. I've got to say the people over at Madison Coal had been watching you close for a while there, but they see the change in you too." Harry seemed happy for me.

"Mr. Goodfellow said the other day that he sees how good you're doing. He had been thinking he might have to let you go for a while there. We all noticed that you had trouble making sentences for some time now. Well, I'm happy for you too, Leland," Joe Bob added.

"Thanks, you guys are helping me along, whether you know it or not. I realized one day that my friends are what's important, so I needed to dry out for that."

Joe Bob patted me on the shoulder as he got up to go get more coffee.

Caleb and Harry started to discuss the Cardinals' chances of putting together a good team this year; I thought it sounded like the world was returning to normal here in Herrin. Now, I just needed to be lucky with the bodies: they had to remain anonymous. Then I could work on getting my life back to the place it had been a year ago.

Chapter 52

In early February, my efforts to dry out were progressing. I was eating better, had put on a little weight, and only drank beer on weekends. It had been a rough few months; I was getting a little more work with Mark but otherwise staying home most of the time. As I cleaned up after work on Friday evening, my thoughts were to go to Vinny's for a good meal, then back home to get to bed early. Saturday would be used to clean the house, which was badly needed. Then the phone rang.

"Leland, darlin' it's little ole me, Charlene. I need your help, if you can."

"Hello, Charlene, it's good to hear your voice. What can I do for you?"

"I'm at the Ly-Mar Hotel, right here in Herrin. Charlie dropped me off a little while ago and he went back to Shady Rest. I was supposed to stay the weekend with a man, he's a mining inspector that's going to inspect a mine Charlie has an interest in, so Charlie wanted him in a good mood when he did the inspection. Well, the man didn't make it down here from Peoria, he's sick or somethin', so here I am in this big room all by myself. Won't you come on over and keep me company till tomorrow? I think you'll enjoy yourself," she said with a promising voice.

"How can I refuse an invitation like this? Of course, I'll be there in a little while. I just got off work and I need to get cleaned up. I'll see you soon."

"Well, you better hurry 'cause I might get outta the mood, if you know what I mean. I'm in room four-one-four, when you get here."

I was determined that I wouldn't drink alcohol, so I needed to make sure she didn't lure me into it. I recalled our last visit, where she had commented on my drinking too much. Just a nice meal, maybe a visit to the cinema, then back to our room for the night. It would be all right.

Charlene opened the door as soon as I knocked, like she had been standing there waiting.

"Am I glad to see you, this room is awful empty with just little ole me." She jumped into my arms and put hers around my neck, kissing me on the cheek. I held her tight and we enjoyed a long kiss; it felt like old times.

Charlene started talking nonstop about the nice room, the nice hotel, the nice people she had met, everything she could think of saying. I thought she was acting a little different from the last time we had been together. And, she didn't want to sit still while she talked; she adjusted the pillows on the couch several times and went to the flowers on the table to rearrange them.

"Charlene, are you all right? I haven't seen you this excited before."

"Oh, that. Yeah, I guess these pills do get me going a little more than I usually am. But I can go all night long when I take them. Charlie thought it might be good for me to take a few with me, in case this inspector guy wanted to go all night. Then I could keep up with him. But if he's an older guy, I usually don't have no problem keeping up with those men." Her face lighted up with an idea.

"Say, why don't you take one of them yourself. If you worked in the mines today, you may need a little extra energy tonight, you know? You don't want to disappoint little ole me."

"I'm all right for now, but thanks. Are you ready to go get something to eat?"

"Do you need to have a drink first? Charlie sent some liquor with me for the inspector."

"No thanks, I'm not drinking anymore."

"Oh, really, can you still have a good time without a drink?" Charlene sounded incredulous.

"I'm sure, let's go downstairs to the hotel restaurant. Then, maybe we can go to the moving picture show?"

The meal was excellent, but Charlene had trouble sitting still throughout. She kept getting up to go various places, then sitting down for a short time. She ordered a glass of wine with her meal—an expensive one. I didn't order one, I was only having water. After coaxing me to just taste the wine—it was very good, she said—I did take a taste. I thought it was delicious, maybe a blueberry taste to it.

At 9:30, we were ready to go to the cinema. We walked slowly to the theater and looked over the fare. It didn't look like something we would enjoy, just another pirate movie. So we walked the long way back to the hotel. When we got to the room, I was getting tired; it was past my bedtime these days, but I hated to not be good company for Charlene.

"Oh, come on, Leland. I'm ready for a good time and you're tired already. Just take one of these pills for me, won't you?"

I did want to have a good time tonight—it had been quite some time since I had been in bed with a female, and what harm could one pill do—so I agreed to try one. I went into the bathroom to get water to swallow it. When I returned, Charlene had already changed out of her clothes and into a sheer nightgown and matching robe. They were obviously intended for the entertainment of the inspector, so it was my lucky night. Charlene was most helpful in getting my clothes off. The heavy boots gave her a little trouble, but by the time she succeeded, I was beginning to feel the effects of the pill. My head was also beginning to hurt a little; maybe I would like to have had a little more of the wine.

Charlene was rubbing my shoulders, but it wasn't feeling good because she was working too hard and too fast.

"I know this sounds funny, but I'm getting a headache from that one sip of wine. Do you have any aspirins?"

"Oh, I know just what you need," she said. "You sit in this chair and put your head back, I'm going to give you a kiss that will solve your headache. Now close your eyes."

I heard her moving over to her table and opening a drawer. In a second she was back, climbing on my chair astraddle of me.

"Now open your mouth for a nice French kiss."

When she put her mouth on mine, she released some sweet-tasting liquid into it. I quickly swallowed it—it was all I could do. I tried to sit up but her body was in the way. I sank back and felt the alcohol hit my system.

"What was that?" I started to be stern with my voice, but that immediately faded as the warmth spread over my body.

"It was peach brandy, isn't it just great. You can really taste the peaches, can't you?"

"Yes, it was very tasty, but like I told you, I'm trying to stop drinking—well, I guess I was trying."

"But darlin', we got to have some fun tonight, and if you're all ready to go to sleep, what am I goin' to do? I know, wait here . . ." She pranced over to the nightstand to get a glass of the brandy and hurried back to me. As she got astraddle of me again she pulled her nightgown apart and dipped one breast in the glass, then offered it to my mouth. "Here's some more brandy for you," she cooed. As I licked the brandy she threw her head back and gave out her contagious laugh—she had me!

Handing me the glass, she walked over to the table to get one for her.

I took the first drink slowly, hoping I could take long enough to finish so she would have had several. Even before I finished the first glass, I was taking big, angry gulps. We finished the first bottle, then started on the second. When the brandy was gone I called room service to have a large bottle of whiskey brought up to the room.

Then she went to the bed to lie down. "Why don't you come over here and smell this expensive perfume I bought?"

I went to her and put my nose near her neck. "Yeah, that smells nice."

She opened her gown. "It smells better down here." She gently pushed my head down her body until my face was against her sweet-smelling, soft breast. She started to breathe deeply.

There was a knock at the door, then the call "room service" came into the room.

I got up and headed toward the bathroom, pausing to take a bill out of my wallet, then handed it to her.

"You take care of it, I have to piss."

When I came back, she had already opened the bottle and poured two drinks.

"I thought I was going to have to help that poor boy get his mouth closed after he saw my nightgown. I bet those room-service guys have something to talk about now!" she giggled.

As I got serious about drinking again, it was like I had never stopped with the whiskey, it went down so smoothly. Charlene was still bouncing around the room pouring drinks and dancing for my entertainment. I sat somewhat upright on the chair, watching her dance as I finished off one glass after another. It seemed like I hadn't stopped drinking at all; the warmth of it flushed through me, made me feel numb, then my eyelids got heavy. Even the pill I had taken had lost its effect.

She asked, "Say, how is it a miner like you has so much money? I know you do some work for Charlie, but you sure can throw money around like it's nothin'."

I reached for the bed, turned and sat on the edge. After a few moments, I leaned back against the pillow and raised my bare feet. My eyes weren't quite focused.

"Oh, I helped with a few bank robberies, did one of my own."

Charlene was also feeling the effects of the drinks, so she came on the bed with me. "You ever killed anybody?"

With my eyes closed, "Yeah, a few men, well, men and a woman, but I don't talk about them."

"During the bank robberies?"

"One was. Later I heard he had a wife and two kids, so I didn't like it at all."

Charlene got up to try to do a striptease dance for me, but she was stumbling too often. My eyes had trouble focusing and I felt my mind was separating from my body; I could see her movements through the slits of my eyes, but I couldn't feel my hands on the bed.

Then she noticed that I wasn't watching her anymore, or talking either, so she came over to the bed to apply her wiles on me. She tried kissing me, but I didn't respond like she wanted. She took off her few clothes and sat astraddle of my chest, then my neck, but she knew she was losing me fast. I realized she was on me, but I couldn't feel her warmth on my body. Next, she moved away to sit on my legs and tried to get me aroused with her mouth. She didn't get any response there either. I sensed that I had started to snore. She slapped my thigh. "Hey, what's goin' on? You can't peter out on me already. I'm just gettin' started."

Now, she was the girl who was pissed.

Chapter 53

On Saturday I awoke early and left Charlene in bed asleep. I went home with a terrible headache, so I quickly drank several cups of coffee and ate some toast. Last night had to be a short fall off the wagon, I told myself. As my head began to clear a little, I cleaned up and went to visit George for a shave and haircut. As I walked toward the pool hall door, I looked at my reflection in the window, then stopped. My appearance didn't seem right. I turned full on to the window and checked the look of my clothes—it all looked normal. Thinking back, I couldn't remember getting dressed, but it all looked like it should, so I went on.

Waiting my turn, I picked up the *Herrin News*. On the front page was a short article about the bodies that had been found. An expert from Springfield was coming to town to help in identifying them, if possible.

I realized that George was saying something to me. "I said you don't look yourself today. Something ailing you?"

"No, no, I feel fine. What have you heard about these bodies that came up out of the mine?"

"Oh, well, the paper says an expert is coming in to help. They already know one of them had one leg shorter than the other, because one of his shoes had extra sole on it. Emory MacIntosh's wife is real excited; she said he had a shoe like that because of a war wound he got in France, that's why he walked a little odd. But that don't mean much, according to the police."

"Is that so . . . How could that be, since he ran off with Bertha?" I tried to sound confused.

"That's what the police told her, too. She's still concerned, though. Guess that's why they called for the expert from Springfield. He'll be here on Monday morning. We might hear more after that."

I got up and headed for the door. "Guess you were right, I'm not feeling well after all. I probably ought to go lie down for a while. We'll do the haircut some other time."

Back at the house, I had just one drink of whiskey before trying to take a nap several times, but only dozed off for short periods. Bertie kept laughing on the couch to wake me up, or the bank guard was talking to his children a little too loud. Around 6:00, I fixed a sandwich and ate part of it—I needed to get back on track.

That evening, I went to the Rome Club for the meeting of the Knights of the Flaming Circle. It was the usual set of speeches and lots of drinking for the members that met each week, although the number had been dwindling since the Klan's power had waned somewhat. After the speeches were over, I went to the downstairs bar area to see my good friend. It would be more comfortable to do my drinking sitting there.

Maryanne had changed over from Vinny's to get away from the people who had become aware of her plight with her husband. Her skin wasn't as fresh and smooth as before: her marriage had taken its toll.

"Are you boys finished with your fun up there?"

"I was finished with the fun before I went in there. Most of those men use the meeting as a good excuse to get out of the house for the evening. I guess you could call what they're doing 'having fun,' but I don't see it that way."

Since reading the article on the bodies in the paper, I wasn't in a good mood. "Will you bring me a whiskey?"

"Are you intending to drink yourself into a stupor like you were a few months ago? For a while there you seemed to be coming out of it, you started to look healthy and you were talking sense. What happened?"

"Some very bad things. Now, can I have that drink?"

When she came back with my elixir, she gazed in my eyes as she set the drink on the table in front of me. Then she turned to go back to working other tables.

In a little while, she returned. "Leland, isn't there something I can say or do to talk you out of this? I can't stand to see you going down this path again. Why are you so depressed?"

I looked past her: Mark Wallops had entered the room. His face was full of fear. He rushed over to my table. As he sat down, he asked Maryanne for a whiskey like the one on the table. She turned to go to the bar.

"Listen, Leland, I just had a phone call from Shorty Malone, one of Charlie's men. Earlier today he had taken a girl back from Herrin to Shady Rest and she said she spent the night with you. She said you told her you were involved in a bank robbery where you killed a guard. It didn't take them long to connect that with the Shawneetown bank robbery and they're looking for you. Charlie's mad as hell about his twenty thousand dollars we took from there. I told them I didn't think you were involved in it and I didn't know where you were, but it's just a matter of time before they get to you, so be careful!"

Maryanne returned with the drink, so we became quiet until she left.

Then it hit me: Could I have told her when we were together? Maybe I had said something in my sleep?

"Yeah, I was on a drinking binge with her last night, but I don't recall saying anything to her. I'll get home and hide the money I've got there so they can't find it, then I can deny everything if they come by. Let's get out of here."

We called Maryanne over and paid our bill, then left in separate directions. As I drove home I was thinking about something I had heard once: 'Man gets used to anything, and he gets used quickest of all to living in a state of degradation.' How well that fit me now. A few years ago, I had high hopes for my future, I was married to a wonderful woman, I was making good money, I had lots of friends; yes, that was a good time. Would it ever return? I wondered.

After entering the house, I pulled all the shades, then poured myself a stiff drink. I pulled out the valise from under my bed and removed most of the money. I left about three thousand dollars in it, as if it was all that remained from the job in Glen Carbon. The rest I stowed in the valise in the heating pipe below the floor grate. Hopefully, they wouldn't find that one.

Another glass of whiskey and I was off to bed. I woke up several times, listened for any visitors, but no humans came, just the demons. Bertie was becoming very active during the nights since her body had been found. At times, I tried to reason with her, only to realize she wasn't really there at all. My only hope was that she couldn't be identified; the same with Emory.

I slept fitfully, at times waking up crying as I thought about Bertie. More and more, I blamed myself for that situation. I could see her face smiling in front of me, so I tried to explain to her why I hadn't told her about my being sterile, but I couldn't get it through to her. I ate little on Sunday, but drank a lot, then got very little sleep that night.

On Monday morning I called in to the mine office saying I was sick. The manager came on the line and told me that he was releasing me, they couldn't depend on me any longer. More drinking with little food the rest of the day.

About 8:00 that evening, Mark called with more bad news:

Charlie's men had called again and they demanded my address from him. "I had to tell them, so I gave them a wrong house number." Then, he recommended that I get out of town quickly, because they had said they were going to kill me. "They'll probably kill you even if you give them the twenty thousand dollars.

"Oh, and also, this afternoon's paper says the female body that has been found has a gold tooth so they are asking if anyone knows of a missing woman who has a gold tooth. I thought you might want to know that, too. The whore told them you said you killed a woman once. Any truth to that?"

"Mark, I've always been alone against the world. My dad beat on me and my mother. My mother left me when I was six when she died. My aunt wouldn't help me when her husband told her to get rid of me. Other people said they would help, but they just used me and then dumped me again. Mrs. Goshen wanted to help, but inside I knew that she would be like the others and turn on me one day. My friend Jimmy was one person I could trust until the federal agents ran me out of town. I thought Bertha was going to be a person I could count on, then she tried to use me too. Mark, you're one person I could count on and now I have to leave you. Well, thanks for your being good to me, my friend.

"So, yes, Bertie had a gold tooth and it's just going to be a short time till her cousin tells them that." I started crying, knowing that the truth was now known by somebody else. "I better get going, if I'm going to get out of here." I hung up the phone.

That's it, I thought. Charlie's men are intending to kill me and the police will soon figure out that the two bodies are Bertie and Emory. Then they'll place the blame on me—who else could have done it?

I threw down another whiskey, got my gun, and sat on the couch to wait for Charlie's men. Cars drove past at intervals, but none of them stopped. My phone rang twice during the evening, but I didn't answer. *What would be the point of that?* I wondered.

As I sat waiting, I thought of the day I had first seen Bertha's gold tooth; it had been a wonderful day, she was so full of life. I also thought of Charlene when I had first taken her to Harrisburg and when we went to Maryanne's wedding. I couldn't blame her for talking about the things I had said—it was my fault for getting drunk with her. Then, there was the look on the bank guard's face when the man felt the bullet I had fired.

The night wore on. I had a visit from Mrs. Goshen telling me to stay away from bad people; I should have taken her advice, but instead I became one of those bad people. She was sitting in the room with me; I apologized for not taking her advice. The tears were streaming down my cheeks. I turned toward Bertie, sitting on the couch next to me, asking her to forgive me for not telling her the truth. She kept screaming at me, telling me not to kill the baby!

I had truly reached a point where I was living in a state of degradation, one I would never get out of, one I had made for myself. When I came to Herrin, I thought I could change from the person I had been in Mule Shoe, but now I realized that couldn't have happened. I was lying to myself to believe I could change who I was.

A car stopped in front of a neighbor's house. Men were whispering outside, I was sure, although my windows were closed. They were coming! I slid to the floor—I needed to try to kill them before they got to me! More killing! What had I become?

My body was craving another drink, but I felt I couldn't take the chance of getting up. For some reason I started to cry as visions of Bertie smiling at me and Mrs. Goshen holding me flashed in my mind. *How much worse could things get?* I asked myself.

I felt the gun in my mouth and heard a bullet being fired.

Website

Marion Illinois History Preservation,
https://www.mihp.org/2013/09/the-ku-klux-klan-in-wil-
liamson-county-part-two/?highlight=Klu%20Klux%20
Klan#more-6320

Wayne's World of History & Genealogy, https://hinton-gen.com/
coal/disasters4.html#sep1922exp2

CPSIA information can be obtained
at www.ICGtesting.com
Printed in the USA
LVHW030354300421
686058LV00006B/546

9 781977 238450